Prepare ... for ... p...erful

storytelling of Sophie Jackson . . .

Sophie Jackson is an E............... Although she read
and wrote furiously a................... n adult, to
scratch the creative i.................... ter reading
the *Twilight* series i.................... r of *Twilight*
fanfics, chapter by chapter, a................... dership.

For more information, visit Sophie's website
www.sophiejacksonauthor.com, and find her on
Facebook at www.facebook.com/SophieJacksonRomance
and on Twitter @sophiejax.

Praise for Sophie Jackson's intoxicating romances:

'Wonderfully written and deeply emotional, *A Pound of Flesh* by
Sophie Jackson grabs you, draws you in, and doesn't let go'
J. Kenner

'[Sophie] writes the type of stories today's reader wants: beautifully
created characters filled with emotion, and a storyline that sticks
with you long after you turn the last page' *Tara Sue Me*

'This book truly was outstanding and I can't express just how
much I loved reading it. It's the kind of book that I felt in my
chest and made me angry when life got in the way of my reading'
Holly's Red Hot Reviews

'Sophie weaves storylincs to build suspense before everything
ultimately comes together, leaving the reader guessing and gasping
until the very end' *J. M. Darhower*

'*A Measure of Love* is beautifully written and addictive; with its
wonde.fully d.tailed ch.......... ....ll.... ....nships, it
hoo...... ....ry last
word ....sexiness'

By Sophie Jackson

a measure of

love

SOPHIE JACKSON

headline
ETERNAL

Published by arrangement with Gallery Books,
a division of Simon & Schuster, Inc.

First published in Great Britain in 2016
by HEADLINE ETERNAL
An imprint of HEADLINE PUBLISHING GROUP

1

Cataloguing in Publication Data is available from the British Library

ISBN 978 1 4722 2469 9

Offset in 10.54/15.31 pt Adobe Garamond Pro by Jouve (UK)

Printed and bound in Great Britain by CPI Group (UK) Ltd, Croydon, CR0 4YY

MIX
Paper from
responsible sources
FSC® C104740

Headline's policy is to use papers that are natural, renewable and recyclable
products and made from wood grown in well-managed forests and other
controlled sources. The logging and manufacturing processes are expected
to conform to the environmental regulations of the country of origin.

HEADLINE PUBLISHING GROUP
An Hachette UK Company
Carmelite House
50 Victoria Embankment
London EC4Y 0DZ

www.headlineeternal.com
www.headline.co.uk
www.hachette.co.uk

For you. Thank you.

ACKNOWLEDGMENTS

What a ride this has been, and it wouldn't have been at all possible without an amazing team behind me. To Micki and Louise and Simon & Schuster, and to Kate and Jo from Headline Eternal, I am forever in your debt. Thank you for all of your hard work and patience.

Special thanks to Lorella, the most amazing agent a girl could ask for. Thank you for your understanding, encouragement, and unending belief in me and my words. I'm not only a better writer but a better person because of you. Here's to the next adventure!

Thank you to my family—I love you—my friends—your support is awesome—and everyone who has ever picked up one of my books. It means the world.

My heart is and always will be yours.

—Jane Austen

a measure of

love

PROLOGUE

He was eight years old when he first saw her.

He stood, captivated, bicycle resting between his legs, as her family unloaded boxes from a U-Haul van outside a house down the street from his school. She twirled on the front lawn. Her blonde hair—sticking out from the sides of her head in pigtails—reached out like two helicopter blades as she whirled. She wore denim shorts, pink jelly shoes, and an even pinker T-shirt with a rainbow emblazoned on the front. She leaped and jumped, sang and laughed in the hot sun. She didn't have a care in the world.

And she was just about the most beautiful creature he'd ever seen.

Looking back, he was pretty sure he fell in love with her that day. She was light, brightly colored, exciting, and new. She was laughter on summer days and adventures after school. Even though his brothers teased him mercilessly, he and the girl became fast friends, riding together on their bikes. The girl even had a skateboard, which she showed him how to ride. She climbed trees, threw rocks at dilapidated buildings, and stole candy from a shop because he dared her to.

She was the coolest thing ever.

They grew up together, fell out together, made up together, and shared their first kiss together when they were fourteen, when he realized he liked her in ways that made his body feel funny. She wasn't just his best friend anymore—she was something more, something he thought about when he was alone and his brother urged him to look at pictures in the magazines his mother had warned him about.

It was on her seventeenth birthday when he finally showed her just what she meant to him. In his truck bed filled with covers and pillows, he slipped into her under the stars, whispering his love for her, promising her that it would never stop. That he would always feel that way about her. That there would never be anyone else for him. She was all he needed, all he would ever want.

With their whole lives ahead of them, naked and panting in the summer air, clinging to one another, they had no idea that, despite their promises, life had other plans.

1

"Harder! Oh God, fuck me harder!"

Riley Moore grinned as he gripped the slim calves resting against his shoulders. "Not God." He pounded into her just as she'd asked, hard and powerful. "Just me."

Dammit, he needed this.

"Oh yes! Give it to me!"

Her hair splayed like a giant black puddle across his pillow as her back arched and she began clenching around him, milking him in such a way that with three more deep, solid thrusts, he came with a loud grunt. He collapsed onto her, panting and gasping into her neck and the sweat collected by her collarbone.

"Holy shit, Moore," she gasped as her legs flopped back down to the bed. She placed a hand between her breasts and shook her head. "You need to call me more often, honey." She patted him on the back of the head.

"Right back at ya," Riley replied, lifting his head and removing himself from her body.

He pulled off the condom and threw it in the trash, before tossing a towel toward the breathless woman splayed across his bed. He watched her wipe her body down from her neck to between her legs. Carla was damned nice to look at and she gave head like a fucking vacuum, but that's where their relationship ended. The sex-based arrangement they'd had for months worked for them both.

Riley smirked while he pissed into the toilet basin, the postcoital glow wrapping around him like a warm hug. He flushed the john, washed his hands, and walked his naked ass back into his room. He nodded in appreciation when he saw Carla was already half dressed, fastening her bra. The zero emotional hurdles between them pleased Riley no end. She pulled on her white blouse and checked her makeup in a small hand mirror, touching the red marks Riley's rough whiskers had left on her neck.

She side-eyed him accusingly and he shrugged in reply. She loved it. Most of the women who came to his bed did. Some even asked him to mark them, which he did without thought. It was sexy as hell to see his lust etched across his lovers.

He picked up his jeans from where Carla had yanked them off at the bedroom door and slipped them on, leaving them unfastened. Fluffing up her hair as she meandered past him, Carla headed toward her purse sitting on his side table. She pulled out her cell and pressed a couple of buttons, frowning.

"I gotta go," she said, casually throwing the phone back into the depths of her bag. "Work beckons."

Riley nodded, checking out her legs wrapped in a knee-length pencil skirt. Lord, she had great legs. The rest of her attire was all dull business. Riley wondered fleetingly how many other men had experienced the wild woman who lurked underneath the conservative outfit. Who knew accountants could be so much fun? Carla turned to Riley, who was leaning nonchalantly against the wall behind her, and let her index finger sneak down the center of his still-damp chest.

"Thanks again, Handsome," she purred before kissing the side of his mouth. "Best lunch date I've had for a while. I'm sure I'll see you soon."

"I'm sure you will," he replied with a wink. She smiled and, with one last flick of her hair, she left. Riley chuckled to himself before going back to the bathroom to wash off the scent of sex that covered every inch of his skin.

Within a half hour, he was back at O'Hare's Body Shop working under a sweet 1965 Ford Galaxie, basking in the loud banging rock music of Guns N' Roses and the contentment he always felt when he worked. He loved working with the vehicles that came into the shop—he always had since he was introduced to his first engine at the age of ten by his father. He'd learned everything there was to know about cars from his dad, who'd made his trade buying classics, tuning them up, and reselling them. Riley was the only one of Park Moore's four boys who'd ever showed any interest in the business and Park did his best to prime him to take it over, including paying for Riley's business degree at NYU.

Not that that shit had worked out.

Riley sighed and picked up a socket wrench, refusing to allow his tenuous relationship with his father to piss on his parade. Besides, he had only his own dumb ass to blame for it. Fifth-degree criminal possession of stolen property and a sentence of eighteen months inside Arthur Kill Correctional Facility killed all of Park's hopes for Riley's business future. That rap sheet wasn't gonna go anywhere fast.

"Yo, Moore, you under there?"

Riley smiled at the frantic sound of Max O'Hare's voice. "Yeah, man, what you want?"

A pair of boots appeared by the side of the car at Riley's ankles. "Need you to go through these receipts with me, dude. I'm about to go fucking cross-eyed."

Riley laughed and stopped what he was doing, using his feet to move the roller board out from under the car. Blinking at the bright lights above him, he looked up at Max, who appeared totally frazzled.

"Math isn't my thing," Max grumbled, wafting a handful of papers at Riley's nose. "Help."

Riley snorted and pushed himself to his feet, taking the papers from his friend. "Sure thing."

Max had inherited O'Hare's after his father died. Running the business had worked for a while, but a little over a year and a half ago, Max was admitted into rehab for his drug addiction. It had been a bleak-ass time, but while Max was getting healthy, Riley, along with financial help from their good friend Carter, had taken the helm of O'Hare's, making sure the place continued to make money.

He and Max had been friends for almost a decade, and helping his buddy was the least Riley could do. After Max came home, the two men decided to combine their business and vehicular knowledge and go into that shit together, with Carter eager to invest financially. Before his stretch inside, having been a graduate of NYU for less than two years, Riley had owned his own small but thriving auto shop business on the other side of the city. Understandably, he'd lost a lot of clientele after his time at Arthur Kill, forcing him to make the decision to close up and sell. He'd used the money to pay off his apartment and all his outstanding debts—not least of all the one owed to his father, who'd footed his hundred-thousand-dollar college fee. It had killed Riley to give up his business like that, but he'd been left with little choice.

He was desperate to get back into the game, and partnering with Max was the perfect solution.

Max was of the same mind, but now that he divided his time between West Virginia and New York, he'd given over most of the administrative responsibilities to Riley, which Riley was more than happy to take over. People often regarded him as nothing more than a tattooed, muscle-headed womanizer—which was partly true. But despite outward appearances, Riley was smart, and the only thing he loved more than women and engines was numbers.

"You ready for tonight?" he asked Max as they entered the office.

"Paintballing?" Max said, shutting the door behind him. "Baby,

I was born fucking ready." He cracked his knuckles. "Prepare to get your ass handed to you."

Riley laughed and dropped into the seat behind the large wooden desk. "You do know my brother is bringing three of his old Marine buddies, right? I'm not sure it'll be just *my* ass."

Max waved him off. "Whatever, man. As long as they aim the hell away from my junk, I'm good."

Riley cocked an eyebrow. "They're Marines. They only ever shoot for the balls."

They both chuckled. It warmed Riley to see Max so relaxed and happy. It hadn't always been that way. Max worked hard every day to stay clean and sober, but his woman, Grace, had given him a new lease on life. And Riley couldn't be happier for them. Of all his friends, Riley had always believed it was Max who deserved happiness the most.

Shit, the past year had brought some major changes to the group of friends with whom Riley surrounded himself. Carter had been married for almost twelve months and, despite a couple of shaky moments at the beginning of the marriage, he seemed more loved up than ever. Then there was Max all content and shit, and the guys in the shop who constantly talked about their women and kids.

Riley supposed it was what happened when a man and his crew were knocking on the door of thirty—shit changed and people grew up. But Riley wasn't convinced he would ever achieve the latter, no matter how old he was. Nevertheless, even with Riley happily throwing himself into work or calling his usual list of ass whenever he felt the need, more often than not, over the past year, he'd found himself wondering what it would be like to finally settle down.

His parents had been happily married for over thirty-five years, with four kids, so the idea of committing to someone wasn't something that Riley shied away from. In fact, it was something he'd first thought about when he was eight years old . . .

"So what do you think?"

Riley looked up to see that Max had taken the seat on the other side of the desk, looking anxiously at the receipts Riley had been staring at but not paying any attention to. He didn't have a fucking clue what they said. He rubbed a hand across his bearded chin and smiled anyway. "Things are good, man. Don't worry."

Max narrowed his eyes. "You sure?" He sat back. "You sure everything's good?"

Riley recognized that tone. Every once in a while Max would pull it out and needle Riley with it. It was Riley's own fault. He'd made some stupid comment a while back, when Max was pining for Grace, about losing love or some other bullshit and Max had, for whatever reason, gripped onto it.

It was only because his friend was worried, but Riley didn't want to talk about his past, even though the dream he'd had the night before—detailing in delicious innocence the first time he'd seen *her*, all blonde pigtails and pink clothes—was still niggling at the back of his mind. It was weird. He hadn't had a dream like that for a while, and it had been the catalyst for his calling Carla for a lunchtime quickie—a fleeting balm to the regret that still rippled through him.

He cleared his throat as images of that same beautiful blonde girl danced over the figures printed on the paper in his hands, coaxing out memories Riley tried his damnedest to keep locked away.

Lexie.

No, he silently chastised himself, that's just what that shit was: the past. And there was no changing that fucker no matter how much Riley wished otherwise.

"Everything's great," Riley said, spreading out the receipts.

Riley wasn't a liar. It was the truth. Everything *was* great. He was working hard. He had great friends and women to warm his bed every night if he wanted, all while living in a city he loved. What was there to be miserable about?

"Stop," Riley commented, his gaze still on the papers. "I can hear your mind whirring from here."

Max snorted and crossed his arms. "Fine. Keep your secrets."

Riley glanced up. "I will." He focused back on the receipts.

"So you were a little late back from lunch," Max pointed out in a nonchalant tone, clearly trying a different tactic. "Who was she?"

Riley barked a laugh and shook his head. "What makes you think there was a she?"

"Because you're like Obi-Wan Kenobi with women."

"Dude," Riley chastised with a frown, looking up. "Please. I'm Han Solo."

"Whatever." Max waved a hand. "So who was it?"

Riley sighed, resigned to the fact that he knew his friend too well to assume he would let it go. "Carla."

Max's eyebrows jumped. "The one with the legs? The accountant?"

Riley scratched the back of his neck with the end of the pen he'd picked up off the desk. "Yup."

Max sat back in his seat. "Nice. She's hot."

Yes, she most definitely was. And a great lay. But as good as it had been, the slight tension that had resided in his shoulders since he'd woken from that damned dream was still there. *She twirled and laughed, colors whirling, blonde hair shining.* Riley felt the beginnings of a smile pull at his lips with the memory of those godforsaken pink jelly shoes Lexie had worn that entire summer. *Jesus.* He rubbed a finger across his brow. They'd been eight years old, with no clue as to what life had in store for them.

And wasn't that sad?

Riley didn't even know where she lived or if she'd stayed in Michigan, where they'd met. At least that was the last place he'd seen her when he'd attended his parents' thirtieth wedding anniversary party five years ago.

Once he'd returned to New York, in honor of Lexie's adamant request that he stay away and not speak to her ever again, he'd resorted to pumping old friends for information about her, but that shit had gotten old for them real fast. Since the night Riley had left her crying on her mother's front porch, he had no right to wonder or worry about Lexie Pierce.

He'd burned those bridges, and Lord knew they were beyond rebuilding. Too much had been said and done. He'd fucked up too many times, made bad choices, and hurt those he loved most.

Besides, Riley scoffed under his breath, finally focusing on the numbers in front of him, the only time a guy won the woman he'd loved for twenty-one years was in those awful chick flicks his mother used to watch.

.   .   .   .

"Jesus fucking Christ, I think you broke my rib!" Carter lifted his T-shirt for the hundredth time, showing off the circular deep black bruise that was growing nicely under his left nipple. "See what they did to me?" he exclaimed to the waitress pouring ice water into Tate's glass. She laughed lightly and shook her head before leaving the table.

The bruise was a result of one of Riley's leaping-through-the-air, Will-Smith-in-*Bad-Boys*–style shots from his paintball gun. It had been awesome, and Carter had been whining about it for nearly three hours. It looked painful as all hell. Riley was still laughing.

"Quit being such a baby," Tate, Riley's brother, commented next to him with a chuckle, while elbowing his Marine friend, Steve, in amusement. "Anyone would think it hurt."

"Fuck off," Carter grumbled, dropping his T-shirt and adjusting his position on his seat. A round of jeers erupted around the restaurant table and Carter reached out again to smack Riley in retaliation.

"I have bruises, too," Riley protested, warding off Carter's attack. "No thanks to this prick." He whacked Tate's bicep with his knuckle.

"Think of it as thanks." Tate smiled with a small shrug.

"For what?"

"For me putting up with you."

"Yeah, awesome." Riley rolled his eyes and sipped from his beer bottle. "That's so thoughtful of you. I should have gotten you to pierce my cock with a white-hot sewing needle while you were at it."

Tate didn't miss a beat. "I have a fork," he said, picking up his cutlery.

"'S okay," Riley retorted. "You can keep it. Add it to the stick and thumb that's already up your ass."

"Jesus," Max complained, running his palms down his face. "I forgot what you two are like."

The two brothers looked at Max as if he were bonkers and said in unison, "What?"

Laughter rippled around the table. Truthfully, Riley was more than a little proud that his brother had gotten in a few shots. After Tate was injured by a roadside bomb while on active duty with the Corps, Riley and his family had spent weeks not knowing if he would ever open his eyes again, let alone kick the shit out of a bunch of assholes on a paintball course. For a guy who had to walk 80 percent of the time with a cane and was a recovering painkiller addict, Tate had pretty much schooled them all.

"Ice it and take some ibuprofen—you'll be fine," Tate uttered toward Carter.

"Thanks, Doc," Carter groused.

"Hey, look at it this way," Ben, Carter's work colleague, said from his seat next to Max. "It's an excuse for Kat to look after you."

Carter pointed at him. "This is true."

"Please," Max snorted. "She'll take one look at you, ask what happened, and laugh her ass off."

Carter shifted his pointed finger to Max. "That is also true." He snickered into his glass of Coke. "It might gain me some macho points, though, right?"

Riley and Max shared a doubtful look, making Carter laugh harder. God, Riley loved this. The boys' nights had started not long after Carter's bachelor party in Vegas. Tonight was a busy one—there were ten of them, including Paul and Cam from the shop. The numbers fluctuated, depending on who had free time, but Riley, Max, Carter, and Tate all tried to get together at least once every couple of months.

Clubbing and drinking were off the list of possible activities due to Max's and Tate's continuing recovery from their addictions, but that didn't matter. They paintballed, went bowling, or just grabbed dinner. The point was, they spent time together, had fun, bonded, and vented about life, work, and women. Not that Riley had much to add to the latter—he and Tate were the only single members of their regular group now. But that hadn't stopped either of them from commenting liberally on everyone else's relationships.

"So you guys still coming to Grace's art show this weekend?" Max asked before taking a mammoth bite of his bacon cheeseburger. His girlfriend, Grace, was a photographer who was gaining a lot of attention in the art world.

Riley nodded. "Got my ticket and everything."

"Sure," Carter commented at the same time Ben gave a thumbs-up. Carter's gaze snapped over to Riley. "Which date you bringing this time, Moore?"

"The Latina?" Paul asked eagerly, gray eyes wide.

"Nah, man, the one who used to be a Victoria's Secret model," Cam added, almost jumping in his seat.

Riley smirked. "I'll bring whoever's lucky enough to get picked."

Carter shook his head while Tate grumbled at his side. Riley threw his arm around his brother's shoulder and squeezed. "Oh, come on now, don't be jealous. I can share."

Tate shrugged him off. "The only thing you'll be sharing is an STD. I hope to God you're wrapping that shit up."

"Always," Riley retorted, throwing a fry into his mouth.

"He single-handedly keeps Trojan in business," Max offered, his brown eyes dancing.

Riley cocked his head, mock serious. "Oh, look who's been in a monogamous relationship for five seconds and thinks he's a born-again virgin." He ducked to avoid the packet of ketchup that flew at him and pointed a finger across the table. "Violence is never the answer."

"Yeah, but it makes me feel better," replied Max, leaning back in his seat.

"Me too," Tate commented before he smacked Riley up the back of the head. Riley raised his hand to hit back and Tate held his palm up. "Ah, ah. Think before you hit the cripple."

Riley barked a laugh and shoved his brother instead. "Some cripple."

Tate grinned before he began rummaging in his pocket. He pulled out his cell and frowned at the lit screen. He pushed back his seat, reached for his cane, and put the phone to his ear as he stood. "Hey, Mom."

While sipping his beer, Riley watched his brother make his way to the entrance of the restaurant, where presumably he'd be able to hear better. An unusual feeling of worry flittered across Riley's throat. It wasn't strange for their mother to call—on the contrary, she called each of her sons at least once, sometimes twice, a week. But something about the timing—it being almost 9 p.m. on a weekday—had the hair on Riley's neck standing up.

"You all right?" Carter asked quietly.

Riley nodded, his eyes still on Tate. "Sure."

When his brother stopped mid-step and his shoulders snapped back, Riley immediately knew something was up. That fear was confirmed when Tate turned back, his brow furrowed, his anxious eyes seeking out Riley around waitresses and other diners. Riley's stomach sank and he stood quickly, scraping his chair across the wooden floor as Tate made his way back to the table. He was still on the phone when he arrived.

"—that's what the doctor said?"

"Doctor?" Riley asked, throwing his scrunched-up napkin down on his half-eaten meal. "What the—?"

Tate shook his head, halting Riley's questions. "Well, that's usual practice. Yeah. And his vitals?" He frowned and swallowed. "Seb's there?"

Riley pulled out his wallet and dropped a couple of twenties onto the table, paying for the two meals they'd barely touched. Carter and Max stood, too, looking ready to do whatever they could. Tate may have been Riley's blood, but that didn't make the two men at his side any less his brothers.

Tate rubbed his forehead with the tips of his fingers. "Yeah, Mom, we'll be there. Just hang tight, okay? We'll get a flight out as soon as possible."

Carter pulled his cell phone out of his pocket.

"What the hell?" Riley asked his brother as Tate ended the call.

Tate sighed. "Dad's had another heart attack."

Riley exhaled shakily, his chest tightening. "Shit. Is it bad?"

Riley watched Tate's face carefully, noticing the medic in him shift and rise to the surface. "They're about to take him into surgery," he replied. It didn't escape Riley's attention that his brother hadn't answered the question. "Seb's already there," Tate added, referring to their younger brother. "We need to get a flight out."

Carter, with his cell phone at his ear, held his hand up, motioning for them all to slow down and wait. "Yeah, expect two passengers," he said to whoever was on the other end of the call. "As soon as the plane's ready. Yeah. Direct to . . ." He cocked a questioning eyebrow at Riley.

"Cherry Capital Airport, Traverse City," Tate offered before turning back to Riley. "He's in Munson. It'll be a fifteen-minute cab ride."

Riley nodded as anxiety and helplessness traveled through him. It was unfamiliar and, honestly, it frightened the shit out of him. His father. In the hospital. Riley's relationship with his dad had been fraught at best since Riley's stint inside, and the thought of losing him before Riley could truly mend their differences filled him with panic. He took a deep breath and closed his eyes. What the fuck would he do if something happened to his father? His mother would be devastated. This was the second heart attack in two years, and the doctors had said the last time that . . .

He pressed a hand to his forehead and cleared his throat in an effort to calm himself.

Carter ended the call and patted the cell phone against his palm. "The company jet'll be ready for you in about ninety minutes."

Riley stared at his friend, overwhelmed with gratitude, before clapping a hand to his shoulder. "Thanks, man."

"Whatever you need."

"Come on," Tate urged Riley, moving around the two men and heading back across the restaurant to the exit. "We have time to grab some stuff from your place before we leave. We'll walk. It'll be quicker than trying to catch a cab."

Riley grabbed his jacket from the back of his seat. "Get a cab, Tate—your leg can't take that distance." He ignored the daggered stare his brother shot back. He was immune. "We've got time," Riley placated. He didn't like pointing out his brother's disability in front of company, but sometimes the asshole was too stubborn for his own good.

Tate sighed and pressed his lips together, his universal signal for "we'll discuss this shit later," and set off again, pushing through the door to the street.

Riley followed, walking backwards as he spoke to the guys who were now standing from their seats around the table. "I'll call you when we get there." He looked to Carter. "Thanks again. Max, dude, I didn't get to— The shop numbers need to—"

"Go," Max said, pointing toward where Tate had exited. "It's okay. I'll take care of it."

Riley dipped his chin, turned, and pushed of out the restaurant door to see the cab Tate had hailed pulling up to the curb. Tate opened the car door and looked back at his brother. He paused for a brief moment and his eyes, always so sure and careful, flickered with fear. It struck Riley cold. The only other time Riley had seen that look on Tate's face was the morning Tate had woken from the medically induced coma he'd been placed in by the doctors treating the horrific injuries he'd suffered while on duty.

"Fuck," Riley uttered. "What if—?"

"Don't," Tate interrupted with a calm voice that reminded Riley of when they were kids. He clapped a hand to Riley's shoulder.

"Tate, man." Riley looked toward the sky. "I haven't spoken to him since . . ."

Christ, it had been almost three years. The fall after Riley's release from Kill, in fact. There'd been heated words, then silence, which was probably worse than the disappointed and angry vitriol that had spewed from his father's lips. When the first heart attack hit, two years ago, Riley had visited the hospital, staying with his mother until his father regained consciousness, but they never spoke. His father had still been too angry with Riley to even look at him. Knowing the kind of man Park Moore was, and his need to stew and come to terms with the disappointment in his own time, Riley had simply kept his mouth shut and left with his tail between his legs.

"Come on," Tate said, gesturing with his hand toward the cab. "We need to move. It'll be okay."

Riley hoped his brother was right because, if he was truly honest, it wasn't the thought of seeing just their father that caused his heart to pound.

2

Twenty-one years ago . . .

He'd watched for three days before she spoke to him.

He'd just completed second grade and it was summer vacation. Each day, he'd make excuses to his parents about going to the park—which was five minutes away and was the only place he was allowed to go sans brothers but "for no longer than thirty minutes"—riding his way to her house and standing at his spot by a tree across the street from it, his bicycle between his knees, watching the fascinating blonde girl dance around her front yard.

She had a dog and a little sister, whom she played with a lot. They looked like they got along really well, which confused Riley since he and his brothers were always wrestling and falling out. Especially he and Dex. Dex was the oldest and thought he could boss Riley, Tate, and Seb around. Seb called Dex a jerk. Last time he had, Mom had overheard and grounded him for the weekend. They'd learned that whispering or using hand gestures was a far safer way of insulting their brother.

Today the girl had a water gun, which she aimed at trees, squirting leaves before turning on the hanging plants outside her front door. She was a good shot, too. Much better than he was. She'd pump the pistol, cock her head, close one eye, stick out her tongue, and fire, giving a huge fist pump every time her aim hit true.

He had a water gun at home and he wondered if she'd mind him joining in. He was busy considering how he would approach her and ask, wondering why that thought made his belly feel funny, when he noticed she'd stopped shooting and was staring at him from across the street, her hand above her eyes, shielding them from the sun.

He froze, like a rabbit caught in headlights, and began fiddling with the handlebars of his bicycle. In his periphery, he saw her start to walk in his direction, stopping at the curb, not crossing over, placing her hands on her hips.

"Hey you!" she called, the water gun upside down at her side causing water to drip down her leg. "Hey boy!"

He looked up, his tongue in knots, his eyes darting around her before pointing at himself in question.

"Yeah, you. Are you lost?"

He noticed how loud her voice was, despite her size. He shook his head.

"Are you homeless?"

He frowned and shook his head again.

"Are you a weirdo?" He blinked and she smiled. "Do you live in that tree? You're there a lot."

His cheeks flamed with embarrassment. It's not like he'd tried to hide, but her noticing him made him feel a little silly.

"Do you play water pistol?" She rested the gun on her hip. All she needed was a cowboy hat to complete the look.

He nodded this time.

"Can you talk?"

He kept his mouth closed and nodded again.

"Are you allowed to cross the street?"

He glanced down the street knowing that he wasn't really allowed, but it was quiet and no one was around. He nodded.

"Well, don't just stand there. Come and play!" She lifted the gun and fired. As powerful as the pistol seemed, the water only just skimmed the toe of his sandal, sprinkling his toes.

He smiled wider and maneuvered his bike, pushing with his feet instead of pedaling, and made his way across to her. As he got closer, he realized how bright her eyes were, like the summer sky above them, and that her hair wasn't just blonde but white and gold and shimmery like the pond in their backyard. He'd never seen anything quite like it. On one of her arms he saw what looked like a tattoo of a flower and, on the other, a pink cat. How had she convinced her parents to let her get them?

She stared at him for a brief moment and nodded at his Batman T-shirt, seeming pleased with what she saw. "So, do you have a name, or do I call you Batman?"

He coughed gently before speaking. "Riley."

She smiled, showing two gaps in her bottom row of teeth. "Hi, Riley. I'm Lexie."

For the next two weeks, Riley saw Lexie pretty much every day, shooting aliens and learning all there was to know about the amazing telescope she had on her back porch, all the while assuring his mom that the park really was that awesome and asking if he could please, please spend every minute there because he was eight and he was sensible.

Standing at the kitchen sink wiping her hands on a striped kitchen cloth as he explained this again, his mother lifted an interested eyebrow.

"Just what is it you love so much about that park, Riley?" she asked with a small smile.

"It's, um, fun," he offered, kicking his toe against the linoleum floor. "Lots of my friends are there."

"And girls."

Riley spun to throw a death glare at his brother Tate, who'd appeared out of nowhere. He laughed at Riley's expression.

"Are there girls?" his mother asked, her voice attentive rather than teasing.

Riley's cheeks heated and he pulled at the hem of the Superman T-shirt he was wearing. "No."

"He doesn't go to the park," Tate added from behind them, his

mouth full of the peanut butter he was eating with a spoon straight from the jar. "I followed him. He hangs out at a tree on Wick Avenue."

Riley turned on his big-mouthed brother and shoved him. Hard. "You shut up!"

"Riley," his mother chastised, shooing Tate away and holding Riley by the elbow. "You keep your hands to yourself, young man."

Riley huffed and shook off his mother's grip while she took the peanut butter away from Tate. Riley stomped to the kitchen table, where he pulled out a chair and dropped himself into it. This sucked. Now that his secret was out, he knew his mother would either ground him or forbid him from going back to Lexie's, and that thought made his stomach twist.

His mother sat down across from him and folded her fingers together on the table. "So," she said quietly. "You wanna tell me what's so interesting about Wick Avenue?"

"No," Riley mumbled toward his lap.

"You sure?"

Riley exhaled heavily. "It's nothing."

"Doesn't sound like nothing. Sounds pretty interesting to have you there every day."

Riley glanced up at his mother to see her green eyes soft and a small smile playing on her lips. She reached into the fruit bowl between them and picked two grapes off the stalk, handing one over to Riley. He took it and threw it into his mouth. Green seedless. His favorite.

"I . . . have a friend who lives there," he muttered, his chin touching his chest. He could feel the heat pulsing through his entire face.

"A friend?" his mother echoed. "What's his name?"

Riley fidgeted. "Her name is Lexie."

His mother stayed silent before handing him another grape. "That's a pretty name."

Riley looked up, surprised. "Yeah," he offered. "She is. I mean, it is. Pretty. Her name."

She laughed, seemingly amused by his discomfort. She reached over *and ruffled the front of his hair. "It's great that you've made a new friend. But I don't want you going to Wick Avenue on your own. It's a long way and that street can get busy."*

Riley swallowed hard. He had a feeling this would happen, but it made him sad all the same. How would he get to see Lexie again?

"Next time you want to go, I'll drive you."

Riley's head shot up. "Really?"

"Really."

Riley sprang from his seat, almost stumbling when his feet got tangled with the legs of the chair. "Can we go now?"

"Now?"

"Yes. I said I'd see her today. There's an important space mission, but we need a spaceship. Lexie knows every planet by name and even some of the stars. Did you know that stars have names? She showed me through her telescope. So we're building a spaceship behind her house in the woods. We're not going too far, though, because her mom said we couldn't, but her dad's cut us some pieces of wood that we can use as long as he can help, even though he calls me 'that boy' instead of my name, so we were going to start it today."

His mother laughed again. "A spaceship for an important mission, huh?"

"Yeah! Lex is the driver. I'm the co-pilot, but I'm still Han Solo."

"Well, why didn't you say so? Spaceships are important business."

"I know!" Riley agreed, relieved that his mother understood his urgency.

"Let's go."

Riley wasn't too embarrassed when their car pulled up at Lexie's house, but he would have happily hid when his mother insisted on meeting Lexie's mom, Christine, before she left. In the front yard, he stood, with Lexie at his side, while the two women murmured and chuckled about something they both seemed to find very funny, and looked at him and Lexie in ways that made him want to hide his face in his hands.

"Maybe Riley can stay for dinner?" Lexie blurted, causing Riley's head to almost topple off his neck in surprise. She glanced back at him quickly and shifted on her feet. "What?" she whispered. "Don't you want to?"

He did. He absolutely did. The only part of the inside of Lexie's house he'd seen so far was the kitchen and the downstairs bathroom. The thought of seeing more was kind of exciting. And spending more time with Lexie could only be a good thing.

"I think that would be fine," Christine agreed with a smile that Riley's mom mirrored. "Okay, Riley?"

"Yeah," he answered quickly. He looked back at Lexie to see her grinning. "Yeah."

"Can we go now?" Lexie asked, all but jumping on the spot, grabbing Riley by his sleeve and pulling him away from their mothers. "We have a mission to complete!"

"I'll be here at seven to pick you up," Riley's mom called after him, but he didn't reply. He simply waved at her over his shoulder as he ran toward the back of the house beside Lexie.

. . .

The plane that Carter had organized for Riley and Tate was fancy as hell. Cream leather seats, of which there were twenty. Full bar, mahogany tables, flat-screen TV, and a cute flight attendant who flushed and giggled every time Riley asked for a drink. He would have been quite happy to kick back and enjoy the view of her in her uniform, but honestly, he was far too distracted.

He sipped his bourbon from a crystal glass as he mused. It had been two years since he was last home. He knew he should have been back sooner, and he wished he weren't such a coward, but, hell, them's the breaks. The trickle of guilt that had appeared when his mother's call came through surged now like a fighter jet. Riley rubbed a hand down his face and dropped his head back against his seat as the plane shook with turbulence.

Tate glanced over. "Dad's gonna be fine, Ri." He sighed and rubbed his bad knee. "Don't brood. It doesn't suit you."

Through the window, the light at the end of the plane's right wing continued to flash intermittently. "I'm not brooding," Riley answered. "I'm worried."

"Me too, man. Me too."

Almost ninety minutes later, they hurried through the main doors of Munson Medical Center, where Tate threw some medical-sounding words and their father's name at a nurse behind the welcome desk.

"Your father's still in surgery," she told them eventually, nails clicking on the computer keyboard. "You can go up to the family room on the fourth floor. The doctor will find you."

It was there that they found their mother.

Riley adored his mom. Was he a momma's boy? Probably, but he couldn't have given a flying fuck. It was a label he was happy to bear. Joan Moore was and always had been a force of nature. Being the only woman in a house filled with four rambunctious boys and a husband who worked long hours would be a challenge for anyone, but she'd always managed to make it look easy.

Riley couldn't remember a time when he'd seen her stressed or unhappy, and he could count on one hand the number of times she'd shouted at him, his brothers, or his dad. She had an infinite amount of patience and optimism, which she used liberally to keep Riley and his brothers in line. And it worked, too. Although the disciplinarian had always been his father, Park, it was always Riley's mother who Riley endeavoured to keep happy.

He would never forget the look on her face the first time she came to visit him in Arthur Kill. It had ripped his heart in two. Despite his towering over her five-foot-five frame from the age of sixteen, Joan's blatant disappointment had reduced Riley to an inch-high asshole who never wanted to see that look in her eyes again.

"Mom?" he said from the doorway.

She looked up quickly, her green eyes tired and red. The thought of her crying twisted something fiercely protective in Riley, something that had his legs eating up the distance to get to her as quickly as possible. He pulled her into his arms and wrapped her up in a tight hug while Tate, who wasn't much of a hugger, hung back. Joan's head fit under Riley's chin, and the familiar scent of the sweet perfume in her ash-blonde hair caused Riley to close his eyes. She felt so small and vulnerable in his arms, and it scared him.

"Oh, Riley," she muttered into his chest.

Riley shushed her gently, squeezing her closer. "It's okay, Mom. He's gonna be okay."

"What the hell happened?" Tate asked from their side, a rare outburst of frustration.

Joan looked up and released Riley, reaching out a hand to squeeze Tate's forearm. "He was fixing the roof on the damned addition."

Riley and Tate both huffed.

"I told him he was a fool for doing it," she continued, rubbing her palms down her jeans and sitting back down. "But you know what he can be like."

"Stubborn old coot," Tate commented, shaking his head. "Where was Seb?"

"He'd stepped out to grab something for dinner. He came back as your father was being put into the ambulance."

Riley took the seat next to his mother. "Did dad manage to get down before he . . . ?"

"No." Joan wet her lips and pressed them together. "I heard him shout and then a loud bang. He landed on the lawn, but it was still a ten-foot drop. He hit his head, and . . . I called 911 right away." Her voice shook before she placed a hand over her mouth. "The doctor said they plan to insert a stent in his valve?" She looked toward Tate, who nodded. "But they don't know how badly damaged his heart is."

Tate sat at her other side and wrapped an arm around her shoulders. "I'm sure it'll be okay," he offered. "They got him here quickly. There's so much they can do for the heart these days."

"I know, but they're concerned . . . It's not long since . . ."

Riley gritted his teeth, hating the shake in his mother's voice. Seeing her so despondent was as terrifying as it was alien. He wished he had something to say that would make it better, but he was at a loss. Even Tate, always the calm and objective one, looked more anxious than he would ordinarily allow people to see.

"Hey, guys."

Standing in the doorway with two cups of machine coffee in his hands was Seb. Riley hadn't seen his baby brother for six months, the last time being when Seb had flown into New York from Chicago at Christmas, and he looked as tired as Riley felt. He approached them, handing one of the cups to Joan, and welcomed the hug Riley offered. Despite his being a professional fitness coach with his own gym and being built like the regular rugby player he was, Seb stood a couple of inches short of Riley's six foot two, which always gave Riley the advantage when they tussled.

"Hey, man," Riley said, patting his baby brother on the back.

"Hey." Seb stepped back and pinched his large shoulders. His gray-blue eyes were dull, he was unshaven, and his brown hair had grown so long that he wore it in a small bun at the nape of his neck. Had the situation been different, Riley would have started ripping him for having hair like a girl. As it was, he kept his mouth shut and watched as Seb shook Tate's hand and asked, "Any news?"

Joan shook her head and clutched the cup closer to her chest.

"Well, that sucks," Seb commented before sipping his coffee. He grimaced and looked down at the cup in disgust. "As does this shit."

The chairs in the waiting room were a chiropractic nightmare, which made for a shitload of pacing from all four of them as they waited for the next two hours. "You heard from Dex?" Riley asked as he looked over a notice board filled with leaflets.

"He's in Thailand for work," Joan replied, running a hand through her hair and suppressing a yawn. "I called him, but with the time difference . . ."

Riley's eldest brother, Dex, traveled around the world, fucking around on computers and making an absolute fortune. He was a hacker or . . . something. He was a glorified computer geek, as far as Riley was concerned.

It was another two hours before the door of the waiting room opened, rousing Riley and Seb from a fitful doze. The doctor was still in green scrubs, the obligatory face mask dangling around his neck. He smiled tightly, making the salt-and-pepper mustache on his lip twitch. At the sight of him, Riley went from dopey to wide awake in three seconds flat. He got to his feet quickly, clasping a hand to his mother's shoulder, holding on to her for his own sanity should the news be bad.

"Mrs. Moore," the doctor said. "My name is Dr. Fitz. I operated on your husband." He glanced at Riley and his brothers.

"It's fine," Joan said, gesturing around herself. "These are my sons. How is Park?"

The doctor crossed his arms and Riley's lungs squeezed. *Shit.*

"He's in the ICU. The surgery went well. I managed to insert the stent and check the valves, which seem fine, but his heart is very weak. In spite of Mr. Moore's fitness, two heart attacks in as many years is a lot for a man of sixty-two."

"Can I see him?" Joan asked immediately.

The doctor sighed gently. "Yes, but only for ten minutes. My patient needs his rest."

Joan stood and began gathering her purse and jacket. Riley watched her and waited for someone else to speak while his pulse pounded in his ears. He closed his eyes and gripped the bridge of his nose in an effort to ease it. Tate spoke first, asking the doctor questions that Riley didn't really understand but appreciated all the same. Not that it eased his worry any. He'd heard the doctor loud and clear: his dad wasn't out of the woods yet.

When he reopened his eyes, the doctor and his mother had gone.

"So what now?" Seb asked, pushing his hands into his jeans pockets.

"We wait for Mom and go home," Tate answered, holding a hand up toward Riley when he opened his mouth to protest. "There's nothing more we can do. He's in the best place. We can come back first thing tomorrow. We all need to sleep."

Riley glanced at his watch to see it was almost 5 a.m., and then at Seb, who shrugged. "Fine," Riley retorted, suddenly feeling really fucking tired. "Fine."

3

Eighteen years ago . . .

Lexie's mom, Christine, opened the front door and smiled. "Hi, Riley. How was school?" Instead of answering, he glanced over her shoulder toward the stairs leading up to Lexie's bedroom. Christine opened the door wider to let him pass.

Riley entered and placed his school bag, as he always did, under the coat rack next to Lexie's, and shucked off his coat and the January cold, hanging it up. "Is she feeling better?"

Lexie hadn't been to school for three days and, Riley had to confess, it sucked ass. His walks to and from the place and lunchtimes were certainly quiet. And boring. He wasn't too cool to admit that he missed her.

"She hasn't been down since lunch," Christine replied, walking toward the kitchen. "I just made some hot chocolate. How about you take it up for her?"

Riley shrugged and followed. He'd always felt at home in Lexie's house, but it was still weird talking to her mom without his friend there. "Is she still sick?"

Christine poured hot water into three cups, glancing back at Riley a couple of times before she spoke. "No. I think whatever she had has passed." She held up a bag of sugar and Riley nodded. He liked his hot chocolate sweet. "So maybe you can help me with something, Riley," Christine added as she spooned the sugar into the cups.

Riley frowned and took a step closer. "Help you?"

Christine hummed and turned, holding out a cup, which he took. She leaned her hip against the kitchen counter and blew into her own hot chocolate. "I was wondering if you know a boy at school named Blake Richards."

Riley pursed his lips at the sound of the name and huffed. Yeah, he knew Blake Richards. Everyone knew him. He was the new boy in fifth grade—he started a little before Christmas break—and he talked to Lexie a lot. He also made her laugh, and Riley really didn't like it. Him. Riley didn't like him. *He was so full of himself. And he had weird hair.*

"Is he a nice boy?" Christine asked.

Riley lifted his gaze. Christine looked worried. "I don't really know him," he muttered. It wasn't a total lie. He simply hadn't made an effort to get to know the douchebag. Lexie seemed to like him. He licked his lips at the sting of that thought. "Why?"

She placed her cup down next to the sink. "Lexie won't tell me because I'm her mom, and I know it's uncool for an eleven-year-old to talk to her mother about stuff, but I think she might talk to you."

Riley was entirely confused. "About what?"

"I think Blake Richards might have . . . upset Lexie."

At her words, something dark and angry squirmed in Riley's chest, causing him to squeeze the cup in his hand. If someone had hurt Lexie, Riley would have plenty to say about it. "What do you mean?"

"It's just a feeling I have." Christine smiled tightly. "It could be nothing. Maybe you could find out for me?" Before Riley could answer, she handed him the last cup of hot chocolate. "Here. Take this up to her. You wanna stay for dinner? I'm making lamb chops."

His favorite. "Sure."

"I'll call your mom and tell her."

Holding the two cups of hot chocolate, Riley crept up the stairs to Lexie's room and knocked on her door with his elbow.

The voice he heard sounded tired and very unlike the Lexie he knew. "What?"

"It's me," he called back. "I brought hot chocolate."

"Come in."

Using the same elbow to push down the door handle, Riley managed to open it. The first thing he saw when he entered was a Lexie-shaped lump on the bed under a bright pink duvet. Actually, most of Lexie's room was pink. Everything from her carpet to her curtains was some shade of flamingo. The only things that weren't were her desk and wardrobe, though she constantly pestered her mom about painting them to match.

Riley approached the bed, rolling his eyes at the new posters she'd put up above her bed next to the Spice Girls and solar system ones she'd had up for ages. They were of that dude from Titanic, the one with the stupid floppy hair. Lexie said he was "dreamy," whatever that meant. In fact, looking at the posters now, Riley was reminded of Blake Richards and the new word Tate had taught him. Douchebag.

He placed Lexie's cup of hot chocolate on her bedside table and moved to the chair by her desk. He swung the chair a little from side to side while fingering the pile of books and CDs on the shelf closest to him. Despite there being a good selection of bands and singers in the music pile, she still listened to the Spice Girls and the Backstreet Boys constantly, but Riley didn't mind. He liked watching her sing and dance along to them.

The duvet moved and Lexie's head gradually appeared. She squinted at him over the edge of the covers and grimaced. Riley had never seen her look so awful. Her blonde hair stuck up in several different directions and her blue eyes were surrounded by large, dark circles. "How are you feeling?"

"Crappy," she answered, her voice hoarse and quiet. She reached for her cup and the pair of glasses she'd had to start wearing three months prior, and sat up against the headboard of her bed with a sigh. As much as Lexie complained about having to wear the glasses, Riley liked them. They were pink, of course, and made her—in Riley's opinion—look sophisticated.

As she adjusted herself on the bed, he noticed she was wearing the Suicide Squad *hoodie he'd loaned her one night when they'd been hanging out in the woods behind her house and she'd gotten cold. For some strange reason, seeing her wearing it pleased him.*

"Are you coming back to school tomorrow?" he asked hopefully.

Lexie lifted one shoulder, keeping her gaze on her drink. "Only if I feel better."

"Your mom said you weren't sick anymore."

She didn't answer but pulled the duvet closer. Watching her, Riley thought carefully about what Christine had said. He couldn't remember ever seeing Blake Richards being mean to her, but that didn't mean it hadn't happened. Lexie and Blake did have three classes together, which Riley hated, so it was entirely possible. But surely she would have said something.

"You'd tell me if there was something wrong, wouldn't you?" he asked, pressing play on her CD player, unsurprised to hear the Spice Girls' "Wannabe."

Lexie frowned instead of singing along. "What do you mean?"

Riley chewed the inside of his mouth, knowing Lexie well enough to realize she might get mad if he told her what Christine had said. "I don't know," he muttered toward his feet. "If someone was, like, mean to you or something."

He looked up at her to see an expression he didn't see on her very often. It was panic. He pressed his lips together, suddenly wanting to find Blake Richards and punch him. Riley had never punched anyone in his life, except maybe his brothers, but that was playing. Or so they told their mother.

"Lexie," he said softly. "Is Blake Richards giving you a hard time?"

"No," she blurted, blinking quickly. "No. Why would you think that? What did he say?"

Riley sat back in his chair, ignoring her lie and hating that he hadn't recognized what was going on with her. "He didn't say anything to me. He never does. I just thought I'd ask."

Lexie narrowed her eyes, which suddenly looked a little brighter. "My mom said something to you, didn't she?"

Riley didn't answer other than to sip from his cup.

Lexie sighed. "He's not giving me a hard time," she said eventually, but her tone had Riley unconvinced.

"But you'd tell me if he did."

"Why?" A smile teased at her lips. "You gonna beat him up?"

"Maybe," Riley replied nonchalantly. "If you wanted me to." And he meant it. Why wouldn't he? Lexie was his friend. She was his best friend. He tapped his fingers against his cup as he shook his head. "I don't know why you like him anyway."

"I don't," Lexie mumbled. "Besides, it doesn't matter. He's seeing Hannah Grand now."

"Hannah Grand?" Riley asked incredulously. "That stupid brown-haired thing who called you fat in third grade?"

Lexie nodded and crossed her arms. Riley remembered how upset she'd been when Hannah Grand had said what she'd said and how he'd watched as Lexie's sister, Savannah, and Lexie's mom had tried to convince Lexie that she was perfect.

Riley shook his head. "Then he's as stupid as she is." Lexie didn't respond while she picked at her thumbnail. Then it occurred to him. "Has she said something to you?"

"Nothing worth mentioning," she replied with a careless shrug.

"Lexie."

"It's fine."

Without any solution or words of comfort, Riley simply repeated, "Does that mean you're coming back to school tomorrow? It sucks without you."

Lexie looked at Riley for such a long moment that he began to fidget. "Pinkie promise," she uttered.

The following morning, Lexie was waiting for Riley on her porch step just as she'd said she would. She looked so much better and even smiled when she saw him walking down her street. She always did *that, but each time it was as if it were the first. They walked to school, talking about the Cardinals game taking place on the upcoming weekend, and the new Superman comic Riley's mom had given him the night before.*

If Riley thought hard about it, it was the walks to and from school that he liked the best. He'd watch Lexie walk along the curb, acting like a trapeze artist, grabbing his shoulder every time she lost her balance, and he'd laugh about her ambitions of being the Harley Quinn to his Joker or the Catwoman to his Batman. He loved that she indulged his comic book obsession. He'd even convinced her to read a couple of them.

"I'd want to have a long tail and cute ears, though," she complained after Riley had explained about Harley Quinn's jester outfit in the animated series. "I don't want bells. That's it. I'll have to be Catwoman."

"That's okay," Riley soothed as they wandered down the school hallway toward their lockers. "I'd rather be Batman anyway." He adjusted his Green Lantern sweater. "You know you could always be Wonder Woman. At least then you'd have stars on your clothes."

"Wonder Woman and Batman? Do you two only ever speak geek?"

Riley's head snapped to where the remark originated to find Hannah Grand standing at her locker, next to the one-and-only Blake Richards. His stupid hair looking as stupid as ever while Hannah smiled in a way that reminded Riley of a snake about to strike. She was a tiny little thing, all skinny legs and big teeth, wearing a sweater that was purple with large hearts on it. He supposed she appeared harmless, but the knowledge that this girl had put the sad look on Lexie's face stirred Riley's anger.

"What's your problem?" Riley hissed.

Lexie's hand on his wrist made him turn. "Don't," she murmured, shaking her head. Her eyes behind her glasses slowly took on that panicked glaze again. "It's not worth it."

"See how she hides behind her boyfriend," Hannah commented with a laugh that was as fake as the friends sniggering at her side.

"He's not *my boyfriend*," Lexie barked back at her. The sharpness of Lexie's words poked at Riley's chest.

"Of course he isn't," Hannah retorted with a hand on her hip. "Why would he want anything to do with you when you don't even wear a bra yet?"

Riley's eyes widened at the same time a gust of breath erupted from Lexie. With secondhand embarrassment heating his cheeks, and having no idea what to say, his gaze flew to hers. Tears filled Lexie's eyes. Riley had only ever seen Lexie cry once before, when she'd broken her arm after falling from their spaceship. To see her hurting so much because of one person had him simultaneously wanting to hug her close while shoving his backpack into Hannah Grand's mouth.

To his relief, Lexie parted her lips to say something that Riley knew would no doubt be venomous, but nothing came. Instead, her shoulders dropped, and she closed her mouth and turned to her locker.

"Nothing to say?" Hannah continued. "That makes a change."

"Lex," Riley whispered, ignoring Hannah and hating the fact that his normally vocal and spirited friend had been reduced to the quiet, helpless girl at his side.

"It's okay," she answered, avoiding his gaze as she pulled books from her bag. "Let's just go."

"Yeah, go," Hannah remarked behind them while closing her locker. "Go and be geeks together. Weirdos. Come on, Blake."

"Listen!" Riley shouted, anger rising through his body, straightening his spine. He thrust a finger toward Hannah and her group of idiots. "Why don't you shut up?"

"Or what?" Blake Richards asked, the smirk on his face boiling Riley's blood further.

Oh, how he'd love to show Blake Richards how not to mess with his friends! But, after a moment of consideration, Riley's hand dropped. He didn't want to get in a fight at school, as much as he wanted to beat them all up for hurting Lexie. His father would go ballistic.

"Oh my God," Hannah exclaimed around a laugh when Riley said nothing. *"They're both pathetic. The Gross Lantern and his sidekick, Spexie Lexie the Braless Wonder!"*

Lexie sniffed at his side, adjusting the glasses on her face as laughter rippled all around them. Without thought, Riley placed a hand on her shoulder and squeezed.

"I'm okay," she uttered, as a lone tear escaped and slipped down her flushed cheek, striking Riley directly in the gut.

Breathing deeply and keeping his eyes on Lexie, he spoke. "Hey, Hannah?" He turned slowly to face her. "I know your secret."

"My what?"

"Your secret."

She scoffed and rolled her eyes. "And what secret is that?"

"About why you're such a bitch."

The gasps that filled the corridor were deafening while the people around them seemed to come to a grinding halt to listen in. Lexie froze at his side.

Hannah Grand blanched. "Excuse me?"

"I get it," he added with a shrug. "You're jealous. And why wouldn't you be?"

"Jealous?" Hannah asked, her voice turning shrill. "Of her?" She pointed at Lexie, who was staring at Riley in utter shock.

"Sure," he answered. "I mean, Lexie here"—he waved a hand at his friend—"has so many options. Don't get me wrong, she's beautiful now, but when she's older, she could ditch her glasses and get contacts or eventually be able to buy as many bras as she wants."

Hannah sneered. "I doubt it. What's your point?"

"Well, what options do you have, Hannah?

"For what?"

"Your face." Riley snorted. "Let's be honest here—you'll always be ugly. Not like a bra and contacts can help that travesty, huh?" Riley turned to Lexie, ignoring Hannah's petty but loud response, and smiled at her wide grin. "Come on. Let's get outta here."

When Riley's mom, via a concerned phone call from school, heard about what had happened that morning, she'd banned him from going out—due to the bad language he'd used, not because she considered what he'd done a bad thing. On the contrary, she was proud that he'd stuck up for Lexie, giving his cheek a kiss, which Riley had appreciated but wiped off his face quickly.

"Use sensible words next time," she'd told him.

Later that evening, when he was lying on his bed reading a comic, he heard the familiar sound of stones gently hitting his bedroom window. He shot up, hurrying to the window, which he pushed opened, and smiled down at the blonde girl with pink glasses standing in his backyard.

"Hey. You come to break me out?"

Lexie laughed quietly, whispering her reply. "No. I can't stay. Mom doesn't know I'm here. I came to give you something." She lifted a soccer ball out of the bag that had been attached to her back. "Catch."

Riley held his hands out and caught it on the first try, realizing as it landed in his hands that there was a piece of paper secured to it by a rubber band.

"Open it," Lexie ordered.

Riley unfolded the paper to see a hand-drawn picture of the Earth, complete with blue sea and green continents. He frowned. "What's this for?" he asked wryly, poking his head back out of the window.

For one unusual moment, Lexie seemed hesitant to answer. She flopped her hands to her sides. "It's to say thank you for today." She scrunched her shoulders. "I know what I said . . . what I said to Hannah . . . about you not—"

"Being your boyfriend," Riley finished. Her words still smarted. Almost like someone had ripped a Band-Aid off his heart.

"Yeah," Lexie nodded solemnly. "It's not that I don't— I just wanted to give you something to explain what you mean to me."

Riley pursed his lips and glanced back down at the drawing. "A planet?"

Lexie shook her head. "No, silly." Her face grew more serious as she said, "The world. All the world."

Riley's breath caught in his throat when he finally understood what she was trying to tell him. You mean all the world to me. *He no doubt looked like a fish with his mouth open and no words coming from it.* "Oh."

Lexie picked up her bicycle and climbed onto it. "Good night, Riley."

She pedaled off into the darkness, leaving Riley warm all over despite the chilly night air. "Good night, Lex."

4

It hadn't surprised Riley that his dreams had been so vivid. He was back in his childhood bedroom, surrounded by the smells of his parents' house, after all. The memory-riddled dreams always occurred when he stayed here, so much so that it had become one of the many reasons he didn't visit more. It wasn't that he didn't like the dreams. If anything, they filled him with a warmth and calm he'd only ever experienced as a kid. They were memories he'd always cherish, reminding him of a time when life was easy and uncomplicated by shit that was, in light of his father's condition, superfluous.

He'd been lucky enough to have a happy, love-filled childhood, and looking around his room, seeing the film posters and the few school, college, and family pictures tacked to the gray walls, and the worn furniture, most of which he'd had since he was fifteen years old, brought a smile to his face. He'd had some awesome times in this room, in this house.

He sighed, rested a hand behind his head, and looked over at the window through which he'd caught Lexie's soccer ball and the drawing that had meant so much. The drawing that *still* meant so much. The drawing he'd kept all these years, folded neatly in a box at the back of a drawer in his New York apartment. The drawing he would allow himself to look at every once in a while just to bring a smile to his face.

Maybe he was a fool for hanging on to a gift that represented something that no longer existed, but who cared? He certainly didn't.

Glancing at the watch on his wrist to see it was a little before 10 a.m., he tossed back the bedcovers and, after rifling through the hastily packed bag he'd brought, threw on a pair of sweatpants. He opened the door, visited the bathroom, and meandered down the hallway to Seb's room.

He knocked once and pushed the door open. Seb was awake, lying on his bed, looking back at Riley over the top of his cell phone as though he were crazy. "Morning," he said wryly.

"I have to say," Riley commented as he entered without invitation, "I'm relieved you have your cell to play with these days rather than yourself. That would have been super awkward."

Seb snorted and shook his head. "If you'd been here twenty minutes ago it would have been a different story."

"Move over," Riley ordered, and dropped down next to his brother once Seb had moved. This was something they'd done almost every Saturday morning when they both still lived at home. Riley would say that, out of all his brothers, he was closest to Tate, but he and Seb had always had little traditions that no one else really understood.

Riley crossed his legs at the ankles and rested his hands behind his head, noticing how his mother hadn't changed the décor much in Seb's room, either. The walls were still light blue and the small glow-in-the-dark stars Seb got on his eighth birthday still littered the ceiling.

"Did Tate stop by earlier?" Riley asked.

Seb placed his phone on his side table. "Yeah, about seven. Told me to stay put." He rubbed a hand down his face and looked over at Riley. "Not much point in us all sitting around at the hospital."

Riley grumbled. He supposed all four of them hovering around the family room wouldn't help his father much, but he still wanted to do something useful.

"So how're things?" he asked Seb instead. "Work good?"

Seb was probably the quietest and least confident out of the four brothers, so Riley was proud of him when he opened his own gym two years ago.

"Everything's fine." Seb's cell buzzed once and he reached over to retrieve it. "Busy." He read the message and sighed before putting it back.

"How long you staying here?"

"It's my weekend off this week, so I booked a flight for Sunday. Freya's watching the place." Freya was Seb's business partner. The two of them had been friends since college, and shit had always been purely platonic as far as Riley knew. Although, how that was possible was beyond him: Freya was a fox.

Seb's phone buzzed again.

"Someone's jonesing for you," Riley commented. "She your new plaything?"

"I don't know what you mean."

Riley laughed. "Bullshit you don't. You work day in, day out surrounded by people with six-packs in skin-tight spandex, which is pretty much like Disneyland for a guy like you. There's no way you're not fooling around with someone."

Seb chuckled and lifted his eyebrows. "No one worth mentioning."

His answer confused Riley. Seb was usually open about who he was fucking, and he fucked a lot. Handsome son of a bitch.

"She not treating you right?" Riley asked seriously. Placing his cell on his chest, Seb kept his stare on the ceiling. Riley prodded further. "*He* not treating you right?"

When he was twenty, Seb had come out as bisexual, much to the surprise of the family. He'd never brought a guy home, but

Riley knew, unlike many others, that Seb had dated a couple of men. How serious those relationships had been, Riley didn't know, but he and the rest of the family supported his brother.

Seb exhaled and turned to his brother. "I'm okay, Ri. Honestly."

Letting it go for the time being, Riley harrumphed and looked down the bed to his bare feet, wiggling his toes.

"What about you?" Seb asked. "You seeing anyone?"

"Not for longer than a lunch hour."

"Still hitting and quitting, huh? And they let you, even with that beard?"

Riley snorted, ignoring the way his brother's words, as true as they were, made his chest tight. Jesus, he wasn't about to yell and boast about the notches on his bedpost, but they were what they were, and he wasn't ashamed. He enjoyed the women who came to his bed and he knew for damned certain that the feeling was mutual. He played safe and treated them right.

Did the fact that his bed was empty after dark more often than it was occupied make him miserable? No. But it didn't fill him with warm fuzzies, either. Having someone to love and hold at night was a comforting idea, of course, and he allowed it to flitter through his mind just as he had the day before at the body shop.

But, as always happened, it fizzled and spluttered before it could gain any traction. For a split second, Lexie's laughing face once again washed through his mind.

You mean all the world to me.

"So, what's the plan? You gonna man up and see her?" Seb asked quietly as though reading Riley's thoughts.

Riley cleared his throat of the anxiety squeezing it. "I don't even know if she's back here. Last I heard, she'd moved with her mom when they sold their house."

"Yeah, I heard the same," Seb confirmed. "You know where?"

Riley shook his head. He didn't dare drive down Wick Avenue in case the house was still empty. That would be a goddamn travesty.

"You gonna find out?" Seb prodded.

Wasn't that the million-dollar question? "I have no idea."

Seeing Lexie after five years of radio silence invited all sorts of feelings that Riley tried his best to ignore, and not because he was emotionally stunted. Far from it. He just didn't see the point of becoming wrapped up in what-could-have-beens, what-ifs, and maybes. Life had provided him and Lexie paths that led in two very different directions and, as much as it sucked, the chance of their paths ever crossing again was minimal, to say the least.

Refusing to wallow, Riley sat up at the same time his belly emitted a furious growl. "I don't know about you," he said as he stood, realizing he hadn't eaten since the night before in New York, "but I need a shitload of food and coffee to strangle the fuck out of the nostalgia in this place."

"I hear ya," Seb mumbled, drawing a cocked eyebrow from Riley. Something in Seb's voice told Riley he wasn't just being agreeable. "Mom said there was food," he continued as he stretched. "But we need to go to the store to stock up. Aunt Carol and Maggie are coming tomorrow."

Riley smiled at the thought of seeing his favorite cousin. "Move your ass, then." He shoved Seb, almost toppling him over the edge of the bed. "I need bacon."

Riley cooked breakfast for himself and his brother before they took their father's Buick Riviera to the store to pick up the essentials. And maybe a few not-so-essentials, like chocolate and ice cream—because Seb and Tate's sweet teeth were ridiculous—and maybe a couple of bottles of alcohol, because Riley needed a buzz after the drama of the past twenty-four hours.

Tate and their mother arrived home a little before 7 p.m. looking tired and despondent, and with little news. There had been no change in their father's condition. He was still unconscious, but his heart was beating. The doctor's opinion was that Park Moore was a fighter, but he still had a way to go.

Guessing that neither of them would have much of an appetite, Riley forwent cooking and ordered a couple of pizzas before pouring his mom a glass of wine. He handed it to her as she curled up in the large armchair in the corner of the living room.

"I didn't know we had wine in the house," she uttered before taking a sip.

"You didn't," Riley said around the lip of his Heineken. "I figured you might need some, to take the edge off."

"Thank you," she said, dropping her head back against the chair. "I do."

"When will they move dad from ICU?" Seb asked as Riley placed the pizza boxes on the coffee table.

Tate lifted the box lid of the meat pizza despite his initial remarks that he wasn't hungry. "Until Dad's condition improves, they'll continue to monitor his progress carefully." He picked up a slice and bit into it. "They'll call if there's any change." Tate's jaw halted mid-chew, as he looked Seb over as though seeing him for the first time. "Where the hell did you get that?"

Seb lifted his pizza-filled hand to display the shirt. "Awesome, isn't it?"

"Yes," Tate agreed, all but drooling over the original *Jurassic Park* T-shirt Seb was wearing. Riley's reaction had been the same. "Where from?"

Seb smirked and chewed his pizza. "I know a guy."

"Just one?" Riley commented. "No wonder you're antsy. By the way, is it still too soon to mention the hair?"

Tate sniggered at the same time Seb rolled his eyes and tucked a piece of his hair back. It was long enough that it sat a little below his earlobe. "Not if you want me to leave that beard alone."

Riley laughed. "Why? My beard is only a teensy bit longer than it was last time you saw me."

"Yeah," Seb replied through a mouthful of pizza. "And now you look a teensy bit like you've stapled a hamster to your face."

"But it's a *really* awesome hamster," Riley remarked, stroking his chin. He'd originally grown the beard in Kill, where, for obvious reasons, razors were in short supply. He liked it enough to keep it. Regardless of what Seb said, he knew it looked good.

Seb looked back at Tate, finally answering his question about the shirt. "eBay."

"You boys and your T-shirts," Joan commented from her seat, ignoring the insults, napkins, and colorful language flying across her living room. On her chair arm, Seb had placed a small slice of cheese pizza on a plate, which she had yet to touch. "I just don't get it."

"Don't worry about it," Riley said with a patronizing tap of his hand on hers.

She narrowed her eyes and pointed at his chest. "I hope to goodness you didn't wear that one to the store."

Riley's T-shirt was one he'd picked up from a small Amish shop on a road trip he'd taken in Pennsylvania before he went to college, and was one of only four he'd left in the closet at his parents' house. The shirt declared "I Love Intercourse" (which was a real, honest-to-God place) and, even at the age of twenty-nine, it still made him giggle like a schoolgirl. He still had a photograph of himself standing next to the Intercourse welcome sign at the side of the highway.

"Of course I wore it to the store, where tons of your friends saw me," he answered his mother with an innocuous blink. "Why, was that bad?"

Joan laughed lightly, her face brightening for the first time since Riley and Tate had arrived.

They sat for a couple more hours, chatting and catching up,

all of them trying their best to forget why they'd all been brought together so abruptly. As nice as sitting in his parents' living room with his brothers was, it brought a sudden wave of melancholy over Riley. He absolutely needed to make more of an effort with his family.

He saw Tate at least once a month, but Seb, Dex, and his parents deserved more than his biweekly phone calls or biyearly visits. Sure, they were all busy, they all had jobs, routines, but Riley's father being ill punched home how much his family meant to him, and how shitty he'd been at keeping in touch.

Joan managed a few bites of her pizza slice and finished half of the wine in her glass before she took herself up to bed. Riley followed quietly to make sure she was okay. "You don't have to baby me," she remarked fondly when she spotted him hovering at her bedroom door.

He smiled and shrugged, leaning on the doorjamb, watching her take off her earrings. "I know," he said. She sat heavily on the edge of her bed and kicked off her shoes. "It's been a long day, huh?"

She nodded and removed her watch, placing it on the side table. Looking around the room, Riley noticed his father's slippers next to the wardrobe upon which Park's collection of ties also hung. He rubbed at a slight ache in his belly and swallowed. "He's gonna be okay, right, Ma?"

His voice trembled and made Joan's eyes soften. She patted the bed at her side. On heavy feet, Riley approached and sat down next to her, welcoming his mother's arm around his shoulder. "If I know your father," she whispered close to his ear, "he'll do everything in his power to get better so that he can finish fixing that damned roof."

Riley huffed a laugh and nodded. Joan squeezed him tightly.

"Last time we spoke was . . ." he began, the rest of his words sticking in his throat, overwhelmed by the moment. He tried again. "I let him down. I let you all down."

"Sweetheart," Joan murmured. "We all make mistakes. I told you that. Your father *knows* that. Believe me, he's made his own share. That man can be stubborn as all hell, but whatever's gone before, your father loves you very much. Don't ever doubt that, okay?"

"Okay," he managed, as she kissed his temple the way she always had when he was little.

.　.　.　.

Riley's aunt Carol and his cousin Maggie arrived before lunch the next day. They wandered into the family room of the hospital where Riley and his mom had been since eight o'clock that morning. Neither Tate nor Seb had argued when Riley said he would accompany their mother.

Carol was Joan's twin sister and Riley's favorite aunt. She was one of those cool aunts who was always more of an older sister. Maggie was the youngest of Carol's three children—her two brothers were in the navy, like her father—and, having grown up the only girl of their generation, could banter and wrestle with the best of them.

Not that she could wrestle much now with her six-month baby belly and her five-year-old daughter, Rosie, clinging to her leg.

Maggie grinned at Riley, her brown eyes dancing. "Hey, stranger," she said as they hugged. "It's been a while."

Riley kissed her cheek. "I know. I suck."

"Kinda like this beard," she commented, poking his chin.

Riley shooed her hand away and laughed, reaching to hug his aunt.

"Don't you listen," Aunt Carol said. "It makes you look very handsome."

"And maybe homeless," Maggie added, cocking her head to the side considering him.

"You're lucky you have these to hide behind," Riley said, pointing to Rosie and then Maggie's belly. "Or I'd have to kick your ass."

Maggie waved him off. "Don't delude yourself. I'd still win."

The teasing quickly lifted the tense atmosphere that had crept into the family room as the hours ticked by with no news about Riley's father, which was the best of a bad situation—no news was good news, after all—but he was still about ready to climb the walls. It was also a relief to fall back so easily into the usual family repartee, despite his not having seen Maggie since his father's last heart attack. That realization brought along another truckload of guilt that Riley knew he deserved.

He looked over at Rosie as Joan lifted her onto her lap and smiled. "Hey, baby girl, you've grown so much since I last saw you."

Rosie's eyes were the same as her mother's—as was the jet-black hair braided down her back. She hid her face in Joan's neck, but Riley detected a smile.

"Don't scare my kid with your beard," Maggie mocked.

Riley barked a laugh. "It's not *that* bad!" He brushed a hand over his whiskered cheek. "You're only jealous because you have to shave yours off every morning."

He yelped playfully when Maggie smacked his arm and again when, apparently done with being shy, Rosie smacked him, too.

They managed to entertain the little girl for an hour before she started getting restless. Not that Riley blamed her; it was boring as shit sitting around the airless family room and there was fuck-all on the wall-mounted TV.

"How about you take the girls and go get some food?" Joan suggested, glancing at Riley as Rosie whined and pushed away everything Maggie was trying to amuse her with. "Get out for a while, take her to the park."

Riley frowned. Although the thought of leaving the godfor-saken place filled him with nothing but joy, he didn't like the idea of leaving his mom or the chance that they might hear something about his dad. "You'll be okay?"

"Go," Aunt Carol ordered. "I'll stay. Get some fresh air."

"And bring me back something sweet," Joan added.

Cranking the AC up to blasting in her car because the air out-side wasn't so much fresh as it was hotter than Hades, Maggie drove the three of them to the nearest McDonald's drive-thru. Riley was more than happy; fast food was his vice.

The park was a fifteen-minute drive from the hospital and, be-cause of the weather and the fact that it was school summer vaca-tion, it was busy. On a blanket Maggie rustled up from the trunk of the car, she and Riley sat in the sun and watched Rosie as she played in the large sandbox, throwing the stuff and building castles with two other children she'd commandeered for the project.

"So how're you doing?" Maggie asked, slurping her chocolate milkshake.

Riley shrugged, leaning back on his hands, watching Rosie through his shades. "Doctors say Dad's a fighter. Can't ask for more than that."

Maggie nodded. "Your mom looks tired."

And it was no wonder. "She's been at the hospital every day for at least twelve hours."

"How long are you staying?"

"As long as she needs."

Riley had spoken to Max that very morning, filling his friend in. Max had told him to take as long as was necessary and Riley didn't argue. He had to be with his family. It was as simple as that.

Riley grimaced as Maggie pulled off the lid of her shake and dipped a fry into it. "These cravings are kicking my ass," she said by way of explanation. Riley chuckled and smiled as Rosie approached, handing him a leaf and a twig she'd collected as she'd played.

"Thank you," he said with a grin. She skipped back toward the sandbox, her pretty pink dress covered in ketchup, chicken nugget bits, juice, and sand. Her hair, which had been tied up in cute, neat pigtails, was now flying around and sticking to her face.

"There's no point in me even trying to keep her looking respectable," Maggie said with a resigned sigh. "She's a hot mess."

"Like mother, like daughter," Riley uttered with a smirk.

Maggie adjusted herself on the blanket, leaning against Riley's shoulder. "And I was going to say how nice it is to have you back in Michigan."

With the blue sky above them, the relative quiet of the park, and the heat, Riley had to agree. Despite the circumstances, it was nice being home. Sure, he missed the bustle of New York, but there was always something about Traverse City that hugged a deep part of him.

"Do you ever think about moving back?" Maggie asked.

"Not really," he answered honestly.

"Best thing I ever did." Maggie had moved back to Michigan from Indiana just before Rosie was born, buying a house with her husband not two hours away from Riley's mom. "I want my kids to grow up here like we did."

It was a nice idea. Riley wasn't sure he'd like his kids to grow up in New York, and Michigan was a nice place to do it. But then he'd have to actually have children, and that wasn't looking all that likely given his current relationship status. Rosie threw off her sandals and began rubbing her small feet in the sand, much to the exasperation of her mother. Riley had to admit, Rosie was as cute as a button, and seeing her play without a care in the world eased the stiffness between his shoulders.

Rosie threw sand into the air, giggling as she did. Riley got to his feet and wandered over to where she was digging and creating

a pile of the stuff between her legs. He crouched and started helping, ignoring Maggie's complaints about having sand all over the
damn car.

Looking back at his cousin to unleash a barrage of "chill the
hell out," Riley noticed a slim woman with light brown hair standing by the slide not fifty feet away. He pulled his shades down his
nose and narrowed his eyes in an effort to see her more clearly, even
though his gut knew exactly who she was. He stood slowly, wiping
his sand-covered hands on the ass of his jeans, noticing the small
blond-haired boy she was playing with. He couldn't have been
much older than four.

Maggie looked over her shoulder to where he was staring.
"Who is that?"

"It's Savannah," he answered, glancing around quickly, his
pulse galloping at the idea that Lexie might be somewhere close
by. But he couldn't see her. When he looked back, Savannah was
staring straight at him, her blue eyes wide as though he were a
ghost.

"Sav," he managed, taking a slight step forward. He had no idea
how she would react to him. She was Lexie's sister, after all, and
there was a shit-ton of water under that bridge.

Savannah didn't reply. Instead, she muttered something to the
little boy as he made to climb the steps of the slide again and
clutched his hand, all but dragging him away, even though the
poor little dude complained about wanting one more go. Rather
than fighting with him, she picked him up and placed him on
her hip.

Riley didn't breathe until they both disappeared in the crowds,
dropping his chin to his chest. *Shit.* Despite the law of averages
stating it was bound to happen, he'd been totally unprepared for
dealing with Lexie or her family. Adrenaline coursed through him,
picking up his heart and throwing it against his ribs.

"You okay?" Maggie's voice came from his side. Riley knew

Maggie didn't know the entire story of his and Lexie's relationship, but he would have put money on his mother having given her the highlights at some point.

He nodded, speechless, and turned back to play with Rosie, praying his burger didn't suddenly make a reappearance in the kids' sandbox.

5

Lexie Pierce leaned her hip against the counter, which stretched halfway across the back wall of the store, smiling at the young woman who'd been debating for the past twenty minutes about whether to buy a ring for her index finger or a bracelet to wear with her watch. For some it may have been frustrating in the extreme, seeing a person um and ah over a piece of jewelry, but for Lexie, it was the best part of her job.

"They're both so pretty," the woman said for the eighth time, holding the ring in one hand and the bracelet in the other, as if weighing their worth.

Lexie had to agree. They were her favorite and newest designs, and both—the ring embossed with the word *laugh* and the bracelet, *sing*—were very beautiful. The woman sighed and dropped her hands. "I can't decide."

Lexie chuckled and placed a hand on the woman's forearm. It was something she tried to do with all her indecisive customers. Touching seemed to help calm them and usually aided in their making a clearer decision. "What's your name?"

"Amanda."

"Amanda, my name's Lexie. Can I suggest something?"

The woman looked instantly relieved. "Yes, absolutely."

Lexie gestured toward the far wall of the store—a wall that was originally covered entirely in mirrors but had, over the three years the store had been open, been slowly buried under hundreds of pink sticky notes. Lexie wandered toward the vast array of pink, smiling at the words written on each one.

"This is the 'love wall.'" She pushed her glasses up her nose before she picked a note and pulled it carefully from the mirror. "I ask each customer who comes in to leave a love note before they leave. Here."

She handed the note over as Amanda asked, "A love note to whom?"

"To themselves," Lexie answered. Some notes made Lexie laugh, others made her cry, and some simply made her thank God for the family she loved and friends who cared for her. "I ask my customers to look in the mirror and write a note detailing at least one thing they love about themselves," Lexie continued. "Each one is signed off already." She placed a finger at the bottom of the note where it read simply:

Love, You.

"The name of the store," Amanda murmured as she read the note Lexie had handed her: *I love your green eyes, your red hair, and your tenacious attitude.* Love, you.

The note that had been next to it merely stated: *Your ass! LOL!* Love, You.

"Some people find it easy to write a few things," Lexie mused. "Some find it hard to write even one."

"This is great," Amanda said, her attention on a note that read: *Your mad kitchen skillz!*

Lexie smiled. "So, my suggestion." Amanda looked back at her and Lexie handed her a love note that was blank, save for the Love, You at the bottom. "Write down three things you love about yourself and I'll knock twenty percent off the bracelet."

Amanda's eyes widened. "You'd do that?"

"If you're honest, sure."

Seemingly panicked by the prospect, Amanda asked, "Wait, three things?"

Lexie placed a hand on Amanda's arm again. "Use the mirror. It might be easier than you think. Come find me when you're done."

Lexie made her way from the "Love Wall" across the store, smiling at her regular customers and stopping to introduce herself to those who were new. She glanced over to a far corner where Jaime, her store manager, was explaining to a young guy who'd bought a necklace for his boyfriend the difference between engraving and embossing. The store did both, and it was usually done while the customer waited. Each piece of jewelry, depending on design, could fit a personal message of up to ten words.

"Lexie?" Lexie turned to see her newest staff member, Annie, looking a little flustered. "I'm sorry, but this gentleman"—she gestured toward a well-dressed man standing by the register—"wondered if you would be able to design a piece for his fiancée—well, his future fiancée. He's going to propose and wants a special ring."

"No problem."

Yeah, it was going to be a busy day. And Lexie loved it. As much as she'd worried and fretted over putting money into a dream she'd had for years, every time she saw the receipts and price tags with her brand, Love, You by Lexie, printed on them, she felt a surge of pride and excitement. It had taken a lot of hard work, patience, and resilience to be where she was today, but it had all been totally worth it.

Catching a glimpse of herself in the mirrored wall as she approached Annie's customer, Lexie found she liked what she saw. Her hair, which she'd twisted up and fastened with two pencils, was still as blonde as it had been when she was small, and the glasses she wore when her eyes were too tired for contacts were the same shade of pink she'd loved forever. The tattoos on her left arm, reaching from her shoulder to her elbow, as well as the ones on the inside of her right forearm, added color and a story to her otherwise boring, pale skin, while the several piercings in each ear and the one in her septum glinted prettily under the store spotlights.

As they had gotten older, her sister, Savannah, described Lexie as having a "sexy edge," and she was happy to agree, especially coming from someone as beautiful and intelligent as her younger sister.

An hour later, the initial ring designs had been approved by the nervous future groom and Amanda's bracelet *and* ring had been paid for and bagged, after her love note, which read, *Your indomitable spirit, your creativity, and your full lips,* had been added to the "Love Wall." Lexie flicked the edge of it proudly. Originally, Savannah had been skeptical of offering a discount for notes, but Lexie's argument for it had stood strong. If it took taking a few dollars' loss on some of her pieces for someone to take a moment and embrace the worth within herself, then so be it. It may have sounded hokey, but Lexie believed in it all the same.

She was adjusting a stand full of necklaces when the front door of the store opened and Savannah walked in. The hair on Lexie's neck immediately stood on end when she noticed her sister's expression.

"What happened?" she asked quickly. "Where's—?"

Savannah put her hands up. "He's fine. He's with Mom."

Lexie swallowed her heart back down into her chest and tilted her head toward a door that led to the engraving and embossing room, a kitchenette, a storeroom, and the stairs up to the apartment Jaime rented from Lexie. Lexie had barely closed the door behind them when her sister spoke.

"Riley's in town."

It was strange how life could move along so peacefully, so perfectly, until someone uttered a few words like, "Your father's dead" or "I'm tired of trying," and in a split moment, everything changed. It had been a long time since it had occurred, but Lexie would recognize it anywhere.

This was one of those moments.

Lexie wasn't sure how long she'd stared at Savannah before she regained the use of her voice. "Where?"

"At the park."

"He saw you?"

Savannah nodded and moved toward a small fridge in the corner of the kitchenette. She pulled out a bottle of water and unscrewed the lid. "Yeah, he saw us."

Us. Her next question didn't need to be uttered; the answer was clear as day on her sister's face. Lexie slumped against the nearest wall, her legs suddenly feeling shaky.

"He was a distance away, and we left before he could come closer or say anything else."

Lexie blanched. "He talked to you?"

"He said my name."

Lexie removed her glasses and clasped the bridge of her nose. "Shit."

A part of Lexie knew seeing Riley again was inevitable—she'd known it the moment she'd moved back to Traverse City three years ago and learned that Joan and Park Moore still lived here. But she'd also hoped that, like the last time Riley was in town, she could avoid him. The last words they'd said to one another hadn't been of the loving and caring variety, and by the time she'd needed to see him and talk, he'd been sent to prison for eighteen months. With everything that had happened since, on top of having an endless list of concerns about reconnecting with a man who'd spent time in prison, time had sped up and slipped away from her, taking the window of opportunity with it.

She'd heard from a friend at the hospital that Park Moore had been admitted, and after Lexie asked about his condition, she'd taken a deep breath and concluded that Riley and his brothers would spend their days five miles away at Munson and everything would be fine.

Never had she considered that he'd be hanging out at the damned park.

"Who was he with?" The question was out before she could stop it, even though she knew she had absolutely no right to ask.

Savannah shrugged, keeping her eyes on the floor. "A pregnant woman I didn't recognize. He was playing with a little girl in the sandbox."

The way Lexie's heart somersaulted in her chest made her reach for the door handle at her side in an effort to stay upright. Her ears rang. *Pregnant woman. A little girl.* He was playing with a little girl in the sandbox. And, sweet Jesus, couldn't she just imagine him with her? She coughed a ragged breath. *No.* She wouldn't allow herself to imagine it or allow the dark questions to creep up into her mind. It hurt too damned much.

Savannah moved closer. "What are you going to do?"

"Nothing," Lexie answered, immediately shaking her head and replacing her glasses.

Savannah blew out a breath that was all frustration. "Lex."

"No. He'll stay until his dad's better, then go back to New York and everything will be fine."

Savannah licked her lips. "Maybe this is the time to tell him. I know you wanted to wait, but school starts in September. That was always your deadline."

Lexie nodded sharply. "I know." But she was terrified. "I know."

"Lex." Savannah moved closer. "What if he decides to take a trip this side of town?"

Lexie's pulse rate soared. "Then we deal with it." She swallowed. "*I* deal with it."

.   .   .

Fifteen years ago . . .

"Riley, come and help me out back, please."

From his slumped position on the sofa, Riley ignored his father, rolled his eyes, and shoveled another spoonful of cereal into his mouth.

"Riley Lincoln Moore, that wasn't a question!"

From the floor, seated in front of the TV, Dex snorted. "Dude, you just got full named and it's not even Sunday."

No, it wasn't Sunday. It was Saturday. The Saturday after a week from hell, and the last thing Riley wanted to do was help his father do . . . whatever the hell it was he wanted him to do. Dex's blue eyes shined with amusement behind his black-rimmed glasses, making Riley curl his lip at his oldest brother. Dex chuckled harder.

"I'm busy!" Riley shouted back in reply. "But Dex is more than eager to help you."

The smile dropped off Dex's face like a stone in water. "Really?"

The smack to the top of Riley's head halted the smart-ass response he was going to fire back at Dex, while simultaneously causing him to flail and spill milk all over the crotch of his The Flash pajama pants.

"Goddammit," he swore, holding his bowl out in one hand, arms wide. He held his breath, realizing what he'd just said in front of his father.

"Get up," his father ordered, glaring down at Riley, apparently letting the curse slide.

"But Dad," Riley began in that whiney voice that could result in another smack.

"But Dad nothing," the man grumbled, pointing a finger in Riley's face. "Get your ass dressed in clothes you don't care about getting dirty and meet me in the backyard in ten minutes. And trust me, son, you don't want me to have to come and get you again."

The look he shot Riley always had all four Moore boys jumping in whatever direction their father wanted at lightning speed and, despite Riley feeling like crap, this time was no exception. With his bowl in the kitchen sink, he thumped up the stairs, dried himself, and then dressed in an old pair of jeans and an old T-shirt before joining his father in the backyard.

Park Moore was a large, formidable man. He had shoulders the width of a barn door, without having to work out too much, and hands the size of shovels. As a kid, Riley had always been in awe of the man's size, but now he was envious. He hoped to God that he'd be the same when he was older.

Riley couldn't be too down about it—he'd definitely had a growth spurt over the last year, hitting almost six feet, but his arms and legs were still lean and gangly. How was it fair that his younger brother, Seb, was already growing muscles at the age of twelve? And Tate, with his dreams of being in the military, was always running and competing in sports at school, so he was fairly ripped. Riley wasn't a slouch—he ran and played football three times a week—but he was still built like a damned green bean.

It wasn't fair.

Life *wasn't fair!*

Riley huffed and looked over the piles of wood and paint that his father was standing next to. "So what are we doing?" he asked petulantly.

"We're building the fence your mother wants."

Riley frowned. "Hasn't she been wanting a new fence since Christmas?" He glanced around himself. "It's May."

"Yes," Park replied with an exasperated sigh. "But I have the time now that I'm on vacation from work and I need your help."

Pushing his hands into his jeans pockets, Riley shrugged. "Help doing what?"

"I need you to knock down the old fence and help me put up the new one."

Riley considered his father for a moment, noticing the large mallet resting against a pile of timber. "I get to use that?"

Park followed Riley's gaze. "Can I trust you not to kill yourself or anyone else with it?"

"I can't promise anything if Dex comes out here, but I'll do my best," Riley offered, glimpsing a small smile twitch at the corner of Park's mouth.

"Then it's a deal."

Riley heaved the mallet over to the old fence, which in reality looked as though a slight breeze could knock it down, and glanced back at his father.

"Hands close to the head of it," Park instructed, clutching an invisible mallet, his hands clenched as fists in the air. "You let it get away from you and that's when the problems start."

Riley did as he was told and glared at the fence before he took a mighty swing and slammed the mallet head into it. The timber and concrete posts gave under the force, yielding a satisfying crack. Riley did it again even harder, until, with just three swings, the fence panel and post were all but rubble at his feet.

"That'll work," Park commented, his tone satisfied if not a little surprised. He twirled his index finger. "Now do it again to the rest of them."

Riley grinned and set about pummeling the fence with everything he had. The delicious burn through his arms and the satisfaction he got from hearing the cracks and snaps almost dissolved the anger that had been boiling in his belly for a week. He almost forgot how hurt he was when he'd learned that Lexie was going to the end-of-year dance with Blake fuckin' Richards instead of him, and the jealousy, which had Riley pinning the guy to a locker when he'd overheard him bragging about Lexie to his buddies, slowly turned from an all-out inferno to a gentle simmer.

Yeah, there was a lot to be said for hitting things to release tension.

When they'd worked halfway around the yard, Park fetched two cans of soda and two sandwiches to eat on the back porch. Riley sat with a groan, his back muscles protesting at the movement, and set about eating his lunch.

"You've done a good job," Park said, looking at Riley's handiwork before sliding his gaze over to him. "Feel better?"

Riley held his breath. He could detect a heart-to-heart coming a mile off, and Riley certainly wasn't about to discuss Lexie with his dad.

It was bad enough when his mother asked questions. "I'm fine," he said in lieu of anything else.

"Your mother's worried."

"I'm fine."

"So you've said, but I call bull."

Riley placed his half-eaten sandwich at his feet and exhaled. "I don't want to talk about it."

"I get that." Park nodded in Riley's periphery. "I do. And I don't want to pry."

Riley huffed and rolled his eyes. "Mom's probably told you everything anyway."

"You're probably right."

Riley had to smirk at that one. "It's nothing."

His dad placed his plate down, too, and moved a little closer until their shoulders touched. "You and Lexie have been friends for a long time."

"Yeah," Riley remarked bitterly. "Which doesn't seem to matter to her."

"And that hurts because you like her."

Riley cleared his throat and shrugged. "She's my friend."

"And a very pretty girl."

The sound that came from Riley was somewhere between a protest and an embarrassed laugh. He shook his head. It didn't matter that his father was right. Yes. Lexie was pretty. He fisted his hands between his knees.

Okay, really pretty.

Over the last few months, Riley had noticed that fact more and more—the way her blonde hair always looked great, the way her nose scrunched when he made her laugh, or how soft her skin was whenever he got the chance to touch it. The list of things he liked about her seemed to grow longer and longer as the days passed, leaving his head in a complete mess. Riley wasn't sure how it had happened or why, but his best friend whom he'd built spaceships with, collected worms with, and climbed trees with was now a girl who, when they touched, made his belly feel funny. He knew he'd always been a little possessive of her—he'd defended and protected her whenever she'd needed him to; she was his best friend, after all—but this was different. He felt different. Being just friends didn't seem enough for him anymore.

He'd done his best to behave normally around her and, as far as he could tell, he'd managed it. No one had said anything, at least. Except maybe his mother and Seb. Whatever. Riley couldn't deny a part of him hoped that maybe Lexie liked him in the same way, but apparently, with her going to the dance with someone else, he was deluding himself.

"It doesn't matter," he mumbled before taking a giant swig of his soda.

"Because of this Richards punk?"

Riley snorted at the way his father spat the name.

"So she picked him to go to this dance over you?"

Riley rubbed his hands through his hair.

His father hummed. "So what did she say when you asked her to the dance?"

Riley frowned. "Nothing. I didn't ask her."

Park narrowed his eyes. "You didn't ask her," he clarified, to which Riley shook his head. "But I thought you wanted to take her?"

"I do. I did," Riley blurted.

"So why the hell didn't you ask her?"

"Because . . ." Riley tried to come up with an answer but was suddenly struck with the overwhelming feeling that he'd truly screwed up. "I just assumed she'd—"

His words were cut off by his father's loud belly laugh. It echoed around the yard and, despite it normally being an infectious sound, it caused a large bubble of annoyance to swell in Riley's chest. "I'm glad you find this all so funny," he griped.

Park clapped a hand against Riley's back before he got up and stormed back into the house. "Oh, Riley." His father tried to calm himself by putting the back of his hand to his mouth. "Son," he muttered *into it. "Listen, if I had to give you only one piece of advice in your entire life regarding women, it'd be to never assume anything!"*

Riley grimaced in confusion. "But we're friends and . . ."

"And she was probably waiting for you to ask her."

His words slowly settled around them. She had *been acting weird recently. She'd snapped every time the dance was mentioned and commented frequently about how she "didn't want a new dress anyway."*

"Oh, shit."

"Yep," his father agreed.

Riley dropped his face to his hands. "What do I do now?"

He didn't care that he sounded desperate. He was *desperate.*

"You go and ask her."

Wow. Didn't that sound simple?

"She's not speaking to me," Riley confessed. "I told her she was an idiot for going with Blake and . . . a few other things." He cleared his throat, hating every barbed word he'd thrown at her the last time they'd spoken. "We haven't talked since Monday."

His father sat forward, reaching into his jeans back pocket, and pulled out his wallet. From its depths he retrieved ten dollars and handed it to Riley. "Then my second piece of advice about women is, flowers always work as an apology."

Riley gaped. "You want me to buy her flowers?"

Park nodded. "And apologize your ass off."

"Then what?"

"Then you ask her to the dance."

"But what if—"

"She won't."

"But how can you be sure that—"

"She will."

Riley stood, the ten dollars clenched in his hand. "Okay." He pointed at his dad. "Flowers. Then I ask her."

Park stood, too, his smile wide and maybe a little proud. "Sounds like a plan."

• • •

Riley grabbed the flowers he'd tied to his handlebars before he dropped his bike on Lexie's front lawn. He ran up the porch steps, lifted his hand to knock on the door, and paused. Christ. *He was suddenly finding it hard to breathe and his heart thumped so hard he could hear it.*

"Grow a set," he grumbled to himself, knowing that's exactly what Tate would have said to him had he been there. He gathered himself and knocked twice.

After a brief moment in which Riley took a few calming breaths, the door opened, and he came face to face with a blue-and-red plaid shirt and a waft of cigar smoke. "Mr. Pierce," Riley muttered, looking at the man with a nervous smile. He hated that Mr. Pierce intimidated him, especially when he saw how nice the man was with his wife and daughters. Lexie found her father's contempt toward Riley hysterical. But then, she was and always had been a daddy's girl.

Mr. Pierce eyed the flowers in Riley's hands and cocked an eyebrow. Heat surged into Riley's face. "Is Lexie in, sir?"

Mr. Pierce exhaled in that disgruntled way he always did around Riley and shouted over his shoulder, "Alexis, that boy is at the door."

Lexie's voice came from the top of the stairs and Riley's throat tightened. "What?"

Mr. Pierce turned back into the house, almost closing the door in Riley's face as he did. "That boy. He's at the door. With flowers."

"He's here with what?*"*

Riley closed his eyes and lifted his face to the heavens. This wasn't exactly how he'd imagined this would go.

"What are you doing here?" Lexie's question had Riley's eyes snapping open. She stood with her hand on her hip, her expression stern. Like her father, she glanced at the flowers with a mixture of suspicion and surprise.

He coughed and lifted them, holding them out to her. "Here. These are for you." She looked at him as though he'd grown a second head. "They're daisies," he said, stating the obvious. "I know you like them."

She looked between the damned things and Riley's face a few times before tentatively reaching out for them. "Um, thanks."

"You're welcome." Riley watched her hold them up to her nose and smell them. "They're to say I'm sorry."

"For what?" Lexie asked quickly. Her expression knew very well what he was apologizing for.

"For being an idiot."

"Riley," she uttered in exasperation. "If you brought me flowers every time you were an idiot, I'd be able to open my very own florists."

Riley couldn't have been certain, but the laugh he heard come from inside the house sounded like Mr. Pierce.

"I know," Riley agreed. "But they're also to say sorry for . . . not asking you to the dance."

For a split second, Lexie looked shocked as hell. "It's okay."

"No," Riley countered. "It's not okay. I should have . . . I should have asked you."

She toed the floor. "But you didn't, so . . ."

Noting her bitter tone, Riley ploughed on regardless. "I know you've agreed to go to the dance with Blake. And I know I said some not-so-nice things to you."

Her head snapped up, eyes blazing. "You called me a desperate sheep, a Hannah Grand wannabe!"

Riley winced, his stare on his feet. The underlying hurt in Lexie's words blatant, now he realized what an ass he'd been. "I know. I'm sorry. I didn't mean it." He shrugged. "Well, I did, but that's only because I was mad because he doesn't deserve to take you, and he only wants to take you because you'll look beautiful and he wants to look good and, Lex, you're better than that and—"

"Riley."

He snapped his mouth shut and took a deep breath. "Look, I was wondering if—"

"If what?"

"If you'd go with me instead."

She pressed her lips together, pursing them to the left. "You think you deserve me looking, what was it you said, 'beautiful' next to you?"

Riley's gaze meandered up the doorframe as he considered his answer. "No."

"No?"

"You'll look beautiful no matter who takes you," he said with a lift of his shoulders. "But that's not why I want to take you."

Lexie sighed, apparently confused and losing patience. "Okay. Then why do you want to take me?"

"Because you're my best friend," he answered quickly. "And because . . ."

Gathering his courage, Riley reached into his back pocket and pulled out the piece of paper he'd kept folded in a box at the back of a drawer for the past four years. "Do you remember giving me this?" he asked as he unfolded the picture of the Earth she'd drawn him on the day he'd defended her.

Something flashed across Lexie's blue eyes as she nodded, something that made Riley's stomach lurch. God, she was so very pretty. "Do you remember what you said it meant, what I meant to you?"

Lexie licked her lips and nodded again. He'd never known her to be so quiet, but he refused to let it worry him. "Well . . . I brought it to give it back."

Lexie blinked as though finally coming to. "What?"

"I'm giving it back," Riley repeated.

The bunch of daisies hit her thigh at the same time a V appeared between her brows. "Why?"

Riley swallowed and lifted his chin, staring straight at her. "Because I wanted you to know that you mean the same to me."

"The same?" Lexie whispered.

"All the world."

For the first time ever, Riley watched as a flush of beautiful pink washed over her cheeks. She shifted on her feet and dipped her chin as though hiding a smile. "Oh."

"So," he breathed and lifted his chest. "I know I've been a jerk, but I wanted to ask . . . would you go to the dance with me?"

The smile started at her eyes and drifted down her cheeks to her mouth. Her mouth, which Riley suddenly had the urge to kiss. His lungs squeezed.

"Okay," she answered quietly.

Riley blinked, meeting her stare. "Okay?"

"I said so, didn't I?"

Riley grinned at her sassy tone. The tone he loved to needle out of her at every opportunity. "Yeah. Okay. Great!"

"Alexis!" Mr. Pierce's voice came from the depths of the house, sounding even more amused. "Tell that boy to go home. You have schoolwork to do, and then we're going to Grandma's."

"Okay, Dad," she called back, still smiling. She turned to Riley and whispered, "I'll come over when we get back."

And without another word, she leaned over and kissed his cheek. Before Riley could do or say anything, Lexie giggled, clutched the daisies to her chest, and closed the door.

6

"Dad's awake."

Tate's voice drew Riley from a deep sleep filled with sweet and vivid memories of daisies, dances, and pink dresses.

As though it were just yesterday, Riley remembered him and his parents picking Lexie up the night of the dance, her amazing dress, the coy glances and torturously fleeting touches, and finally, *finally* getting so close to her that he was unable to resist placing his mouth on hers. Their first kiss. *His* first kiss. She'd been so damned soft, and the taste of vanilla had made his head spin. He'd gripped her waist as she'd squeezed his arm, hoping to God that he was doing it right. Because it had felt *so* right. It always had with her.

The kiss had lasted mere seconds but when they broke apart, breathing heavily and both a little dazed, Riley had known, from the look in her eyes, that everything between them had changed.

He opened his own eyes to find Tate standing at the side of his bed. It was early. The sun had yet to hit his bedroom window, which it always did from 8 a.m., but Tate was fully dressed. Despite his not being an active Marine in over five years, he was still usually up before sunrise.

Tate's words eventually seeped into Riley's consciousness, forcing him to sit up quickly. "Is he okay? Mom all right?"

Tate nodded. "The hospital just called; Mom spoke to them. He's groggy, but he's okay. He spoke with the nurse and the doctor is on his way to see him."

Slumping back in relief, Riley rubbed his eyes with the back of his hands. "You're going to the hospital?"

"Yeah. I'll take Mom. Can you tell Seb?"

"Sure. We'll come up later. Maybe best not to overwhelm him."

And Riley wasn't quite ready to see his father just yet. He would, of course, but he didn't want to add any more tension and stress to an already emotional time. As long as he knew his parents and brothers were okay, he was happy to take a backseat. He and his father would talk, they had to, but not while he was in intensive care recovering from a second heart attack.

"Gotcha," Tate said as he turned to leave. "I'll call you. Maggie's coming over with Rosie. I think she's worried we can't fend for ourselves."

Riley smirked. "We're grown men. Of course we can't fend for ourselves."

Once Tate and their mom had left the house, Riley made his way downstairs, brewed some coffee, and sat with his mug at the kitchen table, trying not to think about what seeing Savannah the day before had made him feel. God, she'd looked shocked as hell when she'd seen him, which shouldn't have surprised Riley all that much—it had had been a long time since he'd traveled back to Michigan. But he couldn't shake the feeling that there was more to it than that. Riley could have sworn he'd seen panic.

And the little boy. That was weird. Riley knew the Pierce family had moved from Traverse City not long after Riley's last visit five years ago, but surely someone would have known about Savannah having a kid. But then, what business was it of his? None. It was none of his business. Riley sighed, glancing out the kitchen window to the yard, where the fence he'd built with his father fifteen years ago still stood tall and strong. He smiled, recollecting what had been a great day. The feelings, though, were so much more potent than usual with the previous night's dream still tap-tapping at his brain.

The house phone ringing jolted Riley from his memories. He hopped off his stool and pulled it from its place on the wall. He had to say hello three times before there was a response.

"Riley? Riley, it's Dex. Can you hear me?"

Riley pushed the tip of his finger into his other ear, blocking out any other sound. "Just."

"It's this crappy cell," Dex grumbled. "Wait a minute."

Riley did as he was asked, hearing white noise, a buzz, and then a beat of silence. When his brother's voice returned to the line it was much clearer. "Jesus, man," Riley teased. "What shitty company are you working for that your cell doesn't work properly?"

Dex snorted. "Tell me about it. The weather's been playing havoc with the Internet and phone lines here. Lemme tell you, for a group of computer nerds and geeks, it ain't pretty."

Riley leaned his forearm against the wall, realizing belatedly how nice it was to hear Dex's voice. "How're things apart from that? Thailand, huh?"

"Yeah," he answered nonchalantly. "Things aren't bad. Busy, you know? How's Dad? I got a text from Mom saying he was awake."

"Yeah, he woke this morning. He's okay. Tate and Mom have gone to see him. I'm here with Seb."

There was a sigh on the other end of the line. "I wish I were there."

Riley nodded despite the fact that Dex couldn't see him. "I know, man, but apart from worrying and pacing, there's not much to be done."

Dex huffed a laugh. "I guess. But knowing he's ill just makes me feel even farther away from home." He cleared his throat. "Good to speak to you, though, Riley. It's been a while."

Riley grimaced. "I know. We should arrange something for when you're next in NYC."

"Sounds like a plan, as long as you don't take me to that club again. There are some things that can't be unseen."

Riley laughed at the memory of the strip joint he'd taken Dex to on Dex's birthday two years before. His face when he'd walked in the place had been a goddamn picture, and he'd nearly had a coronary when Riley paid one of the girls for a birthday dance. Dex could drink and party with the best of them, but, of the four brothers, Dex was possibly the least open about anything sex related. And it wasn't that he couldn't snatch up a hot chick; he just didn't seem interested. It was almost hilarious how oblivious the man was to the attention he got from members of the opposite sex—the geeky, glasses, tie-wearing look was apparently a turn-on.

If it hadn't been for Riley walking in on Dex and a girl he'd met at college one time, he would have wondered if Dex even knew what to *do* with a woman.

"I'll be good, I swear," Riley offered.

"I'll believe that when I see it," Dex retorted, humor in his voice. "You still young, free, and single?"

"Yup," Riley answered, his dream about Lexie flittering through his mind. "Best way to be, man." Seb appeared in the kitchen doorway, hair in disarray, scratching his bare chest. Before Dex could ask any more about Riley's relationship status, he said, "Seb's here. You wanna talk?"

"Sure," Dex said. "You take care, yeah?"

"Always do." Riley passed the phone to Seb and wandered back to his stool, sipping on the coffee that had cooled. He listened to Seb's half of the conversation and his reaction to hearing that Park was awake, until his younger brother said good-bye and hung up the phone.

"So it's just us?" Seb asked with a yawn.

"Maggie's coming later," Riley said, standing and wandering over to the sink, where he placed his cup.

Seb nodded while pouring his own coffee. He leaned a hip against the counter's edge. "So what's the plan until then?"

Riley looked out at the blue sky. The sun was still low, but it was already getting warm through the window. It was going to be a gorgeous day. He smiled. "You feel like getting your hands dirty?"

In fairness, Park hadn't done a bad job of fixing the roof, but there was still a lot of work to do. After clambering up the ladder to the top of the house, Riley and Seb began pulling up the damaged slate and lining, and reminisced about when they were kids. They laughed until they cried about Tate shooting himself in the ass with a pellet gun. *"I was trying to be John McClane!"* And about Dex throwing up after getting drunk when he was seventeen, and their dad making him drink more as punishment. *"Don't you dare vomit and waste that beer, son."* And about a three-year-old Seb getting a toilet-training seat stuck around his neck and the three hours it took for their mother to get it off him again. *"I am not taking him to the hospital with a toilet seat around his neck, Park!"*

After a good few hours' work, both of them shirtless, they lay back on the part of the roof they'd fixed and took a break. Tate texted Riley to tell them their father was being moved from ICU to high dependency, where he would stay under observation, but the surgeon was happy. It was good news, and the tightness that had wound through Riley from the minute he'd heard his father was ill eased a fraction.

"So guess who I saw at the park yesterday," Riley said casually. Seb looked over, one eye closed against the bright sun. "Savannah Pierce."

"No shit."

Riley lifted his eyebrows. "Right? Kind of weird to see her there."

"How'd she look?"

Riley exhaled an amused breath. Seb and Savannah had shared a few drink-fueled nights together during their senior year. Savannah had grown quite attached, but Seb had never been serious about her. "Shocked as hell," Riley replied.

"No doubt, but that's not what I meant."

"I know." Riley closed his eyes against the sun. "She looked good. Did you hear anything about her having a baby?"

Seb's head snapped back as though he'd been slapped, his expression stunned. "She had a baby?"

"She was at the park with a little boy," Riley said with a lift of his shoulders. "You didn't hear anything?"

"Not a thing. I never heard much after they moved."

It was what Riley had figured, and exactly what Tate had said when Riley had asked him, but it frustrated Riley all the same. He hated that he still cared so damned much, but he couldn't adjust his feelings for Lexie any more than he could turn back time and take back everything they'd ever said to each other.

"Anyone home?"

Riley and Seb peeped over the guttering of the roof to see Maggie grinning up at them with her hands at the small of her back so her baby belly stuck out, looking even bigger. With arms in the air, singing to herself, Rosie twirled around the backyard.

"When you two body beautifuls are done sunning yourselves," Maggie called up, "come to the kitchen. I brought Subway."

"Love you, Mags!" the brothers yelled back in unison.

"Yeah, yeah," their cousin grumbled, waddling her way back into the house.

.   .   .

The high dependency unit was a lot more welcoming than the ICU, although Riley put that down to the palpable fear and heartache that seemed to cling to the walls of that particular part of the hospital. Not that the lavender paint and easy-smiling nurses made him feel much better as he walked with Seb and Maggie down the HDU corridor toward his father's room.

In fact, he felt physically sick. It wasn't in his nature to be such a pussy, but Riley was all too aware of the shit-ton of water under this particular bridge and he wasn't sure there was room for more. His mom greeted them all at the door of the room with hugs and cheek kisses and ushered them in, whispering words about them only staying a short time because "Daddy is still fuzzy."

The first things Riley noticed were the wires and machines blurting out sporadic beeps and hisses that were altogether fucking terrifying. There was a patch of white bandage taped to his father's chest and an oxygen tube fixed under his nose. The second thing that Riley noticed was how small his father looked. Small and unbearably weak. He gritted his teeth and pushed his hands into his pockets, fighting off the feeling of helplessness that crashed over him.

Seb approached the bed first, taking Tate's place, and put his hand on Park's forearm. "Hey, Dad." The corner of Park's mouth twitched as he opened his eyes before blinking in reply.

"His voice and throat are a little sore," Joan explained. "He's still not allowed to drink anything."

"Hell of a way to get out of fixing the roof, huh?" Seb said. They all chuckled when Park gave a shaky thumbs-up. "Maybe do it before you get up the ladder next time." Seb leaned over and placed a kiss on his father's forehead.

Joan smiled and glanced at Riley, who fidgeted under her knowing look. "Riley's here, too, Park," she said, rubbing her hand down Riley's arm.

Park's tired, brown gaze slid over to their side of the room. His and Riley's eyes met and, inexplicably, Riley's throat became tight. "Good to see you, Dad," he managed. It was the most cordial thing he'd said to the man in almost five years.

After a tense moment in which Joan's grip on Riley's arm began to tighten, Park blinked just as he had done with Seb, and dipped his chin in reply. The gesture told Riley they still had a long way to go, but it was more than Riley could have ever hoped for.

A plump nurse entered the room with a bag of fluid and squeezed past Riley and his mother. "Don't be crowding my patient now," she warned. "Five more minutes."

"Nancy, this is my niece, Maggie, and these two are my other sons," Joan told the nurse, pointing at them in turn. "Riley and Sebastian."

Nancy eyed the two of them as she changed Park's IV and pursed her lips. "Handsome boys," she commented. "But pretty doesn't make my patient better. Four minutes."

Riley snickered into the back of his hand when he saw Tate's finger move in a circular motion by his own temple.

"Look, why don't we leave and get something nice for dinner, maybe have a mosey around the stores?" Maggie suggested. "I have to pick Rosie up from day care. We'll leave you in peace, Uncle Park. Rosie is desperate to go to the Disney store."

"Urgh, really?" Riley griped, slapping his palms to his thighs in disgust.

"What?" Maggie asked.

"Ignore him," Tate answered with a smug grin. "He's only sore because Disney loves Marvel. Just like I do." He gestured to the T-shirt he was wearing that read, "Who the hell is Bucky?"

Maggie shook her head at Tate in confusion. "Who the hell *is* Bucky?"

Riley barked a laugh in Tate's direction at the same time Seb begged, "Don't, Mags. Please!"

"She doesn't know who Bucky is," Riley said with a loud snort over Seb's pleading.

Tate smirked, crossing his arms over his chest. "She doesn't know who Bane is, either."

"You shut your mouth," Riley snapped with a pointed finger at his brother before glaring at Maggie. "Are you serious? Did you not even watch *The Dark Knight Rises*? Tom Hardy!" All he got from his cousin was a vacant expression. "Jesus, Mags, how are we even related?"

Seb groaned. "Make it stop."

"I concur," Joan added, gently cajoling Riley toward the door while beckoning Tate over with a wave. "Go with Maggie. Sebastian can stay here with me." She cupped Tate's face. "You need some fresh air, sweetheart. And sitting in that chair is doing your leg no favors."

"I'm fine, Ma," he protested.

"That may be so, but I'm tired of your gorgeous face."

"Pffft. I've seen turds more gorgeous." Riley laughed and ducked from Tate's fist that flew toward his bicep. "Dick move, bro," he commented. "You know I can't hit you back because you're a cripple."

"Riley!" Joan exclaimed.

"What?" Riley asked incredulously, pointing at Tate. "He's the one who said it."

But Tate didn't reply, save for his laughter that echoed down the corridor.

• • • •

"This is hell," Riley grumbled, scowling at the Avengers figurine sets packing most of the shelves in the Disney store. "I think my three-piece chicken is going to come back up."

"Oh, stop," Maggie chastised playfully. "Rosie loves it here."

Riley looked over at Rosie flittering and humming around the place, unable to fight the smile that pulled across his face. She was too cute in her sparkling shoes and blue dress.

"Do you know she demands that I do her hair like Elsa every day? She's a queen, too, you know."

"I just bet she is. And what fun that must be," Riley added drolly.

Maggie sighed when Rosie picked up an Elsa doll and hugged it. "Shit, who the hell am I kidding? I'm just praying for the day Disney releases something else so we can all move on and I can finally have some variety of music in the damn car already!"

"*Frozen* sound track?"

"I know it word for word, I swear to God."

Riley laughed and patted Maggie on the shoulder. "God bless Disney." He noticed Tate lift a bobble-head Iron Man and then another that looked like Thor and shook his head. "At least there's *Star Wars* stuff," he mused, eyeing the plush Yodas.

He gravitated toward the *Millennium Falcon* Lego sets, maneuvering his way around kids and other grown adults who were unable to resist the pull of anything created by George Lucas. He picked one up, trying to convince himself that spending over sixty bucks on Lego was outrageous even if it *did* come with an awesome Lego Han Solo and Chewy.

"Dammit, even as Lego, Han Solo looks good."

"I likes Luke Skiesswalker bestest."

The small but resolute voice came from near Riley's knee. Riley looked down to see a blond head of hair burrowing between the lightsabers on the second shelf.

"That's because you don't know any better, kid," he remarked.

The boy reappeared with a blue lightsaber in his hand. "Ham Solo doesn't haves this."

Riley grinned at the way the boy's lisp made his *S*es sound like adorable hisses. "That's true," Riley agreed, waving the box in his hand. "But Han has the *Millennium Falcon*—much better than a lightsaber, wouldn't you agree?"

Still on his knees, and with the lightsaber clutched to his chest, the little boy looked up. His eyes were large and hazel and reminded Riley so much of his own that he was momentarily struck dumb.

"No," the boy replied, his attention dancing between Riley and his toy. "Luke Skiesswalker has The Force." He blinked up at Riley as though daring him to argue.

Riley chuckled and put the Lego set back on the shelf. "I stand corrected. How can I possibly argue with that?"

"You can't," the little boy replied, getting to his feet. "I likes *Star Wars* lots."

"And Batman," Riley commented, noting the T-shirt the boy was wearing. "That's really cool. I have one like it."

The little boy scrunched up his nose. "You can't wear Batman. You have a beard. You're growed up."

Riley grinned. "That's debatable, but I love Batman. I even have Batman socks."

The boy gaped. "Me toos! And pajamas. I get them every Christmas."

"Are you serious? You're like the coolest boy *ever*."

"I know!"

Riley crossed an arm over himself and laughed into his free hand.

"Noah?"

"Uh-oh," the boy uttered, looking behind Riley.

"Noah, I told you to keep hold of my hand and not to— Oh."

Riley recognized the voice before he even turned to see who was standing at the end of the aisle. *Jesus fuck.* She sounded just the same as he remembered and caused his heart to do an honest-to-God cartwheel in his chest. Her name left him as a whisper when he finally allowed himself to turn and found, once he did, that he had to reach out and clutch the edge of the nearest shelf, his legs shook so damned hard.

"Riley." Lexie's eyes flickered quickly between Riley and the boy standing at his side. It didn't make Riley feel any better that she looked as surprised to see him as he was to see her. In fact, she looked plain terrified. "I . . . What—how—how are you?"

Riley cleared his throat. "I'm good." He tried to smile but it felt forced and tight, and holy hell, did she have a septum piercing? "And you? How're you?" he stammered. "You look . . . well."

What a fucking understatement that was. She was beautiful. Her hair was as blonde as it had always been, but now she had bangs that framed her face. The rest of it was long and braided and sat on her shoulder. Her glasses were ones he'd never seen, but they were the obligatory pink he forever associated with her. Despite the frames being thick, they did nothing to hide the blue of her eyes.

She wore a black vest top that showed the ink she'd had tattooed on her arm and shoulder, denim shorts that accentuated her legs, and on her feet? Well. Wouldn't you know it? Black laced Doc Marten boots. His belly bloomed with warmth. No matter what they had done to each other, said to each other, she was still the fearless girl he'd grown up with, the girl who kicked his ass at every sport or game they ever played, the girl who wouldn't stand for anybody's bullshit. Even his.

She nodded sharply. "I'm good."

"Good." Riley rubbed a hand across his forehead, where a righteous headache threatened to begin.

"Noah, we have to go." Lexie held a hand out to the little boy, who, Riley suddenly realized, was the same boy he'd seen with Savannah.

"I found the Skiesswalker lightsaber," Noah exclaimed, holding it above his head.

"I see that," Lexie said with a smile she used to save just for Riley. "But it's not your birthday for another seven months, so put

it back, please. Maybe you can ask Santa for it this year. Let's go—
I've gotta get back to work."

Noah sighed but didn't argue. Very slowly, he placed it back
on the shelf and walked toward Lexie on heavy kid Converse feet.

"A fellow *Star Wars* fan," Riley commented with an awkward
laugh. "He's being raised right."

Lexie's expression, however, was anything but amused. "Yeah.
Okay." She clasped Noah's hand. "See ya."

"'Bye," Riley replied. "'Bye, Noah." Noah waved back, but he
didn't turn as he stumbled after Lexie.

"Damn, was that as awkward as it looked?" Tate asked quietly
from behind Riley.

"Worse," Riley admitted. He exhaled and looked back at his
brother. "Am I bleeding? I feel like I was just fuckin' mauled."

Tate's smile was small and sympathetic. "No, you're okay."

"Christ, I need a beer." Riley winced with the jolt of guilt that
snapped through him when he remembered Tate's addiction recovery meant he couldn't drink. "Sorry."

"Dude," Tate chastised. "If you need a beer, let's go and get you
a damn beer."

"I wish *I* could have a beer," Maggie complained as she approached, keeping her stare on where Lexie and Noah had exited
the store. "Who was that?"

Riley rubbed his beard and sighed. "An old friend."

Maggie wagged a finger toward the exit. "You know, I'm sure
that's the woman who owns the store Mom and I visited last
week."

Riley glanced at Tate. "Store?"

"Yeah," Maggie continued, looking around herself for Rosie.
"That cool jewelry place. Rosie, come here, please. It's where
I got this ring." She held out her right hand and wiggled the
silver ring on her middle finger. Riley leaned closer to see the

word *serenity* embossed across it. It was lovely, and Riley smiled instinctively.

His gaze cut across to his brother. "You up for taking a trip across town tomorrow?"

Tate grinned. "Why not?"

7

Twelve years ago . . .

"Hey, man," Riley said as he walked into the kitchen to find Tate sitting at the breakfast bar eating toast. Tate had been home from medical school for a little over a week and, Riley had to admit, it was great to have his brother back. With Dex working in San Francisco and Seb playing every sport known to man after school and during every free minute he had, the house could get a little too quiet.

"Hey." Riley could feel Tate's gaze follow him around the kitchen. "You look guilty. What's up with you?"

"Nothing," Riley answered over his shoulder as he poured cereal into a bowl. But that wasn't exactly true. "It's Lex's birthday."

Tate crossed his arms on the breakfast bar. "Oh yeah?"

Riley nodded, turned, and leaned against the counter, spooning cereal into his mouth. Tate stared at him, waiting. "What do you need from me?"

Riley craned his neck to look through the kitchen door, checking to see if either of his parents was around. Satisfied that they were alone, he took a deep breath. "Can I borrow your truck?" Tate cocked an eyebrow in question. "It's to help with Lexie's birthday present."

"And your car isn't suitable?" Riley shook his head. "Dare I ask?"

Riley felt his cheeks heat and his stomach clench. "Best if you don't."

Tate shook his head. "Okay, you can borrow the truck on two con-

ditions. One: you clean up any mess before I get it back, and I mean any fucking mess. Two: you pack condoms."

Riley laughed but didn't argue with his brother. He'd been planning tonight for weeks and was equal parts excited and fucking terrified. He and Lexie had been officially a couple since their first kiss the night of the dance three years before, and tonight Riley planned for them to take the next step. Of course, since that dance, they'd done more than kiss, but they hadn't gone the whole way. Riley had remembered Lexie saying something about her birthday and how romantic it would be and . . . well, the truth was, he was desperate for her.

Being friends for nearly a decade, they'd shared so much. Done so much. Experienced so much. Everything except sex. No. Tonight wouldn't be just sex, of that Riley was damned certain. Having seen and felt parts of Lexie's body no other man had, Jesus, he couldn't even imagine what it would feel like to finally push himself into—

"So what's the plan?" Tate asked, placing his plate and cup into the dishwasher.

Riley cleared his throat and his mind of the luscious images he'd conjured and shrugged. "Food. Candlelight. Maybe a little wine."

"You're seventeen."

"Your point?"

"You're drinking and driving."

"The wine's for Lex, nimrod," Riley retorted. "To relax her." He shifted on his feet under the perceptive stare of his brother. "I know she'll be nervous."

Tate nodded as though Riley's words had confirmed what he had suspected: tonight, Riley was going to lose his virginity. Tate moved closer and crossed his arms over his chest. He'd bulked up some since going to med school and his arms were freaking huge. Riley was more than a little jealous, despite having filled out in size himself. He was six foot two and weighed nearly 180 pounds. Being on the school football team sure had improved his fitness.

"You know you can ask me anything, right?" Tate offered in that calm voice Riley unexpectedly realized he missed.

Riley put his bowl down and nodded. "Yeah."

"And you're gonna be safe, right?"

Riley scoffed. "I'm not stupid."

"Hey," Tate said firmly. "I know you're not stupid, Ri. You're anything but. I just want to make sure you're okay, that you're ready."

Riley gazed out of the window toward the yard fence, struck with the memory of building it with his dad and how hurt he'd been that day knowing Lex was going to the dance with Blake fuckin' Richards. He smiled. How far they'd come.

"I'm so ready, man." Riley turned to his brother. "I don't mean that in the way it sounded. I mean it because . . ." The words pushed their way up his throat. "I love her."

Tate's lips lifted at the corners. "I know you do." He clapped a hand to Riley's shoulder and squeezed. "Little brother growin' up."

Riley shoved him off with a laugh. "Shut up."

"Enjoy," Tate added as he threw the truck keys at Riley, left the kitchen, and launched himself up the stairs.

The rest of the day was filled with getting everything ready. Riley managed to convince his mom to cook a couple of Lexie's favorite foods, which she placed lovingly into Tupperware tubs before leaving them in the fridge. Riley packed what he needed into the bed of Tate's truck and drove as close as he could to a spot in the woods that he knew would give them the utmost privacy. It was a spot he and Lexie had discovered once when they were ten-year-old space explorers and it had always stuck with Riley as one of his favorite memories. He doubted Lexie would remember, but there was a part of the forest canopy that opened up, showing millions of stars. Lexie had tried to name every one.

Riley set about making everything perfect, needing it to be perfect. His cell phone chirped with a text message in his pocket. He pulled out his Nokia 3100 and smiled at the screen. Lexie.

Did you know it's my birthday?

> Yes, I did. Even though I texted you at a
> minute past midnight: Happy birthday!

Thank you. Again. Where are you?

> Doing some stuff :)

Stuff? When can I see you?

> I'll pick you up at six as planned.

Can't wait.

With an extra spring in his step, Riley surveyed his work one last time and jumped back into the truck, hightailing it home for a cool shower and some serious chill time. He was about ready to jump out of his skin and the closer it got to six o'clock, the more anxious he became, which was . . . ridiculous, really. Lexie was the one person in the whole world Riley trusted most. Sharing such a private, intimate part of himself with her should be simple, easy, natural even. But that didn't stop his heart from fluttering like a swarm of damned butterflies as he pulled up at her parents' house and honked the horn.

The door opened, and Lexie appeared in a pair of shorts and a pink tank top printed with varying-sized stars of deeper pink. With the summer heat, she'd ditched the usual Docs in favor of a pair of pink flip-flops and had tied her hair up into a messy bun. God, Riley loved her hair like that. He liked the shape of her neck and the fact that he could kiss that part of her. But he also loved knowing that with one tug, her hair would fall down her back and he could lose himself in its smell.

Mr. Pierce stood in the doorway watching Lexie with the eye of a father who suspected his seventeen-year-old daughter's boyfriend was up to no good. Riley tried to smile, but it fell flat when Mr. Pierce glared in reply. Shit. *Even after nine years, the man still called Riley "that boy" and barely spoke to him when he was at Lexie's house. Lexie laughed about it and maintained that Mr. Pierce actually liked Riley—that his bluster was all a façade. But Riley didn't believe that shit one iota. Lexie was a bona fide daddy's girl and the man was scary as hell. For one split second, with Mr. Pierce's all-knowing stare needling him across the twenty feet of the front yard, Riley reconsidered what he'd planned.*

"Hey!" Lexie grinned as she jumped into the truck, slammed the door, and leaned over to kiss Riley's cheek. "I missed you."

With those three words, all of Riley's fears and doubts flew out the window as Lexie waved at her father. "I missed you, too," he admitted, putting the truck in drive and setting off.

Lexie clapped her hands together. "So what's the big surprise? Where are you taking me? What's the plan?"

Riley laughed. "Wait. Were you seventeen today or seven?"

"What?" she protested. "I'm excited. Sue me."

Riley reached across the truck seat and grabbed her hand. Pulling it to his mouth, he placed a gentle kiss on her knuckle. "I'm glad you're excited and we'll be there in about fifteen minutes."

She beamed at him and jumped a little in her seat. She was too adorable when she was like that. As they got closer to the part of the forest where Riley had set everything up, he noticed that Lexie seemed confused. He smirked. "You okay over there? Don't you remember?"

Lexie leaned closer to the window, as if that would help her realize where she was, and her mouth dropped open. "Oh my God, is this where we counted the stars?"

"And you tried to name them all."

"How the hell did you find this place again? What were we, like, twelve?"

"Ten. And why wouldn't I remember?" He turned his head to look at her. "I was with you."

Lexie's face softened as a small smile played across her gorgeous mouth. Riley had always thought Lexie pretty, from the very first moment he saw her. But, over the years, she'd become so beautiful he'd catch himself staring at her just because he could.

"Riley," she whispered. His heart fluttered when she spoke his name and his skin was set on fire when she reached out to run her hand around his neck.

He did his best to focus on the dirt path and finally pulled the truck up to where he needed it. Turning it off, he threw a wide smile at Lexie before jumping out of the truck and moving to her side. He held the door open and closed it behind her when Lexie was next to him. He took a step away, but her hand on his wrist stopped him. He looked at her curiously.

"Come here," she said in that soft, breathy voice that never failed to get Riley's blood pumping.

He did as she asked, dipping his face to hers so they could kiss. Jesus, they'd gotten good at kissing since that first one all that time ago. They knew exactly how to get each other going. Lexie would do this thing where she'd nibble on Riley's bottom lip. When she was really into it and clothes had come off, the nibbles would turn to bites. It drove Riley insane.

They broke apart and Riley rested his forehead against hers. "What was that for?"

Lexie placed her hands on his face. "It was to say that, no matter what happens tonight, you've already made it the best birthday ever."

And didn't those words just make Riley's heart soar? "Come on," he murmured when he found his voice. He pecked at her mouth. "Let's eat."

"Eat?" Lexie asked with an incredulous laugh that got lost on the evening's breeze when she finally saw what he'd done.

Riley had placed a large picnic blanket on the forest floor, directly under the canopy opening so once it got dark, their view of the stars would be brilliant. He'd found some lanterns, just like those from *their junior dance, and hung them on the closest trees ready to be lit, next to pink balloons and pink streamers hanging off branches and leaves. He'd brought a couple of extra blankets in case the temperature dropped later, and there were plates, covered fruit and bread, and the food Riley's mom had prepared still in their Tupperware containers.*

Lexie was quiet for so long, Riley started to become nervous. "Do you like it?"

"It's . . . perfect," she gasped, placing a hand to her chest. "I can't believe you did this for me."

It still blew Riley's mind that Lexie struggled to grasp just what she meant to him. It shouldn't have, considering they'd not ever really said the "I love yous," but honestly, there'd never been a need. It was unspoken between them, residing in their nine-year friendship, fleeting glances, kisses, and touches.

They sat together on the blanket and Riley set about plating the food. "Your mom made this?" Lexie asked. Riley smiled as he passed her the lasagne that was still a little warm. "She's a legend."

"Like mother, like son," he commented and wiggled his eyebrows, causing Lexie to laugh.

The food was awesome, and, once they'd had their fill, Riley lit the lanterns and tea lights he'd stashed. They lay back on the blanket and watched the blue sky turn indigo, talking about everything and nothing until indigo turned to black. Their conversations were filled with laughter and truth, echoing through the woods, while the silences were anything but uncomfortable. She laid her head on his chest, smiling as she listened to his heartbeat and he played with her hair. She pointed at stars and told him stories about them and he listened as intently as he always did. Riley wasn't sure what he loved more—when she was chatty and enthused or when she was quiet and smiling. Not that it mattered; she was perfect either way.

Riley bit into a strawberry she held over his mouth, sucking her fingers as he did.

"Where do you want to be in ten years?"

Riley blinked at Lexie's question and swallowed the strawberry down. "What do you mean?"

"I mean, work, life." She wiped her hands on a napkin. "We have to start thinking about college for next year. You still want to go to NYU?"

With his head resting on his arm beneath it, he turned to look at her. "I want a business degree. Dad says it'd be the best thing for me for the future. You know Dad wants me to take over the shop. I work there enough for him and none of the others want it."

"But is it what you want?"

"Sure," he answered truthfully. "I'm good at it and I enjoy working with cars. But I want to push myself. NYU Stern has the best business program. I'd be able to learn the financial side of running a successful business, more than what I could learn just with my dad. He's happy to pay the bill, so I'm lucky. Plus, with this degree I could have my own business one day. Have a chain of places, a franchise, or even go into something bigger, like parts manufacturing maybe. That's what I'd really want."

Lexie propped herself on an elbow at his side. She watched him carefully, trailing a finger over his Green Lantern T-shirt.

"What about you?" he asked.

"I don't know. I'm still undecided." Riley smirked, knowing that she'd been turning herself inside out with her indecision. "I'd like to do something . . . maybe astronomy."

"Really?" Riley sat up, taking her by surprise. "Because, honestly, that'd be awesome! You'd crush it."

Lexie snickered. "You think?"

"I know! Seriously"—he waved a hand towards the sky—"you know all the names and everything. No one knows more about the solar system than you."

Lexie huffed and lay back down. "Now you're mocking me."

Riley leaned over her. "I'm not." He dipped his head and kissed the tip of her shoulder. "You're like Stephen Hawking or . . ." He thought for a moment, drawing a blank. "Whoever else is really good at space stuff." Her body vibrated under his mouth as she giggled. "I think it'd be amazing," he offered, looking up at her. "No bullshit."

Her annoyed expression softened. "You know, there's an amazing Physics program I've seen," she murmured. Riley hummed into her skin, loving the taste of her skin on his lips. "They do cosmology and, well . . . it's at NYU, too."

Riley froze for a moment before lifting his head. His eyes traveled over her face, knowing every freckle, dip, and small scar by heart. "What?"

"The course. It's at NYU," she repeated, her voice cautious.

Riley drew his head back a little, so he could see all of her. "You'd go to NYU?"

She lifted a shoulder. "I have the grades to get financial aid and it's an amazing school, but . . . more importantly, you'd be there."

Riley tried to swallow past the huge lump of exhilaration and emotion that abruptly lodged in his throat. "You'd come with me. To New York?"

She raised a hand and ran it through his hair, making his eyes roll back into his head. "I'd go anywhere with you."

"Lex," her name escaped his lips before they crashed down onto hers.

Jesus. Riley had never heard news so good and his chest almost burst with relief. He'd worried so much about leaving Michigan to go to college—even considering options closer to home—but he'd all but pushed it to the back of his mind, not wanting to consider what it would do to his heart to be separated from his Lexie. But now? Now all he wanted to do was lose himself to her, and then show her what her words meant to him.

She opened her legs and he dropped carefully between them, wanting her to feel what she did to his body. He was seventeen and, at this point, more than a little familiar with his dick and his hard-ons, but fuck, he was never as hard as he was when he was with Lexie this way. He tilted his hips and pushed against her, the way he knew she loved.

They'd made each other come so many times like this, and each time was incredible. She gasped into his mouth and pulled him closer, her fingertips pinching the skin of his neck and shoulders as his mouth traveled from hers to her cheek to her chin and her throat. He was ravenous.

"Please," she whimpered into his hair, writhing deliciously beneath him.

"Tell me."

"I want you."

"You have me."

"I want you inside . . ."

Riley took a deep breath and pushed himself to his hands at either side of her head. She was beautifully flushed. "You're sure? I mean, I know you said, but—"

Her fingers on his lips stopped him. "I'm ready."

He smiled and kissed her tenderly. "Come with me."

He clambered to his feet and held a hand out for her to take, leading her back to the truck. Telling her to wait by the truck bed, he slipped the keys into the ignition so that the electrics gave a gentle whirr and he plugged a cord into the voltage outlet on the dash.

The laugh he heard from Lexie told him his plan had worked. Around the back of the truck cabin, he'd stuck small pink and white fairy lights. And, in the truck bed itself, once he pulled back the tarpaulin covering it, he'd laid out a couple of large blankets and at least six pillows.

He fidgeted when she turned to him. "I like to plan ahead."

Lexie snorted and started clambering into the truck bed, dropping back onto the blankets. She kicked off her flip-flops and exhaled. Riley watched her stomach and chest rise and fall with his heart in his throat. She was the most amazing thing he'd ever seen, but the enormity of the situation began to weigh heavily. Fuck. They were really going to do this.

Noticing that he hadn't moved to join her, Lexie looked up. "You okay?" she asked, leaning back on her elbows.

He smiled and ran a hand through his hair. "Just . . . watching you."

She smiled. "You going to watch all night, or are you going to join me?"

Without a second thought, Riley kicked off his own flip-flops and climbed into the bed, crawling up her body and making her squeal as he blew raspberries on the parts of her belly that he could see. He kissed her repeatedly until she stopped laughing and dissolved into him, holding him so damned close, clutching him as though terrified he would leave.

"It's okay," he whispered into her skin. "You're okay."

"I love you," she said, her words quiet but fervent. "God, I love you so much."

Riley's breath stuttered from his lungs and his eyes quickly became very hot. He placed his forearms at the sides of her head, framing her, protecting what was so precious to him. "I love you, too," he whispered, nuzzling her temple. "All the world, Lex. Always."

Their clothes came off slowly, both of them taking their time despite Riley wanting nothing more than to go a thousand miles an hour. Lexie pushed him onto his back, taking charge as he loved her to do, and kissed his chest and his throat, driving him beyond distraction. She seemed to grow extra hands when they had hardly any clothes on, rubbing him in ways that had him cursing and pushing his fingers between her legs to touch her until she begged for more. He was still learning and discovering new things about how to make her call out his name, so he loved that she was so vocal. She had never been shy about what she wanted, telling him exactly what she liked: There. More. Easy. Faster. Inside. More. Don't stop. Oh God, don't stop.

She shattered in his arms, his fingers wet with her, his heart full of her and his mouth desperate for more of her. She was glorious under their stars and the lights that seemed to make her skin glow. With shaking hands, Riley rolled on a condom and held himself above her. Staring into Lexie's eyes, her glasses lost among their clothes, he saw what he'd always hoped for: love, adoration, and everlasting friendship.

He lowered his chest to hers, her soft breasts so warm against him, and let his index finger dance across her cheek. "You're so beautiful," he said. "Thank you."

She exhaled a laugh; the movement rubbed her body against his. "What are you thanking me for?"

"For being my best friend," he answered. "For coming to New York and for loving me."

She lifted her head and kissed him. "All the world. Always."

And, as they kissed, Riley pushed his body carefully, slowly, gently into hers, knowing that he would never love anyone else for the rest of his life.

8

Riley's legs powered him forward, the force of his feet pounding the pavement matching every heavy thump of his heart. With every stride, he prayed that the memories of Lexie's seventeenth birthday would fade. But even after running with Seb for over thirty minutes, he'd swear the smell of her from that night was still all around him.

Sweat was dripping down the side of his face by the time they turned down their parents' street and began sprinting toward the house. Seb won the not-really-racing-but-we're-totally-racing race by a mosquito's ball and dropped down onto the lawn, stretching his legs and back. Riley simply dropped to the lawn next to his brother and breathed like an eighty-year-old with emphysema.

"You're getting slow in your old age, son," Seb commented as he stretched his glutes.

"Fuck off."

"It's the beard," Seb continued. "You're not streamlined anymore."

Riley turned to his brother, squinting in the June sun. "You know, the more you bitch about my beard the more I think you actually love it. And the more determined I am to keep it." Seb chuckled and lifted his arms above his head. "Besides, I know you're only jealous because instead of awesome facial hair follicles you have *girl's* hair."

With a tight-lipped smile across his face, Seb flicked him the bird. Riley laughed, rolling onto all fours and pushing himself up. The house was quiet when they entered. Joan was at the hospital with Aunt Carol and, with Park improving day by day, Maggie and Rosie had gone home. Park was still in HDU, but his progress was good. It had been two days since he'd opened his eyes and he was now sitting up and eating. Riley and his brothers were taking turns to be there with their mother. Today, it was Tate who'd gone.

"So Tate told me about the Disney store awkwardness," Seb commented once the two of them were showered and changed. They each sprawled across a couch in the living room, not really watching the programs on the TV.

Riley sighed and nodded. "'Awkward' is one word for it." He winced at the memory and the subsequent recollections that had battered his brain ever since. It seemed grossly unfair to have to deal with remembering the happiest times in his life so vividly when he and Lexie were practically strangers to one another now.

Seb tilted his head. "You seem morose, dude."

Riley threw the TV remote down onto the coffee table. "It just sucks, you know?" He rubbed the tips of his fingers against his temple. "I mean, we were together for so long and now it's like we don't even know one another."

Seb shrugged. "So change it."

"What?"

Seb waved a hand toward the doorway. "Go and get to know her again." Like it was that fucking easy. Seb rolled his eyes when Riley pressed his lips together and looked back at the tube. He scoffed. "You're a fucking coward."

"You're damn right!" Riley snapped, taking himself and his younger brother by surprise. He shifted in his seat, embarrassed by his outburst, but his anxiety about being back home was at an all-time high. He was usually so placid, but between seeing Lex and his father being in hospital, he was wound tight as hell. "Sorry," he mumbled.

"Fuck that." Seb sat forward. "Look, we've been going in circles about this for years. Talk to me. What are you so afraid of? So you said some shit that wasn't so nice. Fine, I get it, but life moves on. You were both idiots back then. Don't look at me like that—you know Lex had her moments, just like you did."

It was true. Lexie could stand her ground and cut to the quick when she wanted, but that wasn't why Riley was so terrified of reconnecting. He ran a hand through his hair and closed his eyes. "I'm just . . . okay, what if we do get to know each other again, become friends? What then?"

"Then you'll feel better?"

"But that's the thing," Riley lamented. "I won't. I was never able to be just friends with her. And that hasn't changed. Besides, I live in New York and apparently she's back living here. It wouldn't work. It wouldn't work now and we both knew it wouldn't then, which is why we . . ."

Jesus, the nostalgia was stifling.

Seb stared at Riley for a long time, his dark eyes astute. "You're scared of getting hurt."

Fuck, it sounded so precious when put that way, but Seb had hit the damned nail on the head. Riley was a fairly open guy and could admit to a lot of things, but the fear of having his heart broken again was not one of them. It was the main reason why he'd never told Carter or Max about Lex. He didn't want to think about the pain or the events that caused the absolute cluster fuck that became his and Lex's relationship.

Riley was silent for a long time before he found the courage to speak. "Do you have any idea what it took to walk away from her?" Seb's gaze dropped to the floor. Pressing his lips together, he shook his head. "It broke me. It was as if I left a part of myself here, and every time I came back and she and I— I never got it back. I never will." Riley rubbed his palms down his face, feeling his cheeks heat with the embarrassment of stating such a thing, but shit, there it was.

"Riley," Seb said softly. "Man, you need to move on." Riley opened his mouth to argue that he had, or was at least doing his best. "Fucking everything with a pulse and tits is not moving on. It's compensating."

"And who are *you* compensating for?" Riley asked sharply.

Seb cocked an eyebrow. "Don't turn this around on me, because you know I'm right."

Riley exhaled heavily and turned to look out the window. "But it's not that simple." He dropped his hands between his knees. "When I saw her the other day . . . Man, it was like everything came back—the fun we had, the laughs, how happy we were." He shook his head of the unease he'd seen in her eyes. "But that was so long ago. I think our time has passed."

"I think you should talk to her." Seb held up a hand. "Just a chat. Clear the air. And then maybe you can move on properly."

"A chat?" Riley slumped back into his seat, a small part of him grudgingly aware that what Seb was saying was right. Maybe he and Lex *could* talk and put whatever happened between them in the past where it belonged. Sure, they'd never be the best friends they once were, but maybe it would help Riley shake off the hurt and guilt that had been skulking quietly within him for years. "I'll think about it," he muttered, although whether it was to Seb or himself, he wasn't sure.

. . .

The following day, Riley drove his mom to the hospital and sat for three hours, awkward and uncomfortable in the only chair that occupied his father's room while his mom perched on the edge of Park's bed. The tension between the two men was still tangible, but Joan did her utmost to clear it, indirectly making the two of them speak to one another. In addition to being ridiculous, it was kind of exhausting.

Riley knew he'd disappointed his father when he'd been sent to Arthur Kill after doing a friend a favor and holding a shitload of stolen car parts in his shop, but what more could he do or say? He'd served his time, apologized to everyone he cared about, cleared his debts, and turned himself around. It was a stupid mistake that he'd paid for, but his father's continuing refusal to speak more than two or three words to him was like a constant bee sting.

In truth, Riley had hoped that his father's ill health might kick the old guy's ass into realizing that life was too damned short to hold grudges, and that he'd decide to clean the slate. But that didn't look at all likely.

"What's on your mind, honey?" Joan asked as they drove back across town. He shrugged in response. "Your father will come around," she added softly, patting his knee. "He just needs to get out of his own way first."

Riley wasn't so sure about that, but he appreciated his mother's confidence all the same.

"Tate told me about the two of you seeing Alexis." Riley's back stiffened a little. He cleared his throat. "You kids need to sort out your differences. It's been too long." Riley leaned an elbow on the window's edge, keeping his eyes resolutely on the road. "A love like that doesn't go away, no matter how much you will it to, sweetheart."

Riley sighed. "She pushed me away."

"She wasn't herself, Riley. She was sick. You know that."

Yeah, he did know that, but it didn't make it any easier.

Joan continued. "Maggie told me Alexis owns a store not far from here—"

"No," Riley interrupted, shutting down the idea immediately. To her credit, his mother didn't push. She never did. Instead she did what she'd always done with her sons: she'd planted a seed. And goddammit, the damned thing only grew bigger and louder as Riley drove. "How far?"

He'd managed to last six whole minutes before asking where Lexie's shop was, not daring to look across at his mother.

"Take the next left."

Riley didn't ask how she knew. It didn't matter.

Ten minutes later, Riley pulled the car into a large parking lot, around which were a number of outlets and restaurants. He turned off the car and sat back, his stare on the small store located between an Old Navy and a Bed Bath & Beyond.

Love, You by Lexie.

Pride and relief clutched his chest. When she was eighteen, due to devastating circumstances out of her control, Lexie had had to let her dreams of becoming a cosmologist go. Riley had to admit that despite his and Lexie's relationship being frayed, he'd worried about what she'd done with her life. Not that he didn't think she'd succeed. Christ, Lexie was the most determined and smartest person he knew. But it had broken his heart to see her turn her back on what she'd always wanted, regardless of the reasons.

Riley and his mother climbed out of the car and made their way toward the store. A smile pulled at his face when he saw the star dotting the *i* of her name on the sign and the moon and stars in elegant white painted in the corner of the storefront window. The display beyond that was stunning. Jewelry of all types glittered, sparkled, and shone as it lay or hung from pink stands, some of which were embossed or engraved with words that made Riley smile wider: *believe, commit, survive.*

"Shall we go in?"

Joan's voice startled Riley out of his thoughts. He took a deep breath and nodded, gesturing for his mom to lead the way. She squeezed his arm briefly as she walked past, and he followed on unsteady legs. The first thing Riley noticed when he entered was the smell of the place. It was all Lexie, sweet and floral, and it threw him headlong into a memory of her undressing for him in her bedroom. They'd been seventeen and so in love. He licked his lips and rubbed a hand down his face.

"Hi, guys." They were approached by a petite woman with deep plum-colored hair, which she wore pulled into a tight bun at the back of her head. "I'm Jaime. Let me know if I can help you today." She reminded Riley of a puppy, all bouncy, smiley, and eager to please.

"Thanks," he and his mother said in unison before Riley moved toward a mirrored wall that was covered in pink Post-its. He realized as he got closer that there were comments written on them:

That you tell it how it is. No bullshit!! Love, You.

Your freckles. Love, You.

Your curly locks and full lips. Love, You.

"This is so cool," he uttered, narrowing his eyes in an effort to read the ones stuck higher up the mirror.

"I'm glad you like it."

Hearing Lexie behind him, Riley whirled around in place, knocking a stand at his side with his arm. "Shit!" He flailed in an effort to grab it before it fell at the same time Lexie dove forward to do the same. They caught it, propping it back up, leaving the necklaces and earrings swinging sharply from their places on the stands.

"Sorry," he mumbled, embarrassment heating his throat.

"It's all right," she replied with an awkward laugh. "It happens. I need to move it or put a warning sign up or something."

Riley looked her over as she spoke, once again noting the septum piercing and the tattoos she'd added to her collection. The tattoo on the inside of his forearm suddenly felt hot, as though it knew she was near. He saw she was holding her own forearm to hide where she'd had the same tattoo inked, on the same day, and his heart pinched a little.

She turned and smiled at Riley's mom. "Hi, Joan. It's been a long time. I was sorry to hear about Park. How is he?"

Lexie's expression was surprised when she was pulled in for a hug, but she quickly reciprocated, smiling into Joan's shoulder. "He's doing better. Thank you. And you look very well, Alexis," Joan commented as they pulled apart. "And your store is wonderful. Congratulations."

Lexie blushed under Joan's praise and pushed a strand of hair behind her ear. Riley had never been jealous of his mom before, but her ease with Lexie was something he would kill for. Why hadn't that been the first thing *he'd* said to her? *Jackass.*

"How long have you had it?" Riley asked instead, shoving his hands into his pockets.

"Almost three years," she answered.

"And you make everything yourself?"

Lexie nodded. "Designed and made on the premises. Unless it's a specific order; then we can outsource it. But we try our best to do what we can here in the store." She crossed her arms. "I'm surprised you found us."

Riley glanced at his mom, detecting the underlying message in Lexie's words: she didn't want him there. "My cousin, Maggie," he offered. "She recognized you at the Disney store. She's been here before and said how awesome it was."

"That was nice of her." Lexie wouldn't quite meet his gaze, fidgeting and fussing with her cuticles. "Feel free to look around some more." She looked over at Joan. "We have some great discounted pieces over there." She pointed toward the back of the store where a group of three girls stood, holding up various pieces against themselves, and Joan took the opportunity to leave her son and Lexie alone. Lexie dropped her hand and slowly turned back to Riley. "And we have some great pieces for guys." Without another word, she headed across the store.

Riley followed obediently, as though he had little choice in the matter. He wasn't ashamed of the fact that he'd always been that way with Lexie. It was simple, really: she chose the direction and he followed.

"We have some really sexy cuffs and necklaces," she said toward the wall of men's jewelry.

Riley took a moment to look at the pieces and a guy trying on a chain before he let his gaze slide over to Lexie. "You look great," he said softly. "Really great. I should have said that when I saw you the other day."

Her shoulders slumped slightly. "Thank you." She lifted her eyes to his. "So do you." She cocked an eyebrow. "The beard is . . . different."

Riley raised a self-conscious hand to his chin.

"But I like it," Lexie finished.

"Thanks."

She nudged her glasses up her nose. "This is awkward, isn't it?"

A cough of laughter burst from Riley. "Yeah."

She swallowed and dragged her top teeth across her bottom lip. It warmed Riley to see it. It was a tic she'd always had, coming out whenever she was nervous. "I don't mean for it to be, but . . ."

"But?"

"But it's been a long time."

Riley nodded. "It has."

"And it was a shock to see you here."

Riley dipped his chin. "I know. I'm sorry."

"Don't be sorry," she murmured. "It's fine. I'm glad you've seen this place."

"It's amazing, Lex. You should be so proud of yourself."

"I am."

Riley turned his body toward hers, the swift and overwhelming need to touch her skin fizzing through him from top to toe. "Listen, Lex, I'm gonna be around until my dad's better and I wondered if—while I'm back, if we could, you know, maybe—"

She was shaking her head before he even finished. "No."

"I just want to talk."

"Riley, I can't."

"Nothing more. I swear." He held up a hand.

Lexie laughed wryly and gazed up at him in a way that made Riley feel a little dizzy. "But we could never just *talk*," she said quietly. "Could we?"

And didn't that look and those words set his blood on fire? She was right, though. Every time they'd met in the past—the last time being when he returned for his parents' wedding anniversary five years ago—with the intention of simply talking and clearing the air, they'd ended up in bed. Or against a wall. Or that time in his car. Riley shifted on his feet, his body hardening quickly. Jesus, nothing changed; the woman was like fucking Viagra.

"No," he managed. "I guess not." He noticed the flush of her cheeks. "But this time I really mean it." And it was the truth. As much as he wanted to lose himself in her, to kiss her and have things back to the way they were when they were teenagers and life was simple, he wanted to be friends with her more. "I miss my best friend."

Her eyes closed for a second. "Riley."

"Just hear me out, okay?"

At that moment the bell above the store door rang. Lexie's eyes widened a little as she looked past Riley. He turned instinctively to see Savannah and the little boy, Noah, in her arms, looking cute as hell with his mouth and cheeks covered in what looked suspiciously like chocolate, and a *Star Wars* balloon attached to his wrist, floating above them.

Savannah froze as the door shut behind them and, after a moment in which no one spoke, Riley began looking between the two sisters, trying to figure out what the fuck they were saying to each other with no words. He glanced again at Noah, who was grinning at him, and something in his stomach twisted at the same time the hairs on his neck lifted.

"Sorry," Savannah said quickly. "I didn't know that— I'll just take Noah—"

"Mommy, look!" Noah exclaimed.

"Noah, don't—" He began wiggling hard enough in Savannah's arms that she was forced to squat and place him on the floor before he fell.

He ran toward Lexie, balloon arm aloft, while Riley's brain suddenly began to move at a million miles an hour.

Wait.

Mommy?

Lexie moved around Riley quickly and bent down to the little boy as he continued to chatter. "The party was so good! I gots a bawoon! And I hads cake."

"I can see that. I can't wait to hear all about it, baby," Lexie said, running a hand through the little boy's hair. "But Mommy's a little busy now with customers. I'll finish up in twenty minutes, and then we'll head home. Go with Aunt Sav and I'll be through in a moment, okay?"

"'Kay," Noah answered without argument, his attention snapping from the balloon to Riley in an instant. "You's the man from Disney. Do you like my bawoon?"

Riley opened his mouth to speak, but found no words came. Noah gazed up at him, waiting for a reply, hazel eyes so familiar, just like they had been in the Disney store. But now, as he looked closer, Riley could see other features of Noah's face that he saw every day he looked in the mirror. Jesus, even Noah's nose and chin were . . .

Riley staggered back as the realization hit him like a fucking sledgehammer, his hip knocking into the display case behind him. How the fuck had he not seen it before? In his periphery, Riley saw his mother moving closer, her wide stare glued to the little boy even as Savannah took Noah's hand and led him to the back of the store and out of a door. Could she be seeing it, too? Could he be . . . ?

When Joan's gaze met Riley's, he knew the answer was unequivocally yes. She looked as shell-shocked as Riley felt. "He looks just like—"

"Lex?" The interruption left Riley on a disbelieving croak. He could barely breathe. Jesus fucking Christ, he couldn't *think*. What the ever-loving hell was going on?

Lexie stood from her crouch, her face pale, her gaze anywhere but on Riley. He pushed his next words out through panic and confusion. "Is there something you need to tell me?"

She inhaled heavily, paused, and then turned to him. "We need to talk."

Riley tried to catch his breath, but his lungs felt as though they'd shriveled to half the size. "Is he—?"

"Not here," Lexie uttered, glancing at the other customers and Jaime, who was hovering behind Joan, seemingly as perplexed by the whole scene as Riley was.

Anger abruptly lit Riley into focusing. He stood up straight and moved closer to Lexie. He towered over her, but she lifted her chin defiantly, meeting his glare. "Not here? Are you kidding me?" he growled, his pulse thundering in his ears. "Fucking say it."

There was a flash of fear across Lexie's face before confidence snapped her shoulders back. "Yes," she said quietly, causing Riley's world to shrink to a pinhead. "He's yours."

9

Eleven years ago . . .

Riley lay on his bed, eyes closed, mouth open, hands gripping the pillows beneath his head. His neck arched and his hips rocked. Lexie's mouth. Fucking hell, *Lexie's mouth. She sucked and licked and kissed and slurped all over his cock, drawing out of him a pleasure so intense all he could utter were sounds, growls, hums of* yes, please, God, don't ever stop what you're doing right now.

She'd gotten so good at this and had admitted on a few occasions that she loved doing it, which, for an eighteen-year-old guy with a near constant hard-on for his girlfriend, was fucking awesome. And, honestly, the feeling was entirely mutual; he adored eating her out. He loved her sounds, her smells, her taste, and when she came on his tongue, clutching at his hair and calling out his name, he felt like a goddamn king. Yeah, sex with Lexie was truly amazing and the two of them—whenever they could—had barely stopped having it since her birthday almost a year before.

She cupped his balls and took his cock deeper. Riley grunted. "Close," *he gasped, lifting his head so he could watch her. She winked at him.* "Oh, fuck me, I'm close. Keep going."

She smirked and took him again and again, fisting the part of his dick that she couldn't take. Her mouth was so wet, so warm, and was just about the most perfect thing in the world. Riley pumped his hips, only vaguely remembering not to make her gag, until his orgasm slammed into his stomach, all but turning him inside out, until he was coming so hard into Lexie's mouth.

He groaned and called out and gasped, and thank God they had the house to themselves, because there was no way in hell that Riley would have been able to keep quiet during that and how fucking embarrassing would that have been? He collapsed on the bed, chest heaving, only slightly aware of Lexie laughing and reaching over for the bottle of water she'd left on his bedside table.

"I swear to God, you're amazing." He closed his eyes as she snuggled in next to him, her naked body warm and soft against his. He wrapped an arm around her shoulders and kissed her forehead. "Amazing."

She laughed again and rubbed a hand across his stomach. "I'm glad you enjoyed it."

Riley managed to open one eye. "Oh yeah."

She reached up, cupped his cheek, and kissed him, the underlying taste of himself on her tongue, as it always did, causing heat to bloom unashamedly in his belly. He hummed against her lips and smiled. If he knew how to bottle the feelings he had for the girl in his arms, he'd have a bestseller on his hands. No one would ever feel miserable again. He knew their happiness was borderline sickening and his brothers had all teased him about it, but Riley couldn't have given less of a shit.

"What time do you have to leave?" he asked, reaching down to pull his comforter over them. It was mid-July and hot, but he liked blocking out the outside world so it was just the two of them.

"Dad wants me back by three," she answered, twirling her finger around his nipple. "Our flight's at seven."

Riley glanced at the wall. It was 1 p.m. "Is it stupid that I miss you already?"

She smiled against his shoulder. "I'll be back in a week. You'll barely notice."

But they both knew that wasn't true. Lexie and her family were flying to Florida for a week as Lexie's graduation present, a last family vacation before she and Riley headed to New York. The family had been saving up since before Christmas, struggling to pay the trip off after her mother was laid off in February. Her father had been working extra shifts at the timber yard, and Lexie contributed from working at the local coffee shop. At one stage, Lexie had asked if Riley could join them, but the expression on Mr. Pierce's face had said it all, especially in light of the fact that he blamed Riley entirely for her new tattoo.

He clearly didn't know his daughter well at all. Of course, the tattoo was Lexie's idea. Riley had simply followed in her wake as he always did.

He held Lexie closer. It didn't matter anyway; they'd be in New York in a handful of weeks, with no parents around, and he'd finally have her all to himself. Excitement pinged through him. He couldn't wait to have more days like today—no interruptions, enjoying Lexie's body, playing hard, and studying at NYU. He'd had it all figured out from the moment they both received their acceptance letters. They'd managed to secure the same dorm—no small feat—and he'd arranged where they'd live on campus while they studied, what they'd do after finals, after graduation, and, after all that, how and where he planned to propose.

It may have been odd for a man of eighteen to have such romantic ideas, but he and Lexie weren't like anyone else. Riley had friends who jumped from one girl to the next, their lives no end of drama, and he couldn't have been less interested. He'd known Lexie was the one for him from the age of eight and, ten years on, not a single thing had changed. Lexie shifted at his side, her breasts squashing deliciously against him.

Well, maybe a couple of things had changed.

He rolled toward her, and kept going until he was lying on top of her, between her legs, pressing gentle kisses across her face, to her mouth and back again. He'd never get tired of how she tasted, the scent of her, or the feel of her hair in his hands. He paused for a moment, his gaze dancing across her face, committing every freckle, dip, and curve to memory. "I love you," he whispered.

She reached out a finger to trace the two-week-old tattoo on his forearm, the tattoo that matched hers exactly. It depicted the world, and sat just above the inside of his elbow. The blues of the oceans and the greens of the continents were bright against his sun-kissed skin. "All the world," she replied, her blue eyes intense. "Always."

Riley drove her home on time. He never failed to be punctual where Mr. Pierce was concerned. And, sure enough, the man was standing on the porch, pretending to water his plants, as they pulled up outside the house. Riley smiled good-naturedly when Lexie chuckled and waved at her father through the window. She turned to Riley and reached for his hand. "I'll miss you," she whispered, her voice a little thick.

"You'll barely notice," he echoed with a smile. He leaned over the gear stick and kissed her softly. She kissed him back, her lips hungry but patient.

They jumped apart when there was a firm tap on Lexie's window. "Alexis," her father said, his voice muffled through the door. "Let that boy go and come and finish packing."

Lexie smiled. "I'm coming, Daddy." She turned back to Riley and kissed him again quickly before she jumped out of the car. Closing the door behind her, she grinned through the window and pressed her tattoo against the glass, mouthing, "I love you."

All the world.

The following days passed at a snail's pace. Riley did his best to keep busy, working out, helping his dad at the car shop, reading, hanging with Seb, but still the clocks in the house seemed to go backwards without Lexie around, especially when he hadn't heard from her in two days. Looking back, Riley should have known something was wrong—Lexie was never quiet for long—but he tried not to worry. She was on vacation after all.

It was at three o'clock in the morning on the fifth day when Riley was woken by his mom's gentle shake. Coming to, Riley rubbed at his eyes, noticing that behind his mother, his father was standing in his bedroom doorway in his bathrobe.

"What's wrong?" Riley asked instantly, throwing a hand out, grappling and searching for his cell under his pillow, then his comforter. Seeing no text or missed call, his heart sank. "Is it Lex?"

Joan shook her head. "No, honey. It's her dad," she answered. "He's dead."

Riley froze, his eyes searching his mother's face for a clue, a prank, a clear explanation to the truckload of what the fuck he was feeling. And, Jesus, his heart hurt. It clenched for Christine, for Savannah, and of course, for Lexie. The girl adored her father. He slumped against his pillows, pushing his fingertips into his eye sockets, hating that he wasn't with her, hating that she was so far away. He tried calling, but her cell phone went straight to voicemail and continued to do so for the next two days.

It had been Lexie's aunt who'd called Joan that night, and she became a source of information for Riley as he watched the hours pass, needing Lexie to be home. Riley was told how Mr. Pierce had died: getting dressed for dinner, he'd suffered a brain aneurism. "He wouldn't have known much about it" were Park's words of comfort, but honestly, they barely stanched the flow of grief Riley felt for Lex.

On the day Lexie and her family arrived back in Michigan, Riley drove to the house and wandered into the forest at the back of her place, eventually finding his way to the spaceship they'd built with Mr. Pierce when they were eight years old. It was still standing, solid and true, unlike Lexie's dad, and Riley allowed a couple of tears to break through for the man, silently vowing to the sky above him that he would love and protect Lexie each and every day of his life.

The sound of twigs snapping behind him had Riley turning and simultaneously breaking his heart. Lexie, hair unwashed, face swollen from crying, stood a few feet away. For a brief moment they stared at one another. Days, weeks, even years later, Riley would understand that those precious few seconds symbolized the moment everything changed—he knew she wouldn't be going with him to New York. Deep in his bones and fractured chest, he knew she'd chosen to stay with her family in Michigan and, as much as it tore him in two, he couldn't be mad. How could he?

"Lex."

She set off at a run and threw herself at him, wrapping her arms around his neck, sobbing louder than he'd ever heard into his shoulder, telling him how sorry she was, God, so sorry that she had to stay with her mom and help, but, please, Riley, go. You're too big to stay. Go. And take my heart with you. I'll wait for you. Every day.

Riley cried, too, holding her so damned tightly, cupping the back of her head and kissing her cheek over and over, explaining how he loved her all the world, more than he could ever explain, and that things would be all right. He promised, he swore to her that no matter what or where either of them was, they would be together forever.

· · ·

The house shook with the force of Riley slamming the front door shut behind him. Joan turned to look at him as she placed her purse and keys on the coffee table in the living room, her eyes sympathetic and worried.

"Did you know?" Riley barked, anger and turmoil tumbling through him. He wasn't trying to be an asshole, and deep down he knew he was lashing out only because he was so fucking terrified, but he couldn't help it. He wanted to hit something, beat something to smithereens, and then scream at the world until he felt better. "Well, did you?"

Joan's mouth all but dropped open. "How can you ask me that? Of course I didn't know."

"You didn't hear *anything*?" Riley exclaimed as he paced. "No nosy gossipers? How is that possible when you know everybody in this shit hole of a city?"

"Riley, she hasn't lived here for years," Joan said calmly. "They all moved after the last time you were here. How would I know?"

And it was obvious now why Lexie had taken off the way she had. *Shit. Shit. Shit.*

Riley clutched at his hair, his head thumping. "Christ, I mean . . . How could she?" he said toward the ceiling. "Mom? I mean, how the fuck? That little boy is— How can I . . . ?"

Joan's chin shook, a mother's heart breaking for her son. "I don't know, sweetheart. I don't know."

Tate and Seb appeared in the doorway of the living room.

"What the hell's going on?" Tate asked, moving to stand beside his mother, concerned frown front and center. "Ri?"

But Riley couldn't answer. He heaved as his stomach turned. His whole world continued to tilt and whirl on its axis as Lexie's words repeated with every pound of the pulse in his ears. *Yes. He's yours. Yes. He's yours.* How could three words have such a devastating impact? How could she have kept this from him? How could he have a son? How could he have lived all this time without knowing the child he'd fathered? How could his heart burst and break all at the same fucking time?

Questions twisted and pummeled him until, unable to contain it, Riley turned and, with a terrifying roar, slammed his fist into the drywall.

Seb was at his side immediately, grabbing his arm. "Fuck, man. Stop! What the hell are you doing?"

Unable to answer, Riley dropped his forehead to the wall and yelled. How was it that the only time he felt remotely like this was when he was back in Traverse City? How was it that it was always because of Lexie? His skin prickled with anger so fierce, he trembled. Seb's hand rubbed his back. "Riley, come on. You're bleeding. Let's clean you up, huh?"

Tate was at his other side with a bag of frozen peas and a damp cloth in his hand. "Let me see." He reached for Riley's arm and quickly wrapped the cloth around his knuckles. Riley figured it should have hurt, and maybe it did, but the rest of him hurt so much more, he barely noticed. "Come on, big guy," Tate coaxed with that doctor voice he whipped out every so often. "You need to sit down. Seb, go grab a can of something sugary and a glass, would ya?"

"Roger that."

On heavy feet, Riley allowed his older brother to guide him over to the sofa. He sat down slowly and let Tate fuss. "Dammit, man, this might be broken."

Like Riley gave a flying fuck.

"I have a son," he whispered in reply.

Tate froze at his side, the potentially broken hand forgotten. "What?" His gaze flickered to Joan, who was sitting at Riley's other side. "How— What did— Hang on. You have a— Why did she not . . . ?"

Riley huffed a humorless laugh. "Yeah, that's just what I said."

A can of Coke and a glass appeared on the coffee table in front of Riley. "Did I just hear right?" Seb asked incredulously. "A *son*?"

Riley dropped his face into the hand he hadn't damaged and exhaled, the throb in his temples keeping a wicked beat. He listened as his mom explained about Noah and how Lexie had convinced Riley to leave her store despite his desire to tear the place to pieces. How she'd pleaded with him not to make a scene. That she would meet him anywhere, anytime, and explain if he'd just leave. In retrospect, Riley wasn't quite sure how Lexie had managed to sway him, but, realistically, what would screaming and shouting at her in front of a ton of strangers have accomplished?

Both Tate and Seb fired out questions that Joan attempted to answer while Riley tried his hardest to slow down his brain.

"And the bitch just kept him a secret?"

"Hey!" Riley's head snapped up. He glared at Seb. "Don't." As much as Riley knew Lexie had fucked up, he wasn't prepared to have anyone call her names.

Seb rolled his eyes in clear frustration.

"He's only saying what we're all thinking," Tate offered as he pressed the frozen peas to Riley's hand and wrapped the cloth around it. "Here, hold this to your chest. Mom, do you have some ibuprofen around the place?"

"Bathroom cabinet, first shelf."

"I'll get it," Seb grumbled, before taking the stairs two at a time.

Riley collapsed back onto the couch, his hand cradled to his body.

"So when are you meeting her?" Tate asked.

"Tomorrow," Riley answered, keeping his eyes closed. "At the park. Neutral ground."

"I've told him all of us will go if he wants us to," Joan said, placing a hand on Riley's shoulder.

"Absolutely, man," Tate affirmed. "If you need us, we'll be there."

Riley nodded. "I appreciate it."

"Is she going to bring Noah?" Hearing the little boy's name now tightened a part of Riley that, until that moment, he didn't know he had. He felt heat, adoration, and a protectiveness so ferocious he could almost taste it. It was something he wouldn't even attempt to put into words, but it was something that meant everything else in the world now meant exactly shit. Everything except for Noah. *Noah*. His small, smiling face flitted behind Riley's eyelids, all hazel eyes and button nose.

Christ, he was beautiful.

"I asked her to," Riley answered finally as Seb came back down the stairs and placed two pills next to the glass of Coke. "Whether she will is another story."

"You need to go to the ER," Tate said, pulling an edge of the cloth down to look again at Riley's hand.

Riley shook his head limply from side to side. "I sat in a hospital for three hours today. Fuck doing that again. It'll be fine." He groaned in annoyance when Tate began to argue. "Listen, Doc, if it's swollen tomorrow, I'll go. Okay?"

The four of them were quiet for a while before Joan stood. "How about I make us all something to eat?"

Seb and Tate both offered words of gratitude, but Riley's stomach grumbled in distaste. "I'm good," he said, sitting forward, grabbing the pills and knocking them back with a swig from the glass. "I'm gonna go and lie down for a while."

His brothers and mother stood around him, looking for all the world as though they were waiting for him to go off like a damned rocket again, but Riley could barely lift his head. The adrenaline had waned dramatically, leaving his body weak and his bones weary. His brain was now groggy and slow and, though he wouldn't say a word about it to Tate, his hand was hurting like a motherfucker.

Still holding it to his chest, Riley glanced at the dent he'd put in the wall. "I'm sorry, Mom," he offered guiltily. "I shouldn't have— That was stupid. I'll pay to get it fixed."

Joan approached him and cupped his cheek. "Don't you worry, honey." She kissed the corner of his mouth gently. "It's been a hell of a day. Call down if you need anything."

He nodded and dipped his chin to each of his brothers before heading up the stairs to his bedroom. He closed the door with a gentle kick, toed off his shoes, and crawled onto the bed. It was only then, in the relative quiet of his room, that he allowed his tears free.

10

He'd broken his damned knuckle.

Through the night, Riley tossed, turned, and took more pain pills before, ready to rip the fucking thing from the socket, he knocked Tate awake to get his professional opinion. One slight press of the knuckle and Riley was cursing a blue streak while Tate got dressed to drive him to the hospital. The good news was that it was fixable without a cast or surgery.

Nevertheless, the idea of having his two middle fingers strapped together for the next three weeks did not improve his mood one iota. He felt stupid and embarrassed on top of being bone tired.

"Stop picking," Tate scolded with a swipe at Riley's curious fingers as they fussed with the tape on his hand.

"Leave me be," Riley grunted, holding his hands out of Tate's reach. "You should be focused on the road."

With Seb leaving that evening, he'd gone with Joan to the hospital to spend some time with their dad. Hell, at least the news there was good. Park was being moved from HDU to a regular room, which also came with whispers about his possible release if he continued to show improvement.

Riley was pretty bummed about Seb's departure, especially in light of the bombshell that was dropped the day before, but his little brother had promised he'd try to get back to Michigan as soon as he was able. Riley didn't want to think about when Tate would have to leave, too. Who knew he could be so needy?

Anxious about his own job, Riley called Max to check in. He

didn't tell his buddy the news, because shit, he was still trying to come to terms with that himself, but he was relieved to hear all was well with the shop. Max assured him that he was welcome to take all the time he needed when Riley explained that his stay in Michigan could roll on for another couple of weeks. He told Riley he was loving the fact that he had an excuse to keep Grace in New York with him—rather than her being in her hometown in West Virginia—while she worked on her next photography project.

Hearing his friend gush about his girl should have warmed Riley, just as it had every other time Max spoke about Grace, but now it stung his exhausted heart, and that was fucked up considering what Max had been through to find her. Why couldn't life be fucking simple?

It took Riley a moment to notice that Tate was pulling into the lot at the back of the park. As it was Sunday afternoon and the sun was baking the place, the park teemed with people and their kids. *Kids.* Riley hadn't thought about having kids for years. Of course, he'd thought about having kids with Lexie, but under very different circumstances.

Panic began to take a stronger hold.

What if Lexie *did* bring Noah? What the hell would Riley say to him—*Hey, kid, I'm your daddy, wanna play Star Wars games?* He smiled a little, remembering Noah's love for the lightsaber he'd hunted down in the Disney store and the balloon he'd had tied to his small wrist. Actually, that sounded kind of perfect for the little guy.

Maybe he should have brought something to give him.

The car engine turning off brought Riley's attention back to the moment. He inhaled and rubbed a sweating palm across his forehead. Tate stayed silent at his side, and Riley was nothing but grateful. No words could calm him down anyway. "Okay," he muttered to himself before opening the car door and getting out. He pulled his Ray-Bans from the pocket of his cargo shorts and put them on, cursing his sore hand as he did.

"I'll just be at Mom's. You call if you need me, okay?" Tate said over the roof of the car.

Riley looked out to the park, spotting Lexie immediately, his gaze drawn to her like a magnet. She was alone. Riley didn't know whether to be relieved or thrilled. "Thanks, man."

Tate nodded and climbed back into the car as Riley set off, keeping his eyes firmly on Lexie. The fact that she looked incredible boiled Riley's blood further. Her hair was up, which had always been his favorite look on her. She wore a skirt, black flip-flops, and a *Sons of Anarchy* vest top that showed off her amazing ink. Stars, planets, flowers, and her father's name littered the top part of her arms, like a map of her life, and it was incredibly sexy.

How unfair was it that he was still so attracted to her? He sighed. How unfair was it that he was still so in love with her? He stutter-stepped as that thought hit. *Jesus.* What the *hell* did that mean and, more importantly, did it even matter? Would it even change anything? He doubted that and, unable to process it, he shook off the thought. His brain was already too stuffed to deal with that shit and, right now, he needed to be on point.

He approached the tree Lexie was standing under. Glancing around, Riley realized they were far enough away from everyone else to have a modicum of privacy. He stopped in front of her, his jaw ticking as he ground his teeth in an effort to keep calm. To her credit, she looked as nervous as he felt. She fidgeted and shifted where she stood, smiling small. "Hey."

Riley sighed, battling between the urge to shake her stupid for being so selfish and thoughtless and his desire to sit with her in the shade of the tree and talk like they used to. He decided to hell with the pleasantries. "I'm here to talk about Noah," he said, noticing Lexie's wince as he spoke.

She pressed her lips together and nodded. She lifted a hand, gesturing behind him. "He's over there with Savannah."

Looking over his shoulder to see the little boy playing on the climbing frame whipped every word straight from Riley's mind. Everything he'd wanted to throw at Lex, accuse her of, evaporated, leaving him standing there like an asshole, watching his son, mouth opening and closing like a fish. Sadness swept through him with the realization that he'd missed too many firsts, too many times when Noah would have done something and Riley should have been present.

"Why?" he whispered, turning back to Lexie. "Why the hell didn't you tell me?"

"I tried so many times," she answered, her voice faltering. "When I first discovered I was pregnant, I picked up the phone to call you. I actually dialed the number, but no one answered."

Riley gradually did the math in his head. "Was that June?" Lexie nodded, and Riley's stomach plummeted. "I was in Kill."

"Yeah. I found out from my mom, who'd heard about your sentence."

Riley crossed his arms, hating that his stupid choices had affected something else important in his life. "When's Noah's birthday?"

"February fifteenth."

"Why didn't you call me when I was released if you knew?"

"I thought about it—"

"Fucking *thought* about it?" Riley snapped.

"Yes," Lexie retorted, her timidity vanishing before his eyes, "I did. Every damned day I thought about it, wanting so badly to tell you, wondering what you'd say when I told you, how you'd feel, all the while scared to death that you'd just walk away from us, from me, just like you've done for years."

Riley almost staggered back, struck dumb by her words and the heat behind them. "*Walked away?* Are you fucking serious right now or are you genuinely not hearing yourself?"

"I can hear just fine."

"Then let me tell you something." He took a giant step toward her. "The only time I ever walked away from you was when you told me to. The only time you asked me to stay away, I listened. I did what *you* asked, so don't you fucking dare throw that back in my face when the last time I saw you, you begged me to leave and never come back."

The fire fizzled and simmered behind her glasses in the blue of Lexie's eyes, before she blinked it away. "When do you *ever* listen to me?" she asked with a shake of her head, looking across the park at Noah.

"It killed me to stay away," Riley admitted toward his feet before he glared at her. "Don't ever make it sound like it was my choice or that it was easy."

Lexie dipped her chin minutely, seemingly contrite. "You're right. I'm sorry." Riley turned, standing at her side, watching Savannah and Noah run around the slide. Lexie took a deep breath. "I was so damned scared, Riley. You have no idea. I knew it would change everything, but then when I heard you'd been sent to *prison* and for *that* long, I had no idea what to do. I was angry with you." She looked up at him. "How could you have been so stupid?" Riley tried not to show how much her words stung or the shame that still slithered through him. "Of course I wanted to call you when you were released," she continued. "I did, but I didn't know how you'd be after time inside, whether you were even the same person. I mean, the Riley I knew wouldn't have even *thought* about breaking the law. I didn't know who you were. I wasn't about to invite a stranger into our lives. Then the days passed and, before I knew it, Noah was a year old, walking and talking. We came back here and I opened my business. I created this perfect bubble for Noah and me. We're happy; my store is successful and . . . I didn't know what bringing you into it would do. Every time before has been a nightmare and I have a good life here, Riley. *Noah* and I have a good life here. I won't let anything change that." She paused, her words settling around them like dead leaves. "I want to do what's best for my son."

"Having his father around would have been the best thing," Riley remarked, his shame turning to irritation. "Surely you of all people understand that."

Lexie's chin snapped to him. "That's not fair."

"Fair?" Riley scoffed. "What's not fair is that you've seen Noah grow. You were there for all the things I've missed. Sure, I was in Kill those first eight months after he was born, but I would have been here after that. Whatever happened between us is nothing compared to how much I hate that you denied me that."

Lexie was quiet for a beat, her expression pained. "I was afraid. I thought I was protecting my son. To you it might sound stupid and selfish, and having you back here now, maybe it is. But that's all I have."

Riley shook his head. "I'm still me, Lex. Doing time didn't change that."

They stood then for a few hushed moments, watching their blond-haired boy as he laughed and giggled and waved when he caught them both watching. As livid as Riley was with Lexie, he couldn't deny the smile that Noah brought to his face. "He looks like me."

Lexie huffed good-humoredly. "Right? My genes didn't stand a chance. It's eerie sometimes. When he looks at me a certain way, I see so much of the little boy I remember." She crossed her arms and hugged herself. "It makes me realize how much I've missed you."

Riley sighed, the heat of his temper weakening with her confession. "I've missed you, too, Lex. I always have. But this isn't about us, it's about Noah, and I want to get to know him."

Lexie nodded. "Of course. He's your son. You have every right to, but I have to know what your plans are."

Riley turned to face her again. "Plans?"

Lexie pushed her bangs to the side. "Look, Riley, seeing you again brings back so much for me. It's nice, but it also scares me to death. We've done this so many times, you and me: you come back, you stay for a while, then everything goes wrong and you leave again." She held up a hand when he opened his mouth to argue. "And that's fine. I can deal with that. It's our thing and has been for years. But I won't deal with you doing the same to Noah. I will not stand by and let you get to know him, for him to fall in love with you, and then for you to take off and leave me to pick up the pieces."

"I live in New York, Lex. I have a life there, a job. I'll have to go back eventually."

"Yes, I understand that. But if you want to be a part of Noah's life, you can't leave years in between visits."

Hurt, Riley pulled his shades deliberately from his face, looking Lexie square in the eye. "Is this my fault?"

Lexie frowned. "Is what your fault?"

"The fact that you think so little of me."

Lexie's expression softened, her gaze nervous as it roamed his face. "No," she answered carefully. "No . . . I don't think so little of you, Riley. I just— I don't want Noah to get hurt."

"I would never do that."

"I know." Lexie looked away, toeing the ground as she did. "I know. I'm sorry. God, I'm so sorry. For everything."

Seeing her struggle, Riley reached out and took Lexie's wrist, pulling it gently from against her body. He wrapped his hand over hers and squeezed. Admittedly, she looked surprised, but she didn't pull away. He tried to ignore the fizz and crackle of her skin against his. "I never wanted us to be . . . like this."

Her chin trembled. "Me, too. I shouldn't have— I should have trusted you. You deserve better from me."

Riley blinked in surprise at her words. "We'll get there," he said, releasing her.

She noticed the tape on his fingers. "What did you do to your hand?"

He shrugged. "Acted like a moron."

"Nothing changes."

Riley cocked an eyebrow in amusement. The tension between them didn't disappear entirely but seemed to lift, allowing them to breathe as they looked at one another. With relief, Riley realized they'd cleared some of the air that had clouded them both for far too long, but he still had to ask the question that had been plaguing him since he'd learned of Noah's existence. "Tell me something."

"Okay."

"If I weren't here right now, would you ever have told me? Honestly."

Lexie exhaled but held his gaze. "Yes, I would have. My plan was to tell you before he started school."

Riley watched her carefully. "And would you?"

She nodded. "He needs his father, Riley." As hard as he looked, Riley couldn't see an ounce of dishonesty. "Would you like to officially meet your son?"

Riley's pulse spiked. "Um . . . yeah."

Lexie's smile grew. "You'll be fine."

Riley wiped his hands on the ass of his shorts. "What do I say to him? I mean, do I tell him that I'm . . ."

Lexie seemed to consider this for a moment. "Look, Noah is a bright kid. He's observant, but we haven't really had the daddy conversation yet. So how about you're just Riley for now and we'll cross that bridge when we come to it."

Instead of feeling disappointment, the panic in Riley lessened. He wasn't sure he was ready to be "Daddy" just yet, as amazing a privilege as that was. He was happy just to take it a day at a time. "Fine."

They set off across the park toward Noah and Savannah. Noah, with arms out wide making plane engine sounds with his mouth, ran toward them. "Mommy, looks at me, I'm a fighting jet!"

"That's awesome," Lexie said with a laugh, reaching out to grab him as he ran past. He dodged her, giggling as he did. "You're so fast!"

Riley nodded toward Lexie's sister. "Hey, Sav."

She smiled back, apparently relieved that Riley and Lexie were both still in one piece. "Good to see you, Riley. Is Seb home?"

Lexie clicked her tongue. "Behave."

Riley watched Noah, captivated. The pride of seeing his son play happily sparked fiercely within him. It was unbelievable to think that this little person was a part of him. Noah existed because of Riley, because of him and Lexie. "It's incredible," he murmured, not meaning for anyone to hear. He startled a little when Lexie's hand squeezed his forearm.

"Hey, Noah, come and say hello to Riley," Lexie called.

Noah spun around in a circle and charged toward them. "The Disney man?"

Riley chuckled at the sound of the boy's lisp. It might have been the cutest thing he'd ever heard. "That's right. The Disney man." Noah came closer, but he didn't stop moving, still shooting and flying in his imaginary plane game. Riley dropped onto his haunches, not wanting to tower over him. "How ya doin', buddy? Where's your *Star Wars* balloon?"

"Tied to my bed," Noah answered conversationally, twirling

on the spot. "Mommy said I could puts it there when I cleaned up the Legos."

Riley's eyes skittered up to Lexie. "Good deal. So what else do you like, Noah?"

Noah paused in his shooting for a moment, his hazel eyes on the clear blue sky before he answered. "Batman, tattoos like Mommy." He lifted his T-shirt to show Riley a transfer tattoo of a lion on his round belly, and Riley was immediately walloped with a memory of Lexie and her sparkly stick-on tattoo obsession. "Hey," Noah added. "You haves some tattoos." He looked over Riley's shoulders carefully. "And that's like my Mommy's." Noah pointed to the world on the inside of Riley's forearm and moved closer. On the breeze, Riley caught a scent of the little boy, all soft sunbeams and fabric softener. "Look, Mommy, it's the sames. You match."

"Yeah, baby," Lexie affirmed softly. "We do."

Riley looked her over, sucking in a breath when he saw the longing in Lexie's gaze. There was no denying what he saw, because he knew his expression mirrored it exactly. He knew she was thinking about that day, the day they chose to permanently mark themselves for one another, after which they made love on a blanket in their spot in the forest. They'd come together hot, loud, and beautiful under the summer sunshine, clung to each other, and then did it all over again. Jesus, he'd moved so hard in her that day. She'd begged him, too, to mark her on the inside to match the mark she had for him outside, so he had, pushing deeper, thrusting faster, needing to get so close to her, *closer* to her.

Feeling a little breathless, Riley's stare slipped down Lexie's arm to where he knew her tattoo was and smiled at the cursive *Noah* she'd had inked in an arc over the top of it. "Nice addition," he said. His attention snapped back to Noah when he felt a little fingertip trace the outline of the designs on his biceps. Riley was amazed at how brave Noah was to do that and, God, he was so close and so real that Riley had the overwhelming and sudden urge to grab him up in a tight hug.

"You like these?" he asked instead, voice a little shaky.

Noah nodded. "They're cool. What's this?"

"That's a dandelion," Riley explained. "See how the parts of it blow up my arm?" The little fingertip moved up and over the artwork. Riley grinned. "Maybe when you're a big boy you can get a real one."

"Maybe," Lexie interjected before Noah could respond. She smiled down at the two of them.

"Do you really have Batman socks?" Noah asked quietly.

Riley blinked. "Of course. I'm surprised you remember that."

Noah's lips twitched and his finger stopped at the tip of Riley's shoulder. His innocent gaze met Riley's. "Do you know what else I likes?"

Riley dropped his voice as though it was a secret. "What?"

"Ice cream."

"Really?" Riley exclaimed. "That's my most favorite thing in the world. What flavor?"

Noah smiled. "Chocolate."

"That's crazy, dude, because chocolate is my most favorite, too."

Noah tilted his head as he regarded Riley. The purity and trust in that one look made Riley's heart skip and trip over itself. The strength of emotion he felt at that moment was almost crushing and made his ribs ache, as though they struggled to contain his heart as it grew.

Over Noah's shoulder, Riley spotted an ice-cream truck in the distance. "Maybe, if Mommy says it's okay, I could take you to get some." Riley glanced at Lexie, who'd also noticed the truck.

"Can we, Mommy?" Noah asked, suddenly all wide eyes and clapping hands.

Lexie laughed. "Okay." She reached into her back pocket for what Riley assumed was her wallet. He stopped her with a shake of his head as he stood.

"This is on me. You want?" She pressed her lips together and he knew immediately what she wanted. "Strawberry?"

"What else?"

Riley turned to Lexie's sister, who had been standing quietly throughout the whole exchange. "Sav?

"Chocolate for me, too."

"Come on, Auntie Sav!" Noah yelled, grabbing her hand. "Disney man—"

"Riley," Lexie corrected.

"Disney man Riley is gettings us ice creams!"

Lexie and Riley followed in their son's wake as he pulled Savannah toward the truck. "You did great," Lexie offered.

Riley nodded, unable to drag his attention away from Noah bouncing and happy. "Yeah, I . . . He's amazing. I can't believe we did that, Lex."

Lexie stopped at his side when they reached the truck. "I know."

"Mommy?" The two of them turned at the sound of Noah's voice. "Can we has them now?" Riley ordered all four of the ice creams and, as cones were given out, he watched Noah and Lexie start to enjoy them.

It was so odd being this close to Lexie again after so long. Within him, anger and disappointment warred with nostalgia and hope. They still had so much to talk about, so much to decide and arrange if Riley was going to have a regular place in Noah's life. And he wanted nothing less. He had to be real; as much as he wanted to reconnect with Lexie, it wasn't just about the two of them any-more—there was Noah to think about, and he was far too import-ant for Riley to mess shit up by being mixed up over Lexie. Things were too complicated, too fragile, to make any silly mistakes. He had to learn to be a father first before he even thought about him and Lexie being more.

And, honestly, did he even want that?

"Thank you, Riley," Noah said with a mouth full of chocolate ice cream and a wide smile. "This is the bestest."

Riley nodded. "You're welcome, bud."

.   .   .

"So that was it?" Tate spat from his place across their parents' dinner table. "*That* was the reason she gave for not telling you about Noah?"

Riley sighed at Tate's tone. "Yeah."

"That's utter bullshit," he retorted with a shake of his head, vehemence apparent in the way he gulped his drink. "She should have told you before now. She kept your *son* from you, man."

Riley simply lifted his eyebrows in reply. Of course his brother was right and honestly, given long enough, when he thought about it, Riley's blood, too, would start to boil. He'd forget what a nice afternoon he'd spent with Lexie and Noah and instead begin to contemplate how hurt and resentful he was that she'd kept him and his son apart.

"I have to agree," his mom said from her seat at his side. "I can't understand why she didn't at least try and get in contact."

Riley lifted his shoulders. "What do you want me to say? I can only tell you what she told me."

"I know, honey," she said, resigned. "But it doesn't make it fair. I thought more of her."

Yeah, so had Riley. But then, Lexie always did make rash decisions when it came to matters of the heart. He pushed his half-eaten plate of food away and sat back, arms crossed defensively over his chest. Riley didn't like feeling so guarded, and God knew he certainly didn't have need to be—he wasn't in the wrong here—but, frustratingly, he'd always been that way with Lexie.

"So what happens now?" Joan asked, her gaze careful.

Riley shrugged. "I've told her I want full access to Noah. I want to get to know him. I've already missed too much."

She nodded, her lips twitching with what looked like the beginnings of a smile. "And do we get a chance to get to know him, too?"

Riley scratched his chin. "I told Lex that I want to bring him here to meet you all, but Noah needs to get to know me first."

"I agree," Joan commented. "He's only a little boy. You don't want to overwhelm him." She pinched her shoulders, the wary expression she'd harbored since Riley's return from meeting Lexie and Noah morphing into something softer, wistful, more maternal. "I . . . can't quite believe I'm a grandmother." She laced her fingers together, resting them under her chin.

Tate huffed a laugh. "At least *I* don't have to worry about giving you grandkids now." Riley tried to smile but it felt too heavy, too forced. He sighed instead and rubbed a palm across his forehead, where the beginnings of a righteous headache had begun to tap ceaselessly at the inside of his skull. "I know this sounds utterly ridiculous all things considered," Tate said gently, his anger at Lexie momentarily receding, "but are you all right?"

Riley shook his head no, because, no, he wasn't all right. He was all over the place—confused, emotional, and completely lost as to how he was going to sort through the cluster fuck of the situation he'd found himself in. He'd known he was a father for all of twenty-four hours, during which he'd been thinking of nothing else, and his brain felt as though it was about ready to slide out of his damned ears. Being an optimistic and lighthearted person most of the time, Riley found the dregs of frustration and fury hard to handle. They left him exhausted and short tempered and desperate for a solution.

Tate's words about Lexie's selfishness and stupidity echoed through Riley, stirring up his own ire, forcing his body into action. He needed to get out, get some fresh air, clear his head.

With a vague "I'm going out" and a short apology for leaving in the middle of dinner, Riley grabbed the car keys and, with a dismissive wave toward Tate, who offered to accompany him because Riley's fingers were still taped together, climbed into the car, reversed out of the drive, and spun its wheels down the street.

For twenty minutes he cruised, his brain racing, his heart hurting. The look of panic in Lexie's eyes when Sav had walked into the store with Noah flashed through his mind, morphing gradually into the face of his son, smiling and laughing and covered in ice cream. How unfair was it that he couldn't even stay angry for that long? Disappointment, however, still bubbled through him, making his heart heavy and his fists clench.

He pulled the car to a stop and climbed out, realizing with a jolt that he was in the hospital parking lot. Pushing his hands into his pockets, he made his way inside the building, climbing into the elevator and pushing the button for the floor he knew his father was on. He had no idea why he was there or what his father would say when he walked in alone, but the relative calm and quiet of the hospital ward tempered the absolute festival that had taken up residence in Riley's head. He approached the nurses' station, grateful to see the familiar face of the nurse he knew was looking after his dad.

"Visiting ends in a half hour," she informed him, then winked. "But my watch is about a half hour slow."

Riley dipped his chin in thanks and wandered down the hall toward his father's room. With a nervous stretch of his neck, Riley tapped a knuckle on the doorjamb. Park was sitting up in bed, reading glasses in the middle of his nose and a newspaper on his lap. The TV played quietly to itself in the corner of the room. He looked over at Riley, his expression surprised.

"Hey," Riley offered as he took a couple of tentative steps into the room.

Park pulled his glasses from his face. "Your mom here?"

Riley shook his head. "Just me."

Park lifted his chin. "I see." He cleared his throat and folded his newspaper before placing it on the wheeled table that reached over his bed. "Are you okay?"

Wasn't that the million-dollar question? Riley made his way over to one of the two chairs in the room and sat down. "I have a lot on my mind. I don't mean to disturb you. I just needed somewhere quiet to go and . . . think, I guess."

Park scoffed. "This is probably the least quiet place you could have chosen. Nurse Ratched is in here every fifteen minutes, pokin' and proddin' me with some kind of implement and asking how I am."

"I can leave if you'd prefer," Riley offered.

Park waved a hand, reaching for the TV remote with the other. "You're here now."

Riley's chest loosened in relief despite the dismissive reply. "How are *you* feeling?"

"I'm fine. I keep telling them all I'm fine, but they won't listen." Riley couldn't help but smile as his father grumbled. He certainly looked better. Still avoiding looking at Riley, he added, "From the sound of it I'm doing better than you."

Riley dropped his hands between his knees and nodded toward the floor. He knew his mom would have told his father everything. "Yeah."

He looked up to see his father's stare on the TV with his lips pressed together as though he wanted to say something but either didn't know how or couldn't. Sadness bloomed in Riley's stomach. Truthfully, he missed his dad, and some fatherly advice right now would have been gratefully received.

Riley slumped back in his chair. Everything felt so messed up. He couldn't remember a time when he'd felt so out of control, so unsure, and he hated it. He let his head loll back and closed his eyes, allowing the background sounds of the place seep into him, trying his best to clear his mind.

He had no idea how much time had passed when he was woken by a hand on his arm.

"You passed out, honey," the nurse whispered. "Visiting time is over."

Riley sat up, rubbing his eyes with the backs of his hands, suppressing the yawn that built in his throat. "I'm sorry."

"Don't be," she replied. "Your dad here told us to leave you."

Riley's eyebrows jumped. He looked over at Park, who was back to reading his newspaper. An empty plate and a half-drunk glass of juice sat on his table. "Seemed senseless to disturb you," Park said nonchalantly toward his lap.

"I appreciate it," Riley said, stretching his arms above his head, the vertebrae in his spine giving a satisfied pop. He stood. "I'll leave you alone. Thanks for . . . letting me in."

Park glanced up, his eyes traveling over Riley quickly before they rested back on his paper. "You need to look after yourself. You have a lot more than just you to think about and be responsible for now."

He may have intended for his words to be harsh, but the way Park said them, all soft and knowing, caused Riley's throat to thicken. "Yes, sir. I know." He floundered a little, wanting to sit and talk more, but knowing they were still too far apart, with more foundations needing to be built before they would be anything like they used to be. Riley threw a thumb over his shoulder. "I'll leave you in peace. Thanks again."

Park dipped his chin in reply. Riley couldn't have been certain, but the last words he thought he heard as he made his way out of the room were, "Take care, son."

11

Twenty years ago . . .

"What are you and that boy doing today?" Lexie's father asked as he placed a bowl of cereal in front of her.

"His name's Riley, Daddy."

"I know," he grumbled as he sat down next to her. "I just like making sure he remembers where he comes in the grand scheme of things around here."

"Scheme of things?"

Her father smiled as he lifted his coffee cup to his lips. "Don't worry about it. So what are you two doing?"

"We're playing in the spaceship," she answered, shoveling cereal into her mouth. "We're traveling to Jupiter."

"Sounds great. You'll be careful, won't you? Mommy and Sav will be back from the store in an hour or so."

"We're always careful," Lexie replied casually.

She leaped from her seat when a small knock came at the front door, throwing her spoon in the half-empty bowl. "That's Riley!"

"He's early. It's only just gone nine."

"Mommy said it was okay, Daddy," Lexie called back over her shoulder. "We have a lot to do."

Her father's chuckle followed her down the hallway to where she opened the front door. Riley and Joan stood on the porch.

"Hi," Lexie said with a smile, which Riley mirrored. The two of them had been playing together for a year and Lexie certainly considered him her best friend.

"Christine said it was okay to drop Riley off," Joan said to Lexie's dad, who was now standing behind her. "Park's at work and I've been called in."

"No problem. Alexis tells me they're traveling to Jupiter today."

"Dad!" Lexie said in exasperation. "It's a secret mission." Both Lexie's dad and Joan laughed, causing both Lexie and Riley to frown. Their parents simply didn't understand. "Come on, Riley," Lexie said. "We have to go."

"Bye, Mom," he uttered quickly before he followed Lexie through the house and out the back door toward the forest and the spaceship they had built with Lexie's father. It sat around ten feet off the ground and, although Lexie and Riley called it their Apollo, her parents called it a tree house.

Lexie began climbing up the pieces of wood that had been fixed to the tree, knowing Riley was right behind her. He always was, and it made her feel very lucky to have such a good friend. They both clambered onto their Apollo and began moving around the boxes, tins, pans, and other bric-a-brac that made up the seats and controls of the spaceship.

"Are we really going to Jupiter?" Riley asked as he placed the pilot's seat (a large box) in front of her.

"Sure," Lexie replied. "We can go anywhere."

"How about Mars?"

Lexie laughed. "Anywhere." She spread her arms wide and spun. "Anywhere. We can see all of the stars and all the galaxies. Together." She spun the other way. "We can explore black holes and travel the universe."

Riley laughed. "And Pluto?"

"Anywhere." Lexie jumped and spun, making herself dizzy and tilting sideways.

She was aware simultaneously of two things. The first thing was that Riley was staring at her as though she was the most terrifying thing he'd ever seen, and the second was that her foot was touching nothing but air. It was a split second later that she began falling. Lexie had never considered how high or how long it would take to fall ten feet, but it seemed like it took forever. She heard a scream, she heard her name, and then she hit the ground, and all she felt was pain.

Her arm was on fire from the inside out and all she could do was shout for Riley, her mom, and her dad. Riley's face appeared above hers, his eyes filled with tears. "Lexie? Lexie? Are you all right?" He took her hand, the hand that was attached to the arm that didn't feel like it was burning up in flames, and squeezed it. "Your dad's coming, Lexie. Hold on to me."

"Lexie!" Her father's voice came next, sounding almost like he was underwater. Then she was moving and the pain in her arm made her scream out. "I know, baby. Just breathe. We need to take you to the hospital. Riley? We need to move."

In the car, Riley sat next to her, holding her hand and telling her he wasn't going to leave her. The journey to the ER and the subsequent wait passed in an excruciating blur for Lexie. She just knew that Riley, as he promised, was with her the entire time, concerned and telling her over and over that she was going to be all right. Of course she was, but the broken arm and the pink cast she was now sporting were going to make the rest of the summer hard. She picked at a small piece of the cast that wasn't quite set and sighed. The color made up for the pain and the embarrassment of it all, she supposed.

"At least it'll go with everything you wear," Riley commented from his spot on the edge of her hospital bed, where he'd been since Lexie's parents had gone to find a doctor to sign something. He smiled, and Lexie was unable to hold her own smile back.

"Yeah. It's going to make climbing to Apollo harder now, though."

Riley's eyebrows jumped. "You want to go back into the spaceship?"

Lexie blinked. "Of course. It's my favorite thing to do with you."

Riley played with the hem of his T-shirt. "I like it, too. But we have to be careful, Lex. You really frightened me."

Lexie watched her friend for a moment as the pain in her arm was overwhelmed by something different, something warm and comforting. She reached out her free hand and placed it on Riley's shoulder. "I'm sorry."

Riley sniffed. "It's okay. It was an accident, but I thought . . . when you screamed. It was really scary."

"I'll be more careful. Promise."

"I'm glad I was there," Riley said softly. "Even though I was scared."

"I'm glad you were there, too."

"Maybe if you promise to always be careful, I'll promise to always be there just in case."

Lexie smirked and held out her little finger. "Pinkie promise?"

Riley snorted and shook his head before he wrapped his own little finger around hers. "Pinkie promise."

•   •   •   •

Lexie stood in front of the full-length mirror in her bedroom, hating every inch of what was reflected back at her. If she could have slapped the woman in the store who'd convinced her that red was her color and that a two-piece was the way to go, she would have. Lord. Was it this small in the store?

She adjusted the top again, standing sideways to investigate how much side boob she was actually showing and pondering how much side boob would be regarded as distasteful at a public pool. The only thing she did like about it was the fact that it showed off her two newest tattoos, the pink orchid that curved up the right side to her ribs from the top of her thigh and the hummingbird on her left hip. The colors popped against her skin, blues and golds, greens and oranges.

The more colorful the better, in her opinion. It wasn't that she disliked simple black; she merely preferred color on her body. Riley only ever had black—save for the world on the inside of his arm—and his tattoos were really nice. Really, *really* nice. He'd had so many new pieces since the last time they'd seen one another—patterns of concentric circles on his shoulders, words she hadn't been close enough to make out on his biceps and forearm, and what looked like a flock of swallows that dove and twisted around his collarbone. When he'd approached her in the park three days before, all ink, height, and Ray-Bans, she'd almost blown a gasket with how hot they were. The man could rock a tat like no one else. And that beard? *Shit*. At first it had been strange not to see that part of his face, a part she was intimately familiar with, but the more she stared at him—and stared she had—the more she understood why men grew them: they were sexy as hell.

Lexie blew out her cheeks and rubbed her fingertips against her temples. It was thoughts like those that were going to get her into a *lot* of trouble. She'd felt the all-too-familiar snap and spark through her body when he touched her, but she knew they had to be sensible. Besides, the hurt and anger she'd seen in Riley's eyes told her that she had a lot of making up and explaining to do before they could move forward. She couldn't allow herself to forget what had been before, or that Noah was the most important thing in the universe to her. Forgetting all of that and falling back into bed with Riley would be a huge mistake. They'd played that scene out too many times, and Lexie knew how it ended.

"Mommy!" Noah called as he sprinted into her bedroom and threw himself at the bed, scrabbling and clawing his way onto it. "Can I wear this?"

He stood, bare feet on her comforter, showing off the Batman board shorts Lexie's mom had bought him instead of an Easter egg. Lexie grinned at how far he'd pulled them up, covering his belly button to almost under his chest.

"Don't you look handsome?" she said as she moved to him, adjusting the shorts so they sat at his waist.

"Riley said he likes Batman, sos I can show him these." He fiddled distractedly with the drawstring ties.

Lexie watched for a silent moment. "Do you like Riley, Noah?" Since meeting at the park, the four of them—Savannah included, because she was the perfect buffer between Lexie and Riley—had met again, just a quick coffee and a juice for Noah in the same coffee shop Lexie had worked in when she was sixteen.

Riley had mentioned that he wanted to introduce Noah to his parents and brothers, which Lexie was more than happy for him to do. Lexie couldn't forget the look of disappointment and shock on Joan's face the day she'd seen Noah. Once again, reason and stupidity clashed around her heart. She'd tried to explain to Riley why she hadn't told him and, honestly, she stood by it 100 percent. Her number-one priority was Noah, and that would never change. Sure, she was more than prepared to build bridges and face whatever Riley and his family threw at her, but she would always protect her son. No matter what.

"I likes his beard," Noah mused.

Lexie laughed and pulled Noah closer, kissing his cheek and taking a deep breath of him. It was strange how sometimes he smelled the same as Riley did when they were kids. So much of her son reminded Lexie of him and seeing the two of them together, as beautiful as it was, was also eerie. Riley wasn't wrong when he said that they looked alike—they were like two peas in a pod—but it was their mannerisms, too. They tilted their head identically when curious about something and cocked their eyebrow in that same derisive way. Even at four years old, Noah had that Moore characteristic down pat.

"I love you," she whispered into her son's hair.

"All the worlds, Mommy. Can we go to the pool now?"

Lexie kissed Noah's forehead and moved back to her closet. "In an hour. Riley is meeting us there, but he's picking up his daddy from the hospital first."

"His daddy is sick?" Noah asked as he thumped back to the floor.

"He's better now. Go and get your stuff. You need to decide what toys you're taking."

And with that Noah took off, leaving Lexie to breathe a sigh of relief, knowing she'd dodged a hell of a bullet.

.　　　.　　　.

"I'm fine, Joan. For Pete's sake, stop fussing!"

Tate snickered and Riley shook his head as the two of them followed their parents through the front door and into the house. Upon his release, the hospital had suggested that once they got home, Park be transported from the car to the house in a wheelchair, but Park had responded with some pretty colorful words of disagreement. As an alternative, Joan gripped his arm as though the poor man were going to keel over at any second, babying him and guiding him with every step. It was clear that Park's patience was running out.

"Oh, stop whining," Joan retorted as they all moved into the living room. "Take a seat."

Park settled carefully into his favorite chair with an eye roll. "It's a few stitches, Joan. Relax."

"*You* relax. I don't want to hear another word. You need to keep your blood pressure down." She turned to Riley and Tate. "I'm making tea." They watched her flounce toward the kitchen and collapsed into almost silent chuckles.

"Yeah, laugh it up, you two," Park commented, adjusting the cushions at his back.

"I *can* laugh it up," Tate said with a grin, moving toward his father so he could help make him comfortable. "She did it with me when I came out of the hospital; now it's your turn."

Park grumbled again and rubbed a hand across his chest. "You okay, Dad?" Riley asked with a concerned frown.

Park nodded and waved an indifferent hand in his direction. "I'd be better if you all stopped looking at me as though I'm gonna explode. Shoo. Go on. Go do something else."

"I'll go and see if Mom wants a hand," Tate said as he limped off in the direction of the kitchen, leaving Riley with their father and an enthusiastic thumbs-up. *Bastard.*

Riley stood for a minute or so, watching his dad and hating the awkward silence, before he took a seat on the large sofa. He sat on its edge, hands clasped between his knees. "It's good to have you home," he offered, to which Park simply lifted his eyebrows. Riley sighed. "Look, Dad, I know Mom has filled you in on what's going on, but I wanted to tell you myself that I'm going to be sticking around Michigan a little while longer. Mom said I'm welcome to stay here at the house, but if you're not happy with that I can make alternative—"

"It's fine, Riley," Park answered with a deep breath. His gaze cut to his son briefly before he dipped his chin minutely. "It's fine."

Riley cleared his throat. "Thank you, sir."

"You do what you have to," Park added. "However long it takes."

Well, hell. Riley nodded. "Okay, well, I'm going to meet Lex and Noah now. I'll see you later."

Park grunted and reached for the TV remote. Riley wandered into the kitchen to find Tate and his mother whispering like two school kids. They stopped when they saw Riley. "My ears are burnin'," Riley quipped, opening the fridge and pulling out a bottle of water. "Anything I need to know?"

Joan shook her head. "No." She sipped her tea delicately. "I was just asking Tate if he knew what was going on with you and Alexis."

"And I told her," Tate said, defending himself, "I know nothin'."

"You know nothin' because there's nothin' to know," Riley sing-songed with a smirk. "I'm getting to know my son. End of."

"And that's wonderful," Joan said, placing her cup on the counter. "But what about you and Lexie?"

Riley lifted his shoulders. "What about us?" He knew he was being obtuse and the purse of his mother's lips told him she knew, too, but he didn't want to lose himself in worrying or wondering about anything other than building a relationship with Noah.

"I worry," Joan said seriously. "You and she have a long history and you've both been hurt. She lied to you about Noah. I just want to know that you're going to be careful."

Riley exhaled heavily. His mother's concern was warming, but it was also unnecessary; Riley was focused on one thing and one thing only: Noah. "You don't have to worry," he told them both. "I know what I'm doing." He didn't stop to wonder why the words almost tasted like a lie.

Joan's stare was probing in the way only a mother's look could be. "Fine," she said, apparently seeing what she needed before she returned to the other room to check on Park.

"I'll see you soon, yeah?" Riley asked his brother as he grabbed his bag and headed toward the front door. Tate was heading back to Pennsylvania that afternoon for work.

"Yeah, man. When will you be back in New York? I've got a meeting with Max at the end of the month." Tate was Max's Narcotics Anonymous sponsor and had been working with him since his release from rehab.

Riley paused. "He okay?"

"Oh yeah, yeah, he's great—we just make a point of meeting at least once a month to catch up, talk about any bad days if he's had them."

"Sure. I'll probably be in the city at the same time, but I . . ." Riley started, running a hand through his hair. The weight of responsibility and questions about how he was going to organize his life now that Noah existed in his world lay heavily on his shoulders. "Seriously, I have no idea what I'm going to do about all of this. I mean, how can I be in New York when Noah's here?"

Tate placed a gentle hand on Riley's shoulder and squeezed. "Don't worry about that yet, man," he soothed. "One step at a time. You'll get there. You spoke to Max and Carter, right? And they're cool. They'll understand."

Riley nodded and pulled his brother into a hug. "Thanks, man." They slapped each other on the back and stepped apart. "Take care, asshole," Riley smiled, opening the front door.

"You too, jerk-off."

. . .

Ten years ago . . .

The squeal that erupted out of Lexie's chest when she saw Riley loping toward her, hair in disarray and his bag on his back, should have been embarrassing. It certainly garnered a few surprised looks from the other people in the airport, but she didn't care.

She ran toward him and leaped at him, wrapping her arms around his neck and her legs around his waist. Jesus, it was so good to see him. She smothered his face in kisses, ignoring his pleas for mercy and com-

mitting to memory the way his loud laugh shook his large shoulders under her hands.

"I missed you so much," she managed through her kisses. "So much." *It had been so long since she'd last seen him at spring break. Lexie had counted every day they were apart, hating each one equally, needing him back with her, needing his hands on her skin and his breath in her ear. The darkness that had followed her like a cape at her back was so much more suffocating when Riley wasn't around, thick and unrelenting, leaving her tired and praying for a hole to hide in. Having him back at her side never failed to ease the unforgiving emptiness that took root when her father died.*

"I missed you, too, baby," he whispered into her neck, holding her tightly. Slowly he let her down, her feet finding the floor. His eyes roamed over her face, concerned and loving. "How are you?"

She wanted to tell him that life was an uphill battle that left her breathless and broken, that sleep was the only thing she ever looked forward to, but instead she smiled, not wanting him to worry about the depression label being bandied about by her doctor. "Better, now you're here."

He curled an arm around her shoulder as she continued to cling to his waist, and they made their way out of arrivals toward the parking lot. Lexie kept her nose close to his chest, breathing him in. His scent had changed a little since he'd been in New York, changing from a more natural, woodsy smell to a metallic, urban aroma that wasn't entirely displeasing. She'd gotten used to it, and even had the T-shirt he'd left on his last visit at Easter under her pillow so she could still take big gulps of his aftershave. She pulled it out when she was missing him—which was pretty much all the time—or when they talked on the phone and she needed to feel like he was near.

It had been a long year since he'd left in September, but now that he was home for the summer after completing his first year at NYU, Lexie could allow herself to forget how difficult the past nine months— sporadic visits aside—had been without him.

"*So I have to take you straight home because your mom wants to see you, but then I get you all to myself,*" *she said as she maneuvered her car onto the freeway.*

"*Sounds perfect,*" *he replied, lifting her free hand to his mouth and kissing the tips of her fingers. She loved it when he did that.* "*And what do you plan to do with me when you get me all to yourself?*"

Her stomach coiled in excitement. "*I've made plans.*"

"*I like plans. Do these plans involve you being naked?*"

She giggled. "*Maybe.*"

He shifted closer, his mouth at the back of her ear. "*Do they involve my face between your legs?*"

Shit. *He was too damned good at saying the exact thing her body needed to hear. Heat pooled in her gut, and Riley snickered when she wiggled in her seat.* "*How about you wait and see,*" *she offered, her voice a little shaky.*

"*Okay. I'll be good.*" *He kissed her neck and his tongue flicked her earlobe.* "*But I swear to God, I can't wait to be inside you again, Lex. It's been too fucking long.*"

"*Riley,*" *she gasped.* "*Stop before I pull over and blow you on the side of the road.*"

Riley laughed loudly. "*Like that's an incentive to make me stop!*"

One of the things that Lexie loved most about her and Riley's relationship was the relative ease with which they fell back into what made them them. *As much as they were a couple, and Lexie loved him with everything she was, Riley was also her best friend. Whenever he came home, despite wanting nothing more than to strip him naked and have her wicked way with him, she also looked forward to just sitting and talking.*

At the Moore house, Lexie was welcomed as she always was by Joan with a kiss and a warm hug. She watched as Riley shook hands with his father. Tate, Seb, and Dex greeted their brother with playful thumps and backslaps. Lexie missed this, too. Joan continually invited Lexie over for dinner when Riley was away, but as grateful as she was, it didn't feel the same without Riley being there. If anything, it made his absence all the more excruciating.

They ate dinner around a banter-filled table, then Riley showered before the two of them climbed back into Lexie's car with the intention of heading to her house. Savannah had been a lifesaver; she'd managed to convince their mother to try the new steak house in town, after which she'd gotten tickets for the newest rom com at the multiplex, leaving the place empty for at least a few hours.

As soon as the front door shut behind them, Riley was on her. He pushed her against the wall, his mouth ravenous, moaning and gasping into Lexie as his hands fought with the button on her shorts. She cursed his belt buckle and his fly, pulling them open, laughing as Riley nibbled and sucked at her neck before she groaned obscenely loudly when his fingers pushed between her legs.

"So wet, Lex," he grunted, and pushed his fingers into her, making her back arch at the same time she called out his name. "That's right. Feel it. Imagine my cock there."

Goddamn. *His mouth was filthy and Lexie loved every minute of it. Becoming truly comfortable with himself when they were in bed, he'd started talking to her that way just before he'd left for New York and would frequently have her panting and moaning down the phone receiver whenever they had the privacy. The man was born for dirty talk and the harder and more turned on he got, the dirtier his words became. She'd lost count of the amount of orgasms he'd brought her to while whispering devilishly hot things into her ear.*

"We're not going to make it to the bed, are we?" she moaned, gripping his cock with two hands, desperate for him.

"How long do we have?"

"Two hours."

"Then no. We're not."

He lifted her up, her legs around his waist, and slammed into her. Her cry echoed throughout the house. Riley tried to muffle it with his mouth, but she was too loud and it felt too good. The emptiness in Lexie dissolved instantly and her lungs expanded, as if finally able to breathe properly now that they were joined together. She grabbed at his hair and pulled his lips to hers as he began to move.

"Yes," she chanted when her back shifted up and down the hallway wall with the force of his thrusts.

"Feels so good," he gasped. "Your pussy feels so good." His hand made its way under her shirt and under her bra. "Feel how hard I am for you." He squeezed her. "Feel it?"

"Yes."

"All for you. Give me that tongue."

She obeyed without thought, letting Riley suck her tongue and twist and turn his own around it. He was everywhere, she felt smothered by him, and it was perfect. She clutched the back of his T-shirt, feeling her orgasm start to build, and began to meet his thrusts, their heaving breaths the only sound save for the slapping of wet skin and the rustle of clothing.

"Oh Jesus, you're close," he moaned. "So tight on my dick." She cried out when he sped up further. "Shit, yes. Come. Come all over me, Lex."

There they were. The words she knew would send her spiraling out of control. It was almost like he had complete power over her body and its reactions and, as he called out to her again and again to come, she gave her body over to him, embracing the snap of her spine, the curl of her toes, and the shouts of exquisite pleasure as she detonated around him. Riley yelled with her, his cock twitching as he came, panting into her shoulder, shaking and thanking God.

Unable to hold them both up, Riley slumped to his knees, still inside of her, before pulling out and collapsing to the floor with his head on her lap. They sat for a few moments, the pair of them trying to regain their breath. Lexie looked down at Riley, seeing his eyes were closed, and began to run her hands though the front of his hair. She chuckled when she noticed his jeans were still around his ankles.

"Welcome home," she whispered.

He smiled a toothless smile. "Thank you." He exhaled contentedly. "Jesus, Lex, it gets better every time."

She had to agree. The feelings the boy before her conjured from her body were indescribable. She doubted very much that anyone else experienced the same when they had sex.

He stretched a little, adjusting and moving her thigh as though it were a pillow. "Who needs London when I've got this, huh?"

Lexie frowned. "What are you talking about?"

He paused, eyes still closed. "Nothing. I'm just playing with you."

"About London? That's random." The shrug he gave in reply convinced Lexie he wasn't simply playing and that there was more to what he'd let slip. "Riley?"

He opened his eyes gradually, saw her expression, exhaled heavily, and cursed, sitting up with a groan. "It's nothing, Lex, I promise. It's just . . ." She crossed her arms over her chest and he laughed uncomfortably. "Okay, so there's an opportunity for all second-year students in my major to work abroad with a company to see another side of business. It's for most of the academic year; it's part of the program and gains the person extra credit, as well as being an all-expenses-paid trip. This year it was Japan. Next year it's London."

Lexie's heart thumped in alarm. "You're going to London?"

"I could *go to London if my grades were good enough and I put my name down, sure."*

And of course his grades were good enough. Lexie knew that for certain. Riley never gave himself enough credit for how smart he was. "Riley." She shuffled closer to him, the black cape pinching at her throat. "Have you put your name down? Are you going?"

He cupped her cheek and kissed her. "No."

For one selfish beat, relief clutched Lexie hard. Riley's being in New York was one thing, but his being in a different country altogether made her want to cling to him like a limpet and never let go. She studied him carefully, and it was then that she saw the glimmer of disappointment in his eyes.

From anyone else, he'd have hidden it well, but she knew him better. He wanted to go. Of course he wanted to go. That much was clear, but he was denying himself for her. In light of the past year, it was no wonder really. Lexie knew she'd been difficult despite her attempts at being upbeat every time they spoke, but it was just so hard having him so far away.

It terrified her that Riley might never come back to her. She'd tried to sound positive in every text and email, too, but truthfully, she was waiting for him to tell her he was staying there, or that he'd found someone else. Which she realized was fucking ridiculous. She knew Riley loved her, just as she loved him, but losing her father had brought home the true bullshit reality of life: nothing lasted forever. And it was scary as hell. Losing someone else in her life, especially Riley, would kill her for certain. Her heart simply wouldn't take it, and yet she knew if she held him back, he'd resent her. The cracks would begin and then it would only be a matter of time.

Lexie took a deep breath and held him close. "You have to go, Riley."

For a brief moment, he looked astonished. "What?"

"This is the opportunity of a lifetime. When will you ever get the chance again?"

"But it's for the academic year," he said quietly, tucking her hair behind her ear. "I know how hard this year has been for you, and I wouldn't be home for a long time."

Lexie swallowed hard, trying to disregard the twist of unease those words caused. "I know, but, seriously, this is your future." Riley was silent for so long Lexie became nervous. "What?"

He huffed a laugh. "I really didn't think you'd react this way." He rubbed a palm down the side of his face. "Are you sure? I mean, do you really mean that?"

Lexie smiled and crawled into his lap, straddling him. "I love you, Riley. All the world. That'll never change. I'm so proud of you." She twirled a piece of his hair around her index finger. "You were always too big for this place." For me. *She rubbed the tip of her nose gently against his, fighting off the panic that thought carried with it. "You need to get out of here. You need to . . . have more."*

Riley's brows met gently above his nose. "Lex. I'll call you every day."

She smiled despite the ache in her chest. "And you'll come back, right?"

He wrapped his arms around her waist and held her close, kissing her so softly, Lexie's heart could barely take it. "If you still want me. I'll always come back to you."

"I'll always want you."

It was the absolute truth, and four months later when Lexie, along with Riley's family, took him to the airport to catch his flight to London, she told him the same thing again. He hugged her tight and whispered his love in her ear, pushing the tears Lexie had tried so desperately to hide from him away with his fingertips. Watching him leave, even though she'd told him to do it, was one of the hardest things Lexie had ever had to do.

And it only got harder.

They spoke on the phone as often as they could, but the differences in time zones and schedules were a pain in the ass. Lexie had begun an online course in business management with part of the money her father's life insurance had paid out, wanting to keep her mind busy and train in something she knew would help her family in the long term. Her mom had only gone back to part-time work, unable to cope with more, and Savannah was still in high school, leaving Lexie the chief breadwinner of the house. She worked a nine-hour shift and then logged on to her course, sometimes falling asleep at her computer or on the phone with Riley when he managed to get through or when she took his calls.

She knew he was frustrated with her and her fluctuating moods, and she didn't blame him. She was so tired and so lost, and because she missed him so damned much, she'd begun to snap when he asked about her course or what she'd been doing with her time. What the hell answer did he expect? He was off seeing the world, enjoying every moment, and she was doing the same shit every day, wearing herself out and spreading herself too thin. The meds her doctor had put her on didn't seem to be working, either. They'd lift her for a time until the black cape began to choke her again, tighter and more acute than before.

In fairness, Riley had the patience of a saint, seemingly under-standing her need to vent her anger and dissatisfaction with everything around her, which ironically only made Lexie more unpleasant. She knew without doubt he didn't deserve her sharp tongue, especially with him being so far away from home, away from his friends, family, and her, but she was just so damned scared that she was going to lose him when he realized what was out in the world waiting to be discovered. She couldn't blame him for any of it. She'd told him to go, for God's sake. She couldn't be mad that he was doing something with his life. He deserved everything coming to him.

Besides, if he hadn't been in London, he would have been in New York, and . . . Jesus!

Lexie threw herself down onto her bed and stared up at the ceiling, trying her best to calm down and stop overthinking everything. She was waiting for Riley's call. It was a Thursday night and he always called. It had become their routine and it should have made her feel excited and happy and, of course, hearing his voice filled the empty spaces in her to a degree, but it also reminded her of what she didn't have.

She didn't have Riley next to her, she didn't have the future she'd dreamed of since she was a little girl, and she didn't have her father. Even with it being over a year since his death, the wounds of his ab-sence were still achingly raw, and it hurt. It hurt so much. If Riley didn't come back, if he decided that he wanted other things and she lost him, too . . .

She wiped at the tears that formed as the words, which had started as a whisper when Riley first left but were now a flat-out yell, marched through her mind: You're not good enough, Lex. You're not good enough for him. He deserves more. He deserves better. Let him go before he leaves you first.

The phone rang, making her jump. She closed her eyes for a brief moment, pressed the answer button, and lifted the phone to her ear. "Hey."

"Hey, beautiful. How are you?"

Lexie smiled, allowing his sounds to fill her hollowness. "I'm okay. Tired. How're you?"

"I'm good. It's been a good day. I miss you."

Emotion collected in her throat. "I miss you, too."

"What's wrong?"

Lexie cursed her shaking voice and pressed a hand to her forehead. "Nothing. I'm okay. Tell me about your day."

And he did. He waxed lyrical about how amazing London was, how the company he was working for was pleased with his progress, and how the family he was staying with had introduced him to black pudding. It sounded gross as hell, but Riley assured her it was good. He sounded so happy, so beautiful and content, pulling Lexie deeper into her own head. She looked over at her bedroom bulletin board, upon which were hundreds of photographs of her and Riley from the age of eight. There were their prom pictures, he so gorgeous in his tux, she smiling and proud at his side. Her father had taken that picture. She remembered it as though it was yesterday.

"Lex?"

"Hmm?"

"You didn't hear a word I just said, did you?" *The smile in his voice was wary.*

"Sorry, I was just thinking."

"About what?"

Lexie closed her eyes and took a deep breath. "Us."

The phone buzzed with dead air for a long time. Lexie counted at least seven heartbeats. "And what do you think?" he asked finally.

Lexie's mind began to fire relentlessly: I think I'm terrified of losing you. I'm terrified of losing myself. I think I'd die if you didn't want me, but I think you deserve more. I think I need to let you go before you hurt me.

"Lex?" he sighed. "Baby, you're scaring me. I know you haven't been yourself . . . I know this year has been really hard for you, but I feel like I'm losing you." Lexie cupped a hand to her mouth to capture the sob that threatened. "Am I?" he asked, his voice small. "Am I losing you, Lex?"

Her answer was as honest as she could make it. "I can't do this anymore."

. . .

Lexie and Noah were standing at the entrance of the public pool, both of them blond and tanned in the blazing sunshine. Riley allowed himself a couple of moments, before he approached, to watch them, astounded by how beautiful they both were. Lexie leaned down and kissed Noah's head, while he looked up at her chattering away, which Riley was learning he did a lot.

If it hadn't been for the obvious physical characteristics they shared, Riley would have questioned whether Noah was his—he was such a smart kid. Even spending such a short amount of time with him, it was obvious. Lexie was right: he was observant as hell, even remembering Riley telling him about his Batman socks. He smiled, unable to stop himself.

Seeing Lexie with Noah when she was oblivious to being watched warmed his very soul. Despite everything, it was so obvious what an amazing mom she was. Noah gazed up at her listening to every word, and she smiled and touched him more often than she was perhaps aware of. The role of mommy seemed so natural for her. And why wouldn't it? She'd always been tactile and loving, but this, this was something else, something deeper.

The heat of Riley's adoration was briefly diluted with a profound sadness when, once again, he permitted himself to think about how things between the two of them could have been so very different. He wondered fleetingly about what her pregnancy had been like, whether she'd craved peculiar things at three o'clock in the morning and whether she'd had morning sickness. Then he'd thought about how her labor might have been, how painful, and who had been with her. It was missing those precious moments of the beginning of Noah's life that hurt Riley almost as much as his missing his son's first step, first tooth, and first birthday.

"Fuck it," he muttered when Lexie noticed him across the street. There was nothing he could do about any of it now, and, honestly, seeing the two smiling faces of his son and his childhood sweetheart made the hurt of the past just about bearable.

"Hey, guys," he said as he drew closer. "Are we ready to swim?"

"I am! I am!" Noah shouted, jumping up and down. Noah pointed to his shorts. "I gots Batman!" Riley curled over an inch of the waistband on his khakis and Noah's eyes grew. "Yous has Batman shorts, too?"

"Only the best, kid." Riley held out his hand and Noah slapped it hard. Lexie laughed, pulling Riley's attention. "No Sav?"

Lexie shook her head. "Just us today." She pulled her bag farther up her arm. "That okay?"

Riley tried not to think about how happy that news made him. It wasn't that he disliked Savannah, far from it, but having Lexie and Noah to himself for the day sounded awesome. "It's great."

"We swims now, Mommy?"

"Yes." Lexie clapped. "We swim!"

"Yay! Come on, Riley!"

Riley's heart all but burst from his chest when Noah's small hand grabbed his. *Jesus.* He looked down at the little boy as he pulled Riley toward the payment booth with more enthusiasm than he'd ever seen. Lexie appeared just as shocked as Riley did as she watched from his side, but the smile that teased her lips calmed Riley enough that he squeezed Noah's hand, holding on to him tightly.

The pool was busy, but thank God, Lexie had had the foresight to reserve two loungers. They settled their towels, placing their bags underneath them, and Riley proceeded to pull off his T-shirt and khakis. He pretended that he didn't notice Lexie's eyes on him, but the trail of hot lust and memories they left as they traveled over his chest was too fucking delicious. Their stares met and his stomach clenched. With Noah on the lounger, smothered in sunscreen and playing with his goggles, she lifted her vest top over her head.

The red bikini top underneath it was perfect. It hugged her in all the right ways, showing off enough of what Riley remembered of her body that his mouth was suddenly a little dry. And sweet mother of God, the ink on her torso was fucking incredible and all but screamed for Riley's tongue to trace every line of it.

His eyes desperately wanted to slip down her and watch the shorts she wore fall to the ground, but, with the will of a titan, he turned away to push his stuff into his bag. *Fuck me.* Would it ever get easier? Would his body ever stop wanting hers? He would guess not, but the least she could do was to help make it painless for him. When he gathered himself and turned back, he moaned.

"Jesus," he grunted, rubbing a palm over his mouth.

"What?"

"You're not playing fair. Not fair at all."

"How can you say that," she retorted incredulously, "standing there looking the way you do?"

Riley looked down at himself and his black Batman shorts, unable to see what she meant. "What?"

Lexie's nose wrinkled as she laughed. She turned back to Noah, removing her glasses as she did. "You ready, buddy?"

"Yes!" He took her hand and the three of them made their way to the pool's edge.

Without preamble, Riley ran and cannonballed into the water, hearing Noah's squeals of excitement and approval when he broke the surface. Riley held out his arms and encouraged Noah to jump, which he did, like a rocket, straight into them, trusting Riley implicitly, without question.

When Riley thought back over the moments in his life that he would cherish, he wasn't afraid to admit that Lexie would feature in most of them—their first night together being a surefire number-one hit. Yet, having his son in his arms as Noah laughed and played in the water, or while Noah held on to Riley's neck and rode on his back like a horse, obliterated them all. This moment, right here, was what he would cherish most for the rest of his life. Even as he chased Noah around the pool, dodging other swimmers and lifting him, throwing him up and catching him, Riley knew that no other memory would come close to this one.

After a good ninety minutes of play in the water, Lexie sat Noah on the lounger and wrapped him in a towel in the shade. He sipped happily from a juice box and nibbled on some fruit she retrieved from her bag. Riley sat on his lounger, watching him and smiling every few minutes. It was strange how simply looking at his son could prompt that reaction. Lexie returned from the poolside bar with two beers in plastic pint cups. Riley took his with a grateful hum and Lexie sat on the lounger at Noah's feet. She murmured and cooed in the little boy's ear, making him giggle before she left him alone.

Riley tipped his drink toward hers and she tapped the side of the plastic with her own. "Cheers."

Riley nodded. "It's been a good day."

Lexie wound her finger through the condensation on her beer cup. "It has."

Riley raised his hand and pointed to the scar he'd noticed earlier, visible just above her bikini bottoms. "You have a C-section?"

Lexie looked down at herself. "Yeah." She patted Noah's foot. "This little guy was breech."

"I was upsides downs," Noah added, without looking up from the small Yoda figurine he was playing with and feeding apple slices to.

"And the doctors didn't want to leave him too long," Lexie continued. "So they decided a section was the way to go."

Riley glanced to his beer, then back at Lexie. "Who was with you?"

"Mom. And Sav." At least she looked apologetic, but Riley's heart stung regardless. Lexie pressed her lips together and sighed. "Riley, in my mind, I made the right decision for me then. Now? I hate that I took that moment away from you. Truly. And I'd give anything to be able to turn the clock back."

Riley looked out to the pool, watching a young couple hug and kiss in the water.

He knew Lexie was waiting for the fight, the argument, the demanding of answers, but he really didn't want to get into it in front of Noah. He sure as shit *would* be insisting on her explaining why she didn't try harder to get in contact at a later date, but sitting in the sun on a cloudless day with the sensation of Noah's hand still burning his palm, Riley was content enough to let it go.

"What did you crave?" he asked suddenly. Lexie blinked. "When you were pregnant, what food?"

"Skittles." She chuckled. "The red ones especially."

"I loves Skittles!" Noah exclaimed, lifting and dropping his feet onto the lounger in excitement. "But I'm not allowed sugars. Only when I've been good as a treats."

Riley laughed into his beer. The little dude sounded like an old man sometimes. Lexie's smile fell gradually as she observed Riley. She had yet to put her glasses back on and her blue eyes were careful.

"Ask me," he encouraged.

"What was it like?" she asked before glancing back at Noah, who was busy playing with his fruit. "Inside."

Surprised by the curve in conversation, Riley turned sideways on his lounger, placing his feet on the hot asphalt, his knees millimeters from Lexie's, and sipped his beer. "Boring mostly. I served fourteen months of an eighteen-month sentence and that was enough for me. Never again."

"Why did you do it? I mean, did you need money *that* badly?"

Riley shook his head. "No. The money was just an added bonus. I was helping a friend out. I stored the car parts in my shops for him, knowing they were hot. I'd done it time and time again without trouble, so I grew cocky and I got busted. End of. It was a stupid choice, but I made it, I owned it, and I served my time."

The answer seemed to appease her enough. "I guess we've both made stupid choices along the way, huh?"

Riley exhaled. "I guess, yeah." He swallowed hard when their gazes stayed connected, feeling her in places inside only she'd ever had the ability to touch. "I thought of you." At his words, her top teeth trailed across her bottom lip.

"I thought of you, too," she admitted.

Fuck, she was so damned gorgeous sitting there all wide-eyed and breathless that Riley wanted nothing more than to lean over and kiss her. He glanced at Noah, who was oblivious and still playing with his apple and Yoda, and reeled the feeling in quickly. It was too damned easy to lose his head around her.

Lexie's mouth opened a little. "My feelings for you never changed, Riley," she whispered. "But things are different now."

Hearing her declare as much pumped Riley's blood around his

body even faster, and he immediately began to disregard all of the concerns he'd voiced to Tate. Of course the feeling was mutual. Dammit, Riley had never wanted a woman more. She'd set a bar that was sky fucking high and no one would ever get close to it. "Maybe things being different is a good thing," he hedged. "Maybe wanting things the way they were is where we went wrong so many times before."

Looking contemplative, Lexie replied, "Maybe."

"Maybe you and I can go out and talk about it sometime. Just us."

Her gaze danced across his. "I'd like that."

12

As it always did during the annual National Cherry Festival, E State Street looked like a cherry had vomited over everything. The place was teeming with people getting ready to watch the parade. The hot afternoon air was cooled by the gentle breeze off the bay and smelled of cherries, burgers, and hot dogs, while the fairground thumped in the distance. It had been too long since Riley had attended the festival and, standing amid the hubbub, dodging balloons and people of all ages and sizes, he realized he'd missed it.

He knew many of the locals hated the noise and the mess the festival traffic left and all that, but he'd always enjoyed it and, being there to meet Lexie and Noah made it all the more exhilarating. His mom was somewhere among the crowds with Aunt Carol, Maggie, and Rosie, but they were keeping themselves scarce, not wanting to confuse Noah too much—despite Joan almost foaming at the mouth in her excitement at getting to know her grandson better—or overwhelm Lexie, while his dad had decided to skip the parade, still not feeling ready to be on his feet for too long. He was more than happy, he said, to stay at home and read a book.

Riley looked down at his cell phone when it vibrated in his hand. It was a text from Lexie. His heart flip-flopped in his chest seeing her name on the screen, which was hysterical, really; it wasn't as if they'd never texted before. It had just been a long damned time since they had.

Look up.

Doing as he was asked, he saw Lexie, Noah, Savannah, and Jaime, the girl from Lexie's store, all waving huge cherry festival foam fingers in his direction from across the street. He waved back before jogging over to join them. Noah was wearing the obligatory Traverse City T-shirt, complete with cherry emblem, as well as modeling an awesome pair of bright red sunglasses that practically covered half of his small face.

Riley crouched down and held out his hand for Noah to slap, which he did without question; it was slowly becoming their thing, and Riley loved it. "Dude, can you even see through those things?"

"Yes," Noah said, his lisp catching the *s*. "I can sees you fine."

Riley ruffled the boy's hair a little and stood back up, looking straight at Lexie. "Hey," he said before smiling at Sav and Jaime. "So what's the plan, guys?"

"Parade!" Noah yelled, jumping at Riley's hip.

"Sounds good," Riley replied, placing a hand on Noah's shoulder. "You all eaten yet?"

"No, we're starving," Jaime commented as she pushed her shades into her hair. "I need to eat before I meet my friends and we start drinking."

"I want cherries!" Noah added. "Can I, Mommy?"

Lexie smiled down at him. "Sure, let's go. But make sure you're holding someone's hand all the time, okay? There're too many people around, and I don't want you to get lost."

"I won'ts get lost," he assured her innocently while wafting his foam finger. "Promise."

"Good boy. Grab a hand."

Riley couldn't hold back the grin when the first hand Noah went for was his. He felt the small fingers wrap around his own and instinctively held on as tightly as he could. He knew nothing would or could break his hold on his son's hand, understanding with a jolt just how protective he was of the little guy. How was it possible to feel something so powerful so quickly? He had no idea, but he embraced it unequivocally.

The five of them wandered toward the cherry stalls, answering Noah's quick-fire questions as they moved: What's that? Why is it cherries and not bananas? Can we go to the fair? Can I get a balloon? Can I have a big burger? He was relentless, and apparently obsessed with food, but Riley found himself utterly captivated, trying to answer what he could without undermining Lexie's rules. It was a tricky line to walk, but Lexie appeared open to Riley's opinion, which eased a small knot of anxiety at the base of his neck.

Taking three baskets of cherries, they decided to make their way around the other stalls, investigating the handmade food and artifacts ranging from pots and glass to pictures and wine. Conversation between Lexie and Riley was light, but Riley couldn't shake the feeling that she was being careful around her sister and friend and, honestly, he wasn't sure how to take it. Their day at the pool had been so relaxed; they'd chatted and played with Noah, all but forgetting the tension between them. Now, however, the unease and apprehension was much heavier.

He was struck with the cold sensation of déjà vu. He should have seen it coming, he supposed. Lexie protected herself and her heart by pushing people away. She'd done it for years; it was why their relationship had been so devastatingly sporadic. Riley knew it stemmed from her losing her father so suddenly, but even after all these years, it still didn't make her cautiousness any easier to take.

"Everything okay?" he asked as they sat on a wooden bench, while Jaime and Savannah waited in the face-painting line with Noah.

Lexie nodded, her focus shifting between her son and the cherries in her hand. She closed her eyes for a beat and sighed. "Actually no."

Riley tried to keep a leash on his dread and pushed a cherry into his mouth. "Anything I can help with?"

"No," she responded quickly. "It's me. I—the truth is, I had a dream about you last night."

Riley swallowed the cherry hard. "Oh."

She looked at him. "It was about when you went to London."

Riley's chest gave a small squeeze of painful melancholy.

Lexie sat back. "I woke up this morning feeling . . ." She cupped a palm to her forehead. "Jesus, Riley, I was—I was a mess back then and I—"

"You were grieving, Lex. Depressed. You'd never given yourself a chance to let your feelings out, looking after your mom and Sav. It had to happen eventually."

"I know," she agreed quietly. "But I shouldn't have pushed you away like I did." She moved her glasses up her nose. "I thought I was doing the right thing." She smiled sardonically. "I seem to do that a lot." She pushed a hand through her hair. "I make bad decisions, obviously. I treated you so badly and there's no excuse for that."

Riley was momentarily speechless. They'd never really spoken about what had happened between them all those years ago. They'd screamed and shouted at each other about it on a few separate occasions, sure—his visit five years ago included—but never spoken like two sensible adults. Hearing her talk about it brought the memories back to Riley thick and fast.

He remembered coming back from London, begging her to reconsider, only to have her push him away even farther as she lost herself in a depression so thick he could barely see the girl he loved. He tried to get through to her for months, calling, texting, even writing her letters, but it was no use. It was like fighting against a tidal wave; the harder he fought, the stronger the dark current became, dragging her down with it.

After almost a year, exhausted and broken, Riley eventually gave up and threw himself headfirst into the social side of college, partying and fucking around in a desperate effort to cleanse himself of the grief and misery that ravaged his twenty-year-old heart. It was about that time he first met Carter and Max.

"I'm so sorry," Lexie whispered. "I'm sorry for so much. You didn't deserve any of it."

Riley's throat was suddenly a little tight. He reached over and took her hand, giving it a gentle squeeze. "You weren't you, Lex. It was . . . It's done. We're okay."

Besides, it wasn't as though he didn't punish her for it enough back then. In his heartbroken state, he'd behaved appallingly, flaunting girls in front of her and saying some truly despicable things. It had hurt every time he'd seen her after that, and all he'd wanted was to make her hurt just as much by pretending she meant nothing. It was either that or drop to his knees at her feet and beg her to take him back. They'd both been young and had hurt each other deeply, despite his loving her with every fiber of his being.

"So listen," Lexie added. "My mom is coming over later this evening. She wants to come to the festival tomorrow to see the second parade with Noah. She's staying at my place and said she'd look after Noah if I wanted to go out."

It took a second for the penny to drop. "Tonight?"

"Yeah, if you still want to. We could. Tonight."

Riley smiled, despite the whirling sensation in his stomach. "Sounds good. Maybe we could go to the Bayside concert. Have a few drinks."

Lexie smiled. "Seven o'clock? I can text you my address."

"Perfect."

"Mommy, look!"

Noah's yell pulled both of their heads snapping toward him. He was running over to them, his face a huge Batman symbol of black, yellow, and glittering silver. Sav and Jaime followed him, each of them with a flower painted on her cheek.

"Look at you!" Lexie laughed as Noah barreled into her.

"Riley, do you see?" Noah asked, patting his palm on Riley's knee. "I asked for Batmans and she did it!"

Riley narrowed his eyes as though inspecting the work. Noah waited patiently for his approval. "That's the most awesome thing ever, buddy. I'm super jealous."

"Yous get one, too?"

"Nah, man," Riley said with a smile, Noah's earnestness almost breaking his heart. "I can't compete. You're Batman today."

Noah laughed and turned to Lexie. "Can we see the parade now?"

"Absolutely," Lexie replied. "Let's go."

"Can you carry me so I can sees them?"

"You're too heavy, baby," Lexie answered as she stood. "You're such a big boy now. We'll find a spot where you can see. I promise."

Riley scratched the back of his neck. "He could sit on my shoulders if he wants."

Lexie blinked up at him, then looked down at Noah, whose eyes had widened so much, Riley feared they might pop out. "Can I, Mommy?"

"Sure. But you have to hold on tight and listen to everything Riley says."

"I swears it!"

Riley crouched down. "Come on then, man. Jump on."

Little feet and fingers grabbed and squeezed, pinching Riley's neck and shoulders as he clambered on, but Riley didn't give a shit. Small knees and legs dangled around either side of his neck while Riley held up his hands for Noah to take. "You ready, Batman?"

He grabbed Riley's hands. "Ready!"

"Hold on." Riley stood carefully and Noah squealed with laughter.

"Yous a giant! And your beard tickles my knees."

Riley laughed with him, noticing the affectionate look Lexie was giving them both. "Let's go see that parade."

• • •

Lexie couldn't help but feel a little pleased with herself that she'd changed her outfit only a couple of times before meeting Riley. She finally settled on a sleeveless, patterned maxidress, a wide brown belt to bring in the waist, and flip-flops. It was a humid evening and she wanted to be comfortable. She knew the Bayside concert would be crammed with people, but she was excited all the same.

A night out with Riley Moore. It was like she was sixteen again, all flushed cheeks and pounding heart. The nerves skittered through her, too, which wasn't surprising. What *had* been surprising was Riley's reaction to her apology that afternoon. It was a shame it had taken so long for her to voice, and the guilt clung tightly, but his swift acceptance of it loosened its hold ever so slightly.

Knowing—and having beaten herself up over the fact—that she'd instigated the heartache between the two of them, she'd appreciated his forgiveness more than she ever thought possible. Over the years, Lexie had seen various counselors and doctors about her grief and subsequent depression in an effort to understand why she wanted to close herself off and push those she loved away.

Of course, the answer was pretty obvious—her father's death had taken with it her natural ability to trust and have faith in people and situations. Unsurprisingly, having Noah helped her massively. Having a precious, fragile creature that relied entirely on her finally gave Lexie faith in something she hadn't had faith in for years: herself. Her next step to gaining back the rest of the control was to open Love, You. Taking on such a project with the support of her mom and Savannah gave her an incredible feeling and convinced her that taking chances on things, and on people, wasn't as scary as she'd thought.

Her job now was to work at building bridges with Riley and his family. She'd loved Riley more than anything, and his family—Joan, especially—had become very important to her. She couldn't forget the look of shock and hurt that had been so pronounced on

Joan's face when she'd seen Noah for the first time, and it killed Lexie that she'd caused it. As much as she had made the right decision for her and Noah when he was born, the regret she harbored was more than a little obvious in the reflection that stared back at her. With a sigh and a plan to right all her wrongs, she turned from the mirror and headed downstairs.

Lexie's mom, Christine, was in the living room with a pajama-clad Noah. She looked up from the coloring book they were both working on and smiled. "I like that dress."

"You looks pretty, Mommy," Noah commented, glancing up quickly.

"Thanks, baby," Lexie said with a smile as she kissed his head. "You go to bed when Grandma says, okay? One snack and some juice if you want."

"Okay," he murmured, his focus still on the crayon in his hand and the picture he was completing.

Lexie grabbed her bag and headed to the front door, sensing her mother behind her. "Are you okay?" Christine asked.

Lexie had told her mom everything, as she always did, about Riley. And, as she always had been throughout her daughter's life, Christine was nothing but supportive. When Lexie had broken up with Riley all those years ago, Christine had tried her best to talk her around. She'd always had a soft spot for the little boy who first appeared across the street when he was eight years old, and she fought his corner with gusto. It had been fruitless, though. Lexie had made her decision.

Lexie breathed and smiled. "Sure. I'm good. Just nervous."

Christine moved closer and rubbed a hand down Lexie's arm. "Sweetheart, don't be nervous. If it's meant to be . . . just don't let your history cloud what you want. Noah's your priority now."

"I know, Mom." She knew her mother was concerned, and maybe she should have been, but Lexie was sure she and Riley could move past what had been before. They had to. For Noah.

She leaned over and kissed her mother's cheek as a knock came at the door. Lexie's heart fluttered as she opened it.

Riley was standing on the porch. He was gloriously sexy in his dark blue jeans, black flip-flops, and a sleeveless red T-shirt that showed off his ink. He looked to have trimmed his beard a little, too, and his hair was pushed back enough that it curled slightly behind his ears. His hazel eyes were playful and reached into Lexie, calming every inch of her.

"Hey," he said with a wide grin that made her a little dizzy. She desperately wanted to reach out and touch him. He smiled over Lexie's shoulder. "Hey, Christine. How're you?"

Lexie's mom moved around her and pulled Riley into a hug. "My goodness, you get more handsome every time I see you."

Riley chuckled, returning the hug. "Thanks. It's good to see you."

Christine pulled back and patted his face gently. "You too, Riley. It's been too long."

"Riley!" Noah barreled down the hallway toward the three of them, arms out wide. Lexie watched in fascinated wonder as he threw himself at Riley, who caught him, picked him up, and threw him into the air before holding him at his hip.

"Hey, buddy!" Riley beamed as they high-fived. "Awesome jammies."

It was such a beautiful thing seeing the two of them together, and it twisted the knot of guilt in Lexie's chest at having kept them apart for so long. She was determined to make up for her mistake in any way she could. She owed both of them that much. Over the past week, having Riley around again, Lexie had allowed herself to wonder how she would explain to Noah about the choices she'd made. Did it frighten her? Of course, but what option was there? She wanted to be nothing but honest with her son and she knew, down the line, no matter what happened between her and Riley, she would have to tell him the truth.

"Are you and Mommy goings out?" Noah asked, pushing a small finger through Riley's beard.

"We are," Riley answered, holding him close.

"Can I come?"

"Maybe next time, dude."

Noah pouted a little. "Can we play again?"

"Absolutely."

"Tomorrow."

"Actually," Riley's gaze slid over to Lexie, "I'm going back to New York tomorrow for a few days. I need to check on some things at my shop."

A feeling of disappointment tickled Lexie's neck.

"You haves a shop?" Noah asked, eyes wide, head tilted. The two of them were so damned alike.

"I sure do."

"A candy shop?"

Riley laughed. "No, man. A shop where I fix cars and bikes."

Noah appeared to consider this. "Can I come?"

"One day."

"And I can see your house?"

"Sure." Riley cleared his throat. "If your mommy says that's okay."

Lexie nodded. "I'm sure it'd be fine."

"Okay, man," Riley said as he carefully placed Noah back on the floor. "We gotta go."

Noah sighed and moved to stand next to Christine. Lexie bent down and kissed his cheek. "Be good. I love you."

"All the world."

When Lexie stood, she noticed the startled expression on Riley's face. "Are you ready?"

He nodded, smiled again at Christine, and held a fist out for Noah to bump. "I'll see you in a few days."

Noah didn't even seem to think about it before he hugged Riley's leg tightly, his cheek against Riley's thigh. "'Bye."

Lexie wasn't blind to the shimmer in Riley's eye as he bent down and kissed Noah's hair and it warmed her very soul. Lexie had been more than relieved that they'd taken so quickly to one another. Not that she should have been surprised; Noah was a social butterfly and Riley was easy to love. He was also going to be an exceptional father. Like most things, he took to it so naturally. It was obvious he was already head over heels for the little boy.

Noah let go, they said their good-byes again, and she and Riley headed down the path toward the car. It was such a familiar thing, having Riley at her side that way, his hand at the small of her back, his aftershave wafting around her subtle and rich. He opened her door, smiling as she climbed in, causing goose bumps to ripple across every inch of Lexie's body. He really didn't play fair. As much as she'd agreed that they had to be sensible and consider the repercussions should they become intimate again, the pull she felt when he was near was almost impossible to ignore. As if an invisible rope connected her heart to his, her chest expanded and squeezed whenever he looked at her in that way of his, gentle and devastatingly sexy.

God knew it had been such a simple thing, falling in love with Riley all those years ago. It had been so easy, so effortless. She likened it to slipping under freshly washed bedcovers in clean pajamas: warm, soothing, safe, and very hard to leave. Once it happened, once she was old enough to realize what her feelings for him meant, there had been no question as to whether she'd love him forever. He was everything she'd wanted and, seeing him now, she knew nothing had changed. She still wanted him. She wanted him desperately. Spending time together had stirred up more heat and excitement inside her than she'd felt in five years. It was a heady combination of lust, longing, and a love she'd tried her hardest to put behind her.

There had been other men during their time apart, before Noah, of course, but none of them had ever come close to invoking the passion and emotion in her that Riley did. The burn, the need, the exquisite desire that slipped lusciously through her veins, deep into her bones, was never there. The man was in her very marrow, and always would be, no matter what happened between them.

She watched him as he drove, keeping her eyes on his forearms and the ink that shifted and moved as he changed gears or turned the wheel. He looked unbelievable in his aviator shades, too. Being fascinated by Riley in that way wasn't a new thing for Lexie, and she allowed herself the pleasure of staring, soaking him all in.

"You okay?" he asked with a quick glance over at her.

"Yeah," she answered quickly, because it was the truth. She hadn't felt as good for a long time and, as content as she had been with her life in Riley's absence, it was clear that her heart had been missing something. "I just like watching you."

He nodded and looked over at her again as they approached a junction. "I like you watching me."

Despite the trouble he seemed to have in admitting as much, when he licked his lips, the smolder in Lexie's belly sparked. "You're not making this easy on me, are you?"

His laugh filled the car. "I didn't know I was supposed to." He leaned an elbow on the window's edge. "Besides, I think we have a lot to discuss before anything else. Wouldn't you say?" He lifted his eyebrows above his shades.

"Absolutely. I just . . . I guess us being together that way is the only thing we do well together."

"That's not entirely true." Riley cocked his head. "We made a pretty great kid."

Lexie bit her bottom lip, his words stirring the craving within her even more.

Riley was quiet for a moment as he drove. "Do you remember the night that we—?"

"Yes."

Of course, she remembered the night Noah was conceived.

She'd thought about it tirelessly now that Riley was around. How desperate they'd been to get closer, to feel more skin, to fuck each other senseless, even with the vitriolic words they'd fired at one another. The heat of their hurt and frustration had exploded between them, resulting in his lifting up her dress and ripping her underwear in an effort to get inside of her. He'd been brutal as he'd taken her and she'd loved every second, ripping his shirt in kind as he slammed into her again and again. They'd come so hard together, she yelling out his name as he groaned beautifully in her ear. She'd been on the Pill and hadn't given the fact that they'd made love without a condom for the first time in years another thought until her period was two months late.

As sex with Riley always was, it had been such an overwhelming experience, messing with Lexie's already confused mind, that she'd told him to leave and never contact her again. They'd played the same game for too long and Lexie's heart had been raw with it. She couldn't face him leaving again, so, as she had done when they were nineteen, she'd pushed him away. He hadn't even argued with her, which told Lexie he was as tired of their bullshit as she was. He looked to consider it for a split second with that pained look in his eyes before he'd fastened his jeans and left.

Now, unthinkingly, Lexie reached out a hand and placed it on his forearm. He turned to look at her, dividing his attention between where she was touching him and the road before he shifted his arm away. She shouldn't have been surprised, but it hurt nonetheless.

The car pulled to a stop in the parking lot and Riley turned off the engine. He sat for a moment, fingers tapping the steering wheel, before he pulled off his shades and looked over at her. "Lex, we both have to stop beating ourselves up for the past. You said shit, I said shit, and we punished each other by fucking. It was a mess for years."

An unexpected burst of laughter bubbled up Lexie's throat.

"Such a way with words." It didn't matter that they were all true. "But I get what you're saying."

"Good." He looked down at where she'd touched his arm. "I want us to be friends, Lex. I really do. But I need to be clear: I can't let *us* get in the way of my getting to know Noah. I would never forgive myself if something happened between us and you stopped me from seeing him."

Lexie's eyes widened. "I would never do that."

Riley's expression saddened. "You already *did* do that, Lex. You chose not to tell me about him. You've kept us apart for four years."

Lexie swallowed hard, fisting her hands in her lap.

"I need to trust you again," he said quietly, his stare on the people walking through the parking lot toward the bay. "I need to understand why, I need to . . . take time and think about what I want."

She breathed deeply, seeing the conflict in his eyes. It killed her that she'd put it there. "Whatever you need," she said gently.

The air in the car began to fizzle as they looked at one another. Her pulse spiked, and the frantic need she had to touch him caused her to reach up and cup his face. The sensation of his beard against her skin made her throat dry. For one breathtaking moment, he leaned into her touch before he sighed and moved back again. "Come on," he said, his voice deep, "I need a beer."

They climbed out of the car and walked the six blocks down to the bay, where the stages were constructed for all the bands. Music filled the evening air, along with the scents of beer and barbeque. Lexie stayed close to Riley's side as they maneuvered through the crowds before deciding on a relatively quiet spot by a railing, where they could watch the show without being pushed and crushed in the throngs of people. Riley bought them both a beer and a hot dog, which they enjoyed in the time it took for the summer sky to darken. Lights hanging from posts and curled around trees began to turn on all around them as they caught up.

Riley talked about his work and his friends in New York, and Lexie told him about her own shop and her dream of expanding. She told him about Noah and the first time he sat up, and when he stood and took his first step. She described how he looked like a dot-to-dot puzzle when he got chickenpox and how he was excited to start school in September. She kept talking, loving the expression of pride on Riley's face, but hating the way his hazel stare would occasionally sadden and twist into something angry and pained. She stopped and leaned her arms on the railing.

"I know you should have been there for all of that, Riley," she murmured.

He mirrored her pose. "Yeah, I should have." His words were clipped and honest. He shook his head minutely. "But you've done an amazing job with him, Lex. You're a great mom."

She didn't appreciate how important that was to hear until he said it. "Thank you. He makes it easy for me." She paused. "And he'll make it easy for you, too. You'll be there for everything else and I'll never keep anything from you again." She'd hidden so much from him over the years—the extent of her depression, her desperate need for him in spite of the fact that she pushed him away, their son.

"You swear it?" he asked quietly. "No bullshit. I have to be able to trust you again."

"I know and I swear it. No bullshit."

Riley sipped his drink. She nudged his shoulder with her own. "So tell me about you." She let her finger trail around the lip of her plastic beer cup. "Have you ever been serious about anyone?"

He shook his head, staring out toward the bay. "Other than you? No. I tried to forget us, tried to move on, and, honestly, I thought I was doin' okay, but . . . no. No one came close." Lexie hated that she felt relieved. She really had no right after the way she'd behaved. "You?"

She shook her head. "There was never any point trying."

As the music echoed from the stage, she and Riley continued to talk. The longer they talked, the easier it became. It was truly lovely to catch glimpses of the friendship she'd cherished, chatting the way they used to. There was no pressure, no tension.

The only other time the conversation became serious was when Lexie asked about Riley's father. There was clearly strain there, which Riley did his best to downplay, and it broke Lexie's heart knowing how important Park's approval had always been to Riley.

"I was wondering what you thought about my speaking to your mom," Lexie hedged. Riley cocked an eyebrow in question. "And your dad, maybe. Your whole family, really. I want to explain. I know you've probably told them my reasons, but I'd like to have the opportunity to clear the air myself. I owe your mom . . . so much. And they're Noah's family, too."

Riley glanced out at the bay. "I think that would be a good idea." He didn't need to say it; she could see it on his face: Joan was disappointed in her.

Lexie pushed her hair back, feeling warm, flustered. "Okay. I'll stop by in a few days. Leave your dad to recuperate a little more."

Suddenly aware of the music playing as they stood there, Lexie giggled. The song emitting from the nearby speakers was the Backstreet Boys' "I Want It That Way." "God, this brings back memories."

Riley chuckled. "It does. You drove me crazy with this damned song."

It was true; she'd put it on replay for at least a week, learning the dance routines with Sav and miming along to all the Nick Carter parts. She'd known Riley had never cared for that type of music, but he'd tolerated it just for her. Innocent and carefree memories flickered through her mind, stealing her breath.

Her cheeks warmed. "My heart had never beaten as hard as it did when I saw you on the porch the evening of the Junior Dance, waiting for *me*." She turned to him. "You know, when I was pregnant," she whispered, "and I remembered some of the things we did together, Noah would kick so hard, like he knew it was you I was thinking about."

For a brief second, longing seemed to flicker across Riley's face, but it was gone as quickly as it appeared. Lexie's heart clenched. "I hated what had become of us."

Riley's shoulders dropped. "I know. So did I. I still do, but—" He opened his mouth but stopped himself, pressing his lips together.

"Tell me," Lexie implored. "Be honest with me. Tell me what you feel."

"I feel robbed, Lex," he blurted, his eyes flaring with heat. "I feel let down. I'm so fucking angry with you, I can't— It's bullshit that you didn't say anything. I mean, okay, you didn't need to tell me in person; I get that, but something, some note, a fucking text, a phone call." He stood to his full height, his anger gaining traction with each word he spat. "You kept the most important thing in my life away from me, a secret." A muscle in his jaw twitched. "What right did you have to do that?"

"None," Lexie replied. "I had none. But I was protecting myself, protecting Noah."

"From what?" Riley exclaimed, incredulous. "I made a mistake, Lex. I served time. Big fuckin' deal. I was still the man you knew, the man who would have done anything for you, been there for you, loved you both without question." His chest heaved.

Lexie's eyes stung. It had been so long since she'd seen him so fired up. She'd almost forgotten how magnificent he was. She watched as the ire in him began to recede. He gulped the last of his beer and chucked his empty cup into a nearby trash can. He pushed his hands into his pockets and shifted from foot to foot. It took a lot for Riley to get so irate and almost as long for him to calm back down. Lexie waited at his side, letting his accusations and vitriol fall around her, knowing she deserved nothing less. They were both silent for a long time before she spoke again. "I'll do everything I can to make it up to you," she murmured. "I promise."

She glanced at him and was struck by the intensity of his stare. It made her want to laugh and cry at the same time. His lack of response weighed heavy and thick between them, and was as loud as though he'd screamed it in her face: he didn't believe her.

13

There had been very few times in Lexie's life when she felt as nervous as she did standing on the Moore family porch, fidgeting and sweating in the godforsaken heat. She closed her eyes for a brief moment and breathed. She just needed to keep calm. She knew the music she was about to face was deserved and overdue, but that didn't go much toward calming her down.

The only thing that did appease her was the fact that, even after so many years, the house was still the same. The lawn was still cut to perfection and was the same vibrant green that Park had always taken great pride in. There were the beautiful explosions of color from the numerous potted flowers—geraniums were Joan's favorite—and the water hose, which Lexie and Riley would play with all summer long, still sat as though paused in history. It was more than a little comforting.

Lexie gathered herself and knocked. She'd asked Riley to tell his parents that she intended to visit and hoped beyond hope they'd give her a chance to explain. If she knew Joan and Park at all, there would be little to worry about. But that did little to ease the knot in her chest.

She was pulled from her frenzied thoughts by the door opening. Joan stood in the doorway, apparently not surprised to see Lexie, her ash-blonde hair short and elegant in constructed waves that made her appear much younger than she was. It had struck Lexie when she'd seen Joan at the shop that she'd changed very little from the second mother Lexie remembered from her childhood.

A wave of shame and regret crashed over Lexie, whipping the air from her lungs, leaving her desperate to be collected into one of Joan's legendary hugs that had always had the power to make her feel better.

Instead she shifted where she stood and tried to smile. "Hi, Joan."

"Alexis," Joan replied. "Riley said you might visit, but I have to admit, I'm surprised to see you." There was a curtness to her tone, but her face was all motherly love.

Lexie nodded. "Is it all right if I come in? I won't stay long."

Joan regarded her for a brief moment before she stood back and gestured for Lexie to enter. The house smelled exactly the same. *Exactly.* It was the fragrance of long childhood summers, stormy nights, baking, and boys. As she looked around at the clean floors and spotless carpeted staircase, Lexie recollected how she'd always marveled at the fact that, even with four sons, Joan managed to keep her house looking immaculate.

"Come in," Joan offered, making her way past Lexie and down the hallway that was littered with photographs of Riley and his brothers through the years, toward the kitchen. "I just poured some juice. Would you like some?"

"Yes, please," Lexie replied, her throat dry and scratchy. She hovered at the kitchen doorway, noting that the large French windows were open, allowing a soft breeze to flow through. She took the orange juice she was offered and clutched the glass. "The house looks great."

Joan looked around herself. "Park keeps telling me that we'll have an addition and the kitchen remodeled when he retires." She sipped her juice. "I'm not holding my breath."

Lexie snickered. "It'll take more than a heart attack to get him to retire." Joan smiled a little. "How is he?"

"He's sitting outside. Come."

Lexie followed Joan out into the bright sunshine to see Park sitting in a wooden deck chair, juice in one hand and a Sudoku book in the other. "Who was——?" His words died in his throat when he looked up. "Lexie."

"Hi, Park. It's good to see you doing so well."

He pulled his reading glasses from his nose. "I'm surprised to see you at all."

Joan coughed gently, drawing a quick look from Lexie. "I asked Riley to tell you I'd be coming over. I wanted to talk to you both."

He placed the Sudoku book down purposefully and sat back. Joan moved to sit in the chair next to him and gestured to the seat at Lexie's side. "Take a seat," she said quietly. The smile she gave Lexie was small, but it was there all the same.

Lexie sat down, gathering herself and the small amount of courage she'd managed to find that morning, trying her best to ignore Park's white-hot stare. He'd always been an intimidating man.

"So," she began, placing her juice on the ground and folding her hands together. "I wanted to come over and try and explain what's going on." She nibbled her bottom lip before continuing. "It's been an emotional couple of weeks. No more than for Riley, I'm sure."

"Emotional?" Park asked, as though offended by her choice of words.

Lexie cleared her throat again. "I never meant to hurt anyone," she said honestly. "I *did* pick up the phone and call him." She sighed. "It doesn't excuse my not trying harder and it doesn't excuse the hurt and confusion I've caused. I . . . know I should have been honest with everyone. I know I should have told Riley about Noah as soon as he was released from Kill. I know I should have told *you* two about Noah."

"But you didn't," Park uttered.

"Park," Joan said quietly before looking over at him. "Let her speak."

He harrumphed and folded his arms over his chest.

Lexie lowered her gaze to her feet. "It's okay. I know you're both angry with me and I know I deserve it. I made a decision that I thought was the right one for me, for Noah. I stand by it, but that doesn't make it right." She sat straighter and looked directly at Riley's parents. "I'm sorry for keeping your grandson from you."

Joan's green gaze softened. She glanced at Park and sat forward, her expression earnest. "You could have come to us about anything, Alexis. You always did as a young girl."

It was true. Lexie remembered when she'd started her period while at the Moore house. She'd thought she was dying. Joan had been amazing, calming her down and getting her what she needed while Riley hovered and fretted and asked what was wrong. Joan had sat Riley down and explained everything to him while Lexie cleaned herself up. It was just one moment out of many where Joan had supported and looked after Lexie.

"I'm so sorry," Lexie whispered, her voice cracking with the memories.

"As much as this apology is overdue," Park said firmly, "it's Riley that deserves it more."

"I know," Lexie replied with a nod. "I promise I'll try and make it up to him."

"You kept his son from him," Park fired back. "As a father of four sons, I can tell you: that's a hell of a lot of making up to do."

"Yes, sir," Lexie offered. "I understand that. And I'll do what I can to make Riley trust me again. But I wanted to tell you both that the last thing I ever wanted to do was hurt anybody, especially to hurt him."

"But you have," Joan murmured, the tone of a protective mother loud and clear. "He may not show it often or even at all, but he's devastated that he's missed so much."

Lexie licked her lips and swallowed her tears back down. Crying would help nobody. "I'm sorry," she repeated because, really, what more was there to say? It was all she had to offer and, as exhausting as it was to assure everyone that she meant it, she would keep doing it until they believed her.

"This may be out of line for me to say," Joan said, bringing Lexie's head up, "but Riley loves you very much. He always has, regardless of what you've put each other through. And I can see that you still feel the same way for him. But I know my son, Alexis, and I can tell you it's going to take more than you simply loving each other to fix this."

Despite the vise that tightened around Lexie's heart, Joan's words were only truth. It was going to take time. But today was another step toward building the foundations for the bridges she was desperate to create. Lexie had resigned herself to the fact that it could be a long, sometimes painful process, but she didn't care as long as it meant that Riley would trust her again. Joan was right; Lexie *did* love Riley. It was simple, really: she'd loved him for twenty-one years and that was never going to change. But that didn't matter. What did matter was that the two most important men in her life—Noah and Riley—were happy and together. Everything else could wait.

. . .

Max and Carter stared at Riley across the diner table they were seated around as if he'd stripped naked, stood on the booth seat, and shaken his shit in front of the other patrons. Riley couldn't help but snicker as he took a huge bite out of his cheeseburger. Christ, nothing beat a New York burger.

Max sat forward, pressing a finger to the table between them. "You're a father? For real?"

Riley wiped at his mouth with his napkin and nodded. "Yeah. He's named Noah. He's the coolest little guy I've ever met."

Max glanced at Carter, who blinked back at him. "Wow." Max sat back and lifted a fry from his plate. "And you had no idea?" Riley shook his head.

"Who's the girl?" Carter asked finally.

"Lexie," Riley offered. "We were together for a long time when we were younger and then . . . her father died and everything went tits up, but every time I went back to Michigan, we'd hook up. The last time was my parents' wedding anniversary. She got pregnant with Noah."

Max nodded, his dark eyes lighting with understanding. "She was the one you were talking about, when you were being all vague and shit about loving someone."

Riley smiled small. "Yeah. That was her."

"You still love her?" Trust Carter to go straight for the jugular when it came to questions.

Riley exhaled and rubbed his hands down his face. "I . . . don't know. I don't know what I feel." The truth was he didn't know if he'd ever not loved Lexie. She'd just made it harder for him to show her over the years.

Carter rubbed a finger across his brow. "I guess it makes sense. All the women you've been with. It could only be rebound."

Riley crossed his arms over his chest. "I was just trying to forget, man. Every woman I went with, I enjoyed and I treated right, but they didn't mean anything more to me."

Carter nodded. "Are you happy?"

"When I'm with Noah," Riley began. "It's like everything in my life finally makes sense, you know?"

"And with the girl, with Lexie?"

Since their day at the festival when he'd finally allowed some of his frustration and anger out, Riley had noticed a marked change in Lexie. She was cooler—no less kind and happy, but it was almost as though she'd taken a step back to allow him to breathe and find his way. "Lex and I have a lot to discuss," Riley said thoughtfully. "A lot to rebuild. My guard is still up. I miss her, but then I always have." He pushed the feeling of melancholy away. "But you wanna see Noah, guys. He's just amazing. He's so smart, and he has this lisp that just breaks your damned heart. And he loves Batman."

Max snorted. "He must be your son."

Carter shifted in his seat. "What's it like being a dad?"

Riley threw a fry into his mouth knowing that Carter was thinking about how he'd behaved when his wife, Kat, had thought she was pregnant when they were first married. "At first, I was terrified about what kind of father I'd make, but when I spend time with him, it just feels right. I mean, I've never felt anything like it."

Max moved so his back was against the wall rather than the back of the booth and draped his arm along its shelf. "So how will this work with them both living in Michigan?"

Riley sat back. He knew that he and Max needed to have a conversation about the shop, but he had no idea where to start. His main priority was Noah. He wanted to get to know his son and Riley knew he couldn't do that living full time in New York, but what was he supposed to do, move back to Michigan? It certainly sounded like a better idea than being a weekend dad, flying back and forth every five days. Either way, he knew he needed an income.

He raised his eyebrows, pushing his plate away, suddenly not feeling hungry. "I don't know."

Max seemed to sense Riley's anxiety and leaned forward. "Look, man. Don't worry about it right now, okay? I can hold down the fort for the next couple of months with Grace in the city working on her art project, and Paul can handle shit when I take any days off. We're partners in this and we can figure something out."

Riley breathed a sigh of relief. "I appreciate that, man." He held a fist out over the table and Max bumped it with his own.

"It's the least I can do," Max offered. "You watched the place when I was away at rehab. I'll do the same for you."

The weight that lifted from Riley's shoulders was awesome. He knew that he'd have to make a decision eventually, but having a bit more time allowed him to breathe a little easier. The three of them hung out for a few more hours, catching up and cutting loose, before Riley headed back to his apartment. It had been a strange experience walking into the place that afternoon. The summer heat of the day had poured through the apartment windows, but it still felt cold, as though it was missing something.

He had a quick shower, then checked the time, knowing that Noah went to bed before seven, and dialed Lexie's number.

He heard Lexie's voice first. "Hold the phone carefully."

"Riley?"

Riley's heart expanded at the sound of Noah's voice. "Hey, man! How're you?"

"Good. Is yous in New Yorks now?"

"I am."

"Whats can you sees?"

"Well, I'm lying on my sofa right now, but if I looked out of my window I would see a busy street and the Empire State Building in the distance."

"Likes Spider-Man!"

Riley chuckled. He couldn't begrudge the kid for liking Spider-Man. "Yeah, like Spider-Man."

Noah was quiet for a brief moment. "Whens you coming back?"

Riley's stomach tightened in a way he'd never felt before. The small voice at the end of the phone caused an ache inside of him that was alien and unnerving. "I'll be back in a few days."

Noah hummed. "And we can play?"

"Sure, buddy. Whatever you'd like to do, we'll do."

"Okay. Comes back soon. 'Bye."

"'Bye, Noah. Be good for your mom, okay?"

"Yeah!"

Riley grinned as he heard the phone being moved around.

"Riley?"

"Hey, Lex."

"His face lit up."

"Mine too."

"Good." The silence between them was like taking a bullet. He hated the distance between them—geographical and emotional. "Are you still able to come back this weekend?"

"Yeah."

They both stayed silent for a couple of beats before Lexie broke the silence first. "I can't wait."

Longing curled in Riley's belly. "Me too."

. . . .

The next few days dragged, despite how busy Riley was at O'Hare's. Max slapped papers on his desk filled with numbers for Riley to organize and look through, which he did quickly and efficiently. Steph, the receptionist Riley had banged during her first week, fluttered her lashes and smiled at him in the way she always had despite him always being clear about where they both stood. She was harmless, and Riley flirted back because, why not? But he couldn't ignore the unfamiliar sensation that clung to him now whenever they spoke or when Carla texted him asking to meet.

God only knew what the hell was going to happen between him and Lexie at this point. Nevertheless, he knew he had to keep his life as simple as possible. He sent Carla a polite text back telling her that he probably wouldn't be in touch for a while, but thanks for the awesome times. She didn't reply and that was fine.

He spoke to Noah every night before the kid went to bed and they made plans to go to the zoo when Riley returned to Michigan. Wanting to spoil Noah and make up for his absence, Riley went to the small tourist store across from the car shop and bought his son a foot-high replica of the Empire State Building and, as much as it killed the DC fan within him, a picture of Spider-Man swinging from the Statue of Liberty. He did his best to get the paperwork at the shop in good order before he left again, knowing, realistically, he wouldn't be back for at least a week. Max assured him a million and one times that he'd call if there were any issues and, *fuck me, man, I have done this before!*

Joan was at the airport waiting for Riley when he arrived back in Traverse City the following afternoon. It was another hot day, and the breeze from the water was more than welcome. Back at his parents' house, Riley put his bag in his room and joined his mom and dad in the backyard. He was pleased to see his father sitting in his usual chair, dressed in shorts and a T-shirt. Joan passed Riley a glass of juice, patting his back gently.

"Did you get everything sorted in the city?" Joan asked, despite having asked the same question in the car on the journey from the airport. Riley knew what she was doing; she was trying to get Riley and his father talking. During his time at home, Riley and Park had spoken only a handful of occasions without outside influences like Tate or Joan.

"Things are good. The place is doing really well," Riley offered, glancing surreptitiously at his father.

"That's great, son," Joan said. "Isn't it, Park?"

Park grunted and sipped his juice. He looked so much better than he had when he'd first come out of the hospital. He had more color and appeared to have regained his broad shoulders. Riley was sure that it was only because Park could sit up properly now, but it was reassuring all the same.

"I'm taking Noah to the zoo tomorrow," Riley said in an attempt to change the subject. "Just the two of us." Riley had been shocked as all hell when Lexie said she'd leave them to spend the day together. He was nervous, but so damned excited.

Joan grinned, and Riley saw a small twitch at the corner of Park's mouth. "That's fantastic, Riley," his mother cooed. "Maybe I can see him before you go? Lexie came over while you were in New York."

Riley dipped his chin. Lexie had mentioned it on the phone but hadn't gone into details. "And? You hear what you needed to?"

Joan tilted her head a little to the side. "Your father and I don't need to hear anything, Riley, other than to know you're all right."

Riley sat back. "I'm okay. You know me. Everything slides right off." It wasn't the complete truth; he was still trying to clear his head and decide what he wanted to do in terms of the whole Lexie situation, but he didn't want his parents worrying. "I'll ask Lex about bringing Noah over."

Joan clapped her hands. "This deserves something a little stronger than juice."

"I can't drink," Park grumbled.

"That's why you'll be having a nonalcoholic drink," Joan retorted before she stood and hurried into the house. Riley smiled after her, shaking his head. He looked back at his father, catching his eye.

"You could meet him, too, if you like."

Park cleared his throat, looking toward the sky. "Okay."

It was one word, but it was progress. "How's the shop doing, Dad? They coping without you?" The question was meant to be in good humor, but it brought a frown to Park's face.

"They're fine," he answered.

Before Riley could needle him further, Joan appeared with a tray of glasses filled with something that looked suspiciously like white wine. She handed them out and tapped the edge of her glass to theirs. "It's good to have you back so regularly, Riley," she said softly.

"Thanks, Mom," he replied. He tapped his glass to Park's. "Cheers, Dad."

Park simply nodded and lifted his glass-holding hand minutely.

The following morning, Riley pulled up outside Lexie's store with Noah's presents wrapped in Batman paper. The bell above the door signaled his arrival and several heads turned in his direction.

Two women not five feet away from him smiled and fluttered their lashes, but his attention was drawn to the beautiful blonde behind the cash register, smiling at the customer in front of her as she placed her purchase in a box and then into a bag.

Riley approached slowly, watching Lexie as she worked, warmed by the happiness she exuded. It was obvious how much she reveled in what she did. He figured it should have bothered him how much seeing her again after a few days made his lungs feel clearer, but honestly, Riley was sick of thinking about it. There were some things that would never change, and he couldn't simply forget how he'd felt about Lexie for so long. Christ, she was the mother of his son, which was, itself, just about the sexiest, most precious thing he could ever imagine. He watched her smile and chat with her customer, her face animated and beautiful, her lips, so soft and plump, stretching with each smile.

He leaned his hip against one of the glass cabinets and allowed his mind to wander, remembering the taste of her lips on his, the feel of her mouth, how she could practically bring him to his knees with one kiss. Did he miss kissing her? Of course. It had always been one of his favorite things, but he knew what one touch of her lips would do to him: he'd be lost all over again, and he couldn't let that happen. Her blue eyes met his and, once she'd said her good-byes to her customers, Lexie walked around the counter toward him.

"Hey," she murmured as she got closer.

"Hey."

"It's good to see you."

"You too."

"Noah's waiting for you upstairs with Jaime," she said, rubbing her hands down the front of the top she was wearing. "You're free to go up and get him. Do you want me to show you?"

"I'll manage." He made his way to the back of the store, through the door, and up the stairs to the apartment above. He knocked and waited, grinning when he heard Noah thumping about and calling for Jaime to open the door.

The door opened and Noah flung himself at Riley, who gave a whopping *oomph* when the small body connected with him. "You're here!" Noah exclaimed as Riley picked him up.

"Of course, I said I would be." Riley's throat tightened when Noah wrapped his small arms around his neck.

"And we're going to the zoo?"

"We sure are. Are you ready?"

"No!" Noah yelled, wriggling in Riley's hold until Riley placed him back on the floor. "I needs my shoes." He dodged Jaime, who was still standing with the door open, and disappeared into the apartment.

"Don't forget your teddy, and put your shoes on the right feet!" she called after him. "He's talked about nothing else," she told Riley with a small smile. "He's so excited."

It was as if his heart grew three times bigger, like the fucking Grinch's, at those words. Noah quickly reappeared, shoes on the correct feet and clutching a plush Chewbacca that Riley was suddenly a little jealous of. Noah took Riley's hand and they made their way back down to the store. Lexie turned from adjusting the Post-its on the mirrored wall and grinned at them both. She bent down and opened her arms for Noah, who hugged her hard.

"Be good for Riley," she told him, kissing his cheek. "Hold his hand, don't get lost, and—"

"I'll bes good, Mommy," Noah insisted.

Lexie glanced up at Riley in a way that said "see how like you he is" before standing up and retrieving Noah's car seat and a bag from behind the counter. "Have a great day," she said as she passed them to him. "I've already put sunscreen on him, but there's more in the bag and a change of clothes because you never know and— Will you be okay?"

Riley nodded. "We'll be fine."

Lexie blinked, appearing contrite. "Of course, sorry. I . . . Just call me if you . . . Just, have fun."

"I'll look after him, Lex."

Lexie sighed. "I know you will."

"Come on, Riley!" Noah called from his place by the store door.

"I'm coming, buddy."

In the car, with the car seat fitted and Noah fastened into it, Riley gave him his presents. He'd never seen such enthusiasm as Noah applauded and laughed at the Spider-Man picture.

"I'll put this picture on mys wall!" he cried as he simultaneously clung to his Empire State Building gift.

The little boy chattered about everything as Riley drove them to the zoo. Lexie was right; he was *very* smart. He took everything in and, despite his young age, had an opinion and comment about all of it. He was hysterical and more than a little adorable as he pointed out the park where they'd had ice cream and a building that turned out to be where he'd attended day care. He explained to Riley that he could count to twenty, and then demonstrated with only a couple of mistakes, as well as describing in detail how he was going to school at the end of summer because he was "a big boy." Riley could have listened to him all day.

"Do you has kids?" Noah asked after a brief second of quiet.

Riley startled, curious as to where the question had come from. How the fuck was he supposed to answer that? "Um, I, well, it's . . . why do you ask?"

Noah kicked his small feet up and down as he kept his stare out of the car window. "You coulds bring them to my mommy's house. I coulds play with them."

Riley's chest squeezed. "Well, I was thinking that maybe you'd like to come to *my* mommy's house and play for a little while later."

Noah's head snapped toward Riley. "I can?"

"Of course. After the zoo we'll go. That sound good?"

Noah's reply was simple; he threw his arms into the air and cheered.

Riley's experience of the zoo with Noah was vastly different from when he'd visited the place before. Seeing the animals through the eyes of a four-year-old was fascinating and ignited a fervor within Riley that he hadn't felt since before Joan had called to tell him about his father being in the hospital. Noah pointed to the lions and giraffes, trying his best to pronounce their names and asking Riley question after question: *Why are their necks long? Can I feed it? Will it eat me? Can I ride it?* He dragged Riley around, wanting to see everything, which Riley was happy to do, and shit got a little dicey only when Noah began jiggling, needing to go pee. Riley helped as much as Noah allowed him to and they both survived.

They ate ice cream, and Riley bought Noah a plush elephant and a blue kids' T-shirt that had the face of a lion on it and read "I had a roaring good time." Seeing the delight on Noah's face was enough to convince Riley that he would spend the rest of his life doing what he could to keep his son happy. And it was the simple things that seemed to work the best, like when Riley carried him on his shoulders around the zoo, or when he lifted Noah carefully onto the railings and held him tightly so he could see the penguins better. Having Noah look up at him as though Riley was the best thing ever caused a buzz the likes of which Riley had never felt before.

"What a beautiful boy," an older woman commented from Riley's side as he watched Noah run around the kids' play area.

Riley smiled. "Thank you."

"Are you a single dad?"

Riley cocked an eyebrow, shocked by the stranger's question. "No," he answered as Noah ran toward him with a wide grin. "His mom is working today."

"That's so nice," the woman replied, watching Noah laugh and charge in circles around Riley. "Too many dads don't make enough effort with their kids. I know my ex-husband never did with ours."

Riley vowed on the spot to never be that way with Noah, or any other kids he had in the future. Noah would always come first, no matter what. As the day continued, Riley took picture after picture of his son on his cell phone, even sending Lexie a couple. His favorite was of Noah with the plush elephant in hand and chocolate ice cream all around his mouth. The sheer glee of the day could be seen on every inch of the small boy's face, and Riley fell even further in love with him. There was no point in fighting it; Riley was a goner.

By the time Riley pulled up outside his parents' house and unclipped and lifted Noah from his car seat, it was mid-afternoon.

"This is yours house?" Noah asked as they walked up the path holding hands.

"No. This is my mommy's house," Riley explained. Apparently, in all the zoo excitement, Noah had forgotten their plan. "Remember? We're gonna hang here for a while."

Noah smiled a little but held his elephant closer. Riley paused and crouched down, meeting Noah at eye level. "Your mommy said it would be okay."

"Is Mommy heres?"

"No," Riley answered, feeling that maybe this wasn't the best idea. He certainly didn't want Noah to feel anxious. "But my mommy is. She's called Joan. My daddy is called Park."

Noah tilted his head. "You has a daddy?"

Riley swallowed. "Yeah, man. They're both really excited to meet you."

Noah's eyes enlarged. "They knows me coming?"

Riley nodded. "Sure." He pulled him closer, loving the smell of him. "You okay?"

Noah dipped his chin. "They has toys?"

"I'm sure we could find something."

The front door opening brought Riley standing to his full

height. He was surprised to see his father in the doorway and not his mom. "I thought I saw a car pull up," Park commented. "Your mother's just gone to the store to get some snacks." His stare snapped from Riley to Noah, and Riley watched in amazement as the man's eyes widened, then shimmered. "You must be Noah. I'm Park."

Noah nodded. "Riley's daddy."

"That's right."

"Do yous have toys?"

Park smiled wide. It was the first time Riley had seen him smile since his return. "Why don't you come in and have a look?"

Riley was surprised when Noah looked to him, seemingly seeking permission. "It's okay, buddy. You can go."

Noah didn't release Riley's hand. "You come?"

Riley smiled down at him. "Of course. Let's go."

Park stepped aside as Riley and Noah entered and closed the door behind them. "Go out the back. I'll get some drinks."

Riley stared at his father a beat. "Thanks, Dad."

In the backyard, Riley chuckled when he saw that the mini trampoline, which had belonged to Seb, had been resurrected from the shed, as well as a small paddling pool that Riley had never seen, filled with water.

"Can I plays in that?" Noah asked excitedly, all but jumping on the spot.

"There aren't any swim shorts in your bag."

Noah snorted. "Mommy says I can swim in my undies," he explained, kicking off his shoes and struggling to pull off his T-shirt.

Riley helped him and, once Noah was undressed, he watched as the little boy ran over to the small pool and clambered in. The water was at his ankles, and Noah immediately started kicking the water all over before picking up the small plastic cups in the pool and using them to pour water on himself. He was adorable.

"Your mother found that at Target." Park's voice came from Riley's side. "She thought he'd like it. You boys always loved the water."

Riley crossed his arms over his chest and smiled with his eyes still on his son. "Yeah. I remember."

Park cleared his throat. "He's your double, Riley." He shook his head a little in wonder. "Standing here it's like looking at you twenty-six years ago."

Riley glanced over at his father, speechless. The tension that had clouded them for so long seemed to ease a bit. "He's amazing, right?"

Park exhaled a laugh. "Yeah, he is."

"Riley!" Noah called, his blond hair darkening under the water he'd poured over it. "Comes play!"

Riley snickered, toed off his shoes, whipped his T-shirt over his head, and charged over to a squealing Noah, who tried to dodge Riley's grabbing hands. He wasn't quick enough, though, slipping a little on the pool's floor. Riley lifted his son before he fell and held him upside down, threatening to drop him back into the water.

"No! Don't drops me!"

"Never," Riley assured Noah as he spun and twirled him. "I've got you."

Noah's laughter was simply beautiful. It was dirty, true, and filled the entire yard.

.   .   .

Riley carried a sleeping Noah to Lexie's front door, holding the small boy closely and breathing in his scent. He'd lasted five minutes in the car after playing and gobbling up the pasta that Joan made them all for dinner. It was safe to say that Noah had won Riley's parents over in about three seconds flat.

He knocked gently before a barefooted Lexie opened the door

with a smile, wearing sleep shorts and a tank top. Her face softened further when she saw Noah in Riley's arms. "He passed out," Riley explained quietly.

Lexie laughed softly. "My heart." She gestured for him to enter and directed him up the stairs. "Second room on the right. Has he been to the bathroom?"

"Before we left Mom's." Riley ascended the stairs carefully and pushed Noah's bedroom door open with his elbow. The room was light blue. The walls were covered half in hand-painted stars and planets and half in Batman posters and stencil shapes. It was the coolest room Riley had ever seen. He placed Noah gently on the small cot bed and stood back as Lexie began to undress him, first pulling off his small shoes and then his jeans. She kissed Noah's temple and pulled the thin sheet over his little body.

Riley moved closer to Lexie as she stood. "I've had the most amazing day," he told her. "I can't put it into words, Lex."

She leaned her shoulder against his as they watched their son sleep. Riley tried to ignore the heat that seemed to permeate his skin. "I know what you mean." She looked up at him, her face shadowed in the dark room. "Would you like a drink?"

Riley paused for a moment, staring at her, torn between his fear and the desperate need to move forward. He took a deep breath. "Sure."

He followed her out of Noah's room, down the stairs, and into the living room. "Take a seat," she offered, pointing to the sofa. "I have wine or beer or juice, water . . ."

"Wine sounds good."

She smiled before she turned away, leaving Riley standing in the middle of the room, taking in the cream and red décor, soft rug, and large fireplace. He smiled at a large blue box by the TV that was filled with an array of Noah's toys, and the small whiteboard standing next to it that was covered with a four-year-old's drawings of what looked like a person surrounded by rainbows and flowers. It also looked as though Noah had been trying to write his name.

Riley wandered toward the mantelpiece, drawn by the photographs filling it from one side to the other. They were almost all of Noah. There was Noah when he was a baby—God only knew how young he was—wrapped in a blue blanket and wearing a skull cap that looked too big for his tiny head. In the next, he was sitting up, cheeks bright red as he gnawed on his fist, drool all over his face and hand. He was gorgeous. Riley watched as his son grew up in each picture, his face changing, his hair growing, him standing up without the help of Lexie, until he was kicking a soccer ball, his expression determined and fierce.

"That one's my favorite," Lexie said softly at his side, holding a wineglass out for him, which he took.

"How old was he there?" he asked, pointing at the first photograph.

"He was a week old," she answered. "Sav got him the hat. It was far too big."

Riley stared at the picture, his heart twisting with grief and love. "He was so small."

"Six pounds, ten ounces. He didn't feel small."

Riley looked over at Lexie. "Same weight as I was."

The side of Lexie's mouth pulled up. "I know. Your mom told me." She sipped her drink and made her way over to the sofa, where she dropped down.

Riley let his gaze dance over the pictures again before he joined her. "Your place is really nice."

Lexie looked around herself. "It's home. It has a great yard for Noah and it's a nice neighborhood. His school is only fifteen minutes away." She shook her head, glancing at the photographs on the mantel. "I can't believe he's going to start school."

"He'll love it," Riley remarked. "He's too smart not to."

Lexie smiled and turned her body to his, tucking her legs under her butt. "He's so excited. He was excited about today. He barely slept last night." She regarded him for a brief moment. "You really enjoyed today, didn't you?"

Riley ran a hand through his hair. "It was so good. Just hanging out with him is amazing. I never knew a kid could talk so much." They both laughed. "He kills me when he holds my hand or hugs me. He trusts me so much. We played in the kiddie pool at Mom's and I was turning him upside and throwing him around—I was really careful with him—and I remember thinking, I don't know when I'd last felt so happy."

Lexie's blue eyes seemed to shimmer. "I'm glad."

Riley looked down at his glass. "Actually, that's a lie."

"What is?"

He huffed a small laugh. "I do remember when I was that happy." He looked over at Lexie, noting from her expression that she knew which memory he was referring to: the night of her seventeenth birthday when they made love for the first time under the stars, and began making all of their plans. Riley shifted in his seat, avoiding her stare. "That was so long ago."

Lexie hummed. "It was." She played with a piece of her hair, twirling it around her finger. "Still feels like yesterday, though."

Riley's gaze drifted over her, trying to see the girl from that night: the girl he'd loved so much he couldn't even begin to describe it; the girl who was his best friend; the girl he wanted to spend the rest of his life with. She was still there, behind her careful blue eyes, underneath the invisible scars of life that he knew they both bore. He blew out a breath before taking a huge gulp of wine. Jesus, he'd never felt so unstable, so fraught with worrying about what the best thing to do was.

"It's okay," Lexie said gently. "Don't wear yourself out. I have no expectations. I don't deserve any. Truthfully, I'm just glad you stayed. I like sitting and talking to you."

Riley had to agree. For all that he missed about being intimate with Lexie, losing himself in her body, he missed their quiet moments even more. They could laugh and play just as much as they could devour one another. It was why they'd worked. The balance had always been perfect. They had been friends first and, sitting with her, Riley was struck with how comfortable he was.

"I have something for you," she said suddenly, placing her wineglass on the coffee table and standing up. "Wait right there."

Riley smiled as she left, and rubbed a hand down his face, willing his heart and his brain to slow the fuck down and start cooperating already. He was exhausted with it all.

Lexie appeared a short while later with a large book in her hands. "Here," she said, her eyes downcast as though she was embarrassed. "I made this for you while you were back in New York."

Riley placed his glass next to Lexie's and sat on the edge of the sofa, taking the book from her. It felt heavy in his hands and he cocked an inquisitive eyebrow. "What is it?"

Lexie dropped down at his side. "Open it," she encouraged, folding her hands together and lifting them to cover her mouth.

Riley opened the front cover to find that it was in fact a photo album. A small piece of paper had been inserted in the first sleeve, upon which Lexie had written *Noah, 0–3 months*. He turned the page over and was met with at least a dozen photographs, all of Noah, from what looked like the minute he was born. Riley's mouth dropped open as he looked at his son's squished face, his hair covered in dried blood, wrapped in a hospital-issue blanket in Lexie's arms.

"He was five minutes old there," Lexie said at his side. "And here—" She pointed to a piece of paper. "That's his foot from the day he was born."

Riley let his fingertip trace the lines of Noah's foot. "So small." His throat tightened as he looked over the pictures and turned the page to find more. In each one, Noah changed, his face rounding, his smiles seemingly coming easier. There were two full pages until Riley reached another piece of paper that read *Noah, 4–6 months*.

"I've done it up to his second birthday. There are so many pictures of him, I couldn't fit them all into this one." She shrugged. "The next one is halfway done."

Riley shook his head, smiling at a picture of Noah on his first birthday, a pointed party hat on his head and a spoon filled with ice cream in his fist. "This is amazing, Lex," he whispered. He looked at her. "You sure I can have all of these?"

Lexie gave a tiny nod. "I want you to have them. You should have been there. I can never make up for that. This is the least I could do."

Without even thinking about it, Riley placed the photo album at his side and wrapped his arm around Lexie's shoulder, pulling her in for a hug. It took her by surprise and she seemed to pause for a moment before she reciprocated. "Thank you," Riley said, the smell of her hair making his eyes close. "It's perfect."

Her arms tightened around him and her nose dipped behind his ear. "Don't thank me. I don't deserve it."

Riley rubbed a hand down her back. "Maybe not, but I appreciate it all the same." He pulled back a little.

She smiled wryly. "Quit being so nice."

Riley tucked a piece of hair behind her ear. The softness of it on his fingertips was so familiar it whipped his breath away. Her small hands fisted in his T-shirt and her tongue peeked out to wet her lips. Riley closed his eyes.

"Lex," he whispered. "We—I can't . . ."

She moved her hands to the back of his neck, pushing her fingers through his hair. She shushed him. "It's okay. Riley, stop. I know. We're okay."

"I want to be sensible," he said, the fight in him waning as her hands moved around his neck and her breath blew across his face. "I do. But I'm struggling to convince my body that it doesn't want you."

Her eyes sparked. "Riley, I won't lie; I want you. I always have, but I know we have a lot to work through before we can . . . be more."

Her words were honest, they were right, sensible even, but Riley's heart thumped in his chest, beating back every one of them. More? He didn't even know what that meant. If it meant kissing her right now, tasting her tongue on his, then, yes, he did want more. After that? Who knew?

"I'm so confused," he admitted quietly, pressing his forehead to hers.

"That's allowed," she whispered. "I only want what you're willing to give me. No more. No less. If that's just us being friends, that's fine, too."

Riley's gaze met hers. "I don't know what I'm capable of right now." He ran his hands down her bare arms and watched gooseflesh appear in their wake. "God, you kill me."

She wrapped her arms around his neck and held him close. Riley sucked in a breath when he felt her lips on his neck. Fuck, he'd always loved it when she did that. But this time, she was tentative, gentle, as though waiting for him to push her away. He knew he should, he knew that letting her do that was sending her the wrong signals, but, Jesus, she'd paralyzed him. All he could do was close his eyes and breathe and think about how, despite it being years since they'd touched this way, natural it felt to have her so close.

"I have to go," he managed, his voice husky and full of lust.

"I know," she mumbled into his skin, before she exhaled and sat back, moving so there was an inch of space between them. Her cheeks were beautifully flushed, but her eyes were guilty. "I shouldn't have done that. Sorry."

"It's okay," he replied, willing his heart to slow down. His lungs squeezed before he spoke again. "I want to be honest with you." She blinked in reply. "I'm terrified."

"Of me?"

"Sort of. But more of this." He waved a hand between them. "Of what this means, of what it *might* mean."

She dipped her chin. "What do you *want* it to mean?"

Riley lifted his shoulders. "I have no fucking idea." Lexie moved back from him a little more. "Lex, wanting you was never the issue. I do; I do want you. I don't think I'll ever switch that part of myself off. But with Noah here now, I can't just push my worries to one side and forget."

"I know," she uttered, smiling sadly.

Riley reached for her hand and squeezed it. "Let's take this slowly, okay? See what happens."

"I'd like that."

Yeah, Riley would, too. At least half of him would. The other half, the half that was still scarred, still wary, wasn't so sure, but, hell, what could he do? It was nothing but the honest-to-God truth when he said he was unable to turn off the part that cared for Lexie, that wanted her and, in many respects, still loved her. All he could do was take his time, be honest, and pray that she wouldn't break his heart all over again.

14

Long Lake on a hot Sunday in July was beautiful. Lexie and Riley wandered along the shore, eating the ice creams they'd bought from Moomers while Noah ran ahead, arms out wide, running in and out of the shallowest parts of the water and splashing like it was the best thing he'd ever done.

"This was a great idea," Riley said, looking out toward the lake. "It's been so long since I've been here." The nice thing about Long Lake was that it was mostly for residents, so, although it did get busy, the water was sand-bottomed, clean, and not dirtied by hundreds of tourists.

"I love coming here," Lexie replied. "When I moved back here I'd bring Noah and I'd sit watching him play." She watched her feet while she walked. "I'd think about you mostly." She shook her head and looked up and out toward the water. "I wasted so much time, Riley. I should have called you."

Riley agreed in the deepest parts of his heart, the most wounded parts, but he couldn't keep looking back to the past. He and Lexie were both different people now with different priorities, different views on what they had been, and what they wanted to be. Her apologies helped him for sure, and he knew they had to make her feel better, but they'd agreed to move forward.

The rest of the day was one of the best Riley had ever had. They spent some of it on the water, swimming and playing together, and then they ate at the lake restaurant. Noah continued to captivate Riley at every turn, and the fact that the little boy was becoming more tactile and open with him was simply incredible. Lexie could barely get a word in edgewise between father and son, but the soft, wistful look in her eye told Riley she didn't mind.

"Are you coming backs to our house?" Noah asked, his mouth full of pizza, from his seat opposite Riley.

"If you'd like me to," Riley offered with a smile.

"Yes," Noah insisted. "Comes and stay with me and Mommy."

Riley looked over the table at Lexie. "I can stay for a little while."

"And has a sleepover? Mommy, can Riley sleeps over?"

Lexie coughed gently into her napkin. Riley smiled at the pink flush that appeared on her cheeks. "Riley needs to go home to his own bed, sweetheart."

Noah frowned at Riley. "You do?"

"Yeah, buddy. I get scared if I'm not in my own bed." He sipped his drink. "Maybe another time."

"Okay." He whipped his head around to Lexie at his side. "Can I has dessert now, Mommy?" He leaned over and placed a small hand on her cheek. Riley wondered how Lexie could resist the little boy when he looked at her that way. Riley knew he'd give the kid just about anything when he busted out those cute Puss in Boots eyes.

"Hmm," she mused. "Did you eat all of your—?" Noah quickly lifted his plate to show her that he'd eaten everything save for a couple of fries and the crust from the pizza.

Lexie chuckled. "Then I guess so."

Noah beamed and clambered up so he was kneeling on his seat and kissed Lexie's cheek. "I loves you."

"All the world, baby," Lexie replied, glancing quickly at Riley before she handed Noah a menu and showed him the pictures of the desserts on offer. Noah quickly decided on apple pie. "Wave to the waitress when she next passes," Lexie said, moving Noah's plate out of the way so he had room to finish coloring in the picture of the lake on the paper place mat he'd been given when they'd arrived.

Riley sat back, watching the two of them, seeing their routines and the love they had for one another in every word and action. It made his own heart beat a little faster, as though the love the two of them shared was slowly seeping into him, too. It was hard to be around them and not get lost in fantasies about the three of them being together, permanently, like a real family.

Shit, was that what he wanted? Sitting with Lexie and Noah now, with the sensation of the sun still warm on his skin, he would say absolutely. But this was just one day. How would it work for the rest of their lives? It certainly wasn't difficult to conjure up old memories of when he'd thought seriously about being with Lexie forever, but they'd lost their potency with all that had happened between them. He had reconciled with the fact that he wouldn't have to fall back in love with Lexie—that shit had never gone away—but things were so different now.

Riley had thought long and hard about what he wanted with her since the night she'd given him the photo album. As each day passed, she continued to try so damned hard to make up for keeping him and Noah apart, and, if Riley were truly honest, her efforts were working. Riley didn't want her to spend every day groveling, as much as others thought she deserved to. It tore him up to see her so submissive, despite how angry he had been with her. He simply wanted to get to know his son. Spending time with Lexie was an added bonus.

Deep down, Riley knew she'd started to create dents in the armor he'd kept resolutely around his heart when she was near, while the trust she'd shattered was slowly healing. For every day that they spent together, every time he watched her play with their son, each time Riley saw what an amazing mother she was, like just now, shards of that trust fused back together.

"Are you all right?" Lexie asked, her expression concerned.

Riley blinked back into the room, allowing the blue of her gaze to solder together more of the faith he'd had in her, in them, and smiled. "Sure. Just thinking."

Her face relaxed. "Good things?"

Riley paused for a beat before he nodded. "Yeah. Good things."

An hour later, back at Lexie's place, Riley offered to help Noah get cleaned up in the bath. It was the most fun Riley had had in ages, playing with all of Noah's bath toys, and he was almost as soaked as the kid was when he picked him up out of the water. He helped Noah choose his pajamas but left him to join Lexie downstairs, after rubbing at his own clothes with a towel in an effort to dry himself.

Lexie laughed when she saw the state he was in. It looked like he'd wet himself. She handed him a glass of wine. "Oh God."

Riley held his arms out wide. "Bath time is officially awesome."

Lexie quickly reached for a dish towel and approached him. "I'm so sorry," she said with a smile as she wiped at his chest. "He thinks splashing is the best thing ever."

Riley held her wrist gently, stopping her fussing. "I said it's okay. I had a great time." She looked up at him and Riley was momentarily struck dumb by how fucking beautiful she was. The curve of her upper lip beckoned him like a siren's call and, before he knew what he was doing, he bent his head to kiss her.

"Mommy!"

Riley's head snapped up at the sound of Noah's feet pounding down the stairs. Lexie stepped away from him and ran a hand through her hair. "In here. Have you brushed your teeth?"

"Yes," Noah replied, skidding into the kitchen.

"Let me smell."

Noah approached Lexie with a reading book under his arm and opened his mouth, breathing out heavily into her face when she crouched down to meet him. "Oh!" she exclaimed. "Nice and minty."

"Can Riley reads to me my bedtime story?"

Lexie glanced up at Riley, her breathing seemingly a little labored. "If you ask nicely, I'm sure Riley would love to read to you."

"Come on, Riley," Noah urged, pulling on Riley's hand and dragging him into the living room. "Sit there," he ordered, pointing to the sofa. Riley chuckled and did as he was told, as Noah scrambled up onto it next to him, still holding the book. He sat as close to Riley as he could and slapped the book onto his lap. Riley smiled. "*The Velveteen Rabbit?*"

"It's my favorite," Noah told him.

Riley looked at his son. "It's my favorite, too."

Noah's face was ecstatic. "Please cans you read it?"

Riley placed his wineglass onto the coffee table. "Sure, buddy. I'd love to." He sat back, wrapped an arm around Noah, and opened the hard-backed book, marveling at the illustrations. Noah pointed with a small finger at the first page. "It starts here."

Riley nodded, looking briefly at Lexie as she sat down in the chair by the fireplace, trying his hardest not to think about what would have happened if he'd kissed her, what it would have felt like. "Okay." He cleared his throat. "*There was once a velveteen rabbit, and in the beginning he was really splendid.*"

Riley read the story, putting on voices that made both Noah and Lexie giggle. As he read, Noah squeezed closer to his side and Lexie leaned over the arm of her seat, her chin in her hand, occasionally sipping her wine. Riley allowed himself to imagine the moment as a small glimpse into what his future could look like. He took a quick photograph in his mind of the scene and stored it, knowing he would pull it out on the days he was away from the two of them.

"'That?' said the doctor. 'Why, it's a mass of scarlet fever germs! Burn it at once. What? Nonsense! Get him a new one. He mustn't have that anymore!'"

"Riley."

Riley looked over to Lexie to see her gesturing with a tilt of her chin toward Noah. He looked down to see the little boy fast asleep, curled up against his side. He was just about the most perfect thing Riley had ever seen. He closed the book and gathered Noah to him, picking him up just as he'd done out of his car the night before.

"He's making a habit of this," Riley whispered as he headed toward the stairs.

"Do you need a hand?" Lexie asked as she stood.

Riley shook his head. "I got it."

In the bedroom, Riley placed Noah on the bed and covered him as he'd seen Lexie do the previous evening. He kissed Noah's head and left the door open a crack before rejoining Lexie in the living room, where she was picking up a few of Noah's toys and books and placing them in the blue box by the TV. She turned to him as he approached. "He okay?"

"Dead to the world."

"Yeah, he's always been a good sleeper."

"Unlike you," Riley commented, moving closer to her.

She shook her head. "No. Thank God. He sleeps just like his father." She pressed her lips together before speaking again. "I love watching you with him," she murmured. She cocked her head a little. "You know he falls asleep on you because he's so comfortable with you, right?"

Riley felt his heart soar. "Really?"

"He only does that with me, Mom, and Sav usually."

Riley took in every inch of Lexie's face, the freckles, small scars, and marks that he knew with his eyes closed. "I like that he feels that way." Riley was more than a little aware of how the atmosphere around them had changed, charged, and snapped as they gazed at one another. "You know, it's going to get harder for me to keep leaving."

"It's already getting harder to watch you leave," she replied. "When do you go back to New York?"

"I know Max said I can stay however long I want, but I can't do that to him. We're partners, and I need a paycheck. I'll stay for a few more days."

She nodded. "Maybe Noah and I can come back with you some time." She smiled. "I've never been to New York."

Riley stared at her in astonishment. "You'd do that? You'd come and see me?"

Lexie shrugged nonchalantly. "Of course. Noah would love it." Her blue eyes darkened. "I'd go anywhere for you. I always would have."

Riley's mouth was on hers before he even realized the need he had to kiss her. And fuck's sake, wasn't it just as he remembered. Her arms were quickly around his neck and she moaned into his mouth.

As always happened when they gave themselves over to their desire, they folded into one another. He pulled her close, her body pressed into his from thighs to chest and, God, she felt so damned perfect, so familiar against him. Their tongues met, first in her mouth and then in his, dancing back and forth like reunited old friends. Her taste. *Her taste.* It was the same. His body pulsed, as though every part of him sang for her, wanting to feel her inside and out.

"Fuck," he panted when they broke apart, pressing himself closer. "We can't."

Her breath flew across his face, hot and gasping. "I'm sorry."

Riley huffed a laugh. "For what? *I* kissed *you.*" He held her when he felt her try to pull away.

"I don't want to pressure you or force you into something, Riley."

"You're not."

"I only want to be honest with you and, the truth is, this is all up to you. I *want* you, I want all of you, but I don't want you to think you have to want me back because of Noah."

Riley let his eyes wander over her, let his hands tighten their grip on her. Was that what he was doing? Was this because of Noah? He kissed her again and she moaned against his lips. No. This was the two of them, how they always were. He could already feel the heat between them start to gain momentum. His mouth moved to her jaw. "I want us." He lifted his head. "But I want us to be patient. No rushing."

The look in Lexie's eyes told him she knew he was right. They had to think carefully about what they were about to do. There were too many variables to consider, Noah being the most important. She kissed him softly. "Okay."

He nuzzled her temple. "Let's take the time I spend in New York as time to think about where we go from here." He sighed and rubbed his hands up and down her arms. "When I get back we can talk more."

"I'd like that."

They sat back on the sofa and for the rest of the evening they talked about easy things, things that weren't scary or dangerous. Every so often, Riley found that he needed to reach out and touch her. His hands ran through her hair or touched her hand. They laughed and reminisced, and, as the hours passed, Riley allowed the hope he'd tried to keep under lock and key back in. Like water from a broken dam it surged around his body, lighting him from the inside out. As scared as he knew he should feel allowing it to happen, Riley knew he'd never felt more alive.

.   .   .

For the next month and a half Riley split his time between New York and Michigan, hating every moment he was away from Noah and Lexie, and living for the days he flew back to see them. Today was one of those days of anticipation, except he wasn't the one doing the flying.

"Jeez, man, what's up with you?" Max sniggered as Riley bopped and dipped across O'Hare's to the rocking sounds of Radiohead. It wasn't that Riley didn't normally dance around—his running man was world famous, after all—but today there was definitely a little more slide and boogie to his moves.

He glanced at the clock on the wall of the shop. "Noah and Lex land at JFK tomorrow morning."

Max smirked. "I know, dude. You've talked about nothing else for a week."

Riley shrugged without apology.

"I think it's sweet," commented Steph as she walked past them back to her desk.

"See?" Riley said with an arm extended in Steph's direction. "I'm sweet. Chicks dig this shit."

"Sure they do." Max rolled his eyes and dropped down into the pit under a 1968 Dodge Charger.

"How's Grace, Max? You still lovin' having her in the city with you?" Riley called, picking up his mug of coffee and chuckling at the narrow-eyed expression and dirty rag that was thrown back at him.

"She's good. And. Yes."

"Great," Riley replied, elongating the vowel just to wind Max up further before turning the volume up on the stereo to drown out his retorts. Riley didn't know why Max still got so touchy about loving Grace, especially since they'd been officially together for nearly a year, but it was funny as hell. He crouched down, catching Max's eye under the car. "You're still gonna bring Grace to meet Lex and Noah on Saturday night, right? Kat and Carter are coming."

"Sure. I think Grace is more excited than you."

The day dragged at a snail's pace, with Riley constantly watching the clock. Every text that Lexie sent him appeared to turn the clock back another hour, driving him beyond distraction, but eventually the day was over and, after he'd shut up the shop, Riley made his way to a couple of stores, grabbing a few last-minute bits for Lexie and Noah's arrival.

It was the first time the two of them had come to New York to visit, and Riley had never been more excited. It was going to be four days of awesomeness and he couldn't wait. He'd even planned a few tourist-type trips for them to take, including to Lady Liberty, whom he knew Noah would lose his shit over. Riley bought a blow-up bed for his spare room, which he'd had to clear of all the junk he'd collected over the six years he'd lived in the apartment. He made sure that his comic-book movie collection was up to date and that his kitchen was filled with everything Noah and Lexie might want.

"I gets to see you tomorrow!" Noah yelled down the phone when Riley called later that evening.

"You do," Riley said with a laugh. "I can't wait. I've missed you, man."

"I missed yous, too. It's been a billion years."

It sure did feel like it, even though he'd seen Noah and Lexie only ten days ago. The longest ten days ever. "I know. It sucks. But tomorrow we can hang out and do whatever you like. Make sure you sleep good tonight, okay?"

"Okay! 'Bye!"

For weeks, Riley had been putting out feelers back in Michigan about possible work, but it seemed that mechanics were an overpopulated race in Traverse City, and, ironically enough, he seemed too overqualified for many to take him on. He'd also worked up the nerve to talk to Max about the shop and what his future options were.

It seemed Riley had two. One: he could cash in his share of O'Hare's and the money it had already made—which wasn't a vast amount in only eighteen months—or two: keep his share and use it as a nest egg, which, as a father with a son to think about, wasn't a bad idea. Either way, they weren't the perfect solutions Riley was hoping for, but he tried not to get too despondent about it; something would turn up. It always did.

The following morning, standing in the arrivals at JFK, Riley heard Noah before he saw him. With only eleven days since their last meeting, Riley could have sworn that Noah had grown again. He charged at Riley, arms out wide, smile beautiful and excited. Riley grabbed him and picked him up, swinging him around and clutching him close, breathing in the scent of sugar, sun, and something that was inherently Noah. He blew a raspberry on Noah's cheek and grinned when he squealed and wiggled to be put down. It was then that he heard Lexie. Her laughter floated toward him, filling the parts of him that belonged only to her.

She was lovely in the New York sun streaming through the windows of the airport concourse. Her glasses, her pink Muse T-shirt, and her pink flip-flops were perfection. She was the girl he remembered, the woman he was getting to know again, to care about again, and everything in between.

Making sure Noah was still at his side, Riley moved toward her, feeling as though his body were in slow motion. Apart from his heart. His heart pounded. He wanted to kiss her—they'd done a lot of covert kissing over the past six weeks, each kiss becoming a little more heated, each one a silent promise of what was to come—but Riley knew he and Lexie still had to be cautious around Noah. The little boy was too smart for his own good, and Riley didn't want to confuse him.

Riley placed a hand on Lex's waist and pulled her to him, furtively kissing the hollow behind her ear.

"I missed you," she whispered.

He stepped back and grinned. He'd missed her, too. "Good flight?" He looked down at Noah as he spoke, always aware of including him in any of his and Lex's conversations—where possible, of course.

"We gots snacks," Noah enthused, grabbing hold of Riley's two middle fingers and swinging their arms.

"Awesome!" He twirled Noah under his arm. "What do you say

we go back to my place, drop off your stuff, and then we adventure around the city?"

Noah paused. "An adventure?"

Riley winked at him. "We may even see Spider-Man."

Noah's mouth dropped open. "We haves to go now!"

He pulled on Riley's hand, dragging him as much as his four-year-old body would allow.

.   .   .

"Welcome," Riley said with a smile and a rattle of his keys. He placed Lexie's bag down and gestured for them to enter. Inviting Lexie and Noah into his apartment was an altogether odd experience, kind of like seeing his past and present merge.

It wasn't odd, however, that seeing them both in his home filled him with something akin to serenity. He and Lexie had discussed her and Noah's trip to New York for a while before they made any concrete plans. They both comprehended what a huge step it was, showing Noah where Riley lived, as well as it dredging up old memories of what could have been had things been different and Lexie gone to NYU with Riley all those years ago.

Watching Lexie and Noah in his apartment, Riley quickly pushed those thoughts away. There was no point mulling over it all now. The anger and the hurt he'd harbored since his return to Michigan had diluted considerably over the past few months and, honestly, Riley was glad of it. Having such negative emotions within him was exhausting. Lexie continued to go above and beyond in terms of helping push his and Noah's relationship forward, while allowing Riley space to consider what he wanted. Despite the effort she was still making with Riley's parents, his brothers were yet to be convinced; the three of them were still understandably protective after Lexie's Noah bombshell.

As always, Dex was objective and logical, always studying a situation from all angles before he made a comment, while Tate called a spade a spade, and Seb took the opinion that if Riley was happy, then fuck it. The four of them were finally getting together for an early birthday celebration for Seb at their parents' house in a few weeks, and Riley couldn't wait.

Lexie stood next to his sofa as Noah investigated the place, skipping around and seemingly touching everything he could. "It's lovely," she murmured. "Noah, watch what you're doing, baby."

"He's fine," Riley said softly, moving to her side.

"This place is great."

Riley looked around as though he'd never seen his apartment before. "Yeah, it's not bad." He kicked his foot against the floor.

Lexie crossed her arms over her chest and nodded. "I'm so happy to be here."

"Me too."

"Can we goes out now?" Noah asked as he ran around the couch and stood with them.

"Sure thing, man," Riley answered. "You ready? I thought we could go to see the Statue of Liberty."

Noah jumped up and down like a jack-in-the-box, clapping wildly.

It had been a very long time since Riley had allowed himself to be a tourist in New York City, but seeing the joy and wonder on Noah and Lexie's faces made it all worthwhile. Noah was awe-struck by Lady Liberty and later ran around like a lunatic as they wandered through Central Park.

Seeing Lexie laugh and enjoy herself reminded Riley of when he'd first moved to New York when he was eighteen. He'd had so many plans, so many dreams about what he and Lexie could do together. The only thing that had kept him even remotely sane when it all fell apart—other than the women and booze—was the fact that the city was easy to get lost in.

Lexie nudged his shoulder with her own. "You okay?"

"Yes. I'm . . . I just . . . I can't wait to rediscover this city with you two."

Her top teeth traveled across her bottom lip as she looked back at him and then toward Noah. "I can't wait, either." She sighed. "Thank you," she whispered before her eyes met his. "For being . . . you. For your patience, your forgiveness. For wanting me around."

Riley stopped walking and turned to her, his fingers itching to reach out and touch her. He allowed his hand to find hers and squeezed it gently. "I meant what I said: I want to try."

She nodded. "You just have to trust me again. I understand." She tilted her head a little. "Do you? Do you trust me?"

Riley regarded her for a moment before taking a step closer to her. "Yeah. I think I do." Forgetting where he was, he bent his head down to graze his lips against hers.

"Mommy!" Lexie didn't flinch away, even though Riley jerked his head back. They both glanced over at the kid, climbing all over the *Alice in Wonderland* statue. "Looks at me."

Riley chuckled. "Be careful, buddy. No broken bones." Noah laughed and sat down, swinging his feet. "He doesn't care, does he?" Riley asked, turning back to Lexie. "He doesn't mind when you and I are . . . like this."

Lexie shook her head. "He told me he likes it when you and I hug."

"He did?" Riley startled.

"Yeah, he was just concerned that I liked your hugs better than his."

Riley let his head fall back as he laughed loudly.

• • • •

The next couple of days in New York were some of the best Lexie could remember. During the day, the three of them ventured about, visiting Ground Zero, walking the Brooklyn Bridge and fastening a padlock to it engraved with their names, riding the subway, seeing the island from the top of the Empire State Building, and eating the most amazing food.

At night they hung out at Riley's apartment, laughed, played, and, after Noah was fast asleep, she and Riley would talk and drink, kiss and rediscover each other in every way they could without falling into bed. It was wonderful becoming friends again, watching his trust for her slowly form behind his hazel eyes. She wanted so badly for him to trust her. It was a hell of a challenge having Riley so close, so tender, and not push for more, but she knew just how damned lucky she was to have him at all, let alone having his mouth on hers and his words of promise in her ear.

It was the most picture-perfect of existences, and it filled her with a hope so profound she could barely contain it. Her adoration and love for her son and his father could no more be measured than put into words.

"You look great."

She turned from the mirror hanging on Riley's bedroom wall to see him leaning against the doorjamb, smoking hot in his ripped jeans and gray T-shirt, which read " 'That's what.' —She."

Lexie snorted and Riley glanced down at himself. "A Christmas present from my asshole brother," he explained. "You doing okay? Still nervous?"

Lexie turned back to the mirror, wondering whether the shorts and white sleeveless blouse were too casual for a dinner with Riley's friends. Was she nervous? Hell yes, but knowing what the evening meant to Riley kept a smile fixed front and center. His wanting to introduce her and Noah to his friends was a massive move. Lexie knew firsthand what Riley's friends meant to him; as far as he was concerned, they were his extended family, and he was as loyal to them as if they shared blood. He'd always been that way, wearing his heart on his sleeve, proud and clear for all to see, taking no shit and protecting those he cared about fiercely. It was one of the things she loved most about him.

She stared at him in the mirror, knowing she didn't deserve the second chance he seemed to be offering her but swearing silently that she'd spend every day she had giving back to the universe. "I'm looking forward to meeting everyone."

He approached and placed his palms on her shoulders, giving them a squeeze. "It'll be great. I know it."

His hair had grown a lot over the past weeks and, with his beard, made him look more than a little sexy. "You look . . . great." She didn't mean for her voice to sound seductive, but hell, she couldn't seem to stop it.

He chuckled. "Thank you. I'll go and make sure Noah hasn't fallen into a *Spider-Man* movie coma and help get him ready."

An hour later they walked into 5 Napkin Burger and were directed toward a circular booth, where there were already four people sitting. Lexie was instantly struck by how good-looking everyone was and instantly regretted not putting in her bigger earrings and more sparkly septum ring. Riley's hand found her lower back and he rubbed gently, seemingly sensing her reticence. Noah, on the other hand, was all smiles and eager to meet all the new people. The fact that he was cute as a damned button helped him fit in just fine.

"Hey, people," Riley said with a wide smile. Four pairs of eyes looked at him before sliding over to Lexie and then to the little boy at their side. "This is Lexie and this is Noah."

Lexie smiled. "Hi."

"Hello," Noah uttered.

Riley then pointed to each person in turn. "Guys, this is Max, my business partner, and his girlfriend, Grace, and this is Carter and his wife, Kat."

"Nice to finally meet you, Lexie," Kat said with a wide smile. Her hair was deep auburn and shone perfectly under the lights of the restaurant. "And Noah, aren't you just the most handsome boy I've ever seen."

Lexie watched in amazement as Noah blushed and dropped his face to his forearms on the table edge. Kat giggled and looked toward her husband, whose blue eyes creased as he chuckled with her. Kat was curvaceous and sexy, and her skin was as unblemished as Lexie imagined skin could be.

Her porcelain skin was the complete opposite of Grace's, whose own was an exquisite caramel color. She smiled widely at Lexie, showing beautiful, straight white teeth, and pushed her long, curly ebony hair over her shoulder. "Riley's told us so much about you both."

"We've been desperate for a variation in conversation," Max teased. He was a little rough around the edges, all wild hair and unshaven scruff, but his dark eyes were playful.

"Shut up," Riley commented with a smile. "Take a seat." He gestured for Lexie and Noah to sit down, and Carter and Kat shuffled around the booth to make room.

"I love your ink," Grace said, her gaze on Lexie's arms. "The colors are amazing. It's so beautiful."

Lexie felt her cheeks warm. "Thank you."

"Have you ever had them photographed?"

Max snickered at her side. "Gracie, leave the poor girl alone."

Grace smirked at him. "What? They'd look fantastic as a part of my show."

Lexie cocked an eyebrow. "Show?"

"I'm a photographer. I have a show here in New York in six weeks."

"Sounds fantastic."

"You should come."

Lexie glanced at Riley, who shrugged good-naturedly. "I'd like that."

Max placed his arm around Grace's shoulder, the pride clear on his face.

"Mommy, can I has a burger?"

Lexie smiled at Noah, who was looking intently at the menu as though he could actually read it. "Have whatever you want, baby."

"He's super cute," Kat uttered quietly, leaning toward Riley. "Like a mini-you."

Riley grinned. "Lucky kid, right?"

Lexie rolled her eyes affably, and the tension that had resided in her shoulders since she'd woken that morning slowly ebbed as conversation moved around the table. Riley's hand continually found a part of her to covertly touch and squeeze, calming her further, even though his friends were more than a little welcoming; the way Grace and Kat cooed over Noah was too sweet.

Noah appeared more than a little taken with Kat, chatting his heart out to her about his adventures in New York, which Kat listened to attentively. Lexie wondered if she and Carter had children or even plans to have them; Kat seemed to be a little broody. "Can we borrow him?" Kat asked, all large green eyes and fisting hands.

Carter shook his head with a smile. "Peaches, he's not a DVD. He's a kid."

Kat shoved his arm playfully. "You know what I mean." She looked between Riley and Lexie. "We could babysit if you two want some time alone together."

Lexie could feel her cheeks heat, and she avoided Riley's stare despite feeling it burning into her. "Sounds good," Carter said, cocking an eyebrow at her. "But they leave tomorrow."

"Well, then maybe next time they visit," Kat offered.

Lexie opened her mouth a couple of times before she found her voice. The momma bear in her reared a little; she'd only just met these people. Glancing at Riley, however, shook her of the feeling. She knew better. Riley would rather die than leave his son with someone he didn't trust. "I—if Noah is okay with it."

"What do you say, Noah?" Kat asked softly. "Wanna hang out with me and Carter sometime?"

Surprisingly, Noah's hazel gaze didn't go straight to Lexie's and instead found Riley's. "It's okay if you don't want to, buddy," Riley assured him in that voice Lexie loved and knew he only ever saved for the little boy.

Noah shrugged a little, looking at Kat, then back at Riley. "Cans we stay at your house?"

"Sure, man, Kat and Carter come to my place loads."

"You think about it," Kat offered. Lexie watched as Carter leaned over and kissed her temple. It was such a tender gesture from a man who looked anything but. "We could bring some games."

"We could?" Carter asked with a raised eyebrow.

"Yes." Kat nudged him. "We could."

Carter looked over at Noah and winked. "We could."

As the conversation continued, Lexie allowed herself to think about what it would be like if she and Noah lived in the city with Riley, living in his gorgeous apartment, hanging out with his friends, and fitting into his life like pegs in round holes.

She knew Riley had been trying to organize moving back to Michigan, willing to change his life without even a second thought, explaining that it would be easier for him to move than her, but guilt teased at her all the same.

"How do you like New York, Lexie?" Carter asked after the waitress had taken their orders and collected their menus.

"I love it," she offered truthfully. "So much more than I imagined."

"Cans we stay forever, Mommy?"

Lexie ran a gentle hand over Noah's head. "You want to stay here forever?"

He nodded solemnly. "Riley is all on his owns."

Lexie heard a small *aw* from both Grace and Kat as Riley held out a fist for Noah to bump. "I'm okay, man," Riley assured him, but Lexie wasn't blind to the sadness in his eyes.

"We'll look after him when you go home," Carter offered, smiling at Noah. "Promise."

Noah's brows drew together as he considered this. "Okay."

Once their food arrived and Lexie talked more with Riley's friends, she began to understand why Riley liked them all so much. Each of them was so different and seemed to draw out various facets of his personality. With Max and Carter, Riley was louder, brasher, but with Kat, he was calmer, speaking to her with an underlying respect Lexie was sure she'd earned when she'd taught him at Arthur Kill.

With Grace, he was teasing, softer and sweet. It was truly wonderful seeing him so happy. He was the Riley of old, carefree and devastatingly attractive. It was becoming increasingly difficult to not allow her desire for him show. She wanted him, of that there was no doubt, but she was terrified of pushing too hard, too quickly. She'd been telling the truth when she'd told him that the ball was in his court. It was all on him and, despite her longing, she would wait as long as it took.

The food they ate was amazing. Why was everything edible in New York like nothing else on Earth? Noah was of the same mind, eating everything that was placed in front of him before he shared a huge ice-cream sundae with Riley.

Before they left, Lexie swapped cell phone and Facebook details with Kat and Grace, promising that she'd let Grace photograph her tattoos the following day while assuring Kat she would send her a catalogue of her Love, You jewelry and design her a version of the necklace Lexie was wearing.

Later that evening, with Noah fast asleep, Lexie and Riley sat on the sofa, he at one end, she at the other, their legs tangled between them. "I had such a good time," she said with a small smile.

"I'm glad. I think Noah has a little crush on Kat."

"Right?" Lexie agreed. "I've never seen him like that before."

"He's gonna have to beat the ladies back with a stick when he's older. Kid's already too handsome for his own good," Riley said with a knowing wink. "He looks like his old man, after all."

Lexie laughed and trailed her finger down the side of her glass of juice. "Can I ask you a question? You don't have to answer it if you don't want to."

Riley smirked. "Sound ominous." Lexie's eyes moved toward the ceiling, then the wall, then back to Riley's face. "Wow. Now I'm intrigued," he said on a chuckle.

"How many . . \ have there been many women?"

Riley's eyes widened for a second before he appeared to regain his composure. *Well.* That wasn't a good sign. He fidgeted and cleared his throat.

"That many, huh?" she asked wryly, knowing that she had absolutely zero right to feel jealous or hurt, despite the pinch in her heart.

"Lex," he began with a long sigh.

"I'm sorry," she murmured. "It's really none of my business. Forget I asked."

He sat forward and placed a hand on her shin. "When we . . . finished after your dad died, I didn't know what to do. I missed you—you know that." Yes, she did know that, and not only because they'd talked and shouted about it over the years, but because she'd lived it, too. "I slept with women to try and forget, Lex. I tried to lose myself in them so that I'd lose the love I had for you."

Pain and regret lanced through Lexie, taking her breath away. "I was . . . so horrible."

"No," he whispered. "You were lost. You weren't the Lexie I knew, my best friend, the girl I loved. It hurt, but I survived it. And we're here now because deep down, no matter how many women there've been between then and now, I always believed we'd find our way back to each other."

The tear that fell down Lexie's cheek was one of apology and gratitude. The faith that he'd always had in her, in them, had always astounded her. When he reminded her of it, she was reminded of how easy it had been to fall in love with him and then to love him every day following.

"I'm not ready for you both to leave yet," he said, watching his hand as it moved up and down her leg.

"Me either." Every time they separated, it tugged on the fear she harbored that she'd lose someone she loved again. It was selfish and admittedly ironic considering her and Riley's history, but there it was. "When will you be back in Michigan?"

His grimace was small but noticeable. "A couple of weeks. Maybe three?"

"Are you asking?" she said with a smirk. "Because you know you're welcome whenever you want, and Noah just . . . he loves you very much."

"I love him, too." Riley exhaled through his nose. "So listen, I thought that . . . maybe on my next visit or the one after, we could sit down and talk to him about who I am. I think it's time. Don't you?"

Lexie bit her lip on a smile. "I think that'd be perfect."

15

Joan Moore was known for three things: her unending patience, her ability to defuse any situation (especially among four brothers), and her ability to throw awesome birthday parties. The last was certainly true on the day of Seb's (two-weeks-early) twenty-seventh birthday. It was the first time all four brothers had been in the same state together, let alone the same room, in far too long, and Riley had been looking forward to it for weeks.

There were balloons stuck to the front door—as their mother had commented, no one is ever too old for balloons—the kitchen table had been extended as it always was when there was a family gathering, and it was set up with a buffet of all the foods Riley and his brothers loved: sandwiches, chips, dip, chicken wings, and ribs, as well as a huge chocolate cake and Jell-O for dessert.

"She does know I'm closer to thirty than three, right?" Seb asked as he handed Riley a set of plates to place on the table and regarded the spread.

"Physically maybe," Riley retorted with a grin.

"Lex and Noah still coming?"

"Yeah, they should be here in an hour or so. Christine's coming, too."

"Wow," Seb said, covertly lifting a chip and throwing it into his mouth. "Just like old times, huh?"

Riley shrugged. "Mom invited them."

Seb nodded. "And you're happy about it?"

"Of course." He glanced at his younger brother. "Why the twenty questions?"

"I'm just making sure you're okay, man."

Riley pinched a chip, too. "I'm good. Really good. Things are perfect at the moment."

"But?"

Riley exhaled a wry laugh. His brother never missed anything. "But I have no idea what I want."

"With Lex?" Seb surmised, crossing his arms over his chest.

Riley lifted his eyebrows in reply. "We're close again, but . . . I don't know. I'm guarded."

"That's understandable, Riley."

He rubbed a hand down his face before reaching for another chip. "I just don't want us to mess everything up. There's too much at stake this time. I don't want Noah caught in the middle of a war if things go tits up."

Seb licked his lips. "And how does she feel?"

Riley raised a shoulder. "She's just waiting for me to make a move."

"Do you want to make a move?"

"Shit, yes," Riley answered quickly, though Seb didn't look surprised. "Wanting her that way was never a problem."

Seb smirked. "Then go for it, man. If it's what you both want, why not?" He took a step closer to Riley. "You'll never know otherwise."

Riley dipped his chin. "I know."

Seb clapped a hand to his arm and squeezed. "If it doesn't work out, you still have Noah together. She'll always be in your life, no matter what." He picked up a chicken leg. "Shit, I'm hungry."

"You two best not be picking at that food." Their mother's disembodied voice came from the living room.

"'Course not, Ma," Seb called through a mouthful of chicken.

Riley snorted and shook his head as Dex's voice rang through the house. "Anybody home?" His question was followed by the sound of their mother fussing over him and Park telling her to *give the poor boy some room, woman.*

Seb and Riley moved through the house to find Dex at the front door being smothered in kisses and hugs, with Tate at his side, bags in hand.

"It's so good to see you," Joan said as she held Dex's face in her hands and kissed his cheek.

"Good to see you, too, Mom."

He stood to his full height, shook Park's hand, and grinned at Riley and Seb, who approached and hugged him in turn. Riley hadn't seen his eldest brother for a long time and, seeing him now, still in a rumpled Tom Ford suit from his flight back from Thailand, he realized he'd missed him. His dark hair was longer, pushed back and curling behind his ears, and he'd grown a goatee that, despite looking more than a little badass, Riley would be mocking before the day was out. His glasses were new, Prada from the looks of it, and the suitcase that Tate had placed by the door was Louis Vuitton. Dex had never been one to shy away from spending money.

"How're you doing?" Riley asked as the six of them moved toward the living room.

"Tired," Dex answered, shrugging out of his suit jacket and placing it on the back of the sofa. "Flight was okay, though." He dropped down onto the seat and looked toward the kitchen. "Is that cake I smell?"

"Chocolate," Joan answered.

"My favorite."

"Even though it's *my* birthday," Seb groused playfully from his place by the door, while sucking the chicken bits off his fingers.

Joan frowned at him. "Have you been eating—?"

"*My* birthday," Seb interrupted with a grin.

"You're looking well, man," Riley told Dex as he sat down.

"Yeah, but I'm not smelling too hot," Dex said with a grimace. "Do I have time to shower before everyone starts arriving?"

"Sure, honey," Joan said, her face all smiles at having her boys home. "I'd better go and throw the vol-au-vents into the oven." She smacked Seb's arm as she passed him. "And stop picking."

Tate dropped down into a chair with a groan.

"You okay?" Park asked.

"Yeah, just my leg acting up."

"Thanks for picking me up, Tate," Dex said as he supressed a yawn. "I appreciate it."

Tate waved him off and rubbed at his knee.

"So what's Thailand like?" Seb asked, perching on the edge of the coffee table as he always had done since he was little.

Dex dropped his head back and closed his eyes. "Amazing. Like a totally different world. The food, the vibe."

"The women?" Riley needled with a finger jab in Dex's side.

Dex scoffed. "If there were, I didn't have time to enjoy them. Work is crazy."

"There's always time for women, man," Riley countered.

Dex looked over at him and narrowed his eyes. "Is there? And how does Lexie feel about that?"

Riley barked a laugh while Seb and Tate snorted. "Touché, my good man," Riley conceded.

Dex clapped a hand to Riley's shoulder. "Okay, let me go get cleaned up," he said as he stood. "Before I fall asleep. Then we can catch up."

He disappeared up the stairs with his suitcase and Riley took a moment to appreciate how nice it was to be in his parents' house with all of his brothers, and the smells of his childhood emanating from the kitchen. It was more than a little comforting. He and Seb set about helping their mom get the rest of the table ready, folding napkins and making sure she wasn't lifting or reaching for anything, while Park and Tate stayed glued to the TV.

Maggie and Aunt Carol were the first to arrive, with a very excited Rosie, who was wearing a pink dress that she twirled around in at every available opportunity. Maggie looked even more pregnant and grumbled constantly about swollen ankles and heartburn. A few of Seb's friends turned up: Gray, his oldest friend from high school, and his new girlfriend, and a few college buddies who were still in the area, who brought beer and presents.

When the doorbell rang again, Riley's chest fluttered. He'd seen Lexie's car pull up and immediately flushed hot all over. He was first at the door and opened it with a flourish. Noah beamed up at him.

"We's here!" he called out, making Riley laugh.

"You sure are," he replied before looking at Lexie, who looked incredible in a navy-blue dress and ballet flats. "Glad you could make it. Hi, Christine. Come on in."

Seb wandered down the hallway, apparently beckoned by the doorbell. He smiled when he saw Lexie and leaned over to kiss her cheek. "Good to see you, Lex. Hi, Christine." He looked down at Noah and grinned. "And you must be Noah." He held out a fist. "I'm Seb, Riley's brother. Nice to meet you, man."

Noah paused only briefly before he knocked his tiny fist to Seb's.

"Do you have something to give to Seb?" Lexie asked.

Noah held up a bag. "This is yours for yours birthday," he said quietly.

"What do you say?" Lexie encouraged.

"Happy birthday."

"Thanks, Noah," Seb said, taking the bag. "That's so nice of you."

"Welcomes."

Riley watched as Seb stared down at the kid and he saw it coming a mile away: he'd fallen for Noah, too. The little boy was just *that* cute.

"Come on through," Riley said. "Everyone is in the backyard."

They joined the congregation in the yard, where the sun shone and music played. Joan and Park both said hello to Christine and Lexie, which didn't feel as tricky as Riley had feared, and he watched as his parents fell about themselves when they saw Noah. Tate and Dex, who were standing by the grill, were the next two to be introduced to Riley's son and both men were immediately taken with him.

"This is Tate and Dex," Riley explained to Noah. "They're my brothers."

"You has three brothers?"

"Crazy, right?"

Noah looked up at Tate and Dex, seemingly flummoxed. Dex spoke first. "How ya doin', Noah?"

"Good."

Dex nodded at Lexie, his blue eyes careful behind his lenses. "Good to see you, Lex."

Lexie smiled small. "You too. I hear you were in Thailand. Sounds amazing."

"It was."

Tate simply sipped his juice, his intense stare on Lexie the entire time, as though he was trying to see straight through her. The small talk was awkward, but at least Riley's brothers were making an effort, which he was more than appreciative of. If he and Lexie were going to try and build a relationship again, his family had to be on board. It was just the way it worked.

"Is that your walking stick?" Noah asked suddenly, as he stared at Tate's cane.

"Noah," Lexie hissed, embarrassed.

Tate smiled. "It's okay." His tone was cool with Lexie, but his grin at Noah was wide and playful. "To the untrained eye it's a simple cane that helps me walk." He lowered his voice and Riley knew what was coming. "But to a Jedi . . ."

Noah's eyes widened. "It's a lightsabers?"

Tate bent at the waist so he could whisper. "I knew The Force was strong in you."

Noah blinked, speechless. He turned to Riley. "Your brother is a Jedi?"

Tate smirked at Riley, while Dex's shoulders shook with his quiet laughter as he said, "He likes to think so." Before Tate could interrupt or say anything else, Riley placed his hand on Noah's head and smiled. "Hey man, there's someone else I want to introduce you to."

Riley took Noah's hand and led him across the yard to where he and Tate had placed some chairs for their guests. "This is my cousin, Maggie, and this is her daughter, Rosie." Noah's eyes widened as he looked at Rosie, who tilted her head a little as she regarded him. "I thought you two could play together." Noah's hand squeezed Riley's. Riley crouched down. "Rosie's a cool girl."

Noah's spare hand found Riley's beard and his small fingers began to twirl around in the whiskers. Riley had begun to understand that Noah did it when he needed comforting. "Does she likes playing soccer?"

"I don't know. Why don't you ask?"

Noah moved even closer to Riley but looked over at Rosie as he asked, "Does you likes playing soccer?"

Rosie nodded. "I play soccer with my daddy."

Noah seemed surprised. "Your daddy?"

"Yes, don't you?"

Maggie's expression softened as she looked at Riley.

"No," Noah answered, making Riley's stomach twist with protectiveness so fierce he had to take a deep breath. He desperately wanted to tell Noah who he was. He and Lexie had discussed it and she was happy for him to tell Noah when he wanted and, Jesus, Riley wanted, but now just wasn't the time.

"Oh," Rosie answered, her face concerned. "I can play soccer with you now."

Noah balked a little. "In a dress?"

Rosie looked down at herself. "Dresses don't stop me playing. I can play anything even though I wear dresses."

Maggie snickered into the back of her hand and pulled Rosie in for a hug. "That's my girl."

"I have a soccer ball in my mommy's bag," Noah told her. "We cans play with that."

"Sounds great, buddy," Riley said and, without thought, kissed his temple. "Why don't you go with him, Rosie?"

She seemed hesitant for a split second before she agreed and followed Noah back toward Lexie, who had been watching from a polite distance. She helped get the soccer ball for Noah and she and Riley watched the two kids move to the far end of the yard and start kicking it to each other. "That might have been the single most adorable thing I have ever seen," Lexie said with a hand to her chest.

Riley smiled, moving closer to her. "You okay?" Christine was standing talking to Riley's parents.

Lexie nodded, glancing at Tate and Dex. "I'm good. I still feel like I'm the big, bad wolf."

Riley looked at his brothers over his shoulder. "Don't worry about them. If I'm happy they will be, too." Riley leaned toward her and kissed her softly, drawn by her understanding and how beautiful she looked in his parents' backyard. She froze for a second before she kissed him back. It was brief, but it was delicious.

"I like you being here," he whispered.

"I like being here, too."

"Mommy," Noah's voice came from behind Riley. He ran toward them, clutching his crotch. "I needs to go."

"Okay, honey," Lexie said, holding out her hand. "I'll be back in a minute."

Riley watched the two of them walk back into the house before he turned, grabbed a beer from the ice bucket, and made his way over to where Tate was still looking like he was ready to throw down.

"Stand down, Marine," Riley commented, shoving his shoulder into Tate's.

Tate shook his head and rolled his eyes. "I don't trust her."

"I know," Riley remarked, pulling at the label that wound around his beer bottle. "But I do."

"Really?" Dex asked. "You're serious about trying again with her?"

Riley sighed, letting his gaze return to where Lexie and Noah had disappeared. "Yeah, I think I am. This is my chance at having a real, honest-to-God family."

"You *have* a family," Tate said. "And we care about you."

Riley's chest squeezed. He wrapped an arm around Tate. "I know, brother. I love your crazy ass, too."

"And this is what you really want?" Dex asked again, his logical brain working overtime.

"Yeah," Riley replied, the word slipping from him with ease and honesty. "She and Noah are what I want."

Dex and Tate shared a look before Dex nodded. "Then I'm happy for you, Ri." He chinked his beer bottle to Riley's. "Just be careful, huh?"

"I will."

"You gonna tell Noah who you are yet?" Tate asked, staring across the yard.

"I want to. I'm just waiting for the right time."

"We'll be there if you need us to be," Tate said firmly.

"I know you will."

Dex lifted an arm, gesturing toward where Seb and Gray were standing alone, apparently having quite the intense conversation. Seb's body language was all closed fists and ticking jaw. Boy looked like he was about to flatten a motherfucker. "What's that about?"

Riley frowned. "No clue."

Before any of them could move across the yard to stop whatever shit was about to fly, Seb shook his head, spat something harsh at Gray, and spun away from him, striding over to where Riley, Tate, and Dex were standing. His cheeks were flushed and his eyes were blazing.

"What the hell's going on?" Dex asked, the eldest-brother streak in him causing a V to form between his brows as he glared over at Gray, who was talking to the girl he'd arrived with.

"Nothing," Seb said before lifting his bottle of beer and draining it. "It's a party, and I'm getting shit-faced. Who's with me?" He cast an apologetic look at Tate, who smiled good-humoredly.

"Why not?" Dex said with a shrug. "This jet lag is already kicking my ass and a hangover tomorrow sounds all sorts of awesome." He wound his arm around Seb's shoulder and guided him toward where all the alcohol was sitting.

"Never a dull moment," Riley commented.

Tate snorted. "Drama, drama, drama."

•   •   •

The rest of the afternoon was perfect. Everyone had a great time, even Seb, who, after Gray and his girlfriend left, seemed to cheer up a little, although the way he was throwing back the Grey Goose and Red Bulls, he would be hurting the day after. Riley had tried to pull out of his brother just what the hell was going on, but he remained close-lipped, which was odd in itself.

Noah and Rosie played the day away. They had umpteen games of soccer before Park pulled out the small pool and the two of them (and a couple of adults) started splashing and throwing water around. Lexie stayed close to Riley for most of the day but let him wander and speak to the other guests, while also making an effort to speak to Riley's family. Joan seemed to be slowly warming back up to her, but Park was still frosty, kind of the way he was still being with Riley. Riley was slowly running out of ideas as to how he could ever gain his father's forgiveness.

At around 8 p.m., Dex and Seb and a few of Seb's friends decided they were going to take the party to a club somewhere. They got changed, booked a cab, and left. Riley was more than a little surprised that Dex had agreed. He was usually so sensible, and almost always the first to go to bed, but it was great seeing him cut loose. Maybe his trip away had shaken some of the pragmatism out of him.

With Maggie and Rosie having left an hour before, Noah was out cold on the sofa, the day's festivities finally catching up with him. Coming down the stairs from a bathroom break, and after checking on the little boy, Riley found Lexie in the kitchen, clearing up the plates and glasses and filling the dishwasher. She wiggled her hips from side to side along to the music that was still playing in the yard, where Riley's parents, Tate, Christine, and a few other stragglers were chatting and drinking.

Riley allowed himself to watch for a moment, enraptured by her ass and the way her waist twisted and curved. She was sexy as hell. He approached her quietly and reached out, placing his hands on her hips, making her jump.

"You scared me," she said with a small laugh.

He hummed in her ear and moved with her. "You look great." He breathed her in. "You smell great."

"You feel great," she said, placing the dish towel down and putting her hands over his.

"Our son is asleep."

"I know. It's late. I need to take him home."

"Can I come?"

She slowed her movement and turned to face him. Riley didn't step back and her chest pressed against his. She pushed her glasses up her nose. "You want to?"

He leaned closer and touched his mouth to hers, squeezing her waist as he did. "Yeah," he answered, nibbling on her bottom lip. "I want to."

Riley lifted his hand and cupped her face. "Let's go."

Riley had drunk too much to drive, but he was more than capable of lifting Noah from the sofa. The little boy was dead-weight, his small arms and legs flopping against Riley as he held him and placed him carefully into his car seat. Riley sat at his side, while Christine rode shotgun. Lexie dropped off her mother and, once Riley had picked a still sleeping Noah from his car seat, they made their way into the house. As was the routine that had slowly built up, Riley took Noah to bed, pulling off his small shoes and shorts and putting the sheet over him. He stood back for a minute watching his son sleep, bowled over by how perfect the kid was.

Riley made his way out of the bedroom to find Lexie standing at the top of the stairs.

"He okay?"

"Perfect," Riley answered.

They gazed at one another for what felt like a million years until, after taking a deep breath, Lexie walked over to him. She reached for his hand and pushed her fingers between his. "I'm so glad you're here, Riley."

"Me too," Riley breathed, his gaze tracing the delicate lines of her collarbone. He remembered just how sweet that part of her tasted.

"Do you want to do this?"

"This?"

"Us," she clarified. "Are you ready for that? For me?"

Riley held his breath a beat. "I think so." Her blue eyes traveled over his face. "I don't want anyone else," he added. "I don't want to *be* anywhere else at this moment."

"Good, because I want you. I've always wanted you." She kissed him then, with slow, warm kisses that caused the blood in Riley's body to pump through his veins faster than he could ever remember. She slowed her mouth on his. "Could you love me again?"

Her question made all the air in his lungs leave him in a rush. "Lexie," he gasped. "I never stopped loving you." He held her face, letting his lips whisper against hers. "I could no more choose to stop breathing than I could forget what I feel for you. And believe me, I tried. For years. But I can't." Lexie slumped in his arms. He could see the words behind her eyes and he was suddenly desperate to hear them. "Tell me," he whispered. "Tell me."

Her voice was hot and husky in his ear. "I love you. All the world."

"Lex." Her name on his lips was a curse, a promise, a goddamn plea, and she heard it, loud and clear.

With her hand still in his, she led him from the top of the stairs and down the hallway to her bedroom. Nerves and excitement thundered through Riley as he entered, turned, and watched Lexie close her bedroom door.

He swallowed in an effort to wet his throat. "Will he wake?"

She shook her head. "Not until six a.m." She reached for the hem of her dress and pulled it up and over her head, leaving her in nothing but her black underwear.

She was just as exquisite as he remembered. In fact, his memories had not done her justice. He'd known her body intimately since he was eighteen, and from teenager to young woman and to her now being a mother, he'd watched in amazement as parts of her softened and altered. Her skin was pale and clear, making the darkness of her nipples even more prominent. He was suddenly hit with the most erotic thought, that the breasts that he knew so well had fed their son. He moaned low in his throat when he remembered the texture of them on his own tongue.

"Let me see you," she whispered, both of them still, breathing heavily in the soft evening air breezing through the open window.

Oxygen shuddered from Riley's lungs as he reached over his

head and pulled his T-shirt up and off. The way Lexie's stare roamed down his chest, over his shoulders, to his hips made his eyes roll. She was four feet away, but he could feel every part that her gaze touched. She was first to move, her body lithe and gorgeous. She bridged the gap between them and Riley closed his eyes in anticipation of her touch. But it never came. Instead, she walked around him, coming to a stop at his back. She blew on the nape of his neck and he inhaled at the sensation.

"I'd almost forgotten how beautiful you are." Her mouth was just inches from his ear.

Riley jumped and sucked in a breath when her hands gripped his waist. They moved up slowly to his rib cage and she squeezed gently. He closed his eyes tightly, trying to calm his body down. It was an exercise in futility; he was about ready to fucking explode.

Lexie's hands moved up farther until her palms were pressed against his shoulder blades. She placed a gentle kiss on his spine and he groaned at the contact. Her lips were warm and felt so fucking good. Riley desperately wanted to turn so he could devour her, but her touch had him all but paralyzed. Her tongue flicked from his shoulder to his neck, and he clenched his fists tightly at his sides.

Lexie moved her arms under his, her fingertips skimming all the way down until she reached his jeans fly. He knew she could feel how hard he was for her as she took hold of the zipper and pulled it down, leaving the material gaping. Her hand snaked into the denim and Riley's entire body tensed while her other hand ghosted over his chest, circling his nipple. Riley panted.

"Jesus, Lex." He could feel her tits pressed against his back and ached to have them in his hands and mouth.

"I know." She moved slowly to stand in front of him, leaving her right hand behind him to trail across his ass before giving it a little squeeze. "It's overwhelming, isn't it?"

Without another word, Riley bent down slowly and let his

tongue flick Lexie's right nipple. She arched slightly and her hands gripped his hair. His tongue twisted and turned over her while his hands moved to her waist. Her skin burned under his palms and made Riley's entire body ignite with want. He lifted his head and moved to her left breast, repeating the movements of his tongue, flicking her, sucking her skin into his mouth tightly, reveling in her sounds of pleasure. He knew he was driving her insane, just as she was him.

Riley lifted his head and stood straight, their faces mere inches apart. He hummed as he licked his lips. "I love your taste." Her breath caught. "Let me see more." He grabbed the edge of her panties and pushed them down. She wobbled slightly. He put his arm quickly around her waist and held her tightly. "Easy, baby."

Her hands held his face. "I've thought about this for so long."

"About what?"

"You."

He pushed his nose to the side of hers. "What did you think about? Tell me."

"Your touch."

"Where?"

"Everywhere."

"Lex," Riley whispered. "Show me."

Without hesitation, she stepped back from his embrace and lowered her hand down her stomach, rubbing it gently over her hip. Riley watched her every move as he pushed his jeans and underwear down. He was unable to resist grazing a hand over himself—his hard-on was borderline painful—and heard Lexie suck in a quick breath.

He smiled, knowing from the look in her eye what she was about to do, and watched as she pressed her middle finger to her clit. *Fuck.* She rotated her finger a few times, whimpering, before her index finger joined the party. He could see how wet she was; her fingers moved so easily. Riley grunted and took a step toward her, imagining it was his hand or his cock that was making her feel that way. He wanted his mouth on her. He wanted to lick and taste her all over and then let her do the same to him.

He imagined his cock in her mouth and groaned louder.

With that thought, Riley tugged Lexie's hand away and lifted her off the floor, grabbing her under the knees and around her back. Her lips found his, frantic and hot, as he carried her over to the bed and laid her down, pushing his tongue into her mouth as he fell on top of her. Her fingers knotted deliciously in his hair and he panted into her mouth. Their movements were fast, disorganized, and impatient. His cock brushed over her heat repeatedly, their hips pushing against one another, frenzied and desperate.

Kissing her soundly, he pushed himself up onto his hands and shifted down her body. Using his fingers to spread her open, he took her clit between his lips and sucked, making her body buck under him. He laid his forearm across her stomach and licked and feasted on her like a starving man. Her wetness coated his face, filled his senses. He pushed his hips against the bed, needing something, needing anything, to ease the pressure.

"Coming!"

Yeah, Riley knew, and as soon as he pushed two fingers into her, she detonated around him. Riley closed his eyes, basking in the heat, wetness, and noise of her. She ground against his face, gasping, and whimpering for more.

"More, Lex?" he gasped, moving back up her body and kissing her neck. He tilted his hips, causing his full length to rub her.

"Yes," she answered, grabbing at his face and pulling it down to kiss him again.

"How do you want me?"

She stopped moving. "Inside. I want." She licked his neck, letting her tongue linger on his jaw. "You inside me. I'm so empty."

Riley's grip on her tightened and his entire body tensed. "Shit.

Can I— Do we need . . . I mean, can we?" He'd only ever gone without a condom once, and that had been with Lexie the night they conceived their son. He was always careful, but he wanted her to feel safe.

Lexie kissed his shoulder and moved her hands around his neck. "Yes. It's okay." She whispered the word like it was a secret between them. He moved his hips again and whispered her name. She moved her mouth back to his ear. "Fuck me, Riley."

As soon as the last letter of his name left her mouth, he spread her legs as wide as they would go and slammed into her. She cried out, wrapping her legs around him, locking her feet around his thighs. He groaned loudly against her shoulder. Then he pulled back and drove into her again, harder than before. "You feel so fucking good." And it was the truth. Of all the women he'd been with over the years, no one made Riley's spine burn or his cock pulse like Lexie.

Lexie grabbed his ass and squeezed as he began thrusting. Like oil, his words seemed to make her body slicker and wetter.

Goddamn. He slipped farther in; he was so deep inside her. "More," she called out before she leaned into his shoulder and bit him hard. He yelled but didn't stop moving, grabbing her face and kissing her as hard as he could, leading her tongue out of her mouth so that he could suck on it. Jesus *fucking* Christ, he couldn't get close enough. He needed more.

He groaned and gripped her hips harder.

"Yes." She moaned against him. "Give me more. I missed it. I missed you."

Riley pulled his hips back until he was almost out of her completely before crashing back into her, over and over. His mouth found her left tit again and sucked on it, biting and nibbling on the skin, before moving to the other. She dragged her nails down his back, then up again into his hair and to his face.

"Lex," he panted, his eyes half closed, "I'm close." He grabbed her wrists and slammed them to the bed before lifting her knees so that they were against his chest, letting him slide deeper.

She cried out his name, loud and beautiful, when his fingers found her clit and began playing her orgasm out of her. She rocked her hips in a way that he recognized and her pussy tightened around his cock. *Oh, thank God.* He never slowed, as his dick grew impossibly hard, knowing that watching and feeling Lexie come around him would catapult him into his own release.

"Come on, Lex. Please. Come." He dragged his mouth down her throat. He shook his head and bit his lip hard, scrunching his eyes closed, feeling his balls tighten and his stomach clench in warning. He was going to come so hard.

Lexie rocked her hips and tensed, as she started to chant his name. Riley's eyes shot open and he drove into her body so hard that she moved at least a foot up the bed. Unable to hold back any longer, he exploded inside of her, gripping her hips and bellowing loudly into the crease of her neck. She moved up and against him, his fingers never stopping on her clit until she arched her back and came with such force, her body almost pushed his out. She opened her mouth and moaned the most beautiful fucking sound Riley had ever heard. Blood thundered in his head as the pressure released from him into her.

Almost immediately, he collapsed on top of her, his head resting on her heaving chest as she breathed loud and fast. His hips finally slowed to long, languid strokes before he stopped altogether. Lexie placed her hand on his head and stroked her fingers through his hair. He was sure she would be able to feel his heart as it hammered behind his ribs.

He took a deep breath and blew it out of his cheeks. "Jesus, Lex. It's the same. Every time. *Every* time. I just . . ."

She snaked her arms around his neck. "I know. Perfect."

He lifted his head and smiled gently, anxiety skulking up his spine. It was usually at this point that the shutters came down in her eyes and she pulled back, pushing him away, and the thought that it might happen again terrified him. "Are we okay?"

She nodded and kissed him softly, letting her tongue graze his lips. "I've never been happier. I don't ever want to be without you again."

16

An hour later, hot, spent, naked, and deliriously happy, Lexie handed Riley the glass of cold juice she'd commandeered from the kitchen and crawled back into bed with him. He took a quick sip before he placed it on the bedside table. He kissed her forehead as she settled in next to his warm body. She wrapped her arms around his neck and pulled him closer, feeling her chest tighten at having him at her side again. The love, desire, passion, and yearning she felt could only be shown through the kiss she gave him when he smiled at her.

Holding his face, Lexie let her lips whisper over his, letting his breath enter her mouth. He sighed and moved closer, their tongues dancing together. His taste was incredible, and exactly as she recalled. Every aspect of their night together had been as good as she had imagined. As few bed partners as she'd had, Lexie knew that no one could or would ever fill her the way Riley did. Her body felt complete, nourished in a way that she only ever experienced with him.

She wrapped her arms tighter around his neck, trying not to think about the panic and hurt that had washed across his gaze when he asked if they were okay. Lexie knew she had only herself to blame and she hated it. She could only continue to reassure him; her body and heart craved him like nothing else. She bent her right knee, bringing it over his hip, and twisted her foot so it was between his legs, locking him against her. She moaned into his mouth when she felt his hard-on press against her thigh. There had never been anything as intense as the thought of her turning Riley on. It drove her insane with desire.

"I'm sorry," he murmured, dropping his lips to her neck.

"What for?" she asked, kissing his temple.

Lexie's heart stammered when he didn't answer. "Riley? What is it?" His eyes rested on the pillow at the side of her head. She ran her hands up his sides, letting her nails graze his skin up to his shoulders. A wave of goose pimples washed over his arms.

She kissed his cheek. "Please, talk to me. We have to talk. Whatever you're worried about, you can tell me."

The left side of his mouth rose. "You can't help, because it's you I'm worried about."

She raised her eyebrows, waiting for him to continue. Riley shifted slightly and Lexie exhaled when his cock rubbed her in the most perfect way. She locked her legs tighter around his thighs, trying her hardest to focus on what he needed to say instead of the insane need she had to take him inside her body again.

He smirked, seemingly knowing exactly where her mind was at. Lexie smiled. "Tell me." She traced an invisible circle on his back with her finger and he closed his eyes.

He sighed and placed both of his hands on either side of Lexie's face. "I don't want you to think that this," he motioned downward with his chin to where their bodies were pressed together, "is all I care about." His gaze was beautiful hazel and full of hope that she understood. "It's so important to me, being with you this way, but it isn't everything."

His caution was heartwarming. Lexie didn't want their reunion to be based on their ability to have amazing sex, either, but it had always been an integral part of who they were to each other. It was going to be a difficult balance, but Lexie knew they could achieve it.

"I don't." She continued to lift her legs slowly up his back so that her feet were resting on his ass. She fought the urge to push him into her and watched as he glanced from her mouth to her eyes and back again. "We can have both. We've done it before."

He closed his eyes, shook his head, and cleared his throat. "I'll always need you like this. I need you to understand that."

The fire that ignited in Lexie's stomach was scorching, deep, and it traveled around her body at lightning speed. Her skin burned and her breathing hitched. She crushed her lips to his at the same time that she pushed her feet against his ass, lifting her hips to meet him. He growled against her mouth as he slipped into her again.

"Riley," she panted, kissing his face, his neck, and his throat. "Want me, have me." She pulled her face from his and waited for him to open his eyes. "I'm yours."

His eyes widened and then he was kissing her again, desperate and hungry. He drove his hips and she bowed her back.

"Fuck." He moaned when she did it again, desperate for the release, *this* release that was building throughout her body. Riley ground against her hard and messy, sensing her need.

"So deep," she gasped.

He licked her from shoulder to ear. "I want to taste you," he panted, pushing into her farther. "Touch you."

Lexie felt her orgasm grow stronger with each syllable that came from his mouth. "Kiss you. Lex." She called out as her body began to pulse hard and relentlessly. He slammed into her one last time and they came together quickly, the sensation intense and scorching hot.

He bent his head back, closed his eyes, and through gritted teeth growled out his release. Lexie swiveled her hips, trying to make the pulses of her orgasm last as long as she could. Her whole body throbbed from head to foot and every space in between. She looked up at Riley. His eyes were still shut as he rode out the end of his own orgasm. Lexie felt her heart swell further. She loved him with a love that couldn't be expressed in words.

As their breathing began to settle and Lexie's heart slowed, his grip on her body loosened and he relaxed, slumping gently against her. He nestled his head under her chin. Lexie wrapped one arm around his shoulders and placed her other hand on his head, stroking his damp hair. The burn on her skin from his beard rubbing all over her was sexier than anything she'd ever felt, and feeling his weight on her was the most comforting feeling in the world. She felt safe, warm, and wanted.

"I need to sleep, but . . . Noah."

Lexie smiled. Yeah, that might be an awkward conversation if Noah came in for morning snuggles to find Riley there. "It's okay," she assured him. "I'll wake you."

They didn't speak again. They didn't need to.

Lexie simply listened to Riley's breathing as it slowed and settled into a sleeping rhythm, knowing that there was no place on Earth she'd rather be.

• • •

Even with his eyes closed, Riley had the weird feeling that he was being watched. He shifted into a small stretch, smiling when he felt Lexie snuggle closer into his side, her hand placed on his stomach, as she nuzzled his neck.

His eyes snapped open when he was poked in the cheek.

Noah stood at the side of the bed, hands behind his back, his shoulders moving back and forth.

Shit. Shit. Shit.

"Um, hey, buddy." Riley adjusted the covers of the bed, making sure nothing was on show.

Noah cupped a hand to the side of his mouth. "Did yous have a sleepover?" he whispered in that loud way kids seemed to do.

Riley smirked. "Yeah. You know, I was so tired after our busy day at the birthday party yesterday that I had to sleep here." It was half the truth. He *had* been tired. Lexie had then zapped any energy he'd had left over. Twice. *Christ.*

"With Mommy."

Riley cleared his throat. "Yeah." He glanced at the alarm clock: 6:45. "So have you been out in the car and picked up breakfast yet?"

"No, silly." Noah shook his head. "I's too small to drive. Mommy makes me cereals."

Riley chuckled. "Okay, man. How about we leave Mommy to sleep, you go downstairs, and I'll join you in two minutes and get you that cereal."

Noah grinned, turned, and ran out of the bedroom without a word spoken. Riley smiled at the sound of his little feet thundering down the stairs. He rolled over gently, making sure Lexie was still asleep. He kissed her softly and she mumbled something unintelligible before he carefully climbed out of bed and threw his clothes on.

Downstairs, he found Noah sitting on the edge of the sofa, feet dangling, watching a cartoon on TV. Riley leaned over the back of the couch. "So tell me, Noah, have you ever had pancakes?"

Wide hazel eyes met Riley's. "I loves pancakes."

"That's good news, because I make the best pancakes in the whole wide world. Wanna help me?"

Noah jumped up and barreled into the kitchen. Riley followed with a grin. "I'll take that as a yes." Noah was already pulling a small bright red step stool toward the fridge when Riley entered after him.

He stood on the steps and opened the fridge door, pointing inside. "Eggs and milk are in there."

Riley laughed softly. "You *do* know how to make pancakes."

"Yep. Grandma showeds me."

Riley grabbed out what he needed and laid it on the countertop. "Where does Mommy keep everything?"

Noah set about showing Riley where everything was and stood on his stool at Riley's side as Riley broke the eggs into a plastic bowl and added milk. "Okay, you're gonna be the head mixing man," Riley said seriously. He cocked an eyebrow. "Are you up to the challenge?"

Noah nodded enthusiastically. "Yes! I cans mix good!"

"Excellent." Riley handed him a silver-handled whisk and stood behind him, holding the bowl steady. "Get to it." Noah was certainly eager to make sure the eggs and milk were whisked well, and managed to get only a little of it on himself. "I'll give it one last mix," Riley offered when Noah's little arms eventually began to slow. Riley laughed when Noah leaned his back against Riley's chest and started making vowel sounds that shook as Riley whisked the eggs and milk hard. Naturally, Riley wobbled faster, so Noah laughed louder.

The two of them spent twenty minutes mixing and whisking, and Riley even allowed Noah to pour the batter into the hot pan, watching every move of his son like a hawk. Noah asked if they could put chocolate in the batter and, unable to say no, Riley allowed him to sprinkle some chocolate chips that he'd found in the pantry.

"Hey guys."

Riley and Noah both turned from the cooking pancakes to see a rumpled-looking Lexie standing in the doorway. Her hair was fastened back in a messy ponytail and even though she was only in a Michigan State T-shirt and gray sweats, Riley had never seen her look more perfect. He noted the red marks on her chin and neck where his beard had scruffed her and swallowed the growl that built in his throat.

"Mommy, we's making pancakes for your breakfast in bed," Noah explained while waving the plastic pancake flipper around. "Go back to sleep!"

Lexie smiled at Noah before she looked over at Riley. His stomach dipped, turned, and bloomed with warmth. "Hey," he murmured with a wink, loving the pink that washed over her cheeks.

"Hey. Can I help?"

"No, Mommy," Noah said with no little exasperation. "Sit downs!"

Riley and Lexie both chuckled before she poured them each a glass of orange juice and began setting the table with knives, forks, and syrup, as well as cutting some fruit to go with the pancakes. Riley carefully placed the cooked pancakes onto a plate and handed the plate to Noah, who, as though he was walking on a tightrope, took them to the table.

"Breakfast! Look. Riley and I mades them."

Lexie helped him with placing the plate on the table and pulled him into a hug. "Thank you, sweetheart. How lucky am I?"

Riley sat down next to Noah and served him two pancakes. "Eat up, buddy. Best pancakes in the whole wide world."

"*All* the world," Noah replied, helping himself to a spoonful of strawberries. Riley stared at his son for a few beats, feeling Lexie's gaze on him, as Noah's words echoed around the three of them. Riley leaned over and kissed Noah's temple.

"You're awesome," Riley told him. It was as close to "I love you" as Riley was willing to risk saying to Noah without confusing him, even though Riley wanted to shout it from the rooftops.

"You's awesome," Noah snickered around a forkful of pancake.

Riley smiled and lifted his juice, looking over its rim at Lexie. "You okay?" Lexie nodded. "Is this—are you all right? Sorry, I . . . fell asleep." His gaze slid to Noah, then back.

She exhaled a laugh. "Don't worry. It's fine. More than fine. I forgot to set an alarm." She chewed her pancake. "Besides, it was lovely to have a sleepover."

"Cans Riley sleep over again in my room?" Noah asked before throwing a strawberry into his mouth, his face earnest. Riley smirked as he ate his pancakes, leaving Lexie to answer *that* gem of a question.

Lexie cleared her throat and shifted on her chair. "Um . . . well, I'm not sure he'd fit in your bed, honey. And he certainly can't sleep on your floor."

Noah and Riley looked at each other and laughed. "You's silly, Mommy."

"Yeah, Mommy," Riley commented with a snort. "You're silly."

He only just managed to dodge the strawberry Lexie threw. "So, do you have plans for today?" she asked with a smile.

Riley shrugged. "Nothing important. You?"

She shook her head. "Jaime's watching the store. I thought we could hang out. Maybe go into town. Maybe go back to Long Lake."

Noah kneeled up on his chair, syrup dribbling down his chin. "Cans we go to the lakes and ride a boat this time?"

Riley leaned closer to Noah. "Sounds great."

After all three of them had helped to tidy the kitchen, Lexie gave Noah permission to watch two episodes of *Dora the Explorer*, leaving her and Riley alone. Seeing Noah run off to the living room, Riley moved quickly, taking Lexie's face in his hands and kissing her hard. Lexie gasped and grabbed the back of his head, holding him close. Riley could smell himself on her. She *smelled* of him. Fuck, she smelled of him all over her. He pushed her against the counter and began to lose himself in her all over again when the sound of Noah's laughter from the living room brought him back to reality.

Their mouths broke apart, but their bodies remained pressed together. "I'm sorry," he breathed. "I just had to do that."

"Riley, don't apologize," she replied, running her hands down his face. She looked at him in a way that caused Riley's knees to weaken. "God, it's so good having you here."

Riley kissed her again. He hugged her and buried his nose in her neck. "Listen, I need to call a cab, go home, and change."

"I can take you."

"No, it's okay. I'll come back and pick you both up in a couple of hours."

Lexie nodded. "We'll be here."

•   •   •

Back at his parents' house, Riley showered and changed. Looking at himself in the mirror as he combed his hair, he noticed how he looked a little different, lighter somehow, less tired. Riley prided himself on being cheerful and positive, but just recently, in light of everything that had happened, he'd seemed to have lost sight of that. Now, he finally felt like himself again.

He thumped down the stairs to find his mom and dad in the kitchen. He opened the fridge and grabbed a bottle of water.

"Just you? Where is everybody?"

"Sebastian and Dex didn't come home until after four a.m.," Joan answered. "They're still in bed. Tate's sitting in the yard with his coffee."

"Party animals," Riley commented with a smile as he looked out of the window to see Tate, who lifted his cup in greeting.

"At least they made it home last night," Joan said. "Unlike you."

Riley laughed loudly and turned to look at his mother. "Jesus, Mom, the year nineteen ninety-eight called, and it wants its conversation back." Park snorted behind his newspaper at the same time Joan rolled her eyes.

"I was just wondering if you were okay," she argued. "No need to be like that."

Riley chuckled and moved to wrap an arm around his mom as he kissed her cheek. She pushed him away but couldn't hide her smile. "I'm fine," he told her. "Great, actually." Joan nodded slowly. He noted the unease in her gaze. "Look, I know you're worried, but, honestly, Lex and I are good. We've talked a lot and we both want to make it work. I'm flying back to New York tomorrow, I'm sure we'll talk more when I get back."

Joan's eyes lit up. "Does that mean you'll be moving back here?"

Riley sighed. Wasn't that the million-dollar question? He'd thought so much about how he was going to figure out being with Lexie and Noah full time, but the numbers just didn't add up. He had some savings, and, of course his cut in O'Hare's, although he was reluctant to cash that in and preferred keeping it as a long-term investment. He knew his parents would support him, but that wasn't fair. Besides, he was nearly thirty years old; he had to stand on his own two feet. His parents had already done so much for him over the past few weeks.

Joan cupped his cheek. "You know we'll help. Won't we, Park?"

Riley's father simply looked over at them. Riley held up a hand. "It's all right. I promise. I'll get my shit together and I'll be fine. I'm sure there's a company of some description out there who'd want me and not care that I have a record."

Joan tilted her head and pressed her lips together. "It'll work out, sweetheart."

• • •

"So I'm not going to be able to come back on Friday," Riley uttered on the phone before dropping down onto his apartment sofa and rubbing a palm across his forehead.

The slight pause before she answered alerted Riley to Lexie's disappointment. "Is everything all right?"

"It's the shop; two of the guys are off sick and we're ridiculously busy, which is great, but I can't leave Max in the shit." He exhaled despondently. "I'm sorry."

"Hey, it's fine." There was a small smile in her voice. "I'm sad you won't be here, but I understand. It can't be helped."

Riley slumped back in his seat. "Do you want me to tell Noah?"

"No need. I haven't told him when you're arriving. He bugs me stupid if I do: 'Is it time yet? Is Riley coming yet?'" They both laughed. "So don't worry. Do you have any idea when you might be here?"

"Maybe Tuesday? I don't know, Lex. It depends on how fast we can get these cars done." He kicked a foot out toward his coffee table, frustrated and pissed. "I miss you both, Lex. I . . . really needed to see you."

"We miss you, too, but you'll be here before you know it. We're not going anywhere."

Riley grinned. "Is Noah there?"

"No, he's with Sav getting some frozen yogurt. I'll tell him you called."

"Tell him I'll speak to him tomorrow."

"I will, and Riley?"

"Yeah?"

"All the world."

.   .   .

"Cheer up, man. You look like you finally realized Robin was Batman's twink."

Riley rolled his eyes at Tate's lame-ass joke and stabbed a piece of penne pasta with his fork. "Why do I even agree to hang out with you when you're here?" he muttered with a shrug.

"It's my sunny disposition, obviously," Tate deadpanned, watching a pretty waitress move past their table. "Which is more than can be said for your miserable face."

"Leave me alone," Riley grumbled. "Let me sulk."

Tate chuckled. "Well, you do it so well."

It was true. Riley had been moping for a full week. Each day he was supposed to be in Michigan and wasn't, felt, despite the chaos at O'Hare's, like a fucking year, making it even more torturous being away from Noah and Lexie. He spoke to them both every day, FaceTiming and Skyping so he could see their faces, but it still didn't fill the void in his heart. It was horrible and, honestly, Riley couldn't figure out how it was going to change.

"You know, I could lend you some cash if you need it," Tate offered, his face open and sincere. "I have my injury and discharge money. Pay me back when you can."

Ordinarily, Riley would have jumped at such an offer, but he knew that a loan would only help in the short term. He needed a job, a fixed income, before he moved back to Michigan. He had a son to provide for, after all.

"Thanks, man. I really appreciate that, but I need to find some damn employment first."

And he'd looked. Finding that there were very few mechanic jobs, he'd started putting out feelers for other things—most of which he was overqualified for, though hell, he'd try anything— but his record made it more than a little difficult to convince anyone, irrespective of his NYU degree, that he was capable and honest.

"You know, you could always bite the bullet and ask Dad," Tate said hesitantly.

Riley shook his head. "Dad can't afford to lend me money any more than—"

"I don't mean to lend you money, Ri. I mean for work."

Riley paused for a brief moment and swallowed his forkful of food. He exhaled and rubbed the spot between his eyebrows, which had been throbbing a lot lately. "He doesn't want me working for the business, Tate. That ship sailed long ago."

"Have you asked?"

"I don't have to," Riley replied. "I've been flying back and forth for months, and he still barely utters six words to me at a time."

"Stubborn old man," Tate grumbled. "It was always the plan years ago: having you take over when he retired. He *needs* someone like you there, someone who truly knows the business inside out, especially now that he's under doctor's orders to take it easy."

Riley was in full agreement, but he knew damned well that his father would never offer him a position at his business after Riley had let him down so badly with being sent to Kill. Riley knew Park and, while his mother considered it unnecessary to keep punishing Riley for his stupid decisions, the man could hold a grudge like it was his job.

"If I'm still struggling for something at the end of the month, I'll ask," Riley offered, even though the thought alone made his stomach roil. "He can only say no, right?"

"Right," Tate agreed through a mouthful of bread. "So you're definitely going to make a go of it with Lex, huh?"

Riley nodded. "When I'm with the two of them I feel like I belong, ya know? It makes sense."

Tate nodded, appearing happy for his brother. "You deserve to be happy, Ri. Just make sure she treats you right."

Riley nodded. "I will. It feels different this time. Like the timing is just right. Who would have thought six months ago I'd be going back to Michigan to be with Lexie and my son."

Tate coughed a laugh. "Not I, man. Not I."

"It blows my mind."

"And Noah knows who you are now?"

"Not yet. Lexie and I had planned to sit him down and explain, but with me not being there it could be fucking Christmas at this point."

"It all happens for a reason, dude. Roll with it."

Riley sighed and sat back in his seat. "I'm trying."

It was later that evening when he was on the phone with Noah that Riley relaxed a little. Hearing his son so excited his lisp made his words bump into one another erased all the stress of the past few days and wrapped around Riley like a warm hug.

"Ands we played on the slide again!" Noah exclaimed, his voice becoming quiet, then loud, as though his mouth was moving to and from the receiver.

"Sounds awesome, man," Riley said with a laugh. "I wish I could have been there."

"Whens you coming back home?"

The word "home" reverberated around Riley's heart, squeezing it until he feared it would burst. It struck him how he was feeling the exact same way he had the first time he moved to New York to begin at NYU: he was homesick.

"As soon as I can, buddy," he replied through a thick throat. "I promise."

"Pinkie promise?"

Riley smiled. "Pinkie promise." Noah giggled in that adorable way of his. "Can I speak to your mommy now?"

"Sure. Mommy? Riley wants you."

"I'll see you soon, Noah, okay?"

"Okays."

Lexie's laughter came onto the line. "Hey."

"Hey, beautiful." It was fucking crazy how hearing a voice could make everything better. "Sounds like you've had a fun day."

"He's so pumped up on sugar I'll never get him to sleep, which is not great considering I have a jewelry event tonight."

"Did you tell me about that?"

"No, it's last minute, I only found out—Noah, stop doing that, please, and go and put your jammies on—earlier today. Sav's being a diamond and babysitting for me. I'm not as prepared as I would have liked, but there may be a few opportunities for new business."

"That's great. You'll kill it."

"Thank you." She blew out a slow breath. "I was wondering if you'd do me a favor."

"If you ask nicely."

"With all your business know-how, I was hoping you'd have a look at my proposals for how I could expand Love, You. Maybe online or a new shop. I haven't ironed out the details yet, but what do you think? I'd pay you, of course."

Riley was silent for a beat. "I'd be happy to. But you really don't need to pay me, Lex."

"Yes, I do. This is business."

Riley smiled. "Okay."

"Thank you. I miss you."

"A few more days and I'll be there," Riley promised. "Jesus, I can't wait to see you."

"Me too." They were both quiet for a brief moment, their longing for one another deafening down the line. "Look, I'm sorry. I've gotta go and get ready, but first I need to make sure your son isn't climbing the walls. I'll text you later."

Riley snickered. "Be safe tonight."

He ended the call and threw his cell phone onto the sofa, hating the silence of his apartment and the fact that Savannah was babysitting his son. It was so damned unfair. "Fuck this," he snarled, pushing himself up from his seat and storming to the freezer. He opened it and pulled out the bottle of Grey Goose he kept for emergencies, such as now when he was feeling like a useless fucking loser. He poured three fingers, tossed in some ice, and made his way back to the cupboard to pull out a Red Bull. There were none. "Shit."

He was pulling on his Vans to go to the corner store when his phone buzzed. He reached over for it, smiling at the photo Lexie had sent of Noah blowing a kiss to the screen. His Batman pajamas were the coolest Riley had ever seen. The message from Lexie beneath it read *Goodnight Daddy xx*

Riley texted back: *Goodnight. All the world. xx*

He pressed send and, after grabbing his keys, headed out to the store to get some Red Bull and maybe some more vodka. It was going to be a long-ass night.

. . .

Lexie awoke with a start, sitting upright in her bed. Her pulse raced and her hands shook with the remnants of a dream she couldn't quite remember, though she knew that it scared her to death.

She rubbed a shaky hand down the side of her face. "Jesus."

In her disoriented state, she sluggishly realized her cell phone was vibrating angrily from its spot on the side table with a number she didn't recognize. Lexie looked at the digital clock. It was almost midnight. Two heartbeats passed before she grabbed at the damned thing, losing her grasp on it twice before she managed to pick it up, the faces of Savannah, her mother, then Riley flashing through her mind.

"Hello?" Her whole body froze when there was no immediate answer. *"Hello?"*

"Lexie?"

Oh, God . . .

"Who is this?"

"Lexie. It's Carter."

She clambered out of bed, raising her voice. "Carter, what's wrong? What is it? Is it Riley? Is it—?"

"Lexie, just listen to me a minute, okay? I'm arranging a plane to bring you to JFK in the next hour. Joan is going to meet you at the airport there in Michigan. I have the details here that you need to write down."

"Wait. What? Joan is . . . Why do I need to come to New York?" Her heart clenched. "Where's Riley?"

"I can explain everything when you're on the plane."

"Tell me now!" Lexie cried, her panic all but choking her. "Tell me, where is he?"

Carter paused before he spoke again. "Lexie, Riley's in the hospital. There's been an accident."

17

Lexie sprinted hard across the hospital parking lot. The pounding of her feet against the asphalt ricocheted through her entire body, making her bones shake and shudder. Sweat prickled her brow while the adrenaline and fear coursing through her veins like nitro kept her heart pumping and her tear ducts dry. And thank God for that. She had to move, keep going, keep the dark thoughts of what might be at arm's length before she fell apart.

She dodged slow-moving cars and even slower people, cursing and frantic in her effort to get to the automatic doors of the hospital, which opened slowly, catching Lexie's shoulder as she barged her way through. Joan was behind her somewhere, hurrying just as Lexie was. There were people everywhere in the ER, bleeding and holding limbs that looked worryingly out of shape, but she couldn't have cared less. There was only one person she cared about, one person she needed to get to.

She shoved her way toward the nurses' station, breathless and bedraggled.

"Riley," she panted loudly to any one of the four people standing behind it. The nurse, sitting at a computer, looked up in alarm.

"Riley," she repeated. "I'm here . . . his mother and I got a call a few hours ago from Wesley Carter."

The nurse's face softened. "Okay, honey, calm down. Do you have a full name for me?"

Lexie nodded and swallowed. The back of her throat burned. "Riley Lincoln Moore." Joan appeared at her side, breathless and pale. "There was some kind of car accident," Lexie added. "He was hit . . . hit by a car. We were told he was in surgery."

The nurse's face changed infinitesimally, and Lexie's stomach was immediately rolling. She'd seen enough TV in her life to recognize that fucking expression. The look sent a spear of frozen fear through her body, buckling her knees and suffocating her chest.

"No," she whispered, gripping the desk. She turned to look at Joan, whose face crumpled and fell. A buzzing sound began in Lexie's ears, deep and loud.

"Sweetheart, it's all right," the nurse said softly, reaching out.

"Alexis," Joan urged. "Breathe."

But Lexie was unreachable. She was quickly falling into blackness, covered only by the animalistic yell that ripped from her throat as she staggered back and lost herself to its embrace.

.   .   .

Lexie awoke slowly, wrapped in a warm blanket, her head resting on a thin pillow. She blinked once, twice, before she shot upright, dazed and utterly discombobulated.

"It's all right," came a soft voice from behind her.

Lexie turned to see Joan. Despite the small smile, her face was drawn, and the lines under her eyes were dark and tired. Seeing her look the way she did made Lexie gasp for breath.

"Is he all right? Can I see him?"

Joan sighed and placed her palms on the silver rails of the gurney Lexie was lying on. She'd feel embarrassed about passing out later.

"The police are here." She licked her lips and exhaled. "They've told me what they know. Riley was crossing the street and was hit by a car. The driver was drunk. He didn't see Riley until it was too late. They've arrested him."

Lexie cupped her hands to her mouth. "Oh God."

"Riley's been in surgery for three hours already, but they won't tell me anything else."

"Is he going to be okay?"

Joan shook her head. "I don't know. I honestly don't know." She bit her lip and wiped a finger under her eyes. "Tate's here. He was in town. Seb and Dex are on their way, but they might not get here for a few more hours. Carter is trying to do all he can."

Lexie shuffled to the edge of the gurney and carefully placed her feet onto the floor, not knowing for sure whether her legs would hold her up. They did. For now.

"He's strong," she whispered, suddenly aware that she had to pull herself together and support Joan as much as she could. She was Riley's mother, for God's sake; Park was still unable to travel, which was why he was back in Michigan; and, if the tables were turned and it was Noah who was in surgery, Lexie had no idea what she would do. Without a word, she wrapped her arms around Joan and pulled her in for a hug.

Joan all but collapsed into the embrace and wept onto Lexie's shoulder. Lexie shushed her quietly and held her close. "He's strong," she repeated, praying to God that it was the truth.

.   .   .   .   .

Lexie placed her arm around Joan's shoulder and held her to her side as they began making their way to the waiting room. When they entered, they found Tate, Carter, Kat, and Max sitting together, all of them looking as terrified as Lexie felt.

Kat stood as soon as she saw Lexie and moved toward her. "Are you okay?" she asked, hugging her tightly.

"I'm okay," Lexie answered as she watched Joan move to sit with Tate, who wrapped an arm around her. Lexie looked over at Carter. "Thank you so much," she said. "Really. Thank you for organizing the plane and—"

He held a hand up. "It's all right. It was the least I could do."

Lexie looked over at Max, who looked like he wanted to be anywhere else but in a hospital waiting room. His leg jumped up and down while he chewed the hell out of his thumbnail. "Where's Grace?"

"West Virginia," he answered quickly.

Lexie allowed Kat to move her to a seat and sat down. "Who has Noah?" Kat asked.

"My mom and sister," Lexie answered. "I didn't want him here, in case . . ."

Carter's hand on hers made Lexie look up. "He's gonna be okay," he offered.

"Yeah," Kat said, her voice small and uncertain. Carter kissed his wife's temple as though trying to calm her.

Lexie nodded, but she was unable to shake the horrible helpless feeling that had clung to her ever since she'd woken in bed. What the hell would she do if she lost Riley? It would be her biggest fear realized, and what kind of bitch was fate to bring them back to each other and then rip him away again?

She placed her palms to her face and tried to breathe, knowing that tears would do nothing to help Riley now. She just had to pray that, as he'd said, he'd find his way back to them all. To her.

. . .

The minutes moved sluggishly, every one of them a moment where Riley was in surgery, another moment where he might never come back. Lexie tried to distract herself from her darker thoughts by getting coffee or trying to talk to Riley's friends, but it wasn't enough. Time ticked on with no word or assurance that Riley was going to be okay.

Lexie was standing, looking out the waiting room window, when Tate moved to her side. Riley's older brother had been more than a little cool with her since he found out that they were trying to make a go of it again, and that was fine. In the years Lexie had known Tate, she knew he and Riley were the closest of the four brothers. She knew how protective Tate was, how loyal, and with that in mind, she reached out a hand and took his, squeezing once before she let go.

Tate looked over at her, his expression one of surprise, before he dipped his chin. A silent thank you that warmed Lexie's heart. "Will we hear something soon?" she asked, hoping that his being an MD would give him more insight into what the hell was going on.

"Riley had some internal bleeding, some . . . broken bones and fractures. He was pretty banged up. They'll spend their time making sure that the bleeding has stopped before they do anything else."

Lexie nodded, but no words came. That all sounded horrific and scary, but she wouldn't allow herself to let it pull her under. No way. She had to be strong. Before she could say anything anyway the door of the waiting room opened with a creak, and a familiar head peeped around its edge.

"Sebastian," Joan breathed, lifting from her seat and moving to her youngest son. Seb was followed by Dex, the pair of them shell-shocked and scruffy. Tate made his way across the waiting room and the four of them formed a circle, arms around one another, words of love being muttered quietly. Joan lifted her head and looked over at Lexie.

"Come over here, Alexis."

"Oh, no, it's okay," Lexie assured her. "You have your moment."

"This is a family moment," Joan countered. "And you are a part of this family."

What the hell could Lexie say to that? She pressed her lips together and as Seb and Joan dropped their arms, she moved between them, allowing their love and warmth to seep into her and fill her with all the strength she knew she needed, the strength the family had continually given her over the years, even when Lexie hadn't realized it.

As they slowly broke apart, the door of the waiting room

opened again. Lexie looked up to see a stout, middle-aged man with pockmarked skin and blue scrubs standing in the doorway. A younger man with blond hair and an arrogant swagger followed.

"Mrs. Moore?" the older doctor inquired.

Joan nodded, as the walls of the room seemed to bend and expand in anticipation and panic. All of Riley's friends stood behind his family and Lexie. They must have seemed like quite the group.

"I'm Dr. Hunt," the doctor continued. "I operated on your son, Riley."

Lexie's heart leaped from her chest to her throat. "How is he?" she blurted without thought.

Dr. Hunt glanced at Lexie briefly before looking at Joan, who nodded in acquiescence. "Riley suffered extensive internal bleeding," he said gently. "There was some blunt-force trauma to his chest, which resulted in some broken ribs and a collapsed lung. There was also some damage to his pelvis. He broke his leg in three places, as well as sustaining a fractured skull."

"Is he *alive*?" Dex asked through gritted teeth.

Dr. Hunt looked over at Dex and crossed his arms over his chest. "Yes, he's alive." Lexie reached out for Joan's hand, gripping onto her tightly as her legs shook. "He was very lucky," the doctor added. "I stemmed the bleeding, reinflated his lung, and an orthopedic surgeon pinned his leg. He's been taken up to recovery as he awakes from the anesthesia and then he'll be moved to ICU."

Seb cupped a weary hand over his mouth. "Can we see him?"

Doctor Hunt shook his head. "Not yet. Get some rest. You can see him in the morning."

"He's going to be okay?" Joan asked.

He raised his eyebrows in quiet respect for his patient. "He's strong. He's a fit, healthy young man. There's nothing to say after some physiotherapy that he won't make a full recovery, but head injuries can be funny things. We'll be watching him very closely for the next twenty-four hours."

"Thank you, Doctor," Tate uttered.

Dr. Hunt turned, but Lexie stopped him with a palm on his forearm.

"Thank you," she whispered. "Thank you so very much."

The doctor nodded. "You're welcome."

18

The intensive care unit of the hospital was unnervingly quiet, save for the occasional beeping of the machines that, in many cases, were keeping their patients alive. Lexie followed a nurse down a long, deserted corridor toward Riley's room.

The nurse stopped at the door and turned. "Dr. Hunt said no longer than ten minutes."

"I know," Lexie answered. "I'll be on the button, I promise."

The nurse smiled and walked away, leaving Lexie standing awkwardly, not moving. The rest of Riley's family were in the waiting room, even Park, who had, unbeknownst to Joan, booked a flight and arrived early that morning. Lexie had stayed at Riley's apartment—Tate had a key—along with his brothers and parents. It had been quite the tight fit, but comforting all the same.

Lexie clasped the door handle firmly before pushing it open. At first, she kept her eyes trained on the floor, unable to look up. She was so afraid of what she would see, despite Joan and Seb insisting that Riley looked okay. Gathering herself took a few moments. Gradually, she lifted her eyes to the bed at the far side of the room and, as though sucked out by a vacuum, all the air in her lungs disappeared.

Riley lay on his back, eyes closed with induced slumber, wires and tubes sticking out from his chest, arms, and mouth. As Dr. Hunt had explained, Riley was on a ventilator. Lexie watched it rise and fall in synchronicity with his chest. His heart was beating loud and clear, each beep of the monitor a beautiful siren reassuring her that he was, in fact, alive.

Lexie walked toward the bed slowly, quietly. She looked him over, searching for any signs of the horrific trauma that he had been through, and saw nothing but a small smear of dried blood on his right arm. Pulling a tissue from her pocket, Lexie wet it with the tip of her tongue and wiped the blood away. She pressed her hands to his skin, feeling warmth and softness. His hair was messy and his mouth appeared stuck in his perfect smirk as the ventilator tube pulled to the left side. A large white bandage covered and wrapped around his chest, a small tube protruding through it, but Lexie couldn't look at that for long. The terror of what lay beneath it was still too raw for her. She breathed deeply and let her palm whisper down the side of his face. He was so damned beautiful.

She smiled wistfully. "I'm here," she whispered.

Lexie's eyes filled with tears when she realized that, stupidly, she'd expected a response from him. He was never quiet. Never. He always had something to say, something crass, funny, or colorful. She loved that about him, how he spoke so freely, so truthfully.

She smiled to herself. Who was she kidding? She loved everything about him. Her heart stammered, seemingly knowing that its other half was so close, but so far away. He was the missing piece to her, her soul mate, her best friend, the father of her child. Living without him was simply not an option.

Fate had kept them apart for so long. She had only just found him again. To lose him now . . .

Halting her thoughts abruptly, Lexie let her fingertips dance up the ink on his arm, curving to his muscular shoulder. He felt so sturdy and tough under her touch, yet he lay utterly vulnerable and helpless. She leaned closer to him, running her fingers through the front of his hair. It felt so soft.

"You get better," she said quietly, near his ear, pushing her hand into his and squeezing with every word. "You hear me? You get better."

She placed a tender kiss on his forehead. This time, with his scent and the familiar tingling of her flesh touching his, there was no stopping the tears.

"I love you, Riley," she whimpered against his skin. "God, I love you so much. I need you." She collapsed against him, burying her face into his neck. "Don't you leave me," she begged. "Please. Don't you leave me."

She prayed to God that he could hear her.

•   •   •

For the next week, Lexie spent her time either sitting in the hospital waiting room anticipating news on Riley or with Noah, who had arrived with Christine three days after Riley's accident. She split the nights between staying at Riley's apartment and Carter's place, where Riley's brothers and parents had taken lodging at Carter's insistence. Having Noah around, playing, cooking, and bathing him, kept Lexie's mind occupied, especially considering how excited Noah was to be back in New York. He was, however, confused as to where Riley was and why they were staying in his place when he wasn't there.

"Riley isn't well, baby," she'd explained the first night they were in the apartment. "He's in the hospital."

Noah frowned. "He has the chicken spots like I hads?"

"No." Lexie had been unable to think quickly enough, wondering what the best thing to say was. She figured the truth was the most important. "He was in an accident, but he's getting better."

Noah thought for a moment. "Shall we gets him a present to make hims feel better?"

Lexie kissed his forehead. "I think that would be a great idea."

"I cans draw him a picture," Noah exclaimed, shuffling off the edge of the sofa and running toward his bag of tricks that Lexie knew contained his Spider-Man doodle pad and crayons. He lifted the two items, laid them on the coffee table, and looked around himself before he set to drawing.

"What are you going to draw?" she asked, watching him.

"Long Lake when we saileds on the boat."

Lexie smiled, remembering what a wonderful day that had been. "That was fun, huh?"

Noah nodded. "The best."

The phone ringing from its place on the wall had Lexie jumping from her seat. She picked up the receiver, heart in her mouth. "Hello?"

"Lexie?" It was Joan.

"Hey. Everything okay?"

"Riley's awake."

•   •   •

Joan and Dex were at the hospital when Lexie arrived. "Where's Noah?" Joan asked.

"With my mom," Lexie replied. "I thought it best to keep him away until we know what's going on. I didn't want him to be scared." Joan nodded. "You've seen him?"

"All he did was ask for you and Noah."

Lexie looked toward the doctor. "How long can I stay?"

Dr. Hunt smiled. "Take your time."

Lexie smiled back gratefully and walked into Riley's room. The heart monitor was still beeping in the corner of the room, but the scary tube that was in his chest the last time Lexie had seen him was now gone. The bandage around his head was smaller, and there were fewer wires stuck in him. He was asleep; his breaths through the oxygen mask on his face were deep and beautiful. Lexie walked toward the side of the bed and placed a gentle hand over his. She leaned over and kissed his forehead.

"I'm here," she whispered.

Riley's eyes moved under the lids, as Lexie continued to whisper secret words of love until, with one slow blink, they opened. Only a half centimeter, but they opened. They were crusty, tired, and confused, but they were beautiful.

"There you are," she said softly as the backs of her fingers whispered down his face.

Riley looked at her through his lashes and tired eyes, and the side of his mouth twitched. Lexie grabbed his hand and squeezed. "I'm here." She kissed his knuckles and placed his hand against her cheek. "I'm going to look after you. I'm not going anywhere, I promise."

She felt him pull on her hand weakly, gesturing toward the oxygen mask. "Is it uncomfortable?" She gently tried to readjust the elastic straps that pressed against Riley's face. "Wait a second," Lexie muttered as she pulled the mask down to his chin, worrying immediately if Doc Hunt was about to barge in and go ballistic. "What is it?" she asked quickly. "Does something hurt? Do you want me to call the nurse?"

Riley shook his head again and pointed to his mouth. Lexie leaned closer, struggling to hear the words he was pushing through his lips. He gasped a breath and his face pinched in pain. His voice was quiet and hoarse. "Lex."

Lexie smiled. "Yeah, baby. I'm here."

Riley swallowed with a grimace and paused. "Pinkie promise."

Lexie felt her eyes sting. She squeezed his hand tighter and nodded.

Riley closed his eyes. "Kiss."

She moved closer and placed a soft kiss on his warm, dry lips.

And it felt so wonderful, so perfect.

She breathed a long breath down her nose, feeling Riley's mouth lift into a small smile.

Pulling back slowly, she carefully placed the mask back onto his face and sat on the edge of his bed. "I missed you."

"Stay."

Lexie smiled and ran a hand over his hair. "Forever."

*   *   *

It had been two days since Riley had awoken, entirely discombob-ulated, in a hospital bed with every inch of his body feeling as if a Mack truck had plowed into it.

Plowed, dragged, and reversed. This apparently wasn't too far from the actual truth. He hadn't seen the car that hit him when he'd crossed the road to get some Red Bull for his vodka. He didn't remember anything but waking up to see a nurse and a doctor, and then his parents and brothers. As good as it had been to see them all, he'd only wanted to see Lexie and Noah.

Needless to say, he was feeling decidedly tender and the con-stant soreness in his chest, head, and leg had him pressing the pain relief button on a regular basis. He'd tried to underplay it to the doctors, nurses, and even Lexie, but the truth was, every breath and movement was a struggle that left a sheen of sweat on his face.

When he awoke that morning, he'd panicked a little when he realized that neither Lexie nor his family were there. A helpful nurse had informed him that Lexie had gone to take a shower and get a change of clothes, leaving Riley feeling guilty at wanting Lexie there twenty-four/seven. He knew from what Tate and his mom had told him that she'd been there almost constantly. She hadn't left his side since he'd woken up, not for one moment, and Riley knew she was exhausted. Dark circles rimmed her eyes and she looked like she needed to eat a good meal, but dammit if she wasn't still the most beautiful thing he'd ever seen.

The door to his room opening pulled Riley from his thoughts of Lexie and Noah. It was his dad. "Hey, son."

"Hey, Dad."

He hadn't spoken to Riley all that much, but Riley knew his father had been at the hospital almost as much as his mother, which meant a hell of a lot.

Park looked him over. "Spent a lot of time in hospitals just recently, haven't you?

Riley exhaled a wry laugh. "Too much."

"How are you feeling?" Park asked, his tone firm but sensitive.

Riley didn't answer immediately. The truth was he was sore; parts of him that he didn't realize he had ached.

"Look at me, Riley." Riley obeyed his father instantly, knowing that no-nonsense voice from when he was a kid. "If you're hurting, tell the doctors. Is your vision okay? Your head isn't hurting, is it?"

"A little."

"Do you want me to get the nurse?"

"No, Dad, I'm okay." Riley glanced toward the door. "Where's Mom?"

"She'll be along in a bit." Park wandered toward Riley's bed and sat down on the nearest chair. He exhaled and cleared his throat before he steepled his hands and pressed them against his lips, staring at Riley in that intense way of his. "I find myself . . . torn here, Riley," he offered.

Riley frowned. "What is it? Are you okay?"

"I'm fine. It's you I worry about." He dropped his hands. "I've always worried about you." He shook his head and looked to the floor. "If you'd . . . Jesus, son."

Riley sat back, a little struck by the curve in conversation. "I'm all right, Dad. The doctor says I could be home in less than a week."

"I know," Park said, nodding, "but it's my job to worry. I'm your father." He sighed. "Out of the four of you, you were always the most sensitive, the most eager to please. You made choices dependent on other people. Your optimism and your selflessness are your best traits, Riley. You think about everyone else before you think of yourself."

"Apart from that one time, huh?" Riley lifted the side of his mouth. It was a risk making light of his time in jail, but he was sick of dancing around the issue.

Park nodded. "Apart from that one time."

Riley sighed. "I am sorry, Dad. I don't know what more I can say or how many times I can say it. I—it was a stupid thing to do."

Park huffed and crossed his arms over his chest. "I don't want to hear you apologize. You did enough of that. And with you being here now . . . I—I know I've not been easy on you."

"I disappointed you, Dad. I get it."

Park closed his eyes for a moment. "But you've paid for it. And if you hadn't—while we were still—while I was . . . I'd never have forgiven myself."

Riley was more than a little surprised by his father's words, as well as the struggle he seemed to have speaking them. "I'm okay, Dad. I'm tough."

The intense stare returned. "Yeah, you are. Thank God for that." He looked at Riley then, and Riley saw all the things that had caused him to idolize his father his whole life. "There's just one thing I want to know."

Riley prepared himself. "Okay."

Park sat forward. "I want to hear what you would do if I gave you the opportunity to work at the family business." Riley blinked. He opened his mouth a couple of times, but no words came. "I want to hear that I can rely on you, that your time inside was a blip, a moment of stupidity that'll never happen again, that you'd take this chance and run with it."

"I would. I swear. I would." Riley licked his lips.

"You worked so hard for it, Riley." Park shook his head a little. "It was always you," he continued. "I always hoped it'd be you taking over from me when the time came. You have the potential to take this business and make it grow into something no one else can. The other boys have tried, but their love wasn't in it." He smiled a little. "Not like you."

"You can trust me, Dad. I promise you, you can."

Park watched him for a long moment before he nodded infinitesimally. "I know I can, son." He patted his palms against his knees. "Okay. Let me sort out the relevant paperwork and we'll take it from there."

Riley hated that he couldn't move to give his father the hug that he wanted. "Thank you," he said instead. "Thank you so much."

Park stood and patted Riley's shoulder. "You're welcome, son." Riley cupped a hand to his mouth, speechless and moved. "Life's too short," Park said. "I knew that already, but seeing you . . . and Lexie, Noah, and— You deserve this. You deserve a chance at being a family."

The room door opened again and Lexie walked in. Her face creased into a large grin when their eyes met before she looked over and saw Park. "Oh, I'm so sorry. I'll leave you—"

"It's fine," Park said with a wave of his hand. "I'm just leaving."

Both Lexie and Riley watched Park leave before Lexie set her bag down and smiled at him again. "Hey."

"Hey." She walked toward him and cupped his cheek, placing the softest of kisses on his lips. She tasted so damned good. The kiss was languid, but ached to be more. Lexie moved her head closer and nipped at his top lip. He moaned softly and he gripped her forearm as the tips of their tongues met.

"I'm so sorry I was away all that time," she grunted into his mouth. "I went back to your place to get you a few things."

"You're too good to me."

Lexie waved him off. "Noah's outside with your mom. Are you up to seeing him?" She fisted her hands together. "You look so much better and I don't think he'll be scared. I know he can be a handful, but he wants to see you."

Noah was delightfully exhausting on the best of days; being in a hospital bed recovering from being hit by a car he was even more so.

"Absolutely," Riley insisted, trying to sit up and hissing at the pain that shot through his chest. Lexie was at his side in an instant.

"Be careful," she soothed. "You don't want to tear any stitches." She helped him sit up a little more and cupped his cheek.

"Before you bring Noah in, there's something I need to talk to you about."

"What is it?"

Riley took a deep breath. "My dad's started proceedings for me to take over Moore's Motors. There's paperwork to be done, but I'll be moving back to Michigan permanently next month."

Lexie didn't speak; she simply gripped Riley's hand and pulled it to her mouth, kissing it over and over. "Is this real?"

Riley chuckled. "Yes, it's real. I'd be there sooner, but I have to stay at O'Hare's until Max finds a replacement . . . but it'll be fine."

"Where will you live?"

Riley blinked. "Until I can get an apartment, I'll stay at Mom and Dad's."

Lexie worried her bottom lip, clearly disappointed. "Oh."

Riley smirked. "Unless . . . what were you thinking?"

"I wasn't."

He snorted. "Lex, I'd know that look in the dark. What is it?"

"My place is so much nicer with you in it."

Riley's mouth twitched and his stomach heated. "You'd want me to live with you and Noah?"

Lexie gave a tiny shrug. "It'd save a lot of money, wouldn't it? And . . . you'd have most likely moved in eventually anyway."

"Most likely," Riley repeated. His smile dropped a little. "Are you sure? This is . . . a big step."

Lexie laughed. "Riley, I think we're way past worrying about big steps, don't you?"

He smirked and lifted their hands. "I guess you're right." He kissed her palm. "So are we really gonna do this?"

Lexie nodded. "I hope so."

Riley's brow furrowed. "We have to talk to Noah."

"I'll get him," Lexie said softly. "Let's tell him everything." She leaned closer, her smell floral and everything Riley wanted. "I should never have kept you two apart and for that I'm truly sorry—let me finish." Riley shut his mouth. "You being here made me realize what we all could have lost, and I'm not prepared to wait another minute not being with the two men I love most in the world."

Riley cleared his throat. "Go get him."

Riley was alone for all of five minutes before he heard the unmistakable laughter of Noah coming down the hospital corridor.

"Riley!" Noah called when Lexie opened the door.

"Hey buddy, how are you?"

Despite his wiggling to be let down, Lexie kept hold of him. "Remember," she said firmly, though her face was soft, "Riley is sore, so we have to be gentle, okay?"

"Okay," Noah said, reaching for Riley all the same. He did as his mommy had told him, though, as he lay next to him on the bed, hugging him gently and rubbing his fingers through Riley's beard. "Is you comings home yet?"

"Not yet," he answered. "Soon, I hope. I miss you so much." He nuzzled Noah's cheek. He smelled of Lexie and it was perfect. "What have you been doing while I've been here?"

"Mommy and mes made pancakes, and then she and Grandma took me swimming. Guess what? I drawed you a picture." He held out his hand, and Lexie handed him a piece of paper that was covered in bright colors and stick men.

"That's awesome, Noah. What is it?"

"It's us at Long Lake. Looks—that's me, you, and Mommy."

"I love it," Riley said, his throat suddenly a little tight. Jesus, it was so good to have his son in his arms.

Lexie looked at Noah, who was fingering the bandage on Riley's arm. "Tell me something," she whispered. "Do you like spending time with Riley?"

Noah leaned closer to Riley and whispered back. "Yes. He's the bestest. Cans I stay here with you tonight?"

"Not tonight, man, but when I get home we can have a sleepover."

"If I've been good, cans I has ice cream?"

Riley snorted. "When I'm out of here we're gonna get the biggest chocolate ice cream we can find." He wrapped an arm around Noah and watched as the little boy snuggled against him. "You okay?" Riley whispered, kissing Noah's temple as Lexie sat down in the seat Park had used not ten minutes before.

Noah looked over at Lexie. "Riley, this is likes a sleepover you and Mommy has."

Riley and Lexie both laughed. "It is," he said quietly. "Can I tell you a secret?" Noah nodded, his eyes crinkling with a smile. "Mommy steals the covers; being with you will be much better."

Noah sighed. His small hands appeared above the covers as he reached out to Riley. "Can I tells you a secret?"

Riley pulled him closer. "You can tell me anything, Noah. Anything at all."

Noah nuzzled Riley's neck and snuggled into his side. "I loves you."

Riley's body froze for an exquisite beat before the emotion he'd been holding back came rushing through him. He squeezed his son to his chest and quietly released his tears into his hair. "I love you, too, Noah. I love you, too."

Lexie and Riley's gazes met. "Hey, Noah, what do you think about Riley coming to live with us?"

Noah lifted his head, his eyes wide. "In our house?"

Lexie nodded. "In our house."

Noah's gaze moved from Lexie to Riley and back again; he was seemingly thinking hard about it. Riley stayed very still, his heart still bursting from Noah's confession. "If you lives with us," Noah whispered, cupping a hand to the side of his mouth as though telling Riley a secret, "cans you be my daddy?"

Riley's breath left him in a huge whoosh as Lexie smiled through tears that gathered in her blue eyes. "Noah," he uttered, "I *am* your daddy."

Noah's small mouth fell open into the shape of an *O*. "And you cans be my daddy forever?"

"Forever, buddy," Riley uttered. "Forever and always."

Noah squeezed Riley, who despite the soreness and aching limbs, laughed and hugged him back, blowing a raspberry onto Noah's neck, making him squeal and giggle. As he did, he looked over at Lexie, knowing in every part of his body and soul that he would cherish every moment he had, knowing he'd never felt as much love for two people in his entire life.

They were everything to him, the two pieces of his heart, his whole world.

All the world.

EPILOGUE

Riley walked along Long Lake, feeling the sun beat down on his arms and face as the water splashed over his bare toes. The smell of the lake surrounded every breath he took and the heat wrapped around him like a comfortable jacket.

He paused for a moment, closing his eyes and allowing himself to take it all in, standing in the summer sun, listening to the lapping water and the birds overhead.

Then the familiar sound of laughter. He smiled.

The laughter was his favorite part. It might have been his favorite sound in the world. It floated on the warm breeze and greeted his ears like an old friend. Without sounding like a complete wuss, the sound of it made Riley feel all the butterfly-type things in his stomach. It always had. And he liked it. It reassured him that the people closest to him were happy. And there was nothing more important.

He opened his eyes, looking down the lake's edge, and his heart clenched when he saw Noah, running—well, stumbling—through the water, giggling as it enveloped his small feet. Riley watched, enraptured. *My God.* He was just about the most perfect thing he'd ever seen.

Noah splashed and laughed, and the sound traveled across the water beautifully. As he always did, Riley caught the sound of his son in his ears and stored it in a place he would visit a long time from now, when Noah was too old to play games and ride on Riley's shoulders. He laughed as Noah stumbled again. He was so inelegant. His hair caught the sun as he twirled and kicked up the water, flashing white and gold.

Riley's laughter brought Noah's head up, and the smile that appeared on the little boy's face damn near floored him. With a wink, Riley held out his arms and Noah took off, running at him as fast as his six-year-old legs could carry him. He stumbled a couple more times before he reached him, and, when he did, Riley lifted him into the air, throwing him to the sky and catching him as he squealed with delight.

Noah placed his small hands on Riley's cheeks and squeezed them. "Daddy." He smiled, all gaps and gums.

Riley placed his lips on Noah's cheek, blowing on it to make a loud farting noise that made him laugh and squirm in his arms. Riley held him tightly to his chest, not wanting him to fall. He held Noah tightly because he loved feeling him so warm and perfect in his arms. Because he always wanted Noah to know that he was safe with Riley; that he loved him more than he ever thought possible. Riley made sure that he told Noah that every day and that his love for him would never change.

All the world.

Like any father worth his salt, Riley knew he'd lay his life down for his son in a heartbeat, loving him with every inch of his soul. That part of becoming "Daddy" was easy. He'd slipped into the role so easily.

Keeping Noah in his arms, Riley continued down to the water. Every Sunday it was the same, and Riley loved it. Spending time with his family, being silly and making memories, was all he'd ever wanted and, since he'd moved back to Traverse City over two years ago, each day seemed to get better and better. Sometimes the three of them would head back to New York to see all of Riley's friends and, yes, he missed them, but Riley's heart belonged to Michigan, where his family lived.

"Is Grandpa coming now?" Noah asked, playing with Riley's beard.

"Later," Riley answered, placing a gentle hand to the back of Noah's head. "He and Nana are coming for dinner."

Being able to say that his mother and father were joining them for dinner was something that Riley had thought would never happen again. It had been a tricky road on occasion, but Riley had worked his nuts off making sure that Moore's Motors ran like a well-oiled machine. He'd officially been the owner for eighteen months and he loved every second, and, with each sale, each moment that Riley proved his capabilities, the more Park opened up. Riley could say with confidence that he and his dad were solid, and the last of the wounds between them were finally healed. Celebrating birthdays and Christmases together again was amazing, especially now that Riley realized how much fun Christmas was with a kid around. He tended to go a little nuts with decorations and shit, but Lexie, God bless her, tolerated the little boy in Riley that got excited about pinning stockings and tinsel to the fireplace.

Riley kissed Noah's hair and chuckled to himself.

It was more than a little crazy. If he'd been told three years ago that his life would be this way, he'd have laughed in someone's face. He sighed as Noah's finger traced the lines of ink on his shoulder. It was a habit he'd developed when he was most tired. Most nights Noah would fall asleep on Riley, one finger in Riley's beard and one finger circling the tattoo patterns on his skin. Those were the best times.

Riley's most precious times.

Noah lifted his head and looked toward the bench they were approaching. "Can I have some more ice cream?"

Riley paused. "Wait. You had ice cream? Without me?"

He shook his head. "Mommy had it. She shared it with me." He lifted his chocolate-stained hands as evidence.

"Mommy did?" he laughed. "I bet. She likes ice cream a lot now, huh?"

"Who likes ice cream?"

Riley looked from his son to Lexie, who was seated on their favorite bench, bowl of ice cream in one hand and a spoon in the other. Dressed in a floor-length, strapless white dress that was almost transparent, she'd never looked so fucking good. It had been a hot summer in Traverse City.

"You do," Riley said with a smile as he placed Noah next to her.

"Have you been telling on me?" Lexie scowled lovingly at their son, who shrugged and laughed. Lexie tickled him, making him giggle more, and Riley's lungs gave a familiar squeeze as he looked between the two of them.

Christ, it still hurt to think he so nearly lost all of this.

He tried not to think about the past too much, but the memories would come back every so often, and Riley would swear to every deity he could think of that he would spend every day being thankful and deserving of what he had.

After stealing two large spoonfuls of ice cream, Noah took off back down to the water. Riley dropped down next to Lexie and wrapped his arm around her, placing his other hand on her beautifully rounded stomach. It was an amazing feeling, knowing there was a new life growing inside of her. A new life that Riley would be there for every step of the way. Finding out about Noah was an amazing yet terrifying experience, but this time Riley felt calmer. He'd played Daddy pretty fucking well. And, truthfully, he'd loved every minute.

Obviously, it helped that Lexie was the most incredible partner, friend, and mother. He rubbed his palm lovingly across her bump and she hummed into his neck. He smiled down at his hand, reading the word "Noah" that was tattooed around his wrist. "Are you okay?" Riley asked as she rubbed her belly and winced.

"I'm great," Lexie replied, kissing his jaw. "Baby just keeps pressing on my bladder."

"She does?"

Lexie nodded, and Riley took the opportunity to kiss her soundly.

And it was just like the first time—all fireworks, heat, and fucking golden.

He pulled back to look at her. "You're beautiful."

"You too." She smiled, holding out a spoon filled with ice cream, which Riley took into his mouth.

"Could you get any more flavors in there?"

Lexie elbowed him in the ribs. "Shush! I like it. And so does your daughter."

Riley laughed and kissed her hair. He pulled her to his side and sat back, looking out to the water to where their son leaped and jumped, sang, and laughed in the hot sun.

Wes Carter: Dangerous, brooding and behind bars, Carter's emotional scars are as permanent as the ink on his skin.

Kat Lane: Vibrant and gutsy, Kat chooses to become a prison tutor in tribute to her father whose murder haunts her.

As teacher and student, any relationship is against every rule. But although their love is forbidden, it won't be denied . . .

Available now from

headline
ETERNAL

Theirs was a love that broke every rule. The searing attraction between Wes Carter and Kat Lane was instant and impossible to deny.

But as they face real life together and share the news of their engagement with those closest to them, Kat and Carter realise that they will still have to fight for their love if it is to survive forever and . . . always.

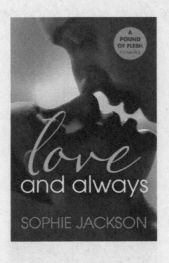

Available now as an e-novella from

Max O'Hare: Tortured by memories of the woman he loved, the child he lost and the drugs that numbed his pain, Max is haunted by his past.

Grace Brooks: An eternal optimist, Grace appears to be the perfect girl, but she keeps the truth of her own difficult history closely guarded.

Bound by their greatest fears and deepest secrets, Max and Grace must learn to trust again. And the key to opening their hearts lies in one another. . .

Available now from

headline
ETERNAL

Tutor and prison student — their love was forbidden but their attraction was impossible to deny.

Everywhere Kat and Carter turn, couples are becoming parents, and the longing in Kat's eyes worries Carter. After his rough childhood, he's not so sure he has what it takes to be a good parent. But fate has brought Kat and Carter together – can their love survive forever?

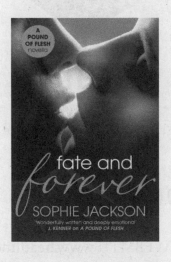

Available now as an e-novella from

headline
ETERNAL

headline
ETERNAL

FIND YOUR HEART'S DESIRE...

VISIT OUR WEBSITE: www.headlineeternal.com
FIND US ON FACEBOOK: facebook.com/eternalromance
FOLLOW US ON TWITTER: @eternal_books
EMAIL US: eternalromance@headline.co.uk